MOURA
and
THE BECKONING

Virginia Coffman was born in San Francisco and worked in the Hollywood studios during the Golden and Silver years. She has worked on many TV scripts as well as acting.

She began writing in 1959 and since then has had over ninety titles published. She now lives in Nevada, where she continues to write enthusiastically, although ancestral ties with France and Britain frequently bring her to Europe.

MOURA
and
THE BECKONING

Virginia Coffman

PAN BOOKS

Moura first published 1959 by Crown Publishers, New York
and first published in Great Britain 1993 by Severn House Publishers Ltd
The Beckoning first published 1994 by Severn House Publishers Ltd

This omnibus edition published 2002 by Pan Books
an imprint of Pan Macmillan Ltd
Pan Macmillan, 20 New Wharf Road, London N1 9RR
Basingstoke and Oxford
Associated companies throughout the world
www.panmacmillan.com

ISBN 1 405 00441 X

1 3 5 7 9 8 6 4 2

A CIP catalogue record for this book is available from
the British Library.

Printed and bound in Great Britain by
Mackays of Chatham plc, Chatham, Kent

MOURA

1

There is this in my memory still when a shadow rises within the moon's glow, and the trees shiver though there is no wind, that on such a night I first heard the name of Moura, and the candle flickered in my hand as if a breath had crossed it faintly. Was this a sign? I am no conjuror to know. But before I came downstairs to answer that midnight summons, almost before I heard the first faint sound upon the circle drive in front of Miss Nutting's Academy for Select Young Females, there was a prescience of demons and apparitions and such like upon me.

I remember the clock on the first-floor landing had just struck the half-hour after midnight, and I was in that state of semi-sleep when an unfamiliar sound is like a lightning bolt to the nerves. The house was very still, so that the thud of a horse's hooves around the drive toward the front door brought me wide awake.

With Miss Nutting and three teachers away at London for the week end, I, as the housekeeper, was responsible for discipline among the girls, and at nineteen I took this task seriously to heart. The girls liked me, perhaps because they could feel superior to an Irish country girl who wore her dark hair free instead of in a Grecian knot, who slept in unfashionable nightgowns rather than shifts, and whose dresses had natural waistlines and full skirts, instead of

1

belting just under the breasts and clinging damply to the figure, with a hem halfway down the calf.

Little Palla Florin, a golden-eyed girl recently sent here from war-ravaged France, had all the stylishness of her native land, and said to me once, "Anne, you'll never come up to scratch!" For she herself was, according to her boast, "all the crack with the gentry." Even Miss Nutting, who almost slept in riding skirts, felt called upon to remark, "Do you want to look like a country dowd all your life? After all, my girl, this is 1815!"

But I had a notion they would not have liked me half so well if I bloomed suddenly into a Miss Nonpareil. Besides, I was young enough to think I should be able to manage anything, as "unfashionable" reputation, a disobedient student, or, as now, a night marauder.

The moon caught the shadow of the fountain in the driveway and sent it creeping over my window sill into my bedroom as I flung my workaday shawl over my nightdress and opened the window. I was concerned for the neighborhood dogs and cats who were always being crushed and maimed in the post road by careless travelers hurrying to and from London. I could no longer hear the horse. The rider must have dismounted and tethered him at the block before the front door. The circle drive, its fountain spraying white in the center, seemed deserted. Nothing moved, and the desolate calm of the autumn moon pervaded the scene. The drive circled inward toward the school from the London post road, some two hundred yards distant. It was guarded by trees which had just begun to quiver as though startled by a passing breeze, though I felt none.

A bad thing it is to have an Irish imagination. In the eight years since I had come to Miss Nutting's as an ignorant, "foreign" scullery maid of eleven, I had never

2

been able to view without a chill that dreadful statue of Ananke, the ancient Greek Fate, in the center of the fountain. One marbled hand was concealed in the folds of the Greek mantle, but the other pointed downward at all who passed, and I was used to fancy that Ananke singled me out especially with her long marble fingers and her marble eyes which had terrible empty sockets where the pupils ought to be.

And then it was I saw that thing like a walking shroud.

Under the distant trees it seemed to mass and lengthen as it advanced from the road to the school drive. A heavily cloaked traveler following the horseman, perhaps. But this dark form drifted nearer with a phantom reality until it was much closer, with a kind of unidentifiable human shape.

My fingers tightened upon my shawl, all my credulous Gaelic imagination alert. Though a sceptic about the possible, I was a perfect repository for the impossible. As it glided nearer, the blackness I had taken for a phantom was surely the cloak and hood of a schoolgirl out late on some escapade, the figure just such as a slim student would have. A moment from now, when the face looked out of its dainty grey hood, one of Miss Nutting's girls would be revealed. I smiled at my silly fright. The driveway curved and the moon illuminated the inside of the hood like a candle thrust on a sudden into a sleeper's face.

Nothing was within that hood.

I stood numbly, staring; for the shrouded thing – whatever it, shadow or phantom or trick of moonlight – was facing toward my window. I was its object. A warning? A visitation? The thing swayed below me, a mass of moon-tinted flecks, like a great mass of dust solidified.

The beat of the brass knocker at the front door sounded through the building, breaking the paralysis of my terror.

Even as I stared at the thing on the drive, it seemed to dissolve into its component parts: the shadow of Ananke on the fountain, a few particles of autumn dust, the shimmering moonlight.

The pounding at the door went on. Though the phantom had vanished, my night rider was not so obliging. I closed my eyes for an instant, felt the cool window frame against my cheek, then looked out once more. All was serene – only the grim statue of Ananke, hovering above the fountain, casting its black pall over the drive and over the worn legend at its base: THE NIGHT COMETH.

There was a patter of footsteps outside my room. Patty, the youngest housemaid, hurried to reach the front door before this midnight visitor broke off the knocker. I came away from the window, put on my everyday work slippers and, although my own mind was in a dreadful state, went downstairs to lend moral support to scatterbrained Patty.

The knocking had stopped by this time. A half-dozen of the older girls crouched on the front stair landing of the first floor, buzzing opinions to each other as they peeked over the stair rail and eavesdropped on the visitor below them.

"What is it?" I asked.

Palla Florin, the fifteen-year-old orphan from our enemy, France, looked up at me, her slanted golden eyes lively. "The devil's in it for you, Anne! We've a tall, handsome foreign gentleman at the door, right out of a romance. And poor Patty's such a fool she does nothing but goggle."

"Well then," said I, pulling my wits together to cope with this unmannerly child, "you are wide of the mark yourself; for you should have called me. Now, off to bed, Miss Palla. Go along! And the rest of you as well."

Palla made faces, but in despite of an extraordinary

4

preoccupation with her pretty self, she liked me, and was used to obeying me. She was a young lady of very strong will and an invariable habit of getting her way. I had heard her boasting once to certain submissive and wide-eyed friends that before she was done she would be more popular than even her mother had been. With no knowledge of her mother, I could still believe her boast. She had all the necessary ingredients: charm, self-confidence, a devious way of going after what she wanted, and a ruthless, even cruel manner of thrusting obstacles out of her way. I don't suppose she ever committed an act that did not further her own happiness in that world of which she was queen. Yet, like so many charming little female dictators, she had a large coterie of admirers among the girls of Miss Nutting's Academy. I doubt, though, that they liked her, as I sometimes did.

When she edged away from the balustrade in answer to my warning, she was followed obediently by the others, to whom she was certainly the bear-leader. Even as I went down to the ground floor, however, I knew the girls would soon be back at their eavesdropping again.

Our visitor stood in the hall between the two parlors, beating against his wide-skirted traveling coat with a very efficient-looking riding crop. With what I thought must be a note of humor in his voice, he dismissed the household as a fine pack of gudgeons to let him stand scraping his heels on a doorstep at midnight.

"Yes'm, indeed, sir. Yes'm – sir." Patty bobbed several times, her screwed-up blonde curls jumping out in an uncontrollable way that made me want to laugh, though I was perfectly sober and as respectable as anyone can be in a nightgown and shawl, with tangled dark hair tumbling down one's back. I took the candlestick from poor Patty who scuttled upstairs to join the giggling pupils waiting to hear me tick off the gentleman. Myself, I expected quite the reverse, for to tell the truth he put me a good deal in awe of him. A tall woman myself, I was not used to meeting men who put me at a disadvantage. I had the handling of all the whey-faced young gentlemen who came calling on the girls. Though they were my own age, they seemed like children to me, with all their fluttering and foppishness in imitation (or so they fancied) of the Prince Regent and his Court. But this person was neither calfish nor young nor subservient, and I was not quite my confident self with him. I thought him splendid looking, except for his dark, curling hair which had been cropped very close not so long ago and was still too crisp and short to be in the style of the moment. His lean, trim body seemed to know something of physical fitness; for he was not young, perhaps all of forty. His movements revealed him as a man used to mastery.

Then I saw his eyes. They were hard and grey and unreadable, and they penetrated to my very soul. I recalled stories told in my childhood that the Devil had such eyes. But I doubt if the Devil ever possessed a smile like this man's. It softened his whole expression as he looked me up and down; then it seemed that those eyes were not so very hard after all.

"You are not the mistress of this establishment. I can't see you answering to 'Honoria Nutting.' Daphne, perhaps. No? Well, then – Aphrodite?" He spoke almost without accent, but there was a foreign intonation that added a certain charm to his excellent voice.

I said coldly, "Anne Wicklow, sir. I am the house-keeper. Miss Nutting is absent. Will you state your business?"

"Anne Wicklow," he repeated, savoring the name

thoughtfully. He took his riding crop between two neatly gloved hands and bent it in an arc. I don't know why, but I suddenly imagined those hands bending a human spine. "Bad enough, but not quite equal to Honoria Nutting. Well, Anne, shall we adjourn to a study? Or do you want those giggling little simpletons abovestairs to hear all that goes on between us?"

"Any dealings you'll be having with me, sir, may be conducted before them, but if you wish, Miss Nutting's bookroom is to my left." I took the initiative and preceded him to the small, south room where the embers of a fire still glowed in the grate. He closed the door behind him and made himself comfortable on the arm of Miss Nutting's favorite chair with his long, booted legs stretched out, while I stood before him with my shawl crossed over my breast in the most uncompromising manner I could adopt with one hand. My left hand carried the candle, and I endeavored to use it in a manner that would light his face and perhaps disconcert him while I remained in the shadows, disheveled and half-dressed as I was.

"Now, sir. Begin."

He said politely, without troubling to shift his position, "Mademoiselle, you are singeing my eyebrows. Come, relax. I am not going to eat you. Not tonight, at any rate . . . How has my niece been behaving? Not a model of female propriety, I am sure." At my surprise, he explained as though I should have guessed, "I see Palla Florin hasn't told you about her French guardian."

As the peace with France was still in the process of discussion, and there were wagers on how long Bonaparte would remain in captivity this time, I was a good deal surprised at the presence of one of the enemy in England.

"She does not speak of France, sir. She came a year ago, as you know, during the 1814 Restoration. We know

7

nothing of her former life in the upheavals of that wretched country."

"Wretched, eh? The propaganda of this little island never ceases to arouse my admiration. I assure you there are many of us who think it was a sad day when you forced us to exchange our Emperor for that fat and, I may say, wholly incompetent Bourbon – who is also a master of cowardice. But I had better guard my tongue. I have just paid a very pretty sum into certain court pockets to assure them of my Bourbon loyalty. I am tired of wars." He paused, stared into the candle flame, and added in a quiet voice that was rather moving in so confident a man, "I am tired of troubles. I want peace."

He laughed without humor. "But I am here on a mission that does not promise a peaceful future. I have come to order my niece home. Achille, the seneschal, had no business sending her out of the country. You know something of Palla's family? The province in which she lives?"

"Very little. I know Monsieur Achille is the seneschal and that the estate is in Auvergne. He has sent her money from time to time, whenever smugglers came through the Channel blockade. Palla told me once that revolution had scarcely touched her estate. I believe it is very old, very distinguished."

"*Her* estate?" he repeated ironically. "Hm. Very old, in any case." He added, "I was in no position to attend to Palla, being myself – "

"Monsieur Achille explained that you were in the Emperor's service."

He seemed to find this an amusing turn of phrase.

"In a manner of speaking." He stood up. I retreated a step.

"Have Palla's things packed and made ready. She is to

8

be sent to me at the King's Cross Inn on Thursday next
. . . or perhaps – yes, I believe I will come for her. I will
escort her from London to the Dover packet – and home."
I wondered why he found the word so unattractive.

"Don't you wish to see her tonight?"

"Good God, why? I shall see her all the rest of my life,
and that is a deal too long."

Before this rudeness I was lost. "But – where is her
home?"

He looked down at me with a faint note of surprise.

"I thought you understood. She goes to Moura."

The wind shifted the candle flame and I shivered; for
my shawl was none too warm, and a prickle had gone
over me, so that I remembered the old saying: "someone
is walking over my grave."

"Very good, sir. I shall see that she is packed and ready.
In the meanwhile, you will be sending to Miss Nutting
some proofs from your solicitors that you are what you
claim to be."

He smiled and opened the bookroom door for me.

"There is an honest Irish glow about you. I like you for
it – and for other things, mademoiselle."

In front of the great door he suddenly stripped the glove
off his hand and took my fingers in his. He had a smile that
warmed and yet embarrassed me; for I did not wish him
to know just how winning that smile was, both merry and
tender, and setting wonderfully well upon the excellent
though somber features of his face.

"But you Irish," he added, "are so damnably suspicious.
Come, Anne, say you believe me honest too." I was too
astonished to withdraw my hand. But when he had gone
and I was bolting the door behind him, I realized that
I had never touched a hand more callused and hard.
This strange, foreign gentleman was no ordinary French

9

nobleman after all, though he might be master of Moura. The name had a sinister sound. Yet, while my hand lay in his, I had felt the impetus of something my blood had never known before, a kind of heightened pulse that made me blush at the stirring with me.

I went upstairs, passing Palla Florin and the other girls who clamored to know what had happened. Jassie Milner said knowingly, "If there's trouble over the two of you locking yourselves in Miss Nutting's bookroom, don't put yourself into a taking. Papa would pay your wages. He told my uncle he would."

"Go to bed, you saucy chit," I told her, and hurried up the stairs to my room on the servants' floor. Palla Florin came after me, padding along in bare feet, with all the Frenchified ribbons of her night rail fluttering behind her.

"Who was it, Anne?"

"I mustn't be telling you until Miss Nutting receives word. Perhaps he's a villain hoping to gain your inheritance."

"Oh, Anne! I told you so. I haven't seen him for ten years, but he is still the same."

"You remember him after ten years?"

"I could never forget Uncle Moura. Those eyes – those dreadful, wonderful, grey bottomless pools! Mama called him the cruel enchanter of the fairy tales."

Trying to untangle this, I said, "Your mama was his sister?"

"Oh, la, how silly! She was his older brother's mistress, of course. Pierre Moura, that's my papa, I think. He and Uncle were not very alike. Uncle was a Bonaparte man. I think for a while Mama wanted to be Uncle's mistress. Mama always wanted things she couldn't have. She wasn't like me – I get them! But Mama said that Uncle was abrupt and insulted her. Mama was very stupid. She never cared about me, or about anybody but herself. Well, then she died. . . ."

Remembering my own sad loss, I could not help saying, "How terrible for you!"

"Oh, not really!" said Palla airly. "You see, she never really loved me, so I couldn't very well love her, could I?" She looked at me with one of those reasonable smiles which are so hard to answer. "And besides, when Mama was gone, everyone said I was the prettiest one at Moura. So it served Mama proper. Anyway, the war with England was on again, and I was alone at Moura with Achille and Matilde."

I refrained from saying that Palla Florin's mother must have been of a piece with all the rest of the French. Everyone knew they had no morals at all. And as for Monsieur Moura, I was resolved to think of him no more. In all likelihood, he had been the lover of Palla's mother also.

"It's an odd name – Moura. Are the Mouras French?"

"Since time out of mind, but" – she shivered with pleasurable fear – "before that, they were a strange people. Huns or Tatars from the East. I heard Achille say that a thousand years ago the Mouras shaved their heads and wore terrible black pigtails and killed men, and ladies too, when they were done with them. How exciting it is to have Moura blood!"

I could scarcely see the present master of Moura in such a role. He was too civilized. Or was he, indeed?

Palla rattled on. "The estate went to Uncle Moura in trust for me, I think. I was so young then. If he married, then his heirs would get it. But he shan't do that. Isn't it fortunate that Uncle and I like each other?"

11

"Remarkably fortunate," I said, remembering Monsieur Moura's aversion to his niece.

"Anyway, he must have liked me. I saw him take your hand and smile. He never did that with many people, but he might do it to please me, knowing I liked you."

In my conceit I doubted this, but it was possible.

"Why have you not mentioned him before, Miss Palla?"

Her golden eyes gave me a side glance and I was aware of a withdrawal from me. She said indifferently, "I didn't think he wanted to be talked about."

"But what would be said of him?"

"Oh – everything," she murmured airily, and kissed me good night.

Surprised and touched by the gesture, I went into my own small bedchamber; and feeling secure enough at last to throw off my cashmere shawl which was my armor against life, I lay down on my cool bed.

The fountain's shadow lengthened in the moonlight across my bed, and I slept.

I remember well the icy sweat of dread in which I awoke hours later, but could not tell what sound had awakened me, and returned to sleep.

In the morning, a few early-rising girls of the school were gathered beneath my window exclaiming over the gardener's find, a small, dead mongrel dog, killed hours before by a hard blow that had crushed its skull. Then I knew what had awakened me in the night. It had been the whimper of the little dog as he lay dying under the vast cold radiance of the moon. Struck down, in all probability, by the flying hooves of Monsieur Moura's steed.

2

How adaptable is youth! Palla Florin was fond of saying in her exaggerated French way that Miss Nutting's school was "a haven and a safe harbor" from her troubled native land. But the summons to Moura swiftly put this haven out of her mind. During the next few days, the girl could think of nothing but her departure. After all, for a girl who would brook no rivals in any field that interested her, Palla had too many potential rivals at Miss Nutting's; whereas, at Moura, she could probably queen it to her heart's content.

As I would busy myself in the bedchambers, showing the new housemaid how to clean without breaking the young ladies' gaudily painted china collections or without dropping albums of ancient, pressed flowers, the little Florin would mention her handsome uncle, if not by name, by indirection. One day, while I was packing Palla's soft cottons, musline and cashmere clothing with the aid of the housemaid, Palla came to the point.

"Frenchmen are so much more romantic than the prosy old English. Isn't it so?" And as I went on folding her new sprigged-muslin round gown, hardly realizing she addressed me: "Anne Wicklow! Stop that nonsense and listen. The girls are out of reason jealous. What a taking they're in!"

"Why?" I said. "Because you must make a tedious journey away from all your friends?"

"How tiresome of you! No! Because they all would like my Uncle Moura to smile at them and take them to far-off places."

"And now you have decided that your uncle is someone very special, merely because the other young ladies admire him?"

Palla made an impatient gesture at my stupidity.

"Who wants to be loved by someone that no one else would look twice at? Mama thought him attractive. He must be so. And you know my disposition very well, dear Anne. When I decide I shall have something, I shall have it!" She pounded on the bed to emphasize this, but her pounding only made her look the more childish. When she glanced up surreptitiously to see how I took this vehemence, I was hard put to it to keep from smiling. Spoiled little minx that she was! One moment completely the egoist. The next, peering at me like a small puppy that wants to be petted.

I felt that her behavior, while charming, deserved a setdown and paid her no heed.

"Mary," I said to the housemaid, "Hand those shawls down to me."

Palla snatched up the shawls and hurled them over my head, and as I clawed my way out of this cashmere forest, in quite a taking myself, she added, "Aren't you going to ask me why they are jealous?"

"You'll be telling me why, no doubt."

She threw herself onto her bed so hard the whole white tester and frame rattled ominously. "You're cross because I've tumbled your hair. But you shouldn't be. You look very pretty – like an abandoned woman." She rested her chin on her elbow, her slanting golden eyes excited by her

14

own daring. "Are you an abandoned woman, Anne? What do you do after we are all abed?"

"That will do, Miss Palla!" How can one answer these French? They think of nothing but things which are not spoken of. And the housemaid, a plump, flaxen-haired baggage, was gaping with curiosity. "Mary, go along. Cook will be wanting you."

"Oh, bother Mary!" said Palla. "But Anne, *chérie*, I'll miss *you*. Truly I will. You try so hard to be stern and prosy but you are sweet, and I like you for it."

I own this pleased me beyond saying, but I thought it well not to let down the barrier of what she chose to call my prosiness, so I went on about the business at my hand.

Curling up on the bed, Palla began romancing again. "It's as though I were the heroine in one of Mrs. Radcliffe's stories. The girls were saying only last night – "

"You know those silly novels are forbidden. All that flummery of clanking chains and armored ghosts!"

"Now, Anne, you shouldn't believe all Miss Nutting says. Some of them are divine – truly. *The Mysteries of Udolpho!* I could swoon to be loved by that wicked Count Montoni. So cold, so distant, so aloof!"

"You are not like to be," said I. "It would be most improper to be loved by one's uncle."

"Ah-ha! You *do* see the resemblance. I never mentioned Uncle Moura, but you thought of him at once." She couldn't see my expression and did not know whether she had scored. I fastened her portmanteau and carried it to the door, where I recalled my duty.

"You are sure to be caught, you know."

She looked up suspiciously.

"At what?"

"You and the young ladies imagine you are fooling me. But I know you read by candlelight, after the lamps are

15

down. One night you will see a more horrible sight than a clanking ghost at your door."

"What, Anne, what?"

"You'll be seeing Miss Nutting in her night rail, with her hair in curlers and her face greased with buttermilk."

She burst into a fit of giggles.

The night before Miss Palla's departure I was busy in the bookroom. Under Miss Nutting's direction I began the cataloguing of her collection of unread *Tatlers* and *Spectators*. It was a muscular rather than a mental task, requiring me to perch myself on top of a ladder.

"A little to the left, my girl," said Miss Nutting. "Aye. There's the set. I must read them one day. I am persuaded I shall find some uncommon truths in them."

Her voice neighed up at me, like one of those fine beasts one sees high-stepping it at Dublin Fair. She had no vanity, for there was nothing false about her. To me she was brusque, rudely kind, penurious with money, and generous with her confidence in my abilities. She was the only parent I had known for twelve years. Not content with raising me from kitchenmaid to my present status by my sixteenth year, she had seen to it that my education likewise proceeded in pothooks, manners, and a curiously equine view of history in which I learned to admire all the great men for their mounts. The glories of a nation that was not "horsey" were lost on me.

I had located the *Tatlers* Miss Nutting referred to, when we were both shaken by a crash on the floor of the chamber about a foot over my head.

"Gad's life! What are they up to now?" Miss Nutting exclaimed.

I had strong suspicions, but not being minded to peach on them, I looked my ignorance.

16

Miss Nutting bolted the dregs of her port and uncrossed her legs reluctantly. "I suppose I must see to them, but I tell you at the outset, I've no taste for managing young females."

Overhead I could make out the tattletale sounds of the girls scuffling around, cleaning up or hiding whatever had made that unearthly crash. It seemed a long time before the sharp knuckles of Miss Nutting beat a staccato rap on the door. The silence was like that in a tomb.

Miss Nutting's voice, muffled to my ears, blasted the inmates. After that, a typhoon seemed to have been loosed in the room. There were some furious words by Miss Nutting, much running, followed by Miss Nutting's piercing neigh:

"Fetch up Miss Wicklow. She'll set it to rights."

I put aside the Addison and Steele papers and had nearly reached the floor when Palla Florin bounded down the great staircase.

"Anne! Oh! Anne! The most famous thing! Do come and see. Charlotte was making cocoa bonbons over the candle and spilled the pan and made a grab for the tester and that came down on the bed, and now it's all over sticky."

I went up with her, reminding her that she was barefoot and did not want to take a chill on the very day she left England.

She was contrite and sought to wheedle me by insinuating her arm around my waist. In a brogue thick as a peat bog, she began, "Annie, me girrrl" – giving me a wicked but very tolerable imitation of myself – "ye're out of reason cross wi' yer little Palla that loves ye."

"Loves me indeed!" said I. "And small way of showing it. Running off to the enemy with your face all smiles."

Her voice was unusually sober. "I don't like many

17

people, but I like you. If ever I was in trouble, I'd come to you. There's a little place inside your heart that's warm and comforting. I feel it." She squeezed me hard, but I was on my guard against her wayward charms and would not admit I was touched. I had known too little genuine affection in my life to let myself believe every protestation.

"Nor will your blarney be helping at all, miss. You'd do better minding Miss Nutting."

"Oh, pooh! Who minds Miss Nutting? She's all boom and bluster."

This, alas, was too true. At least a dozen girls must have crowded into the bedchamber Palla shared with plump, sweets-loving Charlotte Ramikin when we came in. Miss Nutting seemed excessively glad to see me.

"Now we are more like it. Miss Wicklow, clear away this wretched mess and send them off to their beds." As she stalked past me, she added in an undertone, "And Heaven send me a blessed glass of port. Good night."

Once she had gone, I shooed the girls off to their rooms, sending them along with a good hard swipe where it would do the most good. They scattered quickly, giggling and fluttering, but obedient. There was not a bad-hearted girl among them, I thought, and only Miss Nutting's insurmountable aversion to young females had prevented them from obeying her as promptly. Children, like animals, can feel whether you are frightened of them.

Then I went to work on the carpet in Miss Palla's room, and a sad business it was! Palla climbed up into her bed, but Miss Charlotte fussed at having to sleep without a clean white tester overhead. I gave her a cloth and told her to get on with the cleaning. She whined but finished scrubbing the carpet while I tore down and folded what was left of the bed curtains. Palla, meanwhile, whipped a book out from under her own coverlet and resumed what had apparently been her task of reading aloud by the light of her night candle. I was about to stop her but, with very human curiosity, waited to hear more.

It was the *Mysteries of Udolpho* again. I could see what held the girls. I too was captured by it, but at the same time it sent over me a malaise that I cannot describe even now, a kind of foreboding of evil. But in Palla foreboding was balanced by her natural buoyancy.

"I could outwit Count Montoni. I could – " She crinkled up her sturdy little fingers and made clawing signs at Charlotte, who shrieked and backed away from this horrendous sight. "I'd like to be Count Montoni for five minutes and rid myself of every silly, fusty person who troubles me. I know I could do it. I dreamed about it once. And after, I should have everything I ever wanted. . . . Still, my Uncle Moura is much cleverer than Count Montoni. He'd never let me get about so freely as Montoni did in the novel. And Uncle Moura's handsomer too. Isn't he, Anne?"

Although I put her off, I was disposed to admit I thought Monsieur Moura superior in most respects to the fiendish Montoni. But, mysterious though he was, it would be pure fustian to think of Palla's intelligent, highborn uncle as a criminal. I was sure of that after only one meeting.

In my mind's eye I tried to put together the face of Edmond Moura. I could remember nothing of it, not a feature. How then had he impressed me so much? Whenever I thought deeply upon it, my hand still tingled where he had taken it in his in the moonlight of the open doorway, with the shadow of Ananke falling across his face.

But what did it matter? In all likelihood, I should never see him or his golden-eyed niece again. I felt sadly out of sorts at this realization.

"Put by Mrs. Radcliffe and go to sleep," I ordered Palla, and she surprised me by obeying.

As she sank beneath the covers, she said drowsily, "Next to Uncle Moura, I like you, dear Anne. Take care of yourself when I am gone and don't let old Nutting work you too hard." She paused, snuggled down, and grinned. "I'll tell some dashing Frenchy to come and carry you off."

How could I be cross? I sent Charlotte to her bed, tucked the covers around both girls, and, snuffing out the candle, left the room. I knew I should sadly miss the honey-tongued little ambassadress from our great enemy, France.

And now she was gone, the gay, mischievous Palla. She had astonished me by kissing me farewell before Miss Nutting and most of the school, and though I kept my composure, I am sure I flushed with surprise and pleasure. Embarrassed as I was, I could not help feeling at last that her little attachment to me had been genuine. I had a true friend in Palla Florin, perhaps my only true friend in the world.

I scarcely saw Palla's guardian. I had been busy all morning in the preparations for Miss Nutting's monthly tea for the parents and guardians of her pupils. But as the carriage drove around to the front door and Palla was handed in by her uncle, I caught a glimpse of Monsieur Moura's straight trim back. He had his hat off and I was surprised again to note how close-cropped his crisp brown hair was. An outlandish fashion. Probably, unlike our English dandies, he disliked curly hair and had cut it short enough for a convict's crop. It was a remarkably handsome head – or perhaps it was just the manner of his carrying it.

As he was about to step back into the carriage, he spoke to Miss Nutting. She pointed at the window where Patty and I were rehanging the portieres. He looked toward the window and bowed. I think he smiled as well. I went on, very busy, pretending not to see him. I did not know why I behaved so abominably.

Patty squealed.

"Ouch! Miss Wicklow! You pulled the cloth out of my hands too fast. Them things burn!"

"Nonsense!" I said, vastly displeased with myself, for now Monsieur Moura had stepped into the carriage and the coachman was whipping up toward the London post road.

You may think me daft that, for all my interest in my little foreign friend, I had very nearly forgotten her by the end of six weeks, but so it was. There was the day's work to be done from six in the morning until midnight. There were the other young ladies who came to me with their problems, so that I might abet them either in their secret romances, which amounted to no more than the exchange of billets-doux with the callow local swains, or with the loan of a shilling until the inevitable "sweets money" came at the end of the quarter.

The first week or two after Palla's departure, I managed always to be on hand whenever a messenger arrived; for, aside from the pleasure of hearing that Palla had arrived safely, I confessed to a secret hope that somewhere in her duty letter to Miss Nutting would be a mention of me, perhaps even a hint that her guardian had spoken of me.

No letter came. My heart slowed again to its normal, relaxed beat, but I liked less than ever such would-be suitors as the gardener's toothy, twenty-year-old assistant, Miss Zenobia's hip-pinching papa, and the greengrocer's boy who was all of eighteen. I tried to reconcile my dreams to the certainty that I was not like to meet any more romantic male strangers. There had been only this tiny rent in the prosaic pattern of my life, a tantalizing view of a man I could admire and feel my superior, a man of mystery, fascination, and intellect. He was far above my station, and pride, scruples, and teachings prohibited my becoming the plaything of any man. But for a few days it had given me a sensation of delight hitherto unknown to imagine myself in Monsieur Moura's employ: receiving the day's orders from him, keeping his quarters immaculate, being now and again invited into his confidence on the happiest method of seating guests in the great dining room at Moura, or purchasing portieres, or even in managing the high-spirited Palla.

But the weeks passed. Then quite unexpectedly, early in September, the first letter came from Palla Florin.

3

It was a charming, slapdash note painting for us a life untrammeled by the fusty old virtues of schooling and discipline. There were no shadows in that first letter, unless one were minded to question a minor note of mystery near the end, obviously the product of Palla's disordered imagination.

The letter was addressed to me, the second I had received in my life. I was as deeply touched by this fact as by the letter itself:

MA CHERE ANNE:

How do you go on? Do any of the girls speak of that horrid little Frenchy? No doubt, without me, the school is quiet as a mouse, which brings me to mention that the mice in France, at least at Moura, are bigger than those wretched hounds that used to be run down in the roadway at Miss Nutting's.

I was a trifle uneasy in my stomach as we crossed "La Manche," which is what Uncle Moura and the other Frenchies call your Channel, but when we reached Calais all was well.

What a fine thing it is not to have to study every day!

They treat me like a princess here, waiting upon me in every way. I am not allowed to so much as take a

23

step without someone flying to accompany me and do my bidding. The seneschal is named Achille, the very same strange, slithering creature I remembered so well. He always took to me and now asks me what dishes I prefer, as, of course, is proper, since I am truly the lady of the manor and the heiress to Moura.

Moura is divine. It is my very dream of a château. There is so much to see, I have never yet left the grounds. I simply wander and wander, seeing many things I should not, I don't doubt.

I do not often see Uncle Moura. He has no love for his home (I should say *my* home; for one day it will be mine), but when he does come, he is most proper and polite. He tells me – this will please Miss Nutting – that I behave very nicely. My manners are pretty and I am grown into a vastly biddable female. Well, perhaps he does not say quite that, but he says he thinks I may become acceptable, which is the same thing; is it not?

France must be a very curious place since the Emperor is done with. So much to itself these days. You will not credit this, but since I have returned to Moura I have not been presented to a soul, nor, indeed, have I met one guest at Moura. So far as this province is concerned, I may as well be dead and buried, or worse, never have existed. And truly, chérie, I feel ever so alive.

Your naughty friend,
PALLA FLORIN

The letter gave glimpses of so much and yet managed to show so little of Palla's life at Moura. There could be no doubt that she was happy. Her mention of Moura as "divine," a "very dream of a château," brought to mind one of those exquisitely wrought French country houses that I imagined were everywhere in that benighted country before their bloody revolution.

I took the letter at once to Miss Nutting, who sniffed and exclaimed, "Gad's lift! I hadn't thought of it. Now we have the explanation for the good behavior of those young rascals abovestairs. Their bear-leader is safely out of the country."

I felt wounded for little Palla by this surly comment, which seemed to crush all the life and gaiety out of the letter.

"Well, ma'am, that'll hardly be a bit of news to you, now will it?"

She looked along her nose at me.

"Are you being impertinent, miss?"

"Not at all, ma'am. But I'll lay my life Miss Palla is disposed to be sweet and loving to those who offer her friendship."

"Friendship, my foot! That girl is a Frenchy. All they think of is how the rest of the world may be properly used to their advantage. You'll note she makes small mention of me, her loving headmistress."

At this I could not forbear smiling. Miss Nutting, as honest as she was wrank, caught my expression and after a moment's wrestle with pique, gave a loud, whinnying laugh.

"You'd say I was never loving to any child. And you'd be right. Give me a mewling colt, an ancient, spavined, dray horse, and my heart's on my sleeve. But these missish young brats! Well, I should have been born into the equine family."

I liked her for her confession even while I strove hard to keep from joining in her laughter. It is permitted to laugh at one's self, but beware of laughing at the idiosyncrasies of one's superior. And then too, even from the distance of

25

two-score years, I look back upon Miss Nutting with the affection one reserves for an odd but endearing second mother. God rest her.

I took Palla's letter to my room and read it often in the ensuing days, for it was one of the very few objects that belonged exclusively to me. Mine was the superscription on the reverse of the single page, and mine was the name Palla had addressed when she wrote to Miss Nutting's Academy for Select Young Females. I was shamed by my own conceit in this matter, but truly the receipt of a letter was one of those great occasions that marked a kind of anniversary in my life.

Two more such anniversaries occurred before the month was out, and these letters altered the entire course of my life, bringing it near to an end of such horror as still pulls me wide awake in a fit of shivers on moonlit nights, though that evil time is many years gone.

The second letter came into the hands of illiterate little Patty McKissick, who made out only the word *Anne* and dutifully handed it to one of the older pupils, Miss Anna Sophia Fairweather, who had been complaining that her grandpapa's quarterly letter "with funds" was overdue. She too ignored the superscription. Before the letter came into my hands, the whole school was in an uproar.

Charlotte Ramikin had run to Miss Nutting with a tale of murder, poisoning, and I don't know what all. "Those Frenchies" were killing her dear friend Palla (who had always dominated her unbearably) and the Bow Street runners or some such superior being ought to be sent over to France to rescue her. While Miss Nutting digested this startling news along with the contents of Palla's message, I was permitted to read the

26

letter in her presence and that of the twittering young Charlotte.

The contents were puzzling, but the writing itself shocked me. It was weak, ill-formed, not at all what I remembered from Palla's compositions here. The firm, decisive young hand was totally missing.

DEAREST ANNE,

I shall send this by the deaf and dumb kitchen girl who has promised to have it sent on to you from the village; for I am never allowed to leave Moura, unless one of Them is close by me.

I miss you. I miss you all so dreadfully. I am so tired of this hateful place, never seeing anyone but Achille and Matilde, the cook. Once or twice I have seen Uncle Moura's cousin Kate, who lives in the lodge at the entrance to the Moura woods. But I don't think they like her here.

Oh, I wish Uncle Moura liked me. I try hard, but things always come out wrong. I have the most amazing talent for doing the very things that annoy him. Sometimes I hate myself.

I had a governess for several weeks. She was very stupid and when Uncle Moura hired her, she made eyes at him and used to go on to me in a very silly way about him. Naturally, he was polite to her but quite cold, the way he is to me so much. I didn't like her, but still, she was someone different, and now she doesn't come back.

However, that's of no consequence, as Miss Nutting would say, because she was a tale-bearer.

I told her I wanted to go to the village just once, alone, to the fair and market day, and watch the puppets and the stilt-walkers and all. She knew it was a secret but she told Achille and now they won't let me even leave the château. Yes, she was hateful! Hateful! I do not want her back. I am glad she is gone, with her snooping and her mincing, and her silly-eyes at Uncle Moura. But it is lonely.

Achille has tried to be kind but he scares me. When I was so sick and saw the ghosts and phantoms, he told me it was because I had power to see them and others did not. But all the same, I was scared. I don't want to see them again. I am afraid to go to sleep at night because that is when *she* comes, and I can't bear it. Every time I begin to feel sleepy it seems as though I will go into what Uncle Moura calls my "feverish lassitude" and be sick and weak again. So I will not let myself sleep. Uncle was good to me while I had the fever, and often brought me the water and interesting things to drink and make it easier for me to rest. He sat by my bed all night and then I never saw *her*.

But Uncle Moura has gone away again, and though I feel well and strong now, I am afraid.

I wish I had never come to this hateful place. Please, please write to me, dear Anne. I am so lonely I don't think I can bear it.

Your devoted
PALLA FLORIN

I could not look up for an instant after reading that pitiful note. I felt the unfamiliar prick of tears behind my eyelids. Not since my parents died long ago in the overturn of a cart on the road to Dublin Fair had anyone cared for me. I was needed, and by someone who loved me a little. I wanted to cry for Palla's unhappiness, but another part of me wanted to roll up

28

its sleeves and set to work against whatever was hurting the child.

"Well? Well? What do you make of the gibberish?" Miss Nutting asked.

Charlotte let out a shocked squeal which seemed to annoy Miss Nutting more than ever.

I said, "Miss Palla has a powerful imagination, as you know, ma'am. And she has been ill, probably an inflammation caused by the change of climate."

Her eyes narrowed. She looked at me piercingly.

"You think these ravings about 'she' and 'her' are all out of that nonsensical head of hers?"

I was a little startled at what seemed to be a change of front. "Don't you, ma'am?"

"Oh, stuff! I'm not in the habit of seeing phantoms in the night, nor do I believe others do unless they've overindulged in spirits of a more likely hue. I mean, do you think they are persecuting the girl?"

I thought they were.

Not Monsieur Moura, of course. Instinctively, as I had read Palla's letter, my mind kept finding excuses for her uncle. He was home so seldom. He had taken good care of her when she was ill, sitting by her all night, fetching drinks, et cetera. No. The criminal was the ubiquitous seneschal, Achille, who slithered. Or the mysterious Cousin Kate who wasn't wanted at the château but yet lived in the Moura lodge. Or anyone else in that evil France where there must be thousands of likely suspects. But not – surely not the master of Moura.

"Yes," I said. "I think they are persecuting Miss Palla. Not her uncle, of course, but – "

"Why 'of course'? He's perfectly capable of it. She says the estate goes to her upon his death. But what if he contemplates marriage?"

I had a sudden thought.

"Palla speaks of a governess who was dismissed, a woman who may have had a personal interest in Monsieur Moura. Couldn't she have tried to hurt Palla out of anger and resentment at her dismissal?"

"Her natural target would be Moura himself, since he probably dismissed her. And don't overlook the fact that he has an indifference verging on hatred toward Palla. You yourself marked it. No. That uncle bears watching."

I tried not to let her see my indignation as I carefully changed the subject.

"What can we do for her?"

"Do? Good Gad, girl! It's no longer our affair. We are not birds to fly across the Channel and pluck her out of France. Whatever we may think of those wretched villains that've kept Europe in an uproar for a score of years, they are a sovereign country. I shall write to the magistrate of the village of Moura, warning him that I am onto Moura' little game and suggesting that, to preserve the good name of the province, they see that Moura keeps his niece in good health."

I was horrified.

"You will never do such a thing, surely! It would be most improper! He is innocent. I am convinced of it."

I did not like her penetrating gaze.

"Hoity-toity, miss! What ails you? What is Edmond Moura to my housekeeper?"

"Nothing at all, ma'am. But justice is something to me . . . There'll be the work waiting. Excuse me."

I left the room in a fury. I had underestimated Miss Nutting's powers of observation.

*   *   *

It came as we might have expected – the last desperate plea from a sick and frightened child in a country of strangers. It was two weeks after Miss Nutting's rudely effective note to the magistrate at Moura. In all likelihood, Palla's note had crossed Miss Nutting's letter. And, making it even more poignant to me, Palla addressed Miss Nutting, as though she had given up hope of aid from me.

MISS NUTTING,

Oh please please – I am frightened. Clou will take this to the village but though I asked her to indicate to them in the village that I am a prisoner, she doesn't understand. She is deaf and dumb.

They are – they really are – they are trying to kill me. I don't dare to drink anything. When I do, I go to sleep at once, and I see *Her* in my dreams.

I ran away yesterday but it got dark and a peasant and cart came by and I was happy when he took me up. Then I saw it was Achille.

Oh Miss Nutting – if you ever receive this – oh please oh please – I don't want to be dead. I want to go away – help me –

It was the last message we ever received from Palla Florin.

"Mother of God!" I whispered. I stood before Miss Nutting and got out my handkerchief and used it. I felt the child's pitiful plea in my very heart.

"Come, come, this will not help." Miss Nutting rubbed her leathery face with the heel of her hand. "I don't propose to play the spy at my age. But it's plain as a pikestaff, someone must see what they are about."

"They are about killing her!" I cried.

"We don't know that. We know Palla thinks so, and we also know Palla has a vivid imagination."

31

I held out the letter. "Is that the writing of a healthy girl? I have nearly all of my salary for the past two years. It is enough to get me passage across the Channel and into France." I knew that the mention of my own money would be persuasive to Miss Nutting.

"You know what you are suggesting? There may be danger. I don't say there is, mind you, but there may be."

"I shall be careful. Believe me." The idea of the trip was new to my tongue but I realized as I spoke that it had been in my mind since Palla's second letter. "I will visit the château as a friend to Palla. All most innocent and proper."

"Your understanding of French is well enough, but your speaking French is atrociously bad."

"I will then appear more stupid, which is what I wish to do."

She frowned.

"It may serve. I might even advance you a guinea or two for your journey. But you will require schooling in your conduct over there. I'm not at all sure I should let you go. Still, I see only one real objection, aside from your personal safety. I suspect you are susceptible to Edmond Moura."

I flushed. "I've an open mind, I hope."

"Hmph. That's as may be. Just remember this, my girl. So far as we know, the death of Palla Florin would serve only one person at Moura – her uncle. No matter how distinguished and charming he may be, the poisoning of his fifteen-year-old niece must rob him of a little of that charm."

It was humiliating to be so reminded, but I had to accept its justice. In any case, I was in a muddle over my suspicions. On the surface, I reasoned that one of the servants was guilty; but far beneath, in the core of my mind, I had a spreading fear that Monsieur Moura just might be capable of this terrible crime.

Only at Moura would I find the answer.

4

Although a rosy hue still dappled the sky, the Auvergne forest enclosing the road already was beginning to take on that twilight blue which gives eery life to stones and hedges and rotting tree stumps. The weekly coach had moved by fits and starts for the past hour through this desolate region, and as I was the only passenger, I lowered the window and put my head out.

I asked in my bad, schoolgirl French, "Coachman, if you please, can you tell me if we are near the château called Moura?"

"Moura," repeated the fat little coachman with a sudden backward stare at me. "Soon, mademoiselle." He frowned at the forest on either side and whipped up the horses. "It is off the highroad. One walks two kilometers, more or less, through the forest. And then – Moura."

Curiously, I studied the occasional humped shadows beneath the trees crowded along the edge of the ill-kept road. They shifted and moved furtively like great grey dogs. What were they? Two kilometers, while no more than a brisk walk to one accustomed to physical exertion, was a long way to go through an unknown forest when this blue dusk would be darkness within an hour.

"What sort of place is Moura?" I asked in English, and then translated carefully.

"Ah, that," the coachman shrugged. "A château. Very

old. A den of robber lords in the old days. It is not grand. The satin-new Bourbon at Versailles would call it a mousetrap. We Auvergnats call it 'The Devil's Turrets.' "

"Do you think it safe to approach at this time of night?" Not that it signified. It was too late to turn back now.

"Unless one is frightened of wolves. They grow hungry here on the threshold of winter. Does mademoiselle fear wolves?"

I supposed this was provincial humor and tried to answer him in kind. But like many who have lived much in schools where there is no love to spare, I had stored away humor along with love and seldom brought it out without finding it all askew for lack of use. My humor was like that, a hopeful little stab at a joke, and if it failed of its mark I was as serious as a judge for hours after.

"If I were a wolf, I'd not be dulling my teeth on foreign bones when your Auvergnat peasants would make such a hearty dish."

Another shrug. "The Moura wolves ate eleven human beings last winter, mademoiselle. It is not known for a certainty if they made a hearty dish."

I flushed over the setdown. Nor was I made any more comfortable about my destination.

"Have the owners of Moura done nothing about the wolves?"

"You speak of the master, isn't it so?" The coachman's broad toad-face widened in a grin. "But yes. Monsieur would have the wolves killed, only for one thing. There are those who prefer the wolves to Monsieur." He added after a little pause, "Then too, he was not always here at Moura."

"Where was he, then? In Bonaparte's army?"

35

The coachman chuckled. "Not entirely in the army. Ah, that, no!"

"But where, then?"

He shrugged in the way that was becoming familiar to me.

"I am not his keeper, mademoiselle. Monsieur fought for the Emperor at Waterloo. It is enough. It is absolution. All the robber Mouras since the tenth century are absolved by one day in the Old Guard."

His politics were evident and I did not pursue the matter. But his ears must have become accustomed to my weird French with its Irish intonation, for he encouraged me to talk.

"Why does the foreign mademoiselle visit Moura now? It is not a place one goes to for the health. I have told other ladies that. The pretty governess with the yellow hair, for example. But she does not listen either. She goes – then, nothing."

A wraith of fog from the marshy forest bottoms fingered my cheek but I did not withdraw my head. The interior of the coach was airless as a tomb.

"I am to visit Mademoiselle Florin, the heiress to Moura."

"Hmph," said the coachman in a manner that sounded disrespectful. He turned silent again, and as I was more lonely and uneasy than ever, I tried to draw him out, but he wouldn't say another word.

The trees, which interlaced over the road, fell away in one place under the still rosy sky, and revealed here and there a weathered farmhouse crouching along the horizon. After twenty years of war it was not a prosperous country, nor did these early fall days of 1815 herald anything but a fearful winter to come. Crops were already frozen in some provinces. Hailstorms had finished them, and winter not yet upon the countryside. I began to understand those strange, humped shadows in the forest. The wolves were foraging as desperately as men.

Aside from a family of peasants gathering firewood an hour ago, I had seen no human beings since the coach entered the forest. Either the season or the time of day, or possibly the Moura woods themselves, warned away human intruders. I was about to dip my head back into the coach and smooth my ruffled hair when an ancient, vine-covered porter's lodge suddenly appeared at a crossroad in the densest core of the forest.

"Mademoiselle descends here," the coachman bawled loudly, as if announcing me to the unseen forest creatures.

To my alarm, the lodge showed no signs of habitation. Just beyond the low, squat building was a side road wide enough for carriage wheels. A mouldering stone archway framed this road, and keep in the apex of the arch were cut the mouldering letters:

MOURA

I tried to get a good look at the estate road as the coachman let down the steps, but the scramble to get my bonnet on straight and descend from the coach and rescue my ancient portmanteau before the coachman departed required all my attention. Then, as I was about to question the coachman on the danger of prowling animals, he leaped up onto the box with a sobering "God guard thee," and joggling the reins, rattled down the road while my voice trailed after him in English:

"But wait! Do you think . . . ?"

Before the words were out of my mouth I knew there would be no answer, and it gave me a start when a

37

voice from somewhere in the dusk of the crossroad called merrily, also in English, "He thinks so seldom, my lass."

I half expected to find myself alone in spite of that voice, but a buxom, black-haired, dark-eyed beauty was waving an empty water jar at me from a little garden at the back of the lodge. I had never seen any sight so welcome. Taking up my portmanteau, I stepped under the arch and down the Moura road toward the woman. She coughed over the dust stirred in my wake, begged me to "Go gently, gently," and picking up a second water jar, joined me. "If you are for the château, I'll come along. No wolves about yet. But one never knows."

In the distance a last ray of sunlight filtered through the trees and across the straight, unwinding road. Still there was no sign of the château. Seeing the long stretch of primeval forest at the far end of the road, I asked, "Pardon, if you please, madame. Shall I see the château presently?"

"Gad's life!" she exclaimed, for all the world like Miss Nutting. "Don't struggle with your French. My mother was English. Yes. We shall see the château. I haven't noticed your kind here before. Moura doesn't have guests, and they don't need servants. Perhaps they owe you money." She looked me up and down with lively eyes. "But it's unlikely." It was plain that she found no wealth in my black cashmere traveling shawl, my only bonnet, and the sturdiest of my two old-fashioned, full-skirted gowns.

"I am here to visit the heiress, Mademoiselle Palla Florin," I said, enjoying the beauty's rude kindness and the wonderful sanity of the English tongue.

"Heiress? Well, perhaps you should speak to fat Cousin Eustace Moura about that. As for me, my pitchers and I are on our way to Moura to fill ourselves. Call me Kate. I am – or was – an actress. Maybe you saw me in London in my green youth. No? Too many others didn't either. That's why I am home from my Odyssey. I rent the lodge from Achille for a very pretty sou, I can tell you. But the lodge well always runs dry this time of year, and the Moura brandy is good. That Achille is a stingy fellow, as I live! How Edmond can have kept him about the place for so long – ! Well, I suppose he has his reasons. And I don't want to know what they are. Thank God, Edmond will soon be putting things to rights here. He has been gone too long."

The last thread of daylight vanished and night was suddenly upon us. Kate laughed and then shivered, looking skyward.

"Just at the instant of twilight, that is when I don't like to be caught at Moura."

Carefully following a wagon rut to keep from wandering off the road, I put a question that I tried to make amusing nonsense.

"Will you tell me next there are ghosts at the château that come out at twilight, and ladies who lost their heads, and armor that goes 'clank' at midnight?"

"Lord love you, child, no! There is a ghost, but a perfectly reasonable one since she was – since she died only ten years ago. And you'll find the skeletons of some of the Moura robbers who used to watch the highroad from the East Tower and then ride down on rich travelers carrying treasures or women. All this went on from the tenth century when the château was only a wretched little heap of stone walls, until seventy or eighty years ago. Dozens of Mouras were beheaded. Richelieu executed seven all at once when they joined the Languedoc rebellion about a hundred and fifty years ago. Imagine!"

I imagined. That was my great trouble. I was only just able to say calmly, "An exciting family."

"Oh, exciting, I can tell you," said Kate. I felt that she smiled in a secret way, but then she changed the subject suddenly. "There's the East Tower over the treetops under that star. A good three stories higher than the other towers. That is where every Moura used to watch the highroad for his prey – take care. This is the bridge over the river. In the old days, it was a moat. You can easily lose your footing here."

It was no place in which to be left alone. I was out of the forest and over the bridge in no time, almost close enough for my skirt to be caught under the clip-clop of Kate's high, red heels. The acrid odor of reeds and dead vegetation floated up from the bed of an ancient stream twenty feet below; only a trickle of water remained. I was depressed by the fact that not a single light was reflected from any of the recessed window openings above the moat. As far as could be seen, the East Tower and its several slitted embrasures up to the high turret were deserted. So was the lower, crenelated stone building wedged between the East Tower and the decaying turrets to the north and northwest.

Moura was not the modern, eighteenth-century château I had dreamed of. Where were the spacious lawns, the dainty fountains and hedges? Instead, I saw a small, medieval fortress, desolated by time and legend. A perfect robbers' cave for the lawless Moura men.

I murmured, "This is not the thing, at all. I thought châteaux in France had thousands of servants and things."

"So we did here," said Kate quickly. "Moura was always crude, but it was lively enough. The peasants feared the place as they fear the Devil. And with good reason. The Mouras were always doing something mad. Wrestling with gypsy bears, or hunting wolves with a quill knife, or shooting hawks from the parapet on the East Tower. They had town friends down from Paris. Once one of the Bonaparte women was here with Edmond. Crowns or coronets, or straws from a pigsty, the Mouras took any they wanted. Only they preferred an assault to an easy conquest in the old days, and that meant trouble. Coming to Moura before the murder was like attending a village fair. Not formal or grand at all." Kate sighed. "Times change. Already the country is returning to Bourbon formality. Too bad."

"There was a murder? When?"

She frowned. "I shouldn't have mentioned it. I still think it was a good riddance. But, in any case, Laly Florin, the mother of that slant-eyed little hussy, Palla, fell from the high embrasure in the East Turret. Quite a girl was our Laly! Seducing the servants or any other male who walked by. Enchanting creature; though if she could she'd as soon have murdered you as looked at you, if she saw in you a rival. She'd no use for that little daughter of hers. Even at six Palla showed signs of growing into a beauty to beat our Laly, and don't think Laly didn't know it! Did everything she could to make the child appear ugly, but it was no use. Lady Florin had been an opera dancer. Regular tawny-haired little sprite, not much bigger than her child. . . . Here we are at the door. . . . It's Laly who's our ghost, so the servants say. Moura can't hold a decent servant for a fortnight. Nor a governess, nor a housekeeper. Laly's the cause. The Combing Lady, they call her."

The old drawbridge entrance to the fortress had been stoned up. In its place was an iron-bound door with hardly room in front of it for a carriage to turn around. Kate handed me one of her water jars and briskly rapped the wolf's-head knocker. I held my breath. I would not have been surprised to see a vicious Moura robber answer that summons. Or even that ghost they called the Combing Lady.

The heavy door was slow to open. Perfectly proper in a haunted castle, I thought. But at that moment a big, florid face, about as mysterious as a peasant washerwoman's, which it greatly resembled interposed itself in the doorway.

Kate said cheerfully in French, "Good evening, Matilde. You see me begging water and wine, as usual. Don't mix them. Shouldn't like to taint the wine."

"Ah, it's you," said the big, red woman, as one says, "Ah, the devil!" She took the two jars without offering me shelter and was just turning away when Kate pointed out her omission.

"Tell Mademoiselle Palla that Miss Wicklow is here from England. Palla has been feeling poorly of late. A sort of lung fever, I think." This was addressed to me and Matilde looked from one to the other of us, scowling heavily. But I was thinking of Kate's aside to me. Was Palla truly ill then?

Matilde was not going to take Kate's word for the identity of this stray on her threshold. She ordered me very definitely to "Wait!" and left the door ajar so we could hear her heavy sabots clomping the stone floor within. Her harsh voice, reeking with strength and ill-nature, was raised a moment later.

"Achille, there is a thing outside that says it is from England."

A stir, the rattle of a candlestick, and a few minutes later, footsteps very different from Matilde's wooden sabots approached the door. They had a light, gliding sound, rather like the slither of a serpent. I set my bonnet straight once more and removed from my dark shawl imagined particles of dust. I hoped my looks were satisfactory. I was relieved when Kate spoke first to the empty doorway, apparently seeing the person before I did.

"Sorry to bring you away from the fire, Achille, but you will want to welcome Miss Anne Wicklow who is, I understand, to be a guest of the house."

The ribbon of light widened until the door stood open and a slight man of middle height stepped out before us with a lighted candle in his hand. By that flicker we surveyed each other. He must have possessed an extraordinary feline beauty in his youth. He was about forty-five now, his still unlined face framed by unkempt grey hair hanging raggedly to his shoulders. His eyes had the curious opaque shine of new-minted silver. A faint frown ruffled his forehead as he looked at me; yet when he spoke his voice was, like his eyes, silvery.

"What is this, mademoiselle? From England, you say?" Achille stepped back into the house, taking the portmanteau in his slender hands. "Come in, child. Come in."

I obeyed him and found myself jolted by big, red-haired Matilde who handed two full jars to Kate and tried to slam the door in her face.

"Many thinks," called Kate, not in the least offended. She added in English, "Good night, Anne. Happy dreams."

Achille took me by the arm and gently drew me into the center of a long, bare, rectangular stone hall blackened by four or five centuries. Its beamed roof was so high it was lost in obscurity. His voice was sweetly reassuring, but his eyes showed he was puzzled.

"Where are my manners? Welcome to Moura, mademoiselle."

A little of my uncertainty fell away as Achille carefully

43

set down the portmanteau and helped me out of my bonnet, though I would not part with my shawl.

"Come to the fire, child. You must be cold. Matilde! A drop of mulled wine and some biscuits for mademoiselle."

We sat down together at the settle before the hearth and studied each other. I found his gentle manner cloying. I was relieved when Matilde came clomping around the edge of the settle with a wooden trencher of cold porridge and a mug of watered wine.

"No more biscuits."

"At least give the child some sugar for her porridge." It amused me to hear him call me child. I was taller than he.

Exhaling sharply, Matilde pulled from a pocket of her red-striped petticoat a hard little brown block of sugar and set it down on the trencher.

"You are a great fool," she informed the gloomy hall, but whether she referred to Achille or to me, I did not know. I began to eat and found cold porridge quite palatable to a stomach that had taken nothing but vile French tea since morning.

Achille looked around the hall, pursing his lips thoughtfully when he supposed I was not watching.

"I think we will put you in one of the rooms above us. They are much newer apartments, recently done over – in the last century, I believe. You may take your choice. How long do you intend to be with us? Monsieur Moura will not be returning for another few days, I fear."

Over the warm, spiced wine I stared at him.

"But I thought Matilde had told you. I am here to visit Mademoiselle Florin. I was her – her friend at Miss Nutting's school."

To my astonishment he turned pallid, almost as if he

would faint. He recovered after a frightening minute or two.

"Mademoiselle Palla is not here now. She sleeps off the estate these nights – for her lungs, you know. We are closed in by the woods here. Very bad for her. If she remains too long – well, mademoiselle, I fear communication in France has been so sadly cut off since the war's end that you may be gone before she returns. But" – he seemed to take a sudden resolve – "we will talk about it another time. And now, if you are ready, mademoiselle, we go to rest very early at Moura. Off to bed at seven o'clock in the winter. Up at five. It will make you big and strong as Matilde here. You'd like that, wouldn't you?"

His perfect features sharpened a little and I saw his teeth. They were very small and even when he smiled.

There was a chuckling sound behind the settle where Matilde had eavesdropped. "A sly boots, Achille. Watch her. Remember I have warned you, and watch her."

The steward frowned at Matilde and, looking displeased, got up to light me to my room. I noticed again his peculiar tread, almost noiseless, like a serpent body passing. He showed me the Great Hall. The walls looked wet with seepage and mould, but I said in truth that it was very imposing. He opened a door and we found ourselves in a damp and drafty passage which seemed not to have been ventilated since Laly Florin fell from the East Tower.

"By daylight I will show you the courtyard. It would be too chill now. The whole château forms a rectangle around the courtyard. Matilde and I occupy rooms off this passage. This is my door. Hers is at the end of the steps."

I hoped his room was a little brighter than the passage.

45

Perhaps he shared my feelings, for he said presently, "The château has been so little used of late that it is almost uninhabitable. The north end, which we are approaching now, is taken by decay and rodents, all the way from the broken tower to the west battlements. The rodents bite, so you should go warily if you intend to explore as I've heard young ladies do."

I said readily, "I am not afraid of rats."

It was unnerving that I could not see Palla at once, but I did not intend to be frightened away without a try.

He had been watching my reaction and a little frown crossed his brow. "Nevertheless, perhaps it is wisest for you to leave the exploring until Matilde or I can show you through the ruins. Matilde is more than a match for a few rats and toads."

"Toads!" I was no more frightened of toads, which I had found to be friendly enough creatures, than I was of rats, but it seemed curious that no one had put them out or killed them in so many years.

At the end of the passage, where the deserted battlements toward the west were boarded off, a spiked window embrasure looked out upon the countryside. The thick forest huddled there in the rising moonlight.

I followed Achille up the spiral steps of the North Tower. The tower itself had fallen into disrepair above the upper floor, where the passage branched abruptly — on the left to an open parapet under the stars, and on the right to the bedchambers over the Great Hall. Achille lighted me through each of four rooms. I must choose the one I fancied.

The first room didn't seem at all appealing.

"It will not disturb you to hear the wind howling over the north parapet?" Achille asked me in his honeyed voice.

The room was drafty and bleak enough without that.

"Is it a common thing then?"

"Rather like an army marching off to battle."

"Perhaps the next room."

But the next room had a weak floor that threatened to drop the sleeper into the rafters of the room below.

"And it will happen this very night, I daresay."

"Probably not tonight. One never knows when these things will occur in an old house. Aside from its little weakness, it is a charming room. Charming. The morning light from the east comes directly through those portieres. Hm. Dusty." As he was engulfed in a cloud from the ancient velvet hangings, he kept stepping on one particular board that creaked in a plaintive way, like a wailing spirit.

I went out to the passage and tried the next room. It was bigger than the other two. The great, dark-curtained bed stood in the middle of the room with a look that was anything but hospitable.

"What a history this room has!" murmured Achille softly. "Old Monsieur, he that was the father of Monsieur Pierre and Monsieur Edmond, hanged himself to the lintel just where you are standing. He was in political difficulties with Madame de Pompadour."

While I moved rapidly down the passage, he stopped to examine the cause of the draft that beat the candle down to a mere shadow of itself, and when I looked back, he was smiling at my haste.

I could not see an immediate improvement in the next room. It looked exactly like the Hanging Room, and was only a little less drafty than the room next to the tower. When I pulled the bed curtains, I could have sworn they hadn't been touched in ten years.

"What gruesome thing will you be telling me of now?" I demanded at once.

"Nothing, my dear mademoiselle. Nothing. This is just

47

where I hoped you would be. Directly over my room. It was Monsieur Edmond's room. But now, as the master, he has the great chamber. If you are nervous or lonely in the night, I will hear your footsteps overhead. But what can hurt you here? You must not let your imagination run away with your good judgment."

"How can you live with such conditions?"

His delicate hands made an apologetic move. "I am a creature of habit. I have lived here since I was a boy. It is home to me and I am too old to be uprooted now. You are more fortunate. You may always return to London."

"Well then, monsieur – "

"Achille," he corrected me.

"Well then, monsieur," I continued firmly. "I make no complaints! All I'll be saying is, you might at least have shaken the spiders out of the bed curtains."

"But Moura has guests so seldom." He led me away from the bed and over to the window where he flung back the portieres. After the dust settled, I gasped at the lurid, moonlight beauty of the forest through which I had walked with Kate. A golden haze had settled over it like dust. Half a league away I could see the tiny flicker of a light that must come from the Moura lodge where Kate lived. I wondered if Kate's gossip had fed my mind to the point where I was rude to this kind and gentle man who had done nothing for me but good. It was necessary to explain to him.

"This room will answer very well. But you must allow that Mademoiselle Kate's stories of the Moura robbers make me mistrust all of the Mouras. I shall want to run to Kate for protection."

Achille's silvery voice was soothing. "But mademoiselle, didn't she tell you that she herself is a Moura?"

* * *

48

By the time Matilde, with her heavy feet and bad-tempered hands, arrived to make the bedroom habitable, I had all the bedclothes airing out the window and, after some good, honest effort, had shoved the masculine furniture into unaccustomed position so I could dust behind the pieces. Matilde's eyes missed nothing.

"The dusting cloth, m'amselle, what is it?"

I shook out a large bundle of ruffled cambric which put her into a great taking.

"The master's shirt! He leave it here ten years ago. What you say to monsieur if he say 'What have you done with my shirt?'"

"I would say 'go get some more made.' Faith! A man should have a new shirt after ten years."

"You think you say so!" said Matilde. "Everyone in the old days thinks he say this and that to monsieur, but monsieur look at them with his eyes and they think 'no.' They do not say it. Where do you find monsieur's clothes?"

I pointed out a big, cobwebbed clothespress with a bare forearm, for I had rolled up my sleeves so as not to soil them. A smudge on the tip of my nose made me look cross-eyed, and I wiped the smudge on the ruffled shirt, which annoyed Matilde so much she made a great racket beating about the bare floor with her wet bundle of broom straws.

"I ask myself, what is Achille thinking of, to put this M'amselle Who-Is-She in monsieur's old bedchamber?"

I removed my shoes and in my stocking feet waded over to the big bed rehanging the tester and curtains, but I stuck my head out to say, "Matilde, it just isn't the thing somehow. Where would monsieur go for so long that he would not take his clothes?"

"Where would he go? To the army, or the galleys,

or the grave. It is all one. A thousand places he can go."

I shrugged. It was no affair of mine. I went back to work. Between us, we made a livable bedroom out of the dusty chamber before Matilde discovered it was eight o'clock and she had been kept an hour from her sleep. This made her so cross she would not light a fire in the grate, and ignored my "good night" as she rattled her wooden sabots along the passage and down the North Tower steps. Achille rapped gently on the door, paid his respects, and was also gone.

With a sense that all Monsieur Edmond's impressive masculine furniture was watching me, I crawled in between the bed curtains and there changed to my nightdress. I came out and combed the snarls from my hair in front of monsieur's shaving mirror on a small gaming table and went around the room peeking behind every arras that hung over the damp stone walls. My window opened directly over the moat two stories below. There seemed to be no place from which the ancient Moura robbers with all their severed heads might clank in upon me. No place but one. The bolt of the door was broken. It was a little prosaic to picture ghosts wandering through anything as simple as a door; nevertheless I resolved to put up some kind of barrier.

Staggering across the room with the great, high-backed chair, I laid it on its side against the door and then, for extra measure, stacked a little footstool on top of it. When I got into bed and drew the heavy curtains, I began to wonder if I had failed to observe some well-made secret entrance in the wall behind an arras. It was quite possible. I climbed out of bed again and made a chain of three pairs of breeches, some shirts, and a waistcoat left in the clothespress years ago by the master. With the addition of a shirt, which proved to be badly eaten by rodents or something similar, I eked out a rope obstacle long enough to tie between the front bedpost and the claw leg of a card table.

It was only after I had snuffed the candle and tucked myself under the covers that I realized there were three other sides of the bed from which I was vulnerable. I could bear being assaulted from the foot or the window side where I could see what was happening when my eyes became used to the dark, but the great bed stood on its dais in the center of the room, so that ghostly (or even corporeal) fingers might still part the curtains behind my head and descend upon my face. I lay for half an hour, listening and wondering if they spoke the truth about Palla, if she was really staying somewhere else where the air was better.

The night was curiously still. Where I had been led to expect the wind roaring over the north parapet, I heard nothing but the many creaks of an ancient house cooling off when the fires die down. I heard Achille's door open in the passage below and wondered if he couldn't sleep either. Why was he wandering about in the night?

My eyes closed.

5

Something roused me from the first deep, exhausted slumber. It must be near midnight, it was so dark; but it was no longer still. I listened. From a long distance away came the howling of animals, a full pack, somewhere in the Moura woods. I would not admit to myself that they were anything but dogs. Then there was a closer sound. Once, then repeated – a sharp, intermittent scratching very near my own room.

It *was* my room! Was it somewhere inside the chamber with me? With icy cowardice, I flung aside the bedcurtains and tore across the room for the door. A taut rope of clothing caught me across the chest and threw me head over heels into a heap on the floor. I clawed myself out of this cambric monster's clutches and ran for the door where I cracked my knee on the overturned milord chair. Nursing my knee I shouted, "I'm coming, I'm coming. Patience."

The scratching ceased.

"Now what can you be wanting at midnight?" I demanded. But glancing at the great clock in the corner, I saw that it was barely nine. I amended a little more graciously, "Who is it?"

There was no answer.

This made me so out of reason cross that I tore down the barricade and, still rubbing my injured knee, flung the passage door wide, fully prepared to deal with any Moura ghosts.

A pale, starved looking girl of seventeen or so stood there holding a candle, a pewter bowl of water, and a comb that glittered as if crusted with gold. I said crossly, "I don't want anything. Do go away."

The girl made motions with the comb through the water and pointed to my tumbled hair.

"No," I said. "Will you hear me now!" Sounds came from deep in the girl's throat, and I understood that she was deaf and dumb. I patted the girl on the arm and shook my head. The girl seemed to understand and turned away reluctantly.

From the end of the passage, wooden shoes sounded on the north parapet and Matilde came along.

"Clou! What do you do here? You hell's spawn!" She seized the girl by the shoulder so sharply that the water spilled from the bowl, but the girl followed her, doglike.

I called after them. "Don't be unkind to her, Matilde. She only meant to comb my hair."

Matilde did not answer. Her beak of a nose looked fierce.

I leaned against the door thinking about poor Clou, who was probably Matilde's drudge and scapegoat. This was the girl who had tried to aid Palla.

After they had gone, I was stepping back into my room when a glitter in the darkness of the passage attracted me. In a puddle of water I found the long-handled comb that had sparkled in the deaf-mute's washing bowl. I closed the door and took the comb over to examine it by the window. In the moonlight it looked fabulous, solidly crusted with gold, and sparkling with five large diamonds. It was so rich I did not like to handle it and finally hid it under my pillow for safekeeping until tomorrow.

The Moura wolves began to howl again. I could admit their identity now. Poor things! They must be hungry out there in the cold forest. I was amused at the fancy and crawled into bed. Lying there trying to sleep, I could not reconcile the richness of that comb with the poverty of Achille and Matilde, and of Moura. How did Clou happen to have the comb? What sort of creature would use anything so precious at mouldy old Moura – unless, indeed, it was Kate Moura's pet ghost, the Combing Lady?

I didn't wake up until almost six o'clock in the morning, which did not endear me to Matilde. She had left a "soup" of oats and goat's milk upon the chimney piece in the kitchen, and reminded me that at Moura they breakfasted fifteen minutes after they arose. She seemed to be forever in a miff, and I tried to make friends with her by telling her about the comb. But getting into Matilde's good graces was like digging a grave through hoar-frost; my words struck only denials.

"What comb?" asked Matilde, busy in the still-room beyond the kitchen. "When do I lose a comb?"

I showed it to her and then to Clou, who looked perfectly blank as she scrubbed the stone hearth.

"This girl of yours, Clou here, had it last night when she offered to comb my hair. That was before you came and took her away."

"Comb your hair? Why does she do that? No such thing. Isn't it so, Clou?"

Clou looked at Matilde and then looked at the comb. She was puzzled but she must have read something in the big woman's red face, for she shrugged and went on scrubbing. My mouth was open in amazement.

"Will you be telling me she did not knock on my door last night, and that you did not come and take her away?"

54

"Dreams. Dreams."

"And this comb?"

Neither Matilde nor Clou would look at it.

"And my knee?" I pursued them relentlessly, thinking of the greenish bruises on my kneecap. "I fell when I was opening the door to her."

"Clumsy, that one," Matilde remarked to Clou, making me mad as fire.

"There's none can say I'm clumsy. It was dark, and I had the chairs piled against the door, and a footstool on top of – "

I was startled by a purring voice behind me, "My dear child! Surely not a barricade against the poor creatures of Moura!"

Indignantly I told him my story.

Even in the harsh morning light, Achille's face had a young look that was oddly at variance with his shaggy grey hair. Why didn't he cut his hair like other men, or even queue it as was done a few years ago? He took the comb and turned it over. I noticed that the frills of his grey cuffs were of silver lace, but very old and repeatedly darned. He looked up presently and gave me comfort by his simple conviction.

"Matilde, why did you say this was not ours? It is the very comb left here by a lady some years ago. I am afraid you were rude to mademoiselle. You will apologize."

I tried to forestall an act that must certainly make her my enemy. "No. No. It isn't necessary. I understand how it was. I didn't show it to Matilde very clearly."

"Matilde! Make your apologies."

All the hairs on her red face stood out as she mumbled something that might be an apology and then stalked into the stillroom where she threw pots and jars around for several minutes afterward.

"First you will want to unpack, mademoiselle. And after, let me show you to Moura."

Greedy for kindness, I thanked him and went up to my room, but I could not help thinking how quickly he had pocketed those five diamonds and all that gold.

It was amazing what the addition of sunlight did for Monsieur Edmond's long unused room. The bed curtains were no longer dark but a very pretty crimson, and the brocade portieres were only a little faded. All the heavy furniture was beautifully grained, though the lock of the clothespress was broken. I felt perfectly free to open it and lay my own clothes over the careless wardrobe Monsieur Edmond had not thought necessary to remove to the master room when he returned from the wars. My own property was soon put away, and after a few furtive glances over my shoulder, I took out a trim, three-caped greatcoat of a style from some years back and held it up before the mirror. I pictured Edmond Moura as I had seen him on those two occasions at the school.

Achille came into the room. Guiltily, I folded the greatcoat and put it in the bottom drawer, murmuring, "He must have been a strange man to be leaving all these clothes behind him."

After a little pause Achille said, "He could afford others." But in that instant before he replied, I caught in the mirror the oddest confusion on his smooth face, as if he hadn't known what to say.

We went down to the courtyard, dingy and grassgrown between the cobblestones. Achille proudly showed me through the great medieval banquet hall, which occupied the entire ground floor of the south end. Nothing looked inviting amid those great stone columns, with the tattered, ancient banners hanging from the beams high overhead, but I supposed it must have been quite exciting in the days when the Crusaders toasted their quest of the True Cross.

The west side of the fortress was in such bad repair there seemed to be nothing that Achille supposed would interest me, for we avoided its interior.

The grey, weathered stones of the East Tower mounted high over the courtyard, and I recalled Kate's story about the Moura robbers who prowled there in the old days, watching for their prey. Had one of them watched me arrive yesterday?

"I should like to see the tower soon. I wonder if I might do so today."

"All the way up? The energy of youth," he sighed. "Not now. Another day. And perhaps Matilde will give us a little cold meat and a flask of wine for us in the turret. Once I am up, I dread those terrible downward flights."

I craned my neck trying to see the turret. It looked so grand up there against the cold blue sky, where hidden eyes might watch the world below. I suggested hopefully, "I'm sure I should have no trouble. You needn't come."

I was thinking that a good general view of the landscape would help me in the event it became necessary to go myself and visit Palla in her retreat.

"The rats," he began, "and toads – "

I tried to reason away his cowardice. "Surely not in a nice clean tower where the steps have no place to go but up."

"There are a dozen ghost stories about it, my dear. They say each of the Moura robbers takes his turn at guard up there forever, and though one does not see him, one hears his footsteps on the staircase."

"But not in daylight." He was going on like a prosy old fidget. Did he think he talked to a child? I thought his tales obviously calculated to frighten me away.

"Yes, but even so, there was a murder from the turret years ago, and we – "

Matilde's strident voice called to him from the Great Hall.

"Achille, at once! It is of importance I speak to you. Alone."

"Very well. Mademoiselle Anne, you have not seen the carriage house. It is over where the West Tower was in former days. Some of the medieval equipage is still there."

I started over to the carriage house while he watched me, apparently not trusting me to obey. The East Tower must wait.

The ancient vehicles of the carriage house, broken and beyond repair as they were, occupied my attention and my imagination for several hours. It was not until the afternoon was well advanced that I found myself again in sight of the East Tower. After a brief lunch of cold meat and a sour wine, I chanced to look out of the windows of the Great Hall. The tower rose across the courtyard, dipped in the red light of the sunset.

The tower embrasures were the height of a tall man, opening on all sides for a complete view of the country around. There seemed, however, to be only one open embrasure in the high turret. Just there it was that a Moura robber had stood, robed in black probably, a creature with terrible eyes that cast a spell. The vision was so plain that I could almost see the robber standing a little behind an embrasure, where the sunlight would not strike and dissolve him.

I went around to the passage and stepped out into the courtyard, shading my eyes. I saw now that there was something in the turret, shadowed against the grey stone. For a moment I thought of calling Achille. But I could guess as I walked forward that what I had seen was only the shadow of a tiny open parapet jutting out below the turret. I did not know what I had expected to see, phantom headless ladies perhaps, or more especially, the Moura robber.

Reflecting that my time at Moura would be very short, for I knew Achille would contrive to send me packing at the earliest moment, I decided to make my survey of the East Tower now, while the day was still bright and Achille and Matilde were otherwise occupied. From that high vantage point I should gain a general idea of what I had to contend with in locating Palla, or the place Achille had mentioned where "the air was better."

I was very careful in climbing the winding stone flight not to touch the walls, for I knew I should find slimy lichen clinging there.

Now and then I stopped to catch my breath and poke my head out one of those embrasures. From one I got a remarkable view of the great Moura woods; then, from another, a southerly view of the woods; and from a third side, the grain fields.

It was during one of these halts to rest that I first heard a sound on the steps high above my head. It was so far away I could use my imagination freely, and it did resemble a footstep – that peculiar dropping sound as a pair of boots descends a stone flight of stairs. The sound corresponded exactly with Achille's story of the unseen Moura robbers and their footsteps echoing through the tower, and I was angry with myself for yielding to the suggestion. It was just as easy to imagine a woman's footsteps. Why hadn't I?

I thought of turning back, but by this time I was at least halfway to the turret, and a sense of failure dogged me. I continued upward, stopping occasionally to listen. Curiously enough, the footsteps above me stopped too.

But if I moved very carefully, I could hear the boots resume their slow downward march again. I stopped at another embrasure. How close the sound was now! Soon, at this rate, I would pass the other occupant of the tower. Could it be possible that someone was hiding up here? Not liking to venture any closer, I rustled down the steps to an easterly embrasure, hearing the remorseless tread nearer and nearer behind me. It would be impossible to outrun those footsteps to the courtyard.

"I had best wait by a window," I thought. "It would be horrid enough in the light, but not so bad as to have him slither by me in the dusk of one of the turns."

I backed into the embrasure, crowding as far as possible until my shoe gritted on a length of twisted and rusty iron. Long ago someone had tossed aside a broken candlestick and time had rusted it into this serpent-like weapon. I picked it up and hefted it for a blow, should the tower inhabitant prove hostile.

Already the heavy footsteps must be passing the embrasure where I had stood two minutes ago. I looked upward, wielding the candlestick. I was stiff against the mouldering stone wall behind me, determined to stand firm to the last, never revealing my terror. For here was a phantom indeed: the Moura robber going off sentry duty. It was so absurd and yet it was all of a piece with what I had seen and heard.

The footsteps rounded the last wedge-shaped step, and I saw an elegant but dusty male boot, a most gentlemenlike pair of pantaloons, and then, a good-looking gentlemen of thirty or so. We stared at each other, I indignant that I had been led to believe him a ghost, he looking so very amazed that he put me quite in charity with him. He was polite, and apologized in, of all languages, good, straightforward English.

"Good Lord, ma'am! I fear I – I really have startled you. It was unpardonable. I went up for the view. I had no notion of – "

A husky young man with frank eyes, a cheerful look, and a handsome appearance, he was far from alarming. I had to smile and hold him guiltless of being a ghost. There was an openness about him that I liked. Here at last, I felt, might be someone in all this weird and ancient pile that I could trust.

He further won me by his hesitant confession: "May I throw myself upon your mercy? The truth is, I am trespassing."

I smiled. "May I say, sir, that in a sense, I too am an intruder."

He seemed vastly relieved. "Then you are not one of – them?" He indicated the main wing of the château across the courtyard.

"Faith, I'm no Moura. The truth is, I came here from a young ladies' academy in southern England, where I am employed as housekeeper. And I came solely to find out the state of health of a former pupil. We did not like the reports we had of her."

He looked at me for a moment. The tower was so grey, the shafts of autumn sunlight so uncertain, that I could not make out his expression. He seemed about to speak, but cleared his throat instead and began to descend behind me.

He told me his name was Charles Armitage, and that he had gone up to the tower for the view he had so often heard extolled. He was an artist, he explained, on a walking tour of Belgium and France since Waterloo. He added wryly, "I fear my artistic capacities did not impress the seneschal. He refused to let me enter, so I came around to the west portal. Quite deserted. In short, I trespassed.

And, ma'am, I shall be quite safe if I may depend upon your discretion."

I assured him that I should be silent as the tomb. "You see, I too have no love for the seneschal of Moura."

Though he was obviously a member of the Quality, I felt nothing superior or forbidding about him. I remember only too well my timidity and uneasiness when in the presence of that other member of the Quality, the master of Moura. But Mr. Armitage seemed in every way comfortable. I felt I should have no difficulty holding my own with him. Ghosts may put me to rout, but except for Monsieur Moura, few mortal men set me trembling in excitement and fear.

The difference, I think, was that Charles Armitage made me feel he was my friend. Monsieur Moura made me aware that I was a female, and weaker than I had supposed myself to be.

How gaudy the sunset light seemed when we stepped from the tower onto the cracked and grassgrown paving stones of the courtyard! The thick, chill shadow of the tower lengthened across our path with the sinking sun. Mr. Armitage glanced over his shoulder, giving a smile that was half a frown. "I believe the wretched tower is pursuing us."

In one sense it eased my troubled consciousness to know that he too recognized the sinister quality of this place. At the same time, it heightened my own premonition of evil. What was the secret here? A woman's death years gone by, which produced a Combing Ghost and a brooding sense of terror? Or even more and worse things? What could be worse? I had the sensation of staring into a series of mirrors, aged, shadowy and unsilvered, one within the other, each a step deeper into mystery, until the ultimate horror appeared. And I could not yet conceive what they might be.

Mr. Armitage took my hand in a friendly way.

"I hope I shall be able to return legally," he said, "to make a few sketches. And perhaps I may be fortunate enough to see you, ma'am. I shall be staying in the village of Moura for a fortnight, just on the chance that I may return. And, ma'am . . . "

"Yes?"

He was most serious. "If anything should go amiss, I hope you will count upon me to help you mend things." He turned away to leave as he had come, by the crumbling west gate. I watched him through the gate; then he waved, and was gone. He too suspected something here, though he was merely a casual visitor with an interest in sketching.

I was sorry to see him go. It was like losing a piece of home. He was the one breath of clean, British air in this foul, foreign miasma.

When I entered the Great Hall, Achille was stooped before the blackened, grimy fireplace, thrusting in a pennyworth of fuel. He looked up with that slippery smile I did not trust.

"There is heated water in your chamber, mademoiselle. In all likelihood, dinner will be late. We are expecting Monsieur Edmond this evening. You will doubtless wish to change."

I wondered what I should change to on the morrow if I wore my other gown tonight. I said stiffly, "Thank you. I will appreciate the heated water."

Achille had just opened the door into the dark passage and had stepped aside so that he would not bar my way toward the bedchambers, when I was startled to see his whole manner change, his thin, sinuous back stiffen as a cat does upon seeing something it does not understand. He had peered down the passage, and now began to retreat into the Great Hall again, backing toward me with a kind of inexorable, measured pace.

"What is it?" I asked.

With some strain, Achille recovered himself. When he turned to face me, his smooth, ageless face within the silver frame of hair was gleaming with sweat. He tried to smile, but the effort was ghastly.

"Mademoiselle. I thought I saw – I do not know what it was – the light from the broken parapet at the end of the passage. Yes, it was that."

"Really!" said I, laughing with scorn, for I thought I understood this to be more playacting for my benefit. "Are you sure there is no ghost in the passage? Come, let me by. I'll soon tell you."

As I suspected, there was nothing. Only the half-dark passage, partially illuminated by the light pouring down the steps from the upper floor, which led to my chamberpassage and to the broken parapet with its eighty-foot drop into space.

The last reflected glow of sunset was gone when I entered my bedchamber.

Clou had left a pannikin of warm water on the deal table, and I washed quickly, hurying to be gone from this room in which I could find no method of lighting the single candle on the gaming table. It grew steadily darker as I made my ablutions. I thought of Achille and the phantom he had seen. I could not quite convince myself that this sudden fear of his was merely to frighten me out of the château. The mask of terror and sweat on his face was all too real.

I wished again that something as honest-looking as Mr.

Charles Armitage resided here. Just one person in whom I could put my trust.

Meanwhile, I would go down to the Great Hall where, perhaps, I should be in time to see the arrival of the master of Moura, and learn of him, if I could, where Palla had gone. I would not admit for a moment that I was excited at the prospect of meeting him again. For all I knew, he was Palla's ogre. Still, he was not a man to leave me calm and unflurried. As best I could in the semi-dark, I brushed my hair and put it in order, changing my old shawl for my good cashmere wrap, and went out into the passage.

If it was dark in my bedchamber, it was black as a peat-bog in the passage. I had no mind to return the way I had come; the stone steps leading to this passage might easily be mistaken in the dark for the steps leading to the broken parapet. True, if I turned left and went down this upper passage until I reached a staircase, it might be necessary to walk half around the château. But at least this way was all indoors. There were no sudden turnings into space.

I turned left and walked carefully down the passage. I could see nothing, but there were no obstacles in my way. I remembered very well, from the one time I had used it by daylight, that I must be passing several doors, all fastened with ancient, rusty bolts and locks, and all seeming equally unused.

Just at the time when I felt a staircase must be near, I became aware of a faint rim of light outlining a door standing somewhat ajar on my right. The light was strong enough to show me the staircase was indeed beyond the door, and I was about to pass when I recalled something odd: Achille and the other servants slept belowstairs, and when Monsieur Edmond himself arrived he would be occupying the master bedchamber. Who then could be in this lighted room? I was forever wondering about Palla's situation – it was entirely possible she had never left Moura but was kept in some such room as this.

How fortunate for us both, if this were so, that my instinct had made me turn left from my room instead of right!

I opened the door very slowly. It creaked in an irritating way as I stepped into the room itself: a small bedchamber that had been dressed up with pathetic little frills here and there – on the bed tester, on the dingy portieres hiding a small window that must look onto the courtyard, and on the nightstand beside the bed, where a long taper flickered in the draft. A shawl I had often seen Palla Florin wearing was tossed carelessly over the one chair the room contained. It was a forbidding, prison-like room, and with that taper burning, gave me the singular impression of a chapel prepared for a wake.

I moved about the room, examining the touches by which I recognized that Palla lived here, and so I came to the bed with its faded crimson canopy and curtains, thrust them aside – and saw her lying there, white as marble.

She had been carefully laid out in death.

6

I must have made a strangled sound of horror, for it
floated in the air about me. Even as I caught sight of
her, I knew that she was dead. How childish she seemed
with her hands that had always been so busy in life now
folded together in the manner of a child at prayer, on
her breast! She was in her night rail, and her flesh looked
strangely unlike the healthy young Palla I had known. The
bright complexion now was dulled by a pallor that showed
a faintly blue tinge beneath the transparent skin.

I placed my hand upon her forehead, with some thought
that, miraculously, she would open her eyes and call to
me. The flesh was cold and faintly damp. I removed my
hand quickly. There was a frightful pain at my throat; for
I wanted to cry over my little friend, but something of the
awful crime that had been done here made me shudder,
and all I could do for Palla now was to see that this should
not go unpunished.

With a dread that I was ashamed of, I finally got up the
courage to put my hand upon her poor wasted fingers,
remembering how strong they had been once, and how
alive. It helped me a little to be planning vengeance
for her.

"My little friend," I murmured, "you'll not be going
alone. That I swear! Those who did this to you will pay
for it. By all the saints, I swear it!"

In that room of the dead a voice spoke behind me, in

the faint accent, the strange, unreadable quality of tone that had puzzled and confused me the first time I heard it, and before I turned from Palla's deathbed and stared at the door, I knew whom I should see.

"You would do better to comfort the living, mademoiselle. You are made by nature for comforting, not for the furies."

The master of Moura stood in the doorway watching me, still in his greatcoat and travel-stained top boots, handsome and distinguished as I had remembered him, but looking, I thought, a little weary. I was so unnerved that I curtsied low, hoping to gain time and to compose myself as I arose. But it was no use. I could remember nothing polite, no meaningless phrase to lull him. I was out with it in an instant.

"I have no comfort for murderers, sir."

"I'm sure you would have, Anne. I remember your eyes. They hold comfort for all who are in pain."

He came into the room, looked for a moment at the child in that bed, and although I could read no pity in his face, there was concern. I had a curious notion that, for some reason, the concern was for me. As Palla's friend I resented it so deeply that once more I felt I should weep if I did not hold myself. Poor little Palla! The only tears for her, and from a servant who was not even of her own race!

He took my hand gently.

"They were fools to leave the door ajar. It was a shock to you. I would have told you myself. Later."

I was as brusque as might be with my voice cracking in spite of my efforts. "If you must be kind, be kind to her. She has no one. Poor unlucky child!"

"She is more fortunate than she knows. She has one mourner."

I pulled away from him and went quickly from the room, hoping I should be able to find a place where I might be alone and give way to my natural feelings, but as I turned to go back to my room, in some effortless way he was beside me, my warder, and I the prisoner.

"You must not be alone. Come belowstairs to dinner. You will feel better when you have eaten."

"You are callous. Cruel."

"Believe me. I have done all that is humanly possible. Still it was not enough. The lung fever claimed her."

"She was not sick. She was never sick at Miss Nutting's."

He said in a quiet voice, "She was sicker than you know," and as this brought me to a sudden stop on the stairs, he went on. "Even then, the lung fever must have had its start. Do you recall how flushed she used to be, her abnormal periods of enthusiasm, how her cheeks were so red, how she coughed a little when she had been running?"

It was true, and yet – is this not a normal sign of any growing child?

"But what of the physicians?" I asked. "Could they do nothing? There should be a physician to pronounce the causes of her – death."

"The physician of the village, a Doctor Marigny, made the long trip to the château early this morning with Achille. She was dying then. Of course, if you insist, we can delay the burial until he returns from Lyons. But he has gone there for a month, and – I do not advise waiting."

"Don't speak of it!" I said quickly, but added as a last hope, "There must be someone else in the village who could examine the child and testify to her death from lung sickness."

"Believe me, there is no one, mademoiselle. We are not in Paris now. So much must have been obvious to you as you traveled through this country."

We had reached the passage that separated the Great Hall from the medieval dining hall, and as he opened the door into the former, I remembered that Kate Moura had intimated that Monsieur Edmond's fat cousin Eustace was the heir.

"So then," I said, "Palla's return and her death were all encompassed in order to assure Mr. Eustace Moura's place as your heir."

He seemed contemptuously amused.

"I assure you, Anne, that whatever your own opinions may be on the matter, I am still of an age and a condition to beget my own heirs."

I must have flushed to my very toes, for he glanced at me and smiled, then propelled me into the room with a little push that made me aware of the surprising, steelly strength in him – surely, more than enough to snuff out the life of a young girl like Palla. A girl who loved him, found him fascinating, romantic – as I did.

God forgive me, I thought. Or perhaps – God help me.

Though it tasted like food for a king, it was a strange dinner, served an hour later in that medieval great dining hall. At the head of a vast oak table sat Monsieur Edmond, and I, like a gentlewoman, was on his right in a chair considerably too big for a female. Matilde and Clou waited upon us. Matilde was as cross as two sticks because she must wait upon this intruder, this servant, as though I were the equal of the master of Moura. Clou was quiet but efficient, now and then smiling shyly at me.

In the beginning I said very little to Monsieur Edmond,

for it was my first experience of eating with the gentry and I was much afraid I would make some mistake in my choice among the heavy, confusing silverware, or sample too many of the endless wines served.

"She does not like me," I said once of Matilde.

"She thinks you are English. She lost her husband in '93 in the Vendean Rebellion for which we hold the English to blame, and she lost her son at Trafalgar."

It seemed odd to me that the French should resent our killing them fully as much as we resented their killing us. I was so used to assuming we were in the right.

Still puzzling it out, I resumed my dinner. The wretched porridge and the hard crusts that I had been served formerly were certainly not in evidence tonight. This was my first acquaintance with the French cuisine I had heard extolled all my life, and for a short hour I actually forgot that little Palla had died of the lung fever and was lying in that lonely room above us. Perhaps I didn't entirely forget, but I banished the memory; for let me tell you of the food:

First there were three soups of which I best recollect a delightful clear soup flavored with a whisper of some sort of spirits. These were replaced by a baked whitefish whose creamed and succulent shreds melted in the mouth. Then followed the meat, tender young kid broiled delightfully crisp and golden with delicate herbs. Roast hare followed, I believe, and then I do not remember. I was being careful with the wines along about then. But yes, there were tartlets, a small *gâteau*, and another sweet too which was new to my eyes, a kind of pink island of a pudding, soft as a cloud and swimming in cream. As I ate, I noticed Monsieur Edmond watching me. He had refused the pudding but seemed pleased – or perhaps amused is the better word – over my greedy, childlike appetite.

71

But truly, I did not know then when I should ever eat such food again, and suspected I might never in all my life sit down with the Quality after this night.

Through my wine glass I peered down the row of candelabra on this great table, which had one time served a score of hungry Crusaders. If one refrained from looking at the beamed roof and tattered, dusty banners so high overhead, the candlelight itself was almost cheerful.

"It was gold, but now it looks all rosy," I said.

He smiled. "That would be the flames you see. Drink it down. It will do you much good."

I drank. It was sweet and thick, stronger than any wine I was used to. I felt a little heady. I began to wonder about those other wines I had sampled with the fish, the meat, the vegetables. Faith! I should soon be addled at this pace. I became exaggeratedly careful, making all my movements slow, deliberate, so that I should not betray myself.

"You eat very well in France," I said.

"Some do, yes. But there are others."

There was one lying in a small room overhead who was one of the others, and I had forgotten.

"Poor Palla," I said. "I have deserted her – betrayed her. I came to help the child."

"There was nothing you could do. Everything was done. All that remains is the burial tomorrow."

"Yet – " Swimming in my brain on golden waves of wine, was a memory. "She saw things, she said – in the letters she wrote me asking for help. She saw *her*, she said."

He asked pleasantly, "What letters were these?"

"The ones the servant girl had sent from the village."

There was a pregnant stillness.

"Ah, the servant girl, Clou. But of course. I wondered how – You were saying?"

"You'll be laughing at me, I make no doubt, but Palla said that in the night she saw phantoms."

"Than phantasies of her illness. Was that where you picked up this notion that we were all murderers here?"

"I think perhaps it was Palla's own talk, comparing you to one of the villains in a novel, that started it all. This would be before she left the school"

"Tell me, Anne, why did you not come and speak to me that day I came to fetch my niece? It was most uncivil of you."

"I – I did not see you."

"You lie so charmingly. Admit you did not remember me, and all is said."

"I could do no less," I said. Why should he fancy I spent my days remembering him? An hour ago I was suspecting he had killed Palla. Indeed, I was not yet sure he had not. "Certainly, sir, you had forgotten a housekeeper met casually for a brief ten minutes."

"Forgotten?" He set aside my wine glass and looked at me intently. As I reached nervously for the glass again: "No more of that! Look at me." I was puzzled and sleepy, but did as I was told. "Some day, when you know me better, I will tell you what it meant to me to see you that first night in that wretched school, fresh and lovely. You were all the things I had not seen or touched for many years! Afterward, you looked so defenseless, in that bookroom, with your night robes and tumbled hair, but standing up to me as proudly as you stood up for my niece an hour since. Some day, I will show you if I had forgotten you."

He paused then, I think. It was all a little vague.

"Come," he said suddenly, no longer gentle and tender but amused again. "I will have you asleep on my hands in a moment."

He took up a branch of candles from the table and escorted me to my room, staying a moment to light my candle from those he carried.

"Go to sleep," he bade me. "Think of nothing. You understand? Nothing but sleep."

I said something in the polite manner of the Quality, I hope, and slamming the door carelessly, threw myself upon the bed in my day gown, only shaking off my slippers. I was asleep almost at once.

But alas! The heady wines carried me only so far. I awoke deep in the night to find my candle burning down to the socket. My head felt twice its size, and iron clappers seemed to beat inside it. And I had an enormous thirst.

I tumbled out of bed, catching a glimpse of my dress in the faint candlelight. What a sight it was, twisted and wrinkled. My back seemed twisted with it. Never again, I pledged. No spirits will be crossing my lips. No. Nor French wines.

I searched the room. There was no carafe of water, no glass or mug. Nothing to quench this abnormal thirst. There was an ancient, dusty bellpull by the bed, but I could imagine how this would be received by the angry Matilde, if, indeed, it worked at all. I stepped into my slippers and resolved to go down and find water in the kitchen or stillroom. Even in France there must be drinking water. My tongue scarcely found houseroom in my mouth.

Carefully, I opened my door and went out into the passage. It occurred to me that on my way back I might stop into Palla's room and offer a prayer for her. As I came toward an angle in the passage and knew that from there I should see Palla's room, with the single taper burning through the night, my steps slowed, shameful that I should fear the dead – especially a dead child. But so it was. Palla's door was wide open now. I could tell by the light streaming into the passage. Then I heard Achille's voice within the dead girl's room.

"Monsieur – "

"Well?" I recognized Edmond Moura's voice. He must be there too. Was he at prayers for his departed niece?

Achille said, "That young man was here again today."

I pricked up my ears. They were speaking in French, but it was not difficult to follow.

"What young man?" Monsieur Edmond sounded preoccupied. I wondered what he was doing.

"The Englishman."

"Ah – "

"He had some tale about sketching the view from the East Tower."

"That young man becomes a problem."

"I refused him, of course."

"Yes. It was certainly necessary today."

"Monsieur – "

"Yes."

"What is to be done?"

"Do not let it concern you. I will attend to him."

There was a little silence.

"Monsieur, I have thought of something. Perhaps the young Englishman will go to the magistrate of the village for help."

To my astonishment Monsieur Moura laughed shortly. At once, Achille began to chuckle. I retreated a few steps until I was safe from sight around the angle of the passage, and snuffed out what remained of my candle; for in that instant of their amusement, they had sounded to me like two demons, laughing in Hell.

Their voices were now closer, in the passage itself.

"Let me help you, monsieur."

"Pick up the sheet, I have dropped it. Now. Stand aside. You are in my way."

And then footsteps retreated down the stairs to the ground floor.

Cautiously, I went around the corner and along to Palla's room. I went in. I had forgotten my rosary. Well, no matter; this poor soul in the bed before me would not need my help into heaven. Nonetheless, I would pray for her as best I could.

Gently, I pushed aside the red hangings of the bed and looked down.

During a time of terrible confusion in my pounding head, I thought I would faint.

For the bedclothes were badly tumbled about, and Palla's body was gone.

7

There must be a sound reason for all this, I told myself during the dark, cold hours before dawn.

Why had Palla's body been removed in dead of night, and by Edmond Moura himself? Why not leave the task to sturdy peasants on the estate? Was she to be sealed in the coffin before someone (myself?) called for an examination in which the true cause of her death should be found?

I was in a turmoil once more.

Possibly the disappearance of Palla's body could be explained. The effort to have her properly bedded in her coffin for tomorrow's ceremony was understandable. It might even be that they preferred not to hurt me by the sight. Hence these middle-of-the-night doings.

But Edmond Moura's conversation with Achille on the subject of Mr. Charles Armitage was quite another thing. Why was the Englishman "becoming a problem?" Perhaps even my honest, open-faced British gentleman had lied to me with his talk of sketching scenes from the East Tower. What did he really seek here at Moura?

Beneath all this uncertainty, I will confess, was a nagging, evil thought. "Even if Edmond Moura had destroyed his heiress, he never liked her in any case. But he won't destroy you. He shows you his favor. Do not judge him yet. Give yourself a few more hours in his company. You may never know this sensation of delight again. Let him smile upon you just a little longer. He will not kill *you*. He likes you . . . "

I tried to close my mind to this tongue of my wicked secret itself. But it remained vocal.

"Girl!" I thought. "It comes to this: you abandon the only young friend you ever had, for a man who may be a demon. Ah! You disgust me!"

Later, in despite of it all, I slept, and awoke much stronger, ready for the morning, though it was grey, with a mist clutching at the windows and thick white fog hanging low over the Moura woods.

What a farewell for gay Palla!

Shortly after I had dressed in my other gown and my dark shawl, someone rapped softly on my door and there was Clou with my breakfast on a tray. I remembered yesterday's meal in the dirty, soot-stained kitchen with Matilde's scowl for company. And after last night's ambrosial feast I had no appetite. They had gone to some trouble (or someone had) with the eggs, whipped up and feather-light, with a slice of last night's broiled kid, and – these Frenchies! – a full mug of some dark wine the very odor of which turned my stomach.

Suddenly I knew my suspicions of last night must be disproved, and at once. Before Clou could get far down the corridor, I set the tray on the gaming table, and went after her. I took her as gently as may be by the sleeve, and looked into her face. She was older than I had expected, seen close to like this, perhaps twenty-five or more, but there was the childlike, helpless look of one who neither hears nor speaks. I said in French, "It is necessary that I see Miss Palla's body before it is sealed down. You understand?" She did not, of course. I took her by both shoulders and peered down into her gentle, faded blue eyes.

"You will send Achille to me – Achille!"

This time she understood and nodded happily. I patted her thin cheek and let her go.

I returned to my breakfast and dabbled at it here and there, reflecting that this might be my last substantial meal until I arrived at Dover; for the light of day convinced me I'd find no excuse to prowl about and be at proving something once Palla was laid in the tomb. And I would soon know the truth by looking at her again. The difficulty was, every single strange thing that happened after my arrival might be explained logically by a man as intelligent and plausible as the master of Moura.

I remembered a young lady who died of the same lung sickness at Miss Nutting's during my first year as kitchenmaid. She looked very like Palla – wasted, skin like blue-veined marble, calm-faced in death.

What of Paula's letters? Obviously, the product of a disordered and sick imagination. They fitted perfectly into the pattern of her illness.

I must go from Moura. There would be nothing here to hold me when Palla was in the earth – nothing but the face of a man many stations above me, and the voice of him, and the memory.

There was a harsh scratching upon my door and, when I opened it, there stood Matilde, looking as usual like a red-haloed demon escaped from the nether regions.

"You want to see the child? Come."

Sorry now that I had asked for this painful sight of Palla, I followed Matilde down the passage toward the North Tower. In a corner of the lower passage, directly behind those broken steps and lighted fitfully by a candle in a wall bracket, Palla's coffin was laid out on a heavy, ancient table that had doubtless served to feed the Mouras in the years when all of Europe was as black and evil as the

79

Mouras themselves. I knew what I should expect. The very fact that I had been permitted to view the remains once more convinced me that Monsieur Moura had nothing to hide in that regard. How easy it might have been for him, or for Achille, to assure me that she was already sealed in her coffin. The only disturbing thing was the busy corridor itself. There must have been eight to ten people there, taking brief glimpses of Palla in the coffin and then passing on into the Great Hall, probably for refreshments. They did not look to be a friendly breed. Like most of the French I had seen so far, excepting Edmond Moura, they were short, a little inclined to corpulence. They were all hard-faced, as though iron were in their souls. I had not suspected so much strength in this effeminate race. One man looked up at me as I came around the steps. He nudged another peasant beside him. Both were mustached, which was rather a surprise to me, as I was used to clean-shaven men. These two looked as burly as those moustachioed veterans of the Emperor's Russian campaign. And I heard, quite plainly, one of them remark in French:

"Ah, that one, yes. These Mouras and their wenches!"

I could scarcely believe it. Perhaps I had misunderstood. Then, as my cheeks reddened with my indignation, I realized what it must have meant to Edmond Moura to be suspected falsely of something as I was now.

I passed the French veteran, hoping that he had only to glance at me, and especially my garments, to see that I was a working woman, and not a plaything of the Mouras. The two men and a woman behind them, as short-statured as they and as curious over my person, opened up a narrow passage for me to the coffin, and I knew that they would go on thinking what they liked.

"Poor little one! So young," whispered another woman,

80

rather young herself, and pretty, with hands that looked workworn and heavy with chilblains. She was on tiptoe, peering into the coffin, which I saw now was closed to Palla's throat. I was sorry I had asked to see her again. I turned away quickly. I noticed everyone else was doing likewise. The woman who had pitied her was being challenged by a good-looking, florid young peasant I took to be her husband. He spoke such rapid French, and with so many local idioms, that I could not understand him, but there was no mistaking his manner. Something to do with the fact that Palla was a Moura, and none of that accursed race was to be pitied, and that she was the daughter of demons.

I shuddered at these evil, superstitious people, finding them as alien to me as the strange beings I have heard of in faraway China. I could well believe them a party to the dreadful doings of the guillotine. When one of the men stepped aside, making room for me to leave the shuffling group, I thanked him and attempted a rather shy smile, to let him know that I was not an intruder but a friend to the dead child. He only eyed me as though he found me a new and curious kind of insect, and I gave up the French in disgust. Would I ever understand them?

In the Great Hall, which my fingers fairly itched to wipe clean of cobwebs and soot, I found Kate Moura standing with her back to the fireplace and her muslin skirts lifted behind her, warming certain uncovered regions; this in despite of occasional interruptions by a dozen peasants coming in from the inspection of Palla's corpse. They seemed to like Kate, hailing her as something that sounded to me like "Ma'mselle Katta," sometimes toasting her with goblets of Moura wine, which they themselves poured from a huge flagon and drank before they departed.

I watched Kate as she warmed herself. Personally, I

should have thought her more likely to be cold in the lungs than in the nether regions; for her bodice was square-cut and so low her rather overripe charms were almost fully exposed. I realized that this was the new French fashion. Of course, I should never wear the fashion. It would be most improper in my station. But, recalling Monsieur Edmond's gaze last night, I wondered how he would look at me in such a gown. The thought gave me an unaccustomed thrill of delight and unease.

Forgetting the solemnity of the morning, I had to laugh at Kate.

"Good morning ma'am. You'll be after toasting yourself?"

"Painful business all around, my dear, except for the pleasure of seeing you. Gad! Men have their uses, but I enjoy a woman's face for a change. Edmond has asked me to take you to the Moura tomb. Bad place to get to alone in this fog."

So there would be no service for Palla in Moura castle itself. Was she to be buried like a beast of the fields, with as little ceremony?

"Tell me," said Kate. "What do you think of this business?"

"Of what business, ma'am?" I wondered if she was about to mention some suspicions of her own that ran parallel to mine. Curiously enough, an edge came into my voice when I guessed she might somehow put Monsieur Edmond in the wrong. The perversity of me!

"The business of the priest, of course." She took up a longskirted coat from the big chair by the hearth and I helped her into it. "Edmond has had a time of it. Palla being illegitimate – then the poor brat capped that offense by never attending Mass. So far as I know, she may not even have been baptized."

A more unjust situation I never heard of, to blame a child for her birth! I bundled my shawl around me against the creeping fog that met us on the doorstep, half-wondering with another part of my mind whether I should go back for my coat. But Kate was rushing me on.

"It is no fault of Miss Palla's that she was not baptized," I said sharply.

"Ay. The blame lies with the Mouras. But what's to do, now it's done? If I know my cousin, Edmond will manage somehow. You have seen him since his return?"

"Last night."

"Ah." She stopped on the bridge over the ancient moat and gave me a long, thoughtful look. "You find him agreeable?"

I said stiffly, "It is not for me to say." It was bitter cold and the Moura woods did not promise to grow warmer. They loomed all around us now, grey skeletal fingers reaching out of the fog to snag our garments and delay us, catching at us everywhere as we moved down the obscure path.

"Nonsense. I had only to mention your name to him last evening when he passed the lodge. There is something between you. Is it a secret?" She laughed and pretended a playful coquetry, but her bold black eyes were busy. "I might have known you came here for more than a friendly visit to Palla. Tell me, between friends: What really happened at those meetings at school?"

"I only met him once."

"Sly one, aren't you? Well, I can't understand it. He doesn't give a sou for the general run of Pretty Petticoat. Not at all like his late brother. Edmond was always more interested in politics. Of course, he hasn't had much opportunity to be interested in either women or politics, the last few – " She broke off vaguely. "Hmm. Where is the path? Here. What was I saying?" She glanced at me to see if I remembered. I don't think she wanted me to. I could imagine her speculating on what possible attraction I possessed for her aristocratic cousin. "No. To the left. If you keep on straight you will head into some unhealthy country. Thick as a jungle, with a few nasty-tempered wolves. Now and then poachers wander in. Only meat the wolves may count on before spring."

This was probably a lie, one of Kate Moura's attempts at humor, and I refused to be frightened. I felt that I was certainly as brave as she, and Kate did not seem in the least afraid. Nonetheless, I did not like this wilderness, this endless walking through a curtain of fog that parted only inches before us and revealed nothing beyond but thicker curtains. It was tight going – easy to prick ourselves on the outstretched branches, sharp as needles in their nakedness.

But at last I made out somewhere in the fog ahead a little clearing in which stood a group of the peasants I had earlier met at Palla's coffin. They were speaking in low tones around a vine-covered stone building about twenty feet high, and I guessed it to be the Moura vault. The heavy door appeared to be carved out of one enormous block of stone. It stood open on its rusted, clumsy hinges, and I could see its fantastic thickness, the length of my arm. Above the door, carved deep in the stone was the single word as before:

MOURA

The carving was so old that the hollowed letters were half-covered by lichen, but they peered out like deep eyes in a dead-grey face, terrible in their simplicity. I thought of the many Mouras buried here in this tomb after their unquiet lives: the Moura robbers who had spied upon the highroad from the East Tower and then ridden down to plunder and kill . . . The Moura knights who came home from the horror of the Crusades to create their own horror. (What had these godless Mouras to do with the True Cross?) . . . Perhaps even the seven Mouras who were beheaded in the Languedoc rebellion . . . And one more: Palla Florin's unfortunate mother, the opera dancer who had been hurled from the East Tower – was she buried here?

Then I saw the master of Moura standing beside the door of the tomb, talking quietly with a French priest whose vestments were odd and interesting to me – a black cassock and spade hat. In spite of the Worship of Reason during the bloody Revolution, they seemed on excellent terms, the priest and the master of Moura.

Was this Monsieur Edmond actually a blood brother to that evil within the tomb? Out here in the damp autumn air he had none of the Moura look. Hatless, his strangely cropped brown hair grown out a little now and inclined to curl, his eyes masked and reflective, his body looking trim as a youth's in the unfastened greatcoat, he had none of the black, voluptuary look of the Mouras one imagined. I did not know then how he came to possess that particular "trimness" which was that of a steel blade, or how his eyes had acquired their mask. Strange what persuasive factors are one's wishes! Standing there in the clearing before the Moura tomb, I thought the heavy-limbed, dark-eyed woman beside me was a truer black Moura.

Monsieur Moura saw us now and came forward to present us to Père Duclos, who had agreed to offer prayers for the repose of the soul of Palla Florin. I knew then that my supposition had been correct. Fifteen-year-old Palla

Florin was to be sealed in the Moura vault without the service for the dead to which any Christian was entitled. It shocked me, but as I made my curtsy to the little priest I tried not to let him guess how inadequate I found his "prayers for her repose."

I started as I caught a glimpse of a figure, shadowy and vague, moving about within the vault, and was not much reassured to discover it was only Achille, evidently placing the coffin among the other dead Mouras.

A stiff, wet wind began to stir the shrouding fog, and I moved closer to the vault where there seemed a little protection. Kate greeted Father Duclos in her blustery, good-humored fashion, and I was surprised to glean from their conversation the fact that Kate was a good Catholic and attended Mass faithfully in the village of Moura. Monsieur Edmond saw my surprised look, and said,

"What is a good Christian? I wonder?"

I resented his tone, which was both ironic and sacrilegious. "You'll be telling me you're a good Christian."

He was amused. "And you would say I am not."

I thought of his indifference to the tragedy of young Palla. "I would say you never were, nor ever will be."

"You'd be wrong there. When I was young, I was as good a Christian as the next – the next being my elder brother who thought he fathered Palla here."

"That one!" There was no forgetting the talk of the elder Moura. "It's a shameful pack of sinners you are, all the Mouras, with no fear of God."

"My dear Anne, you do not know how comforting I found it to be during the Terror, when your paternal and bearded Old Gentleman was abolished and we learned to worship Reason."

Really! It was too much. I shivered and stepped within the doorway of the vault. It was surprising that "The Old

Gentleman" did not strike him dead for such blasphemy. Yet Monsieur Moura's voice, his very attitude, while ironic and bitter, was not flippant. It was as though he had tried God and found Him wanting.

What were my thoughts coming to? Was I now defending Antichrist? I must leave Moura at once, this very day!

As I looked through the murky grey of the vault for Palla's coffin, I was startled suddenly to feel cloth at my cold throat and shoulders. Edmond Moura had carelessly hung his coat upon my shoulders; the high, standing collar against my cold cheeks was warm from its contact with him.

"Kate is a fool," said Monsieur Moura. "She knew you would be cold."

"No," I said quickly. "I should have gone back for my coat." And a shabby thing it was, too. Nothing like the fine, rich quality of his coat, with the grace of its warm skirt and many capes. It came to my shoetops, but it was blessedly comfortable. I felt guilty in taking it; for I might have informed Monsieur Edmond that in England it was not considered the thing to lend one's coat to a servant.

Perhaps, though, he knew that, and did not care.

Father Duclos's shadow crossed the doorway as he moved to the coffin of naked, new wood, which by daylight looked hastily made and hastily sealed, with pegs and a few nails. It had been laid in the center of this big, square room upon two time-darkened coffins. Outside, the people of the neighborhood went down on their knees with an audible creaking of knee-joints. Kate, Achille, and I knelt before the coffin and bowed our heads. How cold the stone floor was against our knees! Kate padded her limbs with the folds of her wrap, but I was too conscious of the quality of material in my borrowed coat to do likewise.

Instead, I tucked it up around me to protect it from the dirt of the floor, and knelt on my thin skirts. I knew by the silence behind me that Palla's uncle had not moved. If I looked up from my devotions I should see him standing there, gazing at the coffin, his eyes somber but fearing no god, least of all his own conscience. So sure was I of this that I could not resist a single, brief glance over my shoulder. I had never been so set down. He was looking somber as I predicted, but he was studying me. He did not smile when I caught his eyes, but continued his study, with his arms folded and his manner stern, as though unaware that I had intercepted his gaze. Perhaps he did not see me at all. I wondered if he could be mad, or in a trance.

Horribly embarrassed, ashamed at my curiosity – and during prayers, too – I bent my head again and became dimly aware of Père Duclos intoning in Latin. I felt far removed from Palla lying there above me, in her last bed. My prayers were shot through with doubts and questions that had nothing to do with the repose of her soul.

Father Duclos finally finished his prayer, and in that space of quiet, Monsieur Moura suddenly moved. I looked up in surprise to see him staring at the group of people at the door of the tomb. Now I too caught their whispered buzz of comment that had, apparently, gone on under the priest's intoning. They were discussing Edmond Moura and then I caught the words "*la femme anglaise.*" Apparently they objected to his coat about my shoulders. I had never seen Monsieur Moura so angry. His eyes were narrowed, the lineaments of his face like marble, as cold and as hard.

I removed the coat and gave it to him. He looked as though he would refuse it. He was bitterly angry, but he did not frighten me, for I knew I was right. He had done a thing that was improper in their eyes.

The ceremony was over. The peasants of Moura went their way, most of them taking other paths than the one followed by Kate and me. I looked back only once.

Edmond Moura and Achille had closed the door of the vault and Edmond was turning an ugly, enormous key in the ancient lock

I thought: Was this huge door built to keep the living out, or the dead within?

8

One of the fortunate aspects of my position in life was that a sudden removal required very little preparation. I hurriedly packed my portmanteau and, avoiding the Great Hall, left by the somber, ancient front door, saddened at the thought that this wretched place should have been Palla's last view of life.

I crossed the bridge over the moat and was about to take the little wagon-rutted trail to the highroad, when I saw Monsieur Moura striding toward me. He did not see me directly; he seemed occupied with his thoughts. It was an awkward moment. In the circumstances, I would have preferred to avoid him; for there would be only the usual amenities, the polite, meaningless phrases, and what was a casual "au revoir" to him would be a painful "farewell" to me.

In my uncertainty, I paused, half determined upon quick flight, and so gave myself away. He seemed both glad and sorry to see me.

"Then you understood those gossiping fishwives at the vault. I wondered if you had. I could have cut out their tongues."

"You are a savage today, monsieur," I said, and added, "for which I am grateful."

He was puzzled and did not seem to know how to take this.

"Because, monsieur, in my country, I have been taught

that the French were all savages. And here was I, near to believing they were also gentlemen of breeding and politeness."

He laughed.

"Do not go, Anne Wicklow. Stay and be my guest."

"Impossible, monsieur, I must go. I hope I know the proprieties."

He stood there in my path. I was not used to such playing, although I found it to be a wonderful thing.

"The proprieties! And after this pompous little speech you feel that all has been said between us forever?"

"It would be unwise to stay. Alone as I am, and as a guest. Most improper."

"You must still imagine I am a villain. Tell me, Anne . . . " He looked at me in curiosity, but beneath this I could feel a kind of merry tenderness. "Do you actually think me so low that I would try your virtue while you were under my roof, in my protection?"

"We go rather far afield of the matter, sir. Good day to you. And I thank you for your many kindnesses."

"I see what it is. Your pride. Well then, what do you say to the position as my housekeeper here? Look about you. Have you ever seen a place more in need of a housekeeper?"

I had to confess that I hadn't, but I was determined to go.

"The diligence passes only once a week. Do you walk all the way to Moura? Ten kilometers at the least."

"What'll you be taking me for, a city woman?" I asked him indignantly. "I have walked farther on many a summer's day."

"But these are not summer days. The road is lined by the Moura woods, which sometimes encroach on gloomy afternoons."

"You are right, monsieur, to remind me that I must start early."

He laughed again. "At least let me drive you to the village. There is a curricle of sorts here. It has not been in use for ten years but that shall not stop us."

"No. I prefer to walk." I meant it and he must have guessed this. He took my hand.

"I see you are stubborn as a Scot."

"As an Irishwoman, I thank you, sir."

Feeling my hand in his, I was about to give it hearty pump when he brought my hand to his lips and kissed my roughened palm. He had taken unfair advantage of me, besides making me appear an absolute fool, about to shake his hand. But I could not withdraw my fingers without using force and thus compounding my original clumsy behavior.

He examined my hand with his thumb which traced the calluses on my palm. It was humiliating to be reminded of the physical labor which those calluses betrayed, but at the same time I was reminded of a curious thing – Monsieur Moura's hand was no gentleman's either. Where had he got that hardness on the heel of the hand, the red ridges across his palms? It was as if he wanted to demonstrate this similarity, to indicate that we had both known the same servitude. What unaccustomed toil this must have been for a gentleman, a friend of Napoleon!

A part of me wished my hand might be caressed forever by his fingers, but fortunately the other half of me held sway.

I said, "If you please, monsieur." Snatching my hand away, I made a quick little curtsy, and while he watched me in surprise, I went around him and hurried down the road.

"Of course," he called after my retreating back, "as the

housekeeper at Moura, you would have more work than you have ever seen. You do well to run away from it. Coward!"

Wily rogue that he was, hurling his greatest challenge! I could not help laughing, but ran on toward the highroad.

"Stay! Let me get the curricle for you."

I ignored this. There was no sense prolonging our farewells.

It was close on noon and tendrils of sunlight dropped now and then through the Moura woods, burning away the fog. Partly this, and partly my meeting with Monsieur Moura gave me a most sensation of happiness. The vista ahead of me gradually turned watery yellow and then bright, autumn gold, and I felt convinced that all would be well and I should see Edmond Moura again, even that he cared a little for me. It was not all politeness and French gallantry.

As I hurried along the road over decayed red leaves still wet with the morning mist, I fancied Monsieur Moura making a declaration to me, and I, of course, knowing it to be a fantastic mesalliance, refusing gently. I would then live my life out doing useful things, knowing I had once been loved by the man I really believed at that moment must be the ideal.

The sun was directly overhead when I reached the lodge where Kate lived. There was no sign of life about, so I started toward Moura village, not feeling the weight of my portmanteau or the distance I had already come; for I was still in the throes of my dream. All at once, the thick branches alongside the highroad parted, and Charles Armitage stepped out into my path. He was a sad sight, his fine garments all muddied and torn by the angry woods, but he was quite as handsome and apologetic as he had been in the East Tower.

I said calmly, "Good day, sir."

"Look here, miss – I'm most awfully sorry, I don't believe I know your name."

"You are on Moura property."

"Yes. I know. I tried to get in by the postern gate as before, but it is barricaded now. Then I lost the trail returning. You see," he added unnecessarily, "I've been trying to break in."

"To steal the silver, of course. Very meager it is. You'll find it scarcely worth the trouble."

He laughed. He had merry brown eyes and a friendly mouth which seemed easily disposed to mirth. If I had not been so set in my daydream of Monsieur Moura, I should have said this young man was the handsomest I had ever seen.

I can remember now, clearly as in a mirror before me, my glow of happiness that hour, which I carried into these first moments with Charles Armitage. All the while I was bantering with him, and observing his good looks, I was comparing him unfavorably with the master of Moura. There was something so simple, so transparent, about the Englishman. None of the subtle excitement I found in Edmond Moura.

"To tell the truth – " he began.

"The truth, is it?" I said. "You lied to me before. Sketching pictures, indeed. Now, there's a likely story, but you'll be telling it elsewhere. I've a few miles to walk this day."

He tried with little success to brush mud off his excellently cut walking suit. He was sadly stained and the brushing only set the strains. He picked up my portmanteau and walked beside me.

"I did lie to you, miss – "

"Anne Wicklow."

"You see, Miss Wicklow, it's a rather circumstantial tale. My father is Sir Trevor Armitage, an intimate of the Prince Regent. I found the Prince's set a trifle too rich in every sense for me. I was on my walking tour of Europe last year when Waterloo came. I lurked about, sketching, savoring the terror and beauty of those ghastly hours. I know I too should have to join the battle. It was a point of honor. That second night I was in it. When it was over, I was no longer curious about war. I made my way across Belgium into France, carrying in a cart a dying old grenadier who wanted to see his native soil once more."

"But I don't see how this excuses your stealing the Moura silver."

"In a little town south of Chartres, I met my grenadier's daughter, a pretty but somewhat feather-brained young lady named Caroline Durand. Upon her father's death, she told me she was setting out to be a governess. She seemed to think it a great adventure that her first position should be in an ancient château in the south. A place called Moura."

My scalp tingled. All my happiness was fighting within me. Do not tell me more, I thought – I won't listen to you –

"She was a silly little thing, blonde with huge blue eyes that she batted constantly to gain her way. I don't know why I should care what happened to her, but in a way, I stood in the place of her father. When she wrote that the château excited her, that her charge was spoiled but charming, and the master fascinating, I was relieved to be done with silly Caroline.

"Then there was a short letter asking me to meet her at Moura village on a matter of life and death. Miss Wicklow, that appointment was made six weeks ago. I am still awaiting Caroline."

95

I said, walking faster, "This is an effecting story, but it cannot concern me."

"You don't understand. You have the entree to Moura. You can tell me what happened."

"A pack of nonsense! She simply left Moura earlier than she had intended, and for some reason decided not to meet you."

"Then you have not seen her there?"

"I? Certainly not. Nor shall I. I am leaving the province by the first coach."

He set down the portmanteau and cried out as though I had struck him. "You can't! You are my last hope. Miss Wicklow, this young lady may be a prisoner there. I owe it to her father's memory to be quite sure she is not. If I could get in again myself, on any pretext! But they are very careful. That demon, Moura, he is the one! If I could choke the truth out of him!"

I recalled the mysterious conversation between Edmond Moura and Achille last night while they were removing Palla. Was Charles Armitage so great a danger that Monsieur Moura would "attend" to the young Englishman?

As the sun moved overhead, the shadows of the Moura woods shifted, like ragged fences, inch by inch eating away the sunlight on the highroad.

"What do you want me to do?" I asked finally.

He sighed with relief and took my arm in a comradely way.

"Do you have their confidence?"

I thought: I have *his* confidence. I could betray him easily; for he trusts me. But so, evidently, did Charles Armitage.

"Good!" he exclaimed as I nodded. "Then I am sure it would be over in a fortnight. Can you make some excuse to return to Moura?"

"The diligence passes through next week. I might tell him I will wait for it. That would give us five days."

He rumpled up his hair with a muddy hand. "I suppose it must be enough time. If we could search the entire château, we would know at least that she is not a prisoner."

"But I cannot do anything so dishonorable. If he found out, I could never face him again."

He stopped in front of me, looking at me squarely. There was no humor in his candid eyes now. He set down my portmanteau and grasped my shoulders as if to shake me.

"Miss Wicklow, you don't understand. If he finds out, you will not live to face him twice."

I stammered, "He – he wouldn't hurt me."

He did shake me a little. "You stupid girl! Don't you suppose Caroline thought that?"

And Palla, too. Yes. I was sure Palla thought that, almost to the moment of her last pitiful letter. Why should I, a simple, foreign girl, be an exception?

Conceited creature that I was, I made a last futile effort to conquer my own good sense, when Charles Armitage said, "Hush. I hear riders."

We listened apprehensively. Around a bend in the road from the village came two men on horseback, one thin and dried-up, looking like a bookish man, the other elegantly dressed, stout, and massive, jouncing unhappily on his sturdy mare. The fat man seemed relieved at the sight of us.

"Pardon, monsieur – madame – this is the road from Moura to Montemessine?"

I told him it was, that he had left the village behind him. His eyes, like currants in a ruddy pudding, peered at me.

"Quite so, madame. It was our intention. But there

97

was a turn back yonder. I thought perhaps we had gone wrong."

Charles Armitage put in, "You will find Montemessine about fourteen kilometers along this road."

"Thank you, but we are going hardly so far. Good day, 'sieur – 'dame."

As they rode on, Charles said thoughtfully in English, "Now who might they be? I have been in this part of the country long enough to know how seldom they get strangers here."

I was not troubled by them. Things of greater moment occupied me. "It will be awkward returning. How can I face him? I was so emphatic when I quitted the place."

He thought about this, then said brightly, "You could break your ankle."

I was about to retort in anger when I realized that this was the perfect solution. Monsieur Moura would be all sympathy, all kindness.

"I think I will just sprain it," I amended after consideration. "That should keep me there for the next five days."

"Excellent," said Mr. Armitage. "You are a true conspirator."

It was an a ill-chosen word. A mighty suspicious young trespasser was rushing me into treachery, and I knew almost nothing about him. "What proof have you that you are what you claim to be?"

He looked utterly confounded. "Well, I – I don't suppose I have any. Except – I have letters from my father at my room in the village. Whenever you are in the village you may read them."

"What should they tell me, but that you are the son of someone who calls himself your father?" I pursued my advantage. "Perhaps Miss Durand changed her mind and wished to avoid you. It would be a simple thing for her to walk out of Moura toward Montemessine and never see you at all."

"Impossible. She was a delicate and feminine little creature, not a hulking milkmaid able to walk fourteen kilometers."

"Well!" I exclaimed, "a great hulking milkmaid, is it now?" I could not understand how I had listened to this repulsive young man. Detestable creature, with his delicate, feminine little blonde! For I must tell you, with the exception of Palla, I have never had an overfondness toward blondes.

He was all concern and clumsy solicitude.

"No, no, Miss Wicklow, may I be struck dead if I meant it of you! I was thinking of – I had images of quite a different sort. Oh, come, please forgive me. Say you do! I would not hurt you for worlds – I need you too much."

This second bit of information nearly set us at loggerheads again, but by now I was able to think clearly. There would be no point to my going away torn by suspicions of Edmond Moura. Why not discover the truth, once and for all? There was much ranged against Edmond Moura, and when all was said, nothing told against him as damningly as Palla Florin's little notes to us in England. Was I to betray those pitiful pleas? And for what? His lips upon the palm of my hand, his eyes bitterly amused, and now and then tender as they followed me? Was that enough to acquit him in my eyes? I believed it was; for I knew less of the world then than I do now, and it seemed to me that such a feeling as I saw in Monsieur Moura's eyes when he spoke to me could not be false, that no one could look at me with such affection and kindness and be evil.

If I yielded to Mr. Armitage's entreaties, it would be to prove Monsieur Moura innocent, not the reverse.

Mr. Armitage was saying earnestly, "Haven't you observed the hatred – even the horror – in which the peasants hereabouts hold the Mouras? I am a foreigner and I cannot get them to confide in me, but there are hints."

"It was once a family of robbers and murderers, but that was many centuries ago," I protested.

"Not at all, Miss Wicklow! This present master of Moura has killed before. That much I feel sure of. The veiled remarks in the village, the way they make signs to ward off the devil when Moura passes. I've seen these things."

"Have you spoken with the village magistrate about your suspicions?"

"Not yet. I expect to, very soon. He has been called to Paris. When he returns . . . "

I still did not believe him, but I took up my portmanteau and turned back to Moura.

Edmond Moura had got the curricle out after all, and the horses were in harness. I saw the carriage as I came limping up the trail from the highroad. It hurt me to see how gentle he was, and how kind when he thought I had been injured. He told me he would lift me and place me in the curricle, but I said hastily that it was nothing at all, a mere twisted ankle, and with the aid of his hand stepped up beside him. We rode back to Moura most companionably, I resolving that I should carry out the plans Charles Armitage had spoken of, but give Monsieur Moura every benefit of the doubt. As for Moura himself, he was amusing and friendly.

"You would have laughed to see us hitching up, Anne.

I am no man for the job. The curricle itself was in a pretty musty condition. How does it look now?"

"Very nice," I said, pretending to examine it for dust. "But it was not necessary. If I had not stepped on that wretched pebble, I should have been halfway to Moura village by this time."

He seemed to find it amusing that I should be such a sturdy walker. "I'm sure you would have. Do you know how a French lady would behave in the circumstances?"

"Scream and faint, I'm sure."

"And allow me to pack her into the curricle, where I would endeavor to hold her snug in my arms while handling these two obnoxious beasts."

"You would then have the handling of three obnoxious beasts."

"Ah, but it would be in keeping with the heroes in those novels you spoke of."

I said pleasantly, "I do not think you are well cast as a hero. Something about you seems to suggest Count Montoni."

"Not my conduct to you, I hope."

"Your conscience, perhaps."

Neither of us said anything. On the surface of my mind I had meant my remark as a joke. I realized that a little edge had crept into it, and he felt the cut.

"We are not all what we seem," he said after a pause that was uncomfortable to me. "If one knew all the circumstances, perhaps even Count Montoni might be allowed a glimpse of heaven."

I was only too aware that we were not all we seemed; for I had come back to play the spy, and acutely felt my own guilt while pondering his words. We had come within sight of the frowning battlements of Moura.

"Then I may count upon a housekeeper? Or must I continue to live in this wretched pigsty?"

I told him I would be most grateful to act as his housekeeper for the next five days, and by that time he would not recognize the château. It was a perfect opportunity for me to give the ancient pile a thorough search.

He gave me a puzzled glance. "How can you be marching up and downstairs with your ankle sprained?"

Covering this blunder with assurance, I said that my ankle would be perfectly well once I had it tightly bound, and in any case, I could not further trespass upon his hospitality. It must be as housekeeper I remained at Moura, or I would walk away again.

"And I am sure you would, too," he said grimly, but he seemed content with our bargain.

Before we crossed the moat bridge, I saw Achille and Clou leading away two horses, one of which I thought I recognized as that belonging to the fat gentleman on the highroad. I was in a panic at the idea. He would be sure to have noticed the Englishman with me.

"Begin your duties tomorrow, Anne. I wish you to play my hostess tonight. I am entertaining my solicitor and my cousin Eustace, who is – as you once pointed out – the next heir to Moura, and the reason I so carelessly murdered my niece."

"Don't joke about it!" I let him think I was indignant at my own former suspicions, but the truth was I needed time to think of a way out of this. "No, monsieur. I made a bargain with you, and I will not be a guest tonight. I will begin my duties by overseeing the dinner and the serving. That is all."

"Now, Anne," he began coaxingly, but I was adamant.

102

I almost pitied him for thinking me so direct, instead of devious.

When we entered the main passage, I took the staircase to my former bedchamber. He joined the gentlemen in the Great Hall – sure enough, I recognized both.

I spent the afternoon in the kitchens supervising the willing Clou and the furious Matilde as they prepared the courses for dinner. I would be presumptuous to tell them anything about the preparation of the succulent foods, for they knew the subject far better than I; but I did set to work cleaning the kitchen and the dark sculleries until the area looked nearly clean enough to prepare food in. I offered to go down to the cellars for the dinner wines, but Matilde made a great fuss and called Achille, who came, all politeness, and went down the narrow, unrailed flight of stone steps himself to fetch the wines. I watched him from the top of the steps: it was like plunging down into an abyss. He must have owl's eyes, for he took no candle.

After a few minutes he returned with five bottles, all different, and I shuddered at the capacity of these French gentlemen. I had told Monsieur Moura that under no circumstances would I be a party to the dinner, except in the kitchen; so I was understandably surprised when Clou returned from serving the fish and made wild gestures at me.

I vanished into the stillroom. A few minutes later when I came out, Matilde said crossly, while rescuing fresh-baked tartlets from the grate: "The master wants you. You had better go."

"Tell him I am not here," I said, and started to make good my lie, but she got in my way quickly.

"What do you hide, Madamoiselle Anglaise? Go. If it is not tonight, it will be at breakfast or at dinner another day."

This was true. I realized that in my workaday dress, without my coat and bonnet, I might not be recognized as the girl on the highroad. I pinned my hair up so that the heavy, loose knot would rest higher on my neck, and I tried to look ram-rod-stiff. Then I went into the great dining hall. The long table was much too gaily lighted for my purposes. I had put out fewer candelabra, but someone, probably Achille, must have added the others.

I walked down the length of the room and stood in shadow within range of Monsieur Edmond.

"Monsieur sent for me?"

He looked a trifle annoyed at my stiffness, but amusement got the better of him, and he seemed ready to smile. He presented each of the guests to me, but they behaved like perfect gentlemen. I, on the other hand, was behaving like a country oaf.

"Miss Wicklow – my cousin, Eustace Moura." That was the fat one, the one I feared. But he was polite as can be – got up, bowed with a slight creaking of stays, and aside from a puzzled glance, accepted his introduction to a housekeeper as an everyday occurrence. The sour gentleman had a prim, not unlikable little smile. He proved to be Monsieur Edmond's solicitor, and had come to Moura to see about the disposition of the estate upon Edmond's death, the master explained. "He wants to be sure my dear cousin Eustace is not forgotten."

Eustace was not the least embarrassed. He waved a fat, lace-cuffed hand.

"One must be practical, my dear cousin."

Edmond looked just a little malicious. "If only I do not marry, and ruin your chances, dear cousin."

The sour-faced solicitor, Monsieur Trevain, smiled his prim smile and, like a wise man, said nothing. Meanwhile, Eustace Moura's blackcurrant eyes were wandering in that pudding face of his. I did not want them wandering near me, and retreated slightly farther into the shadows.

I saw Edmond look from him to me, in amusement, "Well, Eustace, what do you say? Shall I remain unmarried?" He made a brief motion toward the walls of the room. "And leave this exquisite palace of pleasures to you?"

"That would depend upon which palace of pleasures you refer to . . . Ah, pardon, mademoiselle – would you stand into the light?"

Looking as frozen and formal as I could, I obeyed him.

"I thought so. I've seen you before. Today on the highroad."

Edmond said easily, "Yes. Mademoiselle was in the village ordering supplies to renovate this wretched place."

"Ah, but this was something quite different, was it not, mademoiselle? A lovers' meeting, I'll wager." He was not as stupid as he seemed then, this fat Moura; for he glanced slyly at his cousin who had stopped all movement, and was watching us both with his wine glass to his lips.

"Monsieur is mistaken," I said stiffly. "I was on business."

"But the young, handsome monsieur who carried your valise. Who then was he? A neighbor? Oh, I think not, mademoiselle." His thick lips were moist and red. "Much too handsome. Too foreign. Now, I would guess him to be – English."

Doubtless, Eustace Moura thought he was discouraging any of his cousin's notions to marry me. Edmond Moura set his glass down and looked at me.

I said, "Will that be all, monsieur?"

"For the moment," said Edmond Moura, grimly.

I was about to retire that night when I was interrupted

by a knock at my door. I threw my coat on and opened the door a crack. Monsieur Edmond stood there. He seemed in every way his polite normal self.

"May I speak to you?"

I opened the door wide, but not with enthusiasm. "It is late, monsieur."

He ignored this and sat down in the big chair below the bed. I couldn't quite place his manner. He was not angry; rather, he was on the watch for something.

"Well?"

"I think you owe me an explanation," he said.

"Certainly. If you'll be telling me what offense I have committed."

He took my hand and pulled me closer to his chair, somewhat like an elderly uncle about to scold. But his touch upon me aroused in me no corresponding calm.

"Who was the young Englishman – the handsome Englishman – on the highroad today?"

"A gentleman, monsieur." I warmed to the story I had conjured up since dinner. "He tells me that you at Moura have been most rude to him, not letting him sketch here, or even enjoy the view from the tower. He spoke very badly of you, and to tell the truth, when I turned my ankle, I was half of a mind to walk on to the village anyway, because of the way you treated Mr. Armitage."

He shook my hand a little, studying me. "Is this true?"

I opened my eyes very wide and stared down at him. "What new insult will you make me?"

He said suddenly, "How is your ankle?"

I looked indignant and thrust my bare foot forward, yanking at the stiff cloth binding. "You may see for yourself, monsieur."

Slowly, puzzled, his gaze went down over my person to my ankle below the hem of my gown. The ankle was

106

red and chafed. I had seen to that in the hours after dinner.

Pursuing my advantage, I railed on. "Next you'll say I'm a liar to my face."

He let go my hand and rubbed his face and jaw as if he were very tired. I stared at his nose and his mouth, thinking them beautiful; for my heart went out to him when I saw that gesture. When he looked up again he had that searching, tender expression that I could not resist.

"Are you a liar, Anne?" he said softly. "Not you. Not you . . . "

I felt the tears start in my eyes – not, as he supposed, out of kindness for him, but out of knowledge of my own duplicity. He got up and went to the door where he turned back to say calmly, "They tell me that last night a poacher was torn to pieces by wolves down in the woods. Do not leave Moura unless one of us accompanies you."

He left me then.

It was not until I was in bed, and the distant, hungry howlings became more audible, that I realized Edmond Moura's admonition was somehow familiar.

Palla had recounted it in her second letter. She was never allowed out of Moura without one of them to accompany her.

9

I awoke the next morning, which was Saturday, with a clear plan. Unless the weather threatened on the morrow, they had no excuse to prevent me from going to Mass in the village with Kate; and in doing so, I would get a message to Charles Armitage who was staying at the one inn the village afforded. I would warn him that if he did not hear from me by a reasonable time each day, he must assume I was a prisoner – or worse. He could then, with the aid of the local magistrate or other representatives of the law, take steps to rescue me.

Having satisfied myself on the score of my own safety, I set to work as housekeeper. Immediately after breakfast – we had returned to cold porridge, thanks to Matilde – I began overhauling the upperfloor bedrooms. By noontime, several of the ancient rooms looked habitable, and when denuded of dust and ragged coverings even possessed a kind of old-fashioned charm.

Monsieur Eustace Moura came by as Clou and I were tearing down the faded, bilious-green canopy in the room assigned to the solicitor, Monsieur Trevain.

Eustace stuck his head in the doorway. "I am growing to like the place. A little more, and you will induce me to hurry off my cousin so that I may be master of Moura."

"Hurry off?" I repeated. This was a strange time for such jokes, twenty-four hours after the "hurrying off" of his cousin Palla.

"But yes. Why not? He does not enjoy life as I do. Nor are his financial needs as pressing. Now I – Well then, in effect, I am more suited to Moura."

He had not said a truer word. This Pudding-Face with his voluptuous mouth, his excessive weight, and his roving black eyes was a perfect gargoyle for the Moura chamber of horrors.

He said ingratiatingly, "Such pretty hands should be spared this sort of work, mademoiselle. I understand my dear cousin has ordered the hiring of several local girls and a man or two, to help you in your work. That should give you more time for the amenities. Believe me, we are lonely belowstairs."

Here's a bit of blarney, I thought, that fair sickens the stomach! My pretty hands – indeed! I had lived too long to be flattered by such blatant lies. I went on about my work in the hope of discouraging him, but he was not easily dashed. He stepped into the room and began to probe around among the discarded bedding and draperies. I knew he could not have the least interest in them, but must have something else in mind. It was not long before I guessed what that was.

"Charming room. Charming. Tell me, mademoiselle, will you invite me to rest in this room when you are mistress of Moura?"

I looked at him direct. "I think you have been misled, monsieur. I am the housekeeper here. Not the lady of the house."

He waved his stout hands, and I caught the flash of an enormous ruby. And here was he, carping about his poverty and his cousin's estate!

109

"Of course. Of course. Discretion at all costs, mademoiselle. Believe me, I can be discreet as well. I know you are determined to cut me out. If you marry him, you may succeed." He looked me over as though judging my ability to provide an heir. "But, perhaps, one day, I will give you a better idea." He leaned toward me over a pile of bedding. His breath was so rank that I could not avoid a little shudder of revulsion. Clou was watching us in perplexity, trying to follow the sense of all this.

"My dear," Eustace Moura said, "he is not for you."

I knew perfectly well Monsieur Edmond was not for me, but thus challenged, I could not help asking his cousin, "And why not, pray?"

"But it is so obvious! Do you know nothing of him? Of his life during the past ten years and more? Ah, my poor innocent, he has not told you."

I began to fold sheets vigorously, shaking ten years' accumulation of dust all over the room, so that he went into a terrific sneezing attack and was banished into the hall. He stuck his head in once more, the lower half of his face mercifully masked in his handkerchief.

"You know whose room this was, mademoiselle? You may tell by the green. It was the color she favored. Palla's mother. The one they call the Combing Lady. How Edmond despised her! Small wonder she haunts him. Or is it possible you do not believe in ghosts?"

Having given me what he supposed was something to chew upon, he went his way, his stays creaking madly as he minced down the hall. What an ideal figure he would have cut thirty years ago in silk stockings, satin breeches, and waistcoat! Surely the Revolution had done one good deed, in sweeping out such ridiculous creatures.

I did not see Edmond Moura throughout the day. I was too busy, and I daresay he was as well, though in

110

my ignorance I never could imagine what an aristocrat found with which to occupy himself.

Late in the afternoon, while Eustace and Monsieur Trevain hugged the hearth of the Great Hall, warming their limbs before Achille's modest fire and their innards with incessant glasses of spirits, I went swiftly around the courtyard to the postern gate. If I could open it, Charles Armitage could not only come into Moura, but would also know that I was still free to move about. I was careful to keep under cover and shadow; for I did not like the notion of being spied upon by those new servants that Eustace Moura informed me were being supplied by the master. I had an idea they just might be supplied to act as my warders. Already two strangers had reported to me, both male, husky, toughened veterans of Edmond Moura's own command in what Matilde called proudly, "The Emperor's Old Guard." I did not like their looks. They stared at me, grinned, made comments in some patois of their own, and only after I had behaved like a Dublin fishwife swinging a mackerel would they set to work cleaning the beams and enormously high roof of the medieval dining hall.

The postern gate was now – as Charles Armitage had described it to me – barricaded by a broken-down carriage, while the gate itself was fastened with a lock big enough to shut out a legion. We had an alternate plan if I found it impossible to open the gate. Each day I was to send him a message in a strip of white cloth tied around a heavy object. I was to drop this message through an embrasure of the broken north battlement just off the steps from my bedroom passage. Thus he would know that my movements were not yet confined to one room.

After inspecting and giving up several other methods by which Charles might enter at night for a search, I returned to the main wing of the house and went up to

the first floor, this time taking the staircase on the left
that led to the broken parapet. It was shocking to see how
easily one might walk up those steps and off into space.
I examined this unprotected parapet, studying briefly the
view it presented of the wide dark carpet that was the
Moura woods, and went back down a few steps. In the
north wall was the embrasure I meant to use. I looked
down through its protective spikes. Directly beneath me,
on the bank of the moat, the vegetation was flat; trailing
over the ground was a web of creeping ivy.

I looked carefully, but made out no signs of Charles
Armitage. Somewhere at the bottom of the flight of steps
I heard the hollow sound of wooden sabots. Hastily I
dropped the note I had hidden in my skirts, and scarcely
waited to see it land among the ivy. The message indicated
that things were tightening but not yet critical, and that
I had heard and seen nothing of Mademoiselle Durand.
I stated that I hoped to be in Moura village at Mass
tomorrow. If not, and if the weather were not wholly
impossible, he might regard me as a prisoner.

I hurried up the steps to the first-floor passage and there
proceded serenely to my room. Behind me, I could plainly
hear the clip-clop of the man in wooden sabots. He called
out to me as I opened my door. "Madame," the fellow
ventured. "It is Jehan. This afternoon. You remember?"
He stood in the doorway looking odd, sheepish, not nearly
so insolent as when I first interviewed him. He carried a
stockingcap crushed in his big fist.

"Well? You'll not be telling me you are done already?"
I supposed he came for money and I had not yet discussed
these matters with Achille or the master.

"Yes, madame. That is – done with the dining room,
and I have begun to move the furniture in the rooms off
the Great Hall. Matilde said it would be easier for you to

clean if we moved the heavy things. But it is of those other rooms I wish to speak. Will madame be good enough to answer a question?"

I nodded. It was difficult to understand his peculiar dialect and more difficult to reply.

"Was madame in the last room off the lower passage a moment since?"

Surprised, I said, "No, certainly not. I have been busy up here."

He astonished me by growing alarmed. The pupils of his dark eyes dilated in the light of my candle.

"B-but, madame!" he stammered, "that is impossible. I heard madame combing her hair in one of those rooms, the one next to the steps."

"It was not I," I said with finality, attempting to close the door, but his foot was in the doorway. I looked down and saw his bare brown ankle above the wooden shoe. Here was a sturdy fellow to be disturbed by the housekeeper combing her hair.

"Matilde and Clou, they are in the kitchen, madame. There is no one else but you at the moment."

"You are imagining things," I said in English, not remembering the French of it. I was secretly relieved that he hadn't placed me near the embrasure of the north tower. Resuming what French I knew, I told him I would myself examine the room he mentioned, and he followed me, meek as a huge dog.

Downstairs, we almost walked into Eustace Moura, who had to know what we were up to, and then insisted on following us, chuckling and remarking between breathy gurgles that he had always wanted to see a ghost. Never had, never expected to; now was his first opportunity. Jehan, the workman, looked at him and shook his head at such talk. With his shoe he shoved open the door of a room I had never before seen. Although he was not bred of politeness, he let Monsieur Eustace and me enter first.

It is curious, as I think back upon those days now, that I felt no premonition, no sense of alarm at this absurd Combing Lady. I simply assumed Jehan had listened to the current legends of Moura and convinced himself that a simple sound (perhaps a fly buzzing in the long-unused room) was the sound peculiar to that of a woman combing long full strands of hair. I came into that room without the slightest feeling of dread or fear. It was a large chamber, used in the old days as an after-dinner withdrawing room for ladies while the gentlemen were at their port or whatever.

Except for its size and, of course, a decade's accumulation of dust, the room was comfortable, not at all the kind one associated with ghosts that combed hair in the night. One set of the rich velvet portieres had been thrust apart to permit light to enter from the courtyard, and even at this hour sunset stabbed through the little opaque squares of glass to cast all our faces in a strange, orange glow.

"Where's your ghost, eh? Eh? Where is she?" Eustace kept asking in his sneering way. He went around peering under cushions, examining the hems of drapes, looking up the huge chimney of the fireplace, calling in a nonsensical way for the Combing Lady to show herself.

Putting one hand on the back of a huge chair that faced the fireplace at one end of the room, I said to Jehan, "Where were you when you heard the sound?"

Jehan lumbered over to the opposite end of the room and knelt beside an ancient, highly carved sideboard.

"Now," I said, "where do you think the combing sound came from?"

"From the chair madame is touching."

In despite of myself, my hand leaped as though it had

touched a hot gridiron. "Well then," I said, "our culprit must have left some signs of her passing."

"Not if she *is* the Combing Lady," Eustace taunted. I ignored him. I examined the chair carefully. It revealed no secret except the color of its insides; for the leather was badly cracked. I went on talking as I investigated the worn green carpet beneath and every inch of space around the chair.

"If a woman combed her hair in this chair, it would be most unnatural that no single hair fell hereabouts."

"But if the lady had madame's hair, it might be too dark to see."

"Disabuse yourself of that notion," I said in English, though Jehan understood my tone. "For I have not combed my hair in this room." I tried again in French. "I have never entered this room before. But there are other women at Moura. One of Matilde's red hairs or Clou's chestnut hairs might be seen . . . " Or, I thought, it was just possible that we had stumbled upon our first trace of Caroline Durand, whose hair was blonde.

There were no hairs of any hue, and no signs of anyone having disturbed the dusty carpet except myself.

"Listen!" said Jehan suddenly.

Even Eustace stopped behaving the fool and stood uneasily at attention.

We all heard then faint rustle of something like the folds of a woman's gown, or, perhaps, a comb crackling through long hair. The sound came from the fireplace and I went over and examined it. As I stepped up on the hearth almost inside the huge opening, the sound came again – the spatter of ancient soot dropping onto the hearth, blown down by the wind rattling high in the chimney.

"So much for your Combing Lady," I told Jehan.

He got up grinning, his big white teeth all aglisten,

and came over to me, trying to take my hand with his wretched stocking-cap still crushed in his own palm. He looked different now, not insolent and not terrified but as though he genuinely wanted to be my friend. He took my dusty, soot-stained hand in his own and pressed it before I could stop him.

"Madame, Jehan is your servant. Call upon me at need . . . Combing Lady – ah, the little joke!" and he went off chuckling.

After dinner that Saturday night I managed to catch Monsieur Edmond while he and Achille were busy clearing old furniture and ancient personal belongings out of the second-floor bedchambers. He looked so odd that for a minute I hardly recognized him. Instead of his usual well-cut clothing, he wore a striped seaman's shirt and wide-legged, patched pantaloons like a common seaman, or the dock-workers I had seen in Calais, some of whom had been under guard, like felons. I was so surprised I blurted straight out, "Have you taken to the sea now? If so, you are far from harbor."

Monsieur said cheerfully, "It is a good costume for work that is soiling. I wear it often when I wish to be plain Citizen Nobody."

I wondered if he knew just how attractive the costume was, and what had ever given him the notion of wearing such clothes in the first place. But I brought myself sharply to business and told him I wished to go to Mass in the morning with Kate. He did not seem in the least surprised.

"But why the battle light in your eyes, Anne? Do you think I would forbid a young lady the dubious rites of the Church?"

I had not anticipated his yielding, but I pursued my advantage.

116

"Then may I go down to the lodge to meet Mademoiselle Kate?"

"It would be unwise to go alone. Someone will escort you to the lodge gates. Be ready at seven in the morning."

I thanked him and turned away. He added as I did so, "It is I who should thank you, Anne. In one day you have done an amazing job with this old horror of a building."

I could not help being grateful for his words, and returned his smile a little hesitantly. "I fear you will not think so, monsieur. Your cousin now finds it attractive enough to talk of enjoying the heritage when you are dead."

He said, still in good humor, "Would you be sorry?"

"I shall not be here."

"I mean – if I should die."

I said innocently, "Are you ill, monsieur?"

He gave me an exasperated little slap on the cheek and went his way. I could not help reflecting that this encounter had been a most pleasant break in the day's monotony.

Although I warned myself that night to expect difficulties, even tricks, in the morning, I was really not surprised when Jehan, now bound to prove himself my friend, stood ready at seven A.M. to walk me to Kate's lodgings.

There was really only one blemish on my perfect plan. It was running too smoothly.

I found nothing in the least dangerous about the Moura woods as seen from the road in sunlight and in the company of anyone as bluff and virile as my friend Jehan. I think he was much more alarmed over what topic of conversation he might suitably open to a woman who spoke his language so abominably. He asked me if I liked Moura and was surprised when I said I thought it ought to be consigned to a very large Guy Fawkes Day fire. He said that it used to be a very fine place.

"Not that it didn't have its ghosts, madame. But one grows used to them. And then, one did not know them when they lived – as I knew *her*."

"You knew this Combing Lady you were frightened of yesterday?"

He made an eloquent wave of his big, bronze hands. His dark eyes in that leathery face narrowed to slits. It was his peculiar way of showing friendliness, rather like a large dog who shows frightful canine teeth to indicate pleasure.

"She had a way. No man on the estate, no man in the village, did not know her. She was like that. A way of the body, the walk . . . She was a dancer before Pierre Moura took her. They call them opera dancers. You know of these women?"

I said I did.

"She was very tiny, so little she would come up to here on you." He indicated vaguely somewhere in the neighborhood of my bosom. "With sharp little teeth here and there at the side of the mouth. Ay! I remember those teeth! But she was lovely. And with hair like a golden fox. She loved to comb that hair. The other monsieur spent fortunes on the jeweled combs."

"Was she a good young lady, or – ?"

He shrugged. "One of the others – I saw a portrait once. These – they call them opera dancers, but they – this one had posed with no clothing above the middle, nothing to cover – "

Before he demonstrated, I told him hastily that I understood very clearly, and he was all smiles.

"Ah, good. You have the good understanding of our language. You are a clever young lady. I will tell you something. I do not believe he did it the way they said."

My heart began to beat rapidly. I knew at once who "he" was.

Jehan raised high the low-hanging branch of a tree so that I might walk under it, and went on calmly, "But yes, madame. Monsieur Edmond and Mademoiselle Laly Florin, they used to quarrel. That is to say, mademoiselle quarreled. Monsieur Edmond walked away. I have seen it. But then one day I myself was there when she tried to entice him, and he told her she would be killed one day if she were not careful, that she bored him with her tricks, that she was full of – of artifice, he said, and – Oh, he was always sharp-tongued, was Monsieur Edmond. But he was right. And when she was thrown from the East Tower – You see – back there . . . ?"

I looked over my shoulder at the dark, squat battlements of Moura, the East Tower overshadowing the entire structure.

"Well then, what was one to think? More especially as Monsieur Edmond was in the tower at the time. A few moments after her body went hurtling down, he came from the tower and crossed the courtyard. You see? He claimed, of course, that mademoiselle had fallen accidentally."

"And still you think him innocent?"

"Not innocent. No. But that he had cause. She was evil, madame. Believe me – all evil. She put the eye upon people, and then they would wither and die. Which is why I did not like to meet her – afterward. She would have been twice as deadly, if you take my meaning."

"You cannot believe such things, Jehan. People do not have such power. The Church will tell you differently."

"No, no, madame. She had it, and the Mouras have it.

119

In the village, when Monsieur Edmond passes, they hide the children from his eye. I am not frightened of him. He has suffered enough. But you know how it is with the women. They never forget."

"Was he found guilty of Laly Florin's death?"

"His own brother believed him guilty. The shock of the trial and of Laly's death killed Monsieur Pierre. He died three weeks to the day after Monsieur Edmond was found guilty and sentenced to the guillotine. But Monsieur Edmond was a good friend of the Emperor, and his sentence was – you understand – altered."

"To what?"

"The galleys for life."

My whole body seemed to shudder. I knew vaguely what became of wretches sentenced to that horror. Somewhere, I remember, I had learned that France no longer employed her galley slaves at the oar, but the work was still as degrading, as full of pain and physical suffering, and as full of believable corruption. I could imagine what such imprisonment must have done to a man of aristocratic pride like Edmond Moura. I wondered that he had stood it. But I knew him for a man of resolution and mental strength.

Now I understood the half-finished sentences, the veiled words, the insinuations about Edmond Moura and those lost ten years of his life, even the sailor's easy clothing that he had learned to wear when he was, truly, "Citizen Nobody." I understood, too, the close-cropped hair that he had become accustomed to, and the scarred hands, and something of the hardness that pierced all his warmer, friendlier moments.

"You will see the strangeness of it," said Jehan. "Monsieur Edmond became the master of Moura on the day he entered the galleys."

"But he was pardoned then?"

Jehan beamed. "Ten years later. By the Emperor, during the Hundred Days, when every man who had ever served him was being recruited for the last great stand against our enemies."

I was too full of thoughts to straighten out his politics. I pursued the subject of murder a little further. "It is because of Laly Florin's death that the villagers and the others hate Monsieur Edmond?"

"That and because he is a Moura. Now there is talk of the death of Laly's child, the young Palla. They blame him for that, too. I do not know. But she was Laly's daughter, and Mademoiselle Laly was no better than the worst of women, madame."

"How do you know?" I asked suddenly.

He was embarrassed, looked at his big hands, and then said with a grin, "I talk too much. But this is hard to say. I worked on the estate. Sometimes she would come to me – invite me – you understand. And it was wrong, because she belonged to the master of Moura, Monsieur Edmond's brother. The master suffered from the effects of a disease as a child, and if the master could not satisfy her, the fault was hers to live with him. It was a question of honor, madame. You understand."

It was a peculiar thing to say to a strange woman. But then, I understood that men's honor was peculiar; that it was the accepted thing to take a mistress, but it was not honorable to take the mistress of another man if that man could not satisfy her. According to Jehan's theory, I daresay, it would have been quite the thing for him to accept Laly's advances if the master of Moura had been a young and vigorous man.

"Now," Jehan ended. "You will see why yesterday I wished that the Combing Lady might be you. Because I feared it was Laly, coming to put the eye upon me for refusing her long ago."

So he had refused her! I smiled to myself and was not displeased with him.

We had come to Kate's house, at the Moura gates, and I went up and knocked. There was no sound within.

Jehan reached over my head and rapped smartly on the paneled door.

While he waited, I stepped back and examined the stone building carefully for some sign of life. There was no smoke coming out of the chimney, and no sound anywhere. I called to her and heard nothing but the echo from off the great stone arch over the roadway where the Moura name was carved.

Jehan turned back to me.

"I very much fear, madame, that we will not find Mademoiselle Katta. Her pony cart is gone, and when she goes to the village she always takes the pony cart. When you said you were to meet her, I thought it strange that she should leave so late."

I was so enraged that I vented my spite upon the first handy object, which was this heavy-browed, slant-eyed peasant.

"Now what'll that mean? You thought it strange? Why do you think I came to meet her? Why didn't you tell me she left earlier?"

"But-but, madame, I thought it was an understanding between you. That she would wait for you. I knew – everyone knows – Katta always goes to early Mass. She leaves long before sunrise."

Without her cart, I could scarcely make it to the village – especially in my good dress, my best shawl, and my Sunday slippers. Infuriated, I slapped his shocked and confused face and stalked back toward Moura, muttering to myself.

"I will kill him! I'll be killing Edmond Moura with my bare hands! Lying to me! Thinking he will keep me prisoner. We'll soon see about that!"

Jehan hurried after me, protesting every step of the way and pleading with me not to be so cross.

The infamy of such a trick! I said, "I shall go to the village and lay information against him before the magistrate himself. That is what I will do."

"Oh no, madame." Jehan was terribly worried at my manner, and at my words too. "You cannot go to the magistrate and say such things."

"Why not, pray?"

"Because" – he looked down at me, perplexed that I did not know – "Monsieur Edmond is the new magistrate of Moura."

10

All the way back to Moura I was obsessed with my wrath. In other circumstances I should have felt only the deepest compassion – and more – for a man who had undergone such frightful punishment for a crime he might not have committed. But at last I understood the sinister joke between himself and Achille about the magistrate of Moura village. I must warn Charles Armitage not to try to carry out his plan of laying his complaint with the local magistrate. I could imagine the master's terrible smile as Mr. Armitage thus played into his hands.

The first thing I discovered when I returned was that the message I had left yesterday for Charles had not been picked up. Standing on tiptoe in the embrasure and peering down the sheer walls, I could see the faint mound of white in the ivy just where it had fallen. So the Englishman knew nothing of my plans. And worse, it might be too late to warn him about the magistrate.

Now here was I, making all manner of difficulties, trembling at shadows, when I was rich in support. I had forgotten the sour-visaged solicitor, still a guest here with Eustace Moura. Surely, he had no role in this monstrous plot. At the moment he and Monsieur Eustace were somewhere about the estate, inspecting what Edmond's fat cousin obviously pictured as his own future abode. When he returned, I would give thought to confiding in him.

It was still fairly early in the day, and as I came down from the broken parapet, it occurred to me that with the master and his guests gone, I had a perfect opportunity to oblige Mr. Armitage and myself by searching the cellars and dungeons. If, for any reason, there should be traces of the elusive Caroline Durand, I might find them in those dark places beneath Moura.

I told Achille I must borrow Clou and Jehan to help me in the task of cleaning. He tried dissuading me with his usual tales of rats and bats and such like, but I gave him a picture that would have raised hackles on a ghost of a dungeon near Dublin it had been my task to scrub down at the age of nine. He subsided with one of those slippery smiles of his and hunched up his eloquent shoulders, as one who would say, "I wash my hands of your life. Go and destroy yourself."

He did manage to have the last word, though, by refusing me Jehan.

"I have sent him to the fields to locate Monsieur Eustace and Monsieur Trevain. When they have returned, perhaps." I left him smirking there, a smooth, silvery, reptilian creature.

We descended the steep, plunging flight of stone steps' into the wine cellar, Clou carrying a bed-candlestick and I a serviceable storm lantern. Halfway down my lantern glinted on a ring of ancient keys hanging on a peg driven into the wall. Several of them looked to be capable of opening Westminister Abbey, so huge and rusted were they.

At the foot of the steps I found a sorry collection of old bottles, baskets, and broken glass, all neatly laced over with a Paisley design of cobwebs. I have seen cleaner peat bogs. I made a mental note to send down Jehan and the other new workman to clear this out and bury it.

We made our way beyond this hazard. I glanced curiously at the shelves with their row upon row of wine bottles. Was there a hiding place behind the shelves? No. The cobwebs were all too real; a very large, fat grey spider swung down before my lantern and dangled there, and I sprang back instinctively. Though I knew it must be my imagination, two malevolent little red eyes seemed to stare at me, unblinking, from that bloated grey body.

"Let us go," I said to Clou, who found nothing repulsive in all this. I hurried from the wine cellar into a dank, wet passage that led to another cellar where the winter food store was kept. I examined the walls here and found only what I might reasonably expect to find: namely, solid stones with the mortar somewhat eaten by age.

And at last we descended a still lower flight of steps, slimy with mould. Scurrying little creatures fled from our light to darker havens. We came up sharp against an iron-bound door with a great rusty lock. There was no key in the lock. Under my heavy pushing, the door yielded inward, squawking like a lovesick Dublin tomcat, and beyond and below that door were still more steps, each colder and damper than the one before. At what seemed to be the bottom we were able to make our way around a broken door hanging loose on its rusty hinges – the door to an actual dungeon.

It was horrid enough to be visiting these nether regions, at a depth below even a coffin's earthy bed, but to be kept prisoner in this foul place, without light, without hope, or intelligence of the world above, was beyond my imagining.

Within the cell, which opened at its opposite end on another iron-grilled door, the grey stone walls seemed to throb like a somnolent heart in the sudden glare of my lantern. But I soon saw that the movements were made by tiny creatures of the dark, as they retreated furtively, sometimes in massed clumps that resembled patches of fur on the walls. Lean, starving rats with huge-rope-tails scampered over our feet and darted behind a pile of ancient fetters, or squeezed through holes in the stone floor eaten away by the teeth of former rodents and by underground seepage. Into the opposite wall, beside the farther door, were fastened twin manacles, and in another corner, the broken and no longer serviceable parts of an engine I took to be a rack.

A sharp spike was fixed in the wall about six feet high. Clou lowered her candle toward dark patches on the stone block directly beneath, and made inarticulate little sounds, pointing to the network of blue veins in her neck to indicate blood. Someone had doubtless regaled her with this pleasant tale on a former visit. I knew the spike was sometimes used to impale a human body like the carcass of meat in a butcher's stall, but I shook my head and scuffed at the stains with my shoe. Here and there they became lighter – obviously a rust-colored lichen that had taken root here in the eternal dampness. Still beneath the lichen now removed by my foot, there were other stains. Older, blackened, but the shape of great gouts of blood.

I closed my mind to them, and to these sinister pictures of the Moura history, and went on through the door in the farther wall. This door moved easily, as though it had been oiled. There was a sharp right turn beyond. The walls, carelessly formed of great, ancient stones stuck roughly in mortar, now became our enemy, their jagged edges scratching our arms, tearing at our sleeves.

Here it was, I am ashamed to say, that Clou's eyes proved sharper than mine. As I freed her sleeve from the roughened prong of a stone that was sharp as a hook, she pointed to a tiny wad of cloth almost lost in the darkness of the earth at our feet. I picked it up and examined it. Smoothed out, it proved to be a blue satin ribbon, remarkably fresh for having been here so many centuries. It was stained by water and dirt and a dark, needle-thin streak of what might have been blood or rust; otherwise, it was not in the least faded, and was just such a ribbon as a blonde girl might wear to tie back her hair. It could not be the ribbon of a servant girl. No. This was the property of a lady. Where was she now? It was a little saddening.

Clou smiled and pointed to the ribbon.

Suddenly I had a terrible thought. I said, "Did you know this lady?"

Clou smiled and curtsied, as though to the ribbon's owner.

I said, "Long, long ago when you were a child so high?"

When I had made her understand this, she shook her head, a short, quick shake, and smiled again, making little gestures around her face.

"A pretty girl?" I asked.

She nodded.

It was not the sort of thing Palla Florin would have worn. The shade was a little too obviously innocent for Palla, who had excellent taste and never tried to emulate the simpering blondes of her acquaintance.

Ah, but there was another here recently. Hadn't Charles said she was a blonde?

"Mademoiselle Durand?" I asked Clou. I repeated the name. I put down my lantern and made motions of reading a book. She nodded, pleased that she had understood my charade.

"This belonged to the governess, Mademoiselle Durand? What was she doing down here?"

Clou looked at me. She did not understand, or seemed not to, but in her faded blue eyes there was no look of puzzlement. It was as though she had schooled herself to look perfectly blank. I took her by the shoulders and shook her.

"Have they killed mademoiselle? Look – " Using my thumb and forefinger, I made motions of shooting. She shook her head. "Well then, did they stab her?" I indicated as much by a downward stroke. "Clou, do you understand me? Did they kill her?"

Clou looked at me, unblinking. Her face reminded me of a drab little doll I once dropped accidentally into a bucket of water. All her features seemed washed out of that pale face. After a few moments, I desisted. She became herself again, smiling, friendly, eager to help me. I folded the ribbon, clean side out, and tucked it into my bodice. We went on and eventually found ourselves approaching light.

The passage ended at another flight of steps, twisting and turning upward, lighted by what seemed to be sunlight far above. There was still another passage leading further into the dark, but I was on my way toward the light above when I heard a sound I could not place, whether made by an animal or a human being, I did not know. Then Clou pinched my arm, pointing upward and making dreadful little sounds that showed her excitement.

"What is it?" I asked. I finally made out that she wanted me to follow the darker passage, but I paid her little heed. Surely she could not consider the out-of-doors more dangerous than those dreadful underground passages! Hanging the lantern handle over my arm, I scurried up the steps as fast as I could, with Clou scrambling behind me. Breathless, I reached the top step, only to find myself in the bottom of a kind of well with two boards carelessly stretched over the top about fifteen feet above. Moura was worse than England with her priest holes. Secret passages! Secret exits!

There was a ladder of sorts, with many rungs missing, that took me up the side of the well but it was an ordeal, and for a few minutes, I thought gentle little Clou would not make it. But once we removed the boards over our heads, she was as glad as I was to be out in the sunlight, though she still made gestures of danger.

We were somewhere in the Moura woods. I looked around, found myself in the center of a tangled berry thicket that had grown so high that we could not see our way over it. However, a path had been laboriously cut through the thicket, although I had to walk bent over, for the berry vines were all tangled together overhead. As we made our way along what I took to be some forgotten field, I began to understand the sounds I had faintly made out in the deep dungeon passage.

They were plainly those of a human being screaming for his life.

There were suffling sounds now too, and beating . . . and the sounds of growling.

Coming out of the thicket into a gentle grove of trees, I saw that Clou had been right to be alarmed. Down that path was a terrible sight.

Two big grey dogs were attacking the wizened solicitor, Monsieur Trevain, who lay writhing in the grass at one side of the path, while Charles Armitage, of all people, was trying vainly to beat off the dogs with a walking stick. Above the gradually decreasing force of Monsieur Trevain's screams, were the sounds of the struggle, the thud of blows by Charles, and above all, the hideous slavering sounds of the dogs – which were, I now realized, wolves.

Eustace Moura was nowhere around, and I assumed he had gone for help. I knew there was nothing for it but to find weapons, and pulled hard at a rotting branch of a tree overhead. Clou looked on, trembling. I pushed her away, pointed back toward what I supposed must be the direction of Moura.

"Go for help," I told her.

She seemed to understand, and much to my surprise, instead of taking the path that must lead eventually to Moura, she boldly went back into the thicket, intending to return through those dreadful dungeons. I gave her full marks for courage, and came up beside Charles. He had seen me but did not turn his head for an instant. He kept beating at the wolves, and I joined him, but I swung my lantern from the end of the stick. The smaller of the two animals, scorched suddenly across the ear, flashed around at me. I have never seen such great, white tusks, gleaming in a fiery mouth that looked to me at the moment like a cavern in Hell. I belted him again and he twisted, seemed half of a mind to attack me, but then contented himself with backing away, growling like a ravenous dog. As he retreated, I saw that he was terribly gaunt; the bones of his ribs seemed to protrude through his shaggy coat.

The larger of the two animals, however, was less easily alarmed. I began upon him as Charles popped him a great crack on the skull. Between us we managed to get him off the unfortunate Monsieur Trevain who, by this time, had fainted under the pain and fright of his experience.

Now it was like the bull-baiting I had seen in my childhood. Charles, keeping me rather behind him, managed to hold the animal at bay, but now and then the huge, scrawny body would lurch forward and the great canines would snap at Charles' hands. I could see that his hands were bleeding, but he seemed otherwise unhurt.

I screamed very loudly several times, hoping to bring to our aid any peasants in the woods, but the sounds only infuriated the wolves and brought the second one loping back, hoping to sink its teeth into me. At last, one swipe of a giant forepaw smashed the lantern, and left me with only the most inadequate defense, the blunt ended stick I had broken off the tree. The greater wolf reared back on his hindquarters, and I knew he was about to spring. Charles leaped backward, knocking me down, and the springing wolf missed him by inches. The next thing I knew, the snarling canine face was glaring down at me, the teeth bared, and a very long tongue switching back and forth as the creature panted for breath – or for me, who was very likely to be his next meal.

I heard a crack of what I took to be Charles' stick – although I didn't see it strike the animal – and was amazed when the creature crumpled up on top of me. I was still beating the air like an overturned turtle, unable to get up with this great body on my chest, when I felt myself gathered up, dead wolf and all, by the workman, Jehan. There was another crack and a sickening, whining sound as the second wolf died more slowly. Then, over Jehan's arm I saw Edmond Moura put down a pair of smoking travelers' pistols and turn his attention to me. For an instant he seemed more worried than my state warranted; but then, as he saw me squirming indignantly under the weight of the dead wolf, he smiled.

With Jehan's aid, I succeeded in freeing myself of the animal, and got to my feet unaided, smelling horribly of the dead wolf's blood and of the stench of the unwashed animal. I could still hear, not far off, the terrible whimpering death agony of the second wolf. Monsieur Edmond put the wretched creature out of its misery with one hard

132

blow of his pistol-butt, and then with Charles examined the unconscious solicitor.

"It is grave but not fatal, I think," said Edmond. "They should never have ventured so far without guns. That would be my fool cousin. Greedy as ever to see what he may inherit. I am surprised he got back in time for me to be of any use." He unwound his muslin cravat and applied the snowy folds to the wounded man's throat, then looked at me. "Do you mind giving me some cloth? We will need to staunch the bleeding first."

He went back to his work, having bound the cravat to the ragged, bleeding wounds at the unfortunate solicitor's throat, and now his left thumb pressed hard on the vein or artery above the wound at the point of his breastbone. Charles, who was dressed carelessly for hard walking, wore no cravat, and was about to tear off his ruffled shirt collar when I pointed out that my petticoat contained much longer strips for bandages and I would need help with the stiff, white fabric. He reddened slightly, but, after finding a seam in the skirt, helped me tear away long strips from the hem. Jehan watched with interest and Edmond looked up occasionally to see how we were progressing. He noted the way my proper young Englishman avoided sight of my ankles, then glanced at me, having seemed to find this amusing. I gave him back a frosty look. I was not forgetting this morning's long walk to Kate's place, nor the murderous Moura devices in the dungeons.

11

"Appalling business," said Eustace, finishing off a tall goblet of a thickish red wine as he watched Matilde and me tuck the sleeping Monsieur Trevain into bed for the night. "How fortunate that I was able to get help, or you might all have been devoured! I saw the beasts first, you know, and took to my heels. Poor Trevain here was not so active. He stumbled and – But you know the rest. My timely race to fetch Edmond – who arrived none too soon from the village – winded me, too."

Monsieur Edmond rolled down his sleeves after examining his guest's wounds and renewing the bandages, but none of us said anything to this astonishing summary of Eustace Moura's heroic retreat. Having thus graced the sickroom with his sagacious comments and drunk up the wine Matilde brought to strengthen the patient, Eustace strutted out. Presently I heard him in the next bedchamber, where I had no doubt he was filching Charles Armitage's bedside wine. In spite of the discourse between Monsieur Edmond and Achille the night before Palla's funeral, Charles was now a guest at Moura.

I was in a mood to laugh as a kind of release, being so completely tired and at the same time prey to such inner trembling that there were moments when I felt I could have used that rich wine to good advantage. Nor did this room help to restore me; for it was the chamber hung with green, the one once occupied during her lifetime by Moura's lively ghost, the Combing Lady.

Edmond Moura did not share my trepidation, however; for he had looked after his departing cousin with such contempt and hatred that I should not have liked to stand in the fat man's boots at that moment. Matilde shuffled out with the medications, and after helping Edmond on with his coat I was about to do likewise when he spoke.

"I have not thanked you for your courage today."

"You repaid me fully," I said, and looked him in the eye. "You let me go to Mass with Kate."

"Ah, that. Jehan told me how angry you were. I am sorry. I did not know Kate's habits."

"And yet," I said, "every inhabitant of Moura to the poorest peasant seems to know them."

"But you see, for many years I have not been resident at Moura."

I felt hot with shame that I should remind him of those dreadful years. Faith now, how should a man in the galleys know Kate's religious habits? She had told me herself that during her earlier years she was an actress and often away from Moura.

I wanted to make amends and said to him as warmly as I might, "I beg your pardon, sir. But I was so very angry."

"Then we are friends again?"

The meanness of the man, being tender and merry again to work upon my silly self! And me with my wretched thoughts of the satin ribbon that I still kept with me! So I said, "It is not my place to say whether we are or not, monsieur."

"I see." The tender moment was gone. I recognized the underlying bitter hardness that was so much a part of his everyday manner to the world. "Like your country and mine, the best that can be said of us is that we are not now at war."

I was wanting to say – oh, many things, to bring back the qualities I had seen him display to no others except myself; but I knew my own weakness against that wondrous and special warmth of his, and I could not yield. I dared not. I had Caroline Durand to think of, and my little dead friend.

I realized suddenly that I was remiss in my own gratitude and said as we entered the passage, "I have not thanked you, monsieur. But for you, I would have provided dinner for those poor starving beasts."

"Do you think I would let anything happen to you?" he asked in such a matter-of-fact tone that I did not know how to take him.

We were passing the next room and I stopped, intending to pay a brief call upon Charles Armitage. It was essential that I tell him the identity of the magistrate of Moura, though he must be much more exhausted than I, and with those injured hands as well. I could see at once that Monsieur Edmond did not like this call.

"Your room is some doors beyond," he said.

"I would like to see how Mr. Armitage is doing for himself."

"Young men of his sort generally do very well for themselves, especially with susceptible young ladies."

"Oh, bosh!" I said inelegantly. "He saved poor Monsieur Trevain's life, and mine as well."

"But what was he doing there in the first place, I ask myself."

I did not like his tone. It promised nothing good for poor Charles.

"Surely, the Moura woods are not so sacred that one

136

cannot walk through them. Mr. Armitage is a great walker. He is fond of difficult paths."

"He has chosen a rugged one in coming to Moura," said Edmond ominously, and opened the door for me.

Just as I expected, we found Eustace standing at the bedside guzzling Charles' glass of wine.

"Good God!" Monsieur Edmond exclaimed upon seeing him. "Isn't there enough to drink downstairs? Must you steal everyone else's property as well as mine?"

Eustace set the glass down with a snap and said haughtily, "I did not think you were so parsimonious, cousin, but very well. Keep your wine!" and he made a grand exit past both of us.

Out of pure curiosity I took up the glass he had set down, and turned it upside down. Not a drop came out. From his comfortable place among the pillows in that crimson-decked bed, Charles Armitage laughed.

"I'm afraid I was not fast enough." He turned his head and gazed at Edmond Moura pleasantly. "I hope you will forgive me, sir. I know I trespass upon your good nature. By tomorrow I'll be quite myself again."

"How are your hands?" asked his host, making no effort to deny that he was an unwanted guest.

"Tolerably well. Stiff, I think. That will be the greatest problem. Gad! It's been a strenuous day! I was on a walking tour, you know, sir. They told me in the village that I might find some remarkably interesting fauna hereabouts."

Edmond glanced at the door, where his cousin had departed, and remarked, "Some of the fauna are rather worse than others. You may find the Moura wolves the least of your troubles here."

Charles and I exchanged glances. This did not elude Monsieur Edmond, who frowned unbecomingly. I said, before Charles could make any blunders: "You must speak to the magistrate of Moura, Mr. Armitage. And what could be easier? For here he is in person."

Charles succeeded admirably in concealing his shock at this announcement. He lowered his gaze to the sheets before he said coolly, "But that would be bad manners to complain of my treatment, when I occupy one of the best beds at Moura."

"Hardly that," said Edmond who seemed determined to be difficult. "It is an inferior room."

"For inferior people?" asked Charles, smiling a little.

Edmond shrugged, apparently too cross to bother with the amenities. I had never seen him behave like this and was very much puzzled. He glanced at the old gold-banded clock on the mantel and remarked that Charles must be sleepy and would need his rest.

"Come, we will let him sleep," he said to me, holding out his hand in a manner I could not mistake.

"Yes. I find myself rather tired. Good night to you." And Charles sank back onto the pillows weakly.

We were both about to leave the room. Edmond had the door open already, when Charles called to me.

"Would you mind, just a moment? I seem to have these sheets twisted, and my hands are so stupid I can't do a thing with them."

I knew he was calling to me, but Edmond was determined not to leave us alone, and started back into the room, only to be halted by Charles' very definite request.

"Miss Wicklow, if you please."

Edmond studied the two of us, his mouth hard, his eyes narrowed with anger. Then he shrugged and went into the passage, closing the door upon us.

I hurried to the bed but found Charles quite himself, and in need of nothing but advice and company.

138

"You must know why I was out there in the woods today. A villager told me there was an outside entrance to the cellars – through a well, or some such nonsense."

"There is. I found it."

"But is it true? Is he actually the magistrate?"

I said it was true.

"Then we are trapped."

"Worse than that," I said, and brought out the blue ribbon that Clou and I had found in the dungeon passage. "Do you recognize this?"

He took it and examined it in his clumsily wrapped hands.

"It is such a ribbon as Caroline used to wear. She had very curly hair and often caught up a handful in a kind of Grecian knot with blue ribbon."

"It is stained," I said. "Do you mark the stains?"

"Mud . . . and water . . . What do you think this one is? The long, thin streak here?"

I let him guess.

He sat straight up in bed. "Do you think it could be blood?" he asked, and then winced at the picture it brought to his mind. "That poor child! That poor, stupid, blundering girl! If only I had known – been here in time! Why, these men are monsters!"

"One of them is, at any rate," I said.

"My God! What infamy! To kill a helpless young female like that! And then to go on living here!"

I ventured slowly, "It is just possible that Edmond Moura is not guilty. There may be reasons we don't suspect. Or Miss Caroline could have left for some other purpose. This stain may not even be blood."

He sat there propped on one elbow and looked at me.

"Do you really believe all this regamarole you're telling me?"

"No," I confessed. "I don't – but I wish I did."

Charles said, with more wisdom than I expected, "I've no doubt you find him attractive. Devils usually are."

I imagined that after the exertions of the day I would sleep the sleep of the dead, but it was not to be. I dozed off for an hour or so, and then, fancying I heard stealthy movements in the passage outside my door, I leapt out of bed and ran to look out, preferring to meet head-on whatever danger threatened. Of course nothing was to be seen. The passage was utterly deserted, the only sound the whisper of the wind rustling around corners.

I had just returned to bed when I became aware of the howling of wolves. They appeared to be rather closer than I remembered from previous nights.

I got up and went to the window, pushing aside the heavy portieres and then throwing open one of the casement windows. It gave me a genuine start to see a number of the gaunt, grey bodies ringed in a circle near the moat bridge below my window. As I looked out they became absolutely still, glaring upward, their muzzles glistening wet with saliva in the starlight, as their long tongues moved slowly back and forth hungrily. Then I saw their movements shift to my direction. Their attention had been occupied by something on my left, apparently in one of the rooms occupied by the guests of Moura – Cousin Eustace, or the injured solicitor, or Charles Armitage, or even something on the parapet. I could see nothing to betray the source of their interest, and looked back down at them. In that moment great chunks of something were hurled through the air from my left, to land in their midst. It seemed to me to be scraps of food. I stuck my head out of my windows and studied the blank stone face of Moura beside me. I could not see any windows ajar, or anything to betray the person who fed these man-killing beasts below. The wolves tore into what had been thrown them, and soon were snarling and slavering among themselves.

What kind of person, I wondered, would feed wolves rather than shoot them?

I closed the window and retired into my room. Thinking it over, I felt that this feeding of deadly wolves deserved investigation; so I stepped into my shoes, took my heaviest shawl, and went out in the passage, being careful not to tread on any yielding boards in the floor. Eustace Moura's room was silent, but as I passed Charles' room the door opened a crack and he peered out. He was ludicrously wrapped in a blanket with his curly dark head sticking out above its folds like a Red Indian. He seemed more shocked to see me than I to see him.

"Good Lord, you startled me! Did you see that below? Someone feeding those accursed animals."

"I think it came from along this passage."

"The parapet. By the by, I have been worrying the last half hour or so about our friend next door. It seemed to me I could hear him groaning. May have been only a bad dream, of course."

We opened the door into Monsieur Trevain's room, and went to the foot of his bed, watching him closely. He groaned a good deal in his dreams, which was not surprising after the horror he had so narrowly escaped this afternoon. But otherwise he seemed sound asleep.

We tiptoed out and along to the flight of steps leading to the broken parapet. Below us the thick, dark woods lay serene under the silver light, and we could see the wolf pack slinking away into the shelter of the woods.

Charles whispered in awe, "I should like to command beasts in such a fashion. Do you realize what this means,

141

that someone in this terrible place has domain over those creatures?"

"But – " I protested, knowing whom he meant, "he shot two of them today. If he had command of them he would have got them off in some other fashion."

"Why? Wasn't it easier to play the dashing rescuer? Why shouldn't he sacrifice two of his creatures? Look out. Don't step there."

As so often happens when one is warned in such a fashion, I immediately trod upon something that gritted between my shoe sole and the stone of the parapet. I shifted quickly. Clutching tight to his ridiculous blanket with a bandaged hand, Charles picked up the object with his other hand, and examined it. It was a bone, with shreds of meat still clinging wetly to it. A veal bone. Someone at Moura did feed those beasts.

"But why?" I asked dumbly.

"To keep them near, of course, For his – purposes."

"You mean they are the instruments to kill his victims, or something of that sort?" I simply could not believe it. A murder of necessity, perhaps, or in deep hatred. But not the monstrous, purposeless feeding of those vicious beasts. It was utterly fantastic, like the hideous tales told around a fire in a great hall about the past, the distant, terrible past when men were not civilized. How could Edmond Moura be one of those? A man of his dignity and breeding and family.

And family? I remembered the cellars and dungeons which existed below us, in these enlightened days of 1815.

I ventured once more, "It might be the sort of thing Achille would do. You must have remarked how weird he is, and he has lived here for many years. Monsieur Edmond only recently returned."

Charles said stubbornly, "Then why hasn't Moura stopped him? Or is our fine host able to sleep through all this racket?"

I still clung tenaciously to the theory of Achille's guilt, but Charles was rambling on.

"If I can get this story to someone in higher authority than a local magistrate . . . I still don't see how Moura could have been appointed magistrate when his record under Napoleon is so well known."

"Monsieur Moura intimated to me that he bought his pardon from the king, and probably along with it the magistracy of this area. I understand such things can be done."

"Oh, anything is possible with these Frenchies," said the chauvinistic Mr. Armitage.

A midnight wind had sprung up suddenly, ruffling Charles' hair and piercing my shawl and night robes. In the prospect of danger neither of us had given thought to our appearance. We looked at each other, and he said, "I beg your pardon. I have no right to be in your presence in such a condition."

I thought it rather late for these apologies, and turned away from the now chilling parapet with relief. In my room I should perhaps think of some explanation for all this business of the wolves.

As we started back along the first-floor passage, Charles hesitated. We were passing Monsieur Trevain's door.

"He is dreaming again. Poor fellow."

I could hear muttered sounds beyond the door, punctuated by what was undeniably a human groan. We opened the door and peered in. To our surprise and uneasiness, Edmond Moura still fully dressed, though it must be after midnight, stood at the foot of the solicitor's bed. He looked up as we came in. His glance took in all of

143

Charles and he seemed almost on the verge of a smile. Then he looked from Charles to me as though speculating on why we should be together, and in such deshabille.

I said quickly, "Is Monsieur Trevain suffering? I heard sounds, and met Mr. Charles in the passage. He tells me – "

Charles spoke for himself.

"Good Gad, man! I couldn't sleep. The poor fellow is in pain."

"Not in pain at all," Edmond assured us coolly. "He has been dreaming. I gave him something to drink. It should see him comfortably through the night. And give you no more occasion to wander about the house."

Charles stiffened with anger. "Very well, sir. If you will allow your guests to be disturbed by wolves howling at your very gates, I say no more. Good night to you." He stalked out majestically in his blanket and bare feet.

Edmond Moura laughed after his retreating back. "So much for that fool. Did the wolves trouble you as well, Anne?"

"Not so much as the other things," I said quietly.

"Ah?" He raised an eyebrow in what I took to be a question, and moved toward me. I was oppressed and confused by his shadow over me; for his back cut off the light of the candle.

"What troubles you?"

"Yourself, sir."

He took my chin gently between his thumb and forefinger. In his darkened eyes I read many things, but none of them had any possible bearing on man-killing wolves, and cellars with secrets, and the rest of the horrors at Moura.

"Be patient, Anne. Patient and trusting. It is all I ask of you."

I knew that I was being enveloped in the personal magnetism he held over me, but I could not find the strength to break away. He gave my chin a little twist to one side, and before I knew what he was about, he had bent his head and kissed me softly on the throat, just above the fold of my shawl. He did not touch me in any other way, and yet, if I were weighted by fetters I could have been no more securely bond; there was a trembling in my limbs.

Suddenly, behind him in the sick-bed, the old man scrambled up, breathing hard. I thought for an instant he had seen us and was protesting, but when Edmond looked around with an impatient exclamation in French, he saw at once that Trevain was troubled by other matters. His rheumy eyes stared into space. He breathed in great, hard clutchings for air.

"She was there – sitting on the foot of the bed! She was there – I saw her."

Edmond went to his side and settled him back on the pillows.

"You saw Mademoiselle Anne. There was no one else. You understand? No one." His voice and quietly decisive manner had its effect on the sick man; he relaxed slowly, though he still muttered.

"She was there . . . combing . . . combing . . . "

"Sleep!" said Edmond.

The old man's eyes closed. Gradually the heavy breathing grew gentler, and he truly slept. Edmond arranged the jumbled bedclothing thoughtfully.

"I will take you to your room," he told me then, quite businesslike, as though nothing had happened between us.

I said, "It will not be necessary. I know the way," and left the room.

I passed Achille in the passage. He was running. I don't believe I ever recall seeing him run before. He went into Trevain's room and I quietly followed him back, listening at the door like any gossiping parlormaid.

Inside the room Achille gasped out, "All safe."

An instant later, I was astonished to hear the unmistakeable crack of a stinging slap. There was a sound like a gasp, and Achille's voice again, muffled, almost incoherent, as though he nursed his cheek and mouth.

"Monsieur, I have told you. An accident – an accident!"

"There are too many accidents," said Edmond Moura, in a voice that froze my blood. I heard footsteps coming toward the door, and I ran.

I had only just closed my own door when I heard Edmond Moura's purposeful footsteps pass my room.

12

I suppose few people have opened their eyes in quite so startling a fashion as I upon that next morning. But boys will play at being Bow Street runners, and Charles Armitage was no exception, though a trifle old for such nonsense.

In my dreams I had been part of an absurd but intricate plot involving Edmond Moura. I think he was in the act of pilfering Miss Nutting's store of *Tatlers* and *Spectators* with my connivance, and Palla Florin was watching us, sober-faced but with her tawny eyes dancing as they were used to do when she was caught at mischief. Only, in this case, we were the culprits. It saddened me to see her; for I knew, even as I dreamed, that she was dead.

Then came the hard hand upon my mouth, another hand upon my shoulder, so that I awakened a prisoner, unable to cry out. I opened my eyes, with my heart thundering in my bosom, and there I looked up into the face of Charles Armitage who, for all his violence to me, had the effrontery to whisper: "Hush!" There was nothing for it but to listen to his explanations, lame as they must be.

"I don't wish *them* to hear."

So much was obvious, even to me. I lay there frowning up at him, not in the least concerned that my hair was tousled and the neck of my night robe all awry. How much more uneasy and nervous I should have been if the master of Moura stood in place of Charles! It does not seem to me, even now, that this was precisely complimentary to my handsome English friend. Seeing my calm demeanor, he took his hand from my mouth.

I said drily, "I must say you are grown vastly familiar with my person, Mr. Armitage."

"I know – I know. But this is important!" I had never seen him more serious. There was no lurking laughter in his brown eyes. "Of the utmost importance."

"So is my person, to me."

"Listen. I spent the night roaming through this chamber of horrors."

"All of it – and at night?" He was either an extraordinarily brave man, or completely nerveless.

"Everything. Followed every dashed winding passage. Narrowly missed that accursed grey-haired steward once. He was returning to his chambers with the toothache."

"Not the toothache," I put in, remembering the hard slap I had heard beyond the door last night.

"Well, I've found something odd, something that will injure *him*, you may be sure. Can you dress and come with me?"

"Now? I shall be missed."

He looked at me steadily with rather more shrewdness than I'd have credited to him.

"Yes. I've remarked it myself. He does keep a close watch on you. And not out of fear – quite the reverse."

I changed the subject.

"Where is this thing you have found?"

"In a passage under the carriage house. This place is a honeycomb of dungeons and cellars. Good Lord! I lost myself a dozen times."

"When did you sleep?"

"I have not. Do you think I could get an hour's sleep

in this tomb when somewhere they have buried my poor stupid little Caroline?"

I felt guilty that such matters had not prevented me from getting several hours of rest, and I said, "Give me five minutes and I will go with you."

"Only five? You are a remarkable lady! Indeed you are!" He was genuinely enthusiastic. But not at my character, I could not fail to observe; rather at my haste to serve in the line of duty.

"Because I am not a *lady*, I am able to dress in five minutes. Wait in the passage."

"I can't, someone may see me."

"Well then, keep your face to the door. I'll contrive very well behind you."

"My dear Anne, all haste, no questions – you are unexceptionable!" He hugged me in a friendly way, begged pardon for such familiarity and turned a broad back to me while I made good my boast, dressed and joined him five minutes later.

"What is it we are to find?"

He motioned me to silence, picked up my bed-candle, and I followed him uneasily into the passage. I did not like the extreme bleakness of his normally kind face. Whatever his discovery, it promised disaster for Edmond Moura.

To my surprise, Charles had found other passages down to the cellars. Behind the stone steps leading to the broken north parapet was a small door I had supposed must open into a storeroom. Instead, it plunged downward into more cellars. There were no torture chambers here, for which I was profoundly grateful. In their place were utilitarian stone-walled rooms that had once concealed implements of war. In one cellar were the remnants of a wheeled siege-tower, and in another, a kind of apparatus of iron pots for pouring boiling pitch upon luckless invaders.

149

When we were approximately under the carriage house, we found the wretched but spacious area apparently still used for storage of old junk that one should burn but never quite does. There were iron-bound trunks, some with the locks sprung and the faded contents spilling out. A rare piece of green damask caught my eye. If Charles had not shaken my arm impatiently, I should have had out the entire brocaded gown, with thoughts of using it to cover pillows. He pointed to a small portmanteau that had been more neatly placed than the great trunks and cases beneath it.

"I know that portmanteau," Charles said grimly. "It belonged to my grenadier friend. I remember the day Caroline packed it. Look inside, but don't disorder it in any way. I want it to be found by others exactly as we found it."

I mounted several trunks that served as steps, and opened the portmanteau. It was full of girlish frills and furbelows, pastel muslins, laces and ribbons, the wardrobe of a blonde young coquette.

This is evidence. Deadly evidence, I kept thinking to myself.

With great care I unfolded what was left of a pretty shawl, bright and gay as a daffodil in this dreary place.

"How strange! Half of it is burned away."

"I know," said Charles. "I'll wager they intended to burn all of those things, but probably some servant girl, hungry for fripperies, pulled the shawl from the fire and rescued the other belongings in time. Either that or the shawl was stained or worn by Caroline herself when they – "

"Spare me that," I said hastily. "I take your meaning."

"We must hurry now. It is a long walk back to the

village and I should be there when the prosecutor – the king's attorney – arrives."

"The king's attorney? But – in Moura village?"

"Why not? Apparently, he has heard rumors. They say he was in Lyons on the king's business, and he comes now into Auvergne. He's expected within a day or so. That big fellow, Jehan, told me last night when he brought my bath water. Seems there is a street-fair tonight, with puppets and such mummery. The villagers are sure the king's attorney will wish to arrive in time. I doubt that. In any case, Jehan thinks his visit is a great compliment to Edmond Moura. Seems they are acquainted."

"Do you think then that Edmond will put the evil eye on the king's attorney?"

"I shall personally remind this fellow of Moura's record under the Empire. A notorious Bonapartist."

If Edmond Moura had bought his way back into the good graces of the Bourbons, certainly the highest judicial authority in the land must know of his past record, but I did not remind Charles. He was so sure of himself.

"And I'm to stay here alone, is it?"

He said griskly, enthralled with his plan, "Of course!" And clasped me by the shoulders. "Dear comrade, we shall slay this dragon together, you by spying upon him from within, and I from without."

I felt a good deal like the squire to some crusading knight. My skirts were of no account. To Charles I was a comrade – inferior of course, so that I might be sacrificed to his holy crusade if the dragon slew me in his fury.

I said calmly, "You think it safe for me to remain here?"

He was astonished. "What else is there to do?"

"Perhaps you are right. I have always wondered what it would be like to lay my life upon the altar of heroism."

"Oh, nonsense. He likes you. There's no danger to you from that quarter."

I forbore reminding him of his warning to me in the high-road a few days ago, that if Edmond Moura found me out I should not live to regret it. Ah, well! That is impetuous youth for you. I felt eons older than the thirty-year-old Charles Armitage.

"Now then!" He had put everything back where we found it; now he took my arm and led me through the grey-dark of the passages, lighted only by the flickering glow of the candle. "By week's end we shall have this monster under lock and key, and you are free to return to England."

What a sad setdown that would be! I realized for the first time that I had no desire to return to Miss Nutting's school.

"You will be a heroine, a true Joan of Arc. Believe me, no other woman would have the strength for what you must do." He hugged me a little, a sop to quiet his faithful squire.

It was one thing, indeed, to boast that I could take care of myself, but quite another to be taken at my word, and by a man. It would serve Charles properly if Monsieur Edmond murdered me too and tossed my wretched shawls and gowns in a heap into his ancient dungeons. I dwelt on the idea a moment, fancying I heard Charles' regretful sigh, his fierce determination to be revenged for the death of his brave "comrade." I could not help laughing at the dismal picture.

He looked at me in surprise. I caught myself quickly. "Hysteria."

"Oh." He seemed to think this quite natural in the circumstances.

We were approaching that small upward flight of steps

152

which opened into the little entry hall on the ground floor of the main wing. I was in such a muddled state I hadn't the faintest idea of how to proceed in the following days. But I underestimated my friend.

"Your task will require a minimum of effort. Nothing with which to concern yourself." (Nothing but my life, I thought.) "Mine is more complicated. Let's see now. I return to the village. I await the arrival of the prosecutor. Before Edmond Moura can reach him, I present our case. We proceed to Moura where – "

"You find me eaten alive by the Moura ghost. There is one, you know. They call her the Combing Lady."

"Come, you want to tease me. Combing ghosts! I should like to see a Combing Lady, indeed. In any case, the king's attorney and I will proceed to Moura where – "

"Monsieur Edmond sees you from the East Tower, and rushes down and strangles me, the sole witness against him. Whereupon – "

"Not if you are clever and take care to arouse no suspicions." His padded hand clapped me between the shoulder blades. He smiled, but there was a purposeful look that gave his handsome features strength – or was it pigheadedness? I could not decide. "You are joking with me, and believe me, Anne, it is no laughing matter. But do not fancy I don't appreciate your effort to make light of your bravery. You are the best – the – well, let me be honest. You are just like a true English-woman! I am proud to have known you."

"That sounds like my obituary."

"No. No. I would not let you stay if I did not feel that you, at least, are safe with him. Why, I do not know. But I believe it. Now, to get on. The prosecutor and I will arrive. You and I then reveal to him the evidence we have just seen in these cellars, and he will have a thorough search made – especially in the Moura burial vault."

"Good God! Not the vault too!"

"Certainly. It is the logical place in which to entomb a human body."

It was a stifling thought.

"After which, I have no doubt, Edmond Moura will then be arrested and guillotined," he continued.

I shuddered.

As we reached the top of the steps, he looked at me curiously. "I think, Anne, you are being unwise."

Yes. I was unwise to remain here. He realized at last what danger I ran.

"I seem to detect a certain sympathy with this monster. Believe me, you only complicate matters by it. You must always bear in mind what Edmond Moura has done."

In my disappointment in him, I could have murdered Charles myself.

He opened the door and I stepped into the hall. I was so shocked at what I saw that I came to an abrupt stop and poor Charles piled into me.

In the hall, Edmond Moura stood leaning comfortably against the wall, his arms crossed and his eyes upon us. There was a kind of grim amusement in those grey eyes.

"I – we – " began Charles.

Ever the correct host, Edmond said, "During the Terror, tours were conducted through the Moura cellars. A fee of one assignat was collected for the benefit of the local Committee of Public Safety. Would you say the tour was worth an assignat?"

We were too dumbfounded to say anything.

"With our bankrupt treasury, an assignat, of course," went on Edmond smoothly, "was a worthless piece of paper. The tour, I think, is on a par with it. But perhaps

154

you have found something worth the admission?" He looked from one of us to the other.

At least we had the sense not to betray ourselves. Charles said huffily, "Scoff if you like, but somewhere in this accursed house I know evidence will be found against you."

"Evidence of what?"

"Of – of – anything, damn it! If one had time to search more thoroughly – But I suppose I am ordered off the premises now?"

Once in a great while Charles surprised me by the conviction of his acting.

"It might be wise," said Edmond.

This was my chance for escape. Common sense advised me to take it, whatever my heart might protest. "I shall be ready in ten minutes, Charles."

"I think not," said Edmond. "I will see to mademoiselle's departure – in my own time."

He took me by the wrist and more or less propelled me over to his side. It was like crossing a boundary from safe, home country into a mysterious and beautiful, perhaps deadly foreign land. I saw by Charles' glance at me that this suited his plans. He bowed stiffly to Edmond and was already moving up the steps to his room when Edmond called after him,

"One of my men accompanies you. He will be at your room in half an hour. By good luck, you may reach the village in time for their carnival tonight."

"It is not at all necessary. I am perfectly capable of finding my own way back to the village."

Edmond said politely, "I insist. Your bandaged hands would be of no use to you if you met with more of our wolves."

"I prefer them to any two-legged wolves you may send.

I'll wager the fangs of the Moura wolves are not so sharp as Jehan's knife."

Edmond laughed. On the whole it was quite a pleasant laugh.

Charles stopped by the kitchen in the company of Jehan, very much like a criminal in the charge of a jailer. Edmond Moura, like the hangman, watched from the doorway. Charles said, "Don't worry now. All goes well. Be prudent. I shall see you soon."

I took the hand he offered and agreed that I would be prudent. I looked at Jehan, ignoring Edmond Moura.

"Are you my friend?"

Jehan said briskly, "You know it, madame."

"Then may I have your word that Monsieur Charles is safe with you?"

"Really, Anne," Charles protested, half amused, half vexed that I should treat him like a helpless child. "I assure you I can take care of myself."

"Promise me, Jehan."

Jehan glanced at Edmond, shrugged his big shoulders and said, "I am not the only one who goes, Madame. Victor also goes."

That had a bad sound to it. I saw Edmond's face and knew by the tightening of his features that it was true.

"Promise me, Jehan," I said again.

"I will do my best, madame."

Charles, despite his bravery, had reacted to the hint that he must count upon two enemies on the long walk back to Moura village. He gave me one look which was good-by, and I felt my selfish fears for my own safety pass away before this greater fear that Edmond meant to destroy Charles, whom I knew he hated.

I ran after the two men and caught Charles by the sleeve.

"God guard you," I said, and seeing the childishly brave face Charles put upon the matter, I reached up and kissed him on the cheek. It was a silly thing to do, for I realized at once it antagonized the watchful Edmond Moura. Charles would have returned my kiss had not Edmond spoken sharply.

"Jehan. You are expected back here by nightfall. You understand?"

Jehan pulled the forelock hanging below his stocking cap, apparently his salute, and he and Charles started down the hall. Charles looked back and waved to me.

I said to Edmond, when we were alone, "As God is my judge, if you harm him – "

"Well?"

"I'll be killing you myself."

He was amused. "I believe you would."

I went past him to the door. He stopped me.

"Answer me one question straight out as you are an honest girl. Are you in love with that fellow?"

I said sharply, "This has nothing to do with my duties as housekeeper."

I thought he would shake me, but he smiled at last, and let me go. "I am inviting my cousin Kate to dinner tonight. Eustace seems to think it proper to establish the Mouras as a family again with a small, private dinner. A ball in miniature. For ourselves and Kate. Eustace insists it will not be legitimate without your presence. What do you say?"

I thought of many reasons why it was preposterous. I was not used to parties, at least as a guest. I had no gowns whatever that would be suitable. And, in any case, I was a servant, not a guest. Still, in spite of my fears for Charles, in spite of my tormenting doubts about Edmond Moura, I wanted very much to attend that dinner, to let him see me just once in a ball gown – not one of those new fashionable gowns that were so disgusting, but a gown that showed me happy and laughing, instead of my dark and dismal self.

Well, there it was. Shameful truth.

"Impossible, monsieur."

"I wish you there."

"You know it is impossible. It would be most unsuitable. I am, after all – "

"If you please! No more talk about knowing your place and other such amiable stupidities. They are the talk of a scullery maid."

"I was a scullery maid, monsieur, and not so long ago."

He said quietly, in that tone which is impossible to contradict, "I intend to have you, Anne." I began to move away again, not quite sure how he meant that. He saw my difficulties and added, "I intend to have you grace the dining hall tonight."

"In the first place, my gowns are – "

"Clou or Kate will find you something suitable. There have been many women at Moura."

I could believe that. "Will you swear to me that you have not sent Jehan to harm Mr. Armitage?"

"Jehan? Certainly. I swear it."

"Well then – "

Before his persuasion and my own desire, I weakened.

158

13

It was less simple than Monsieur Edmond imagined to find a gown I could wear. Not a single one in the wardrobe of past Moura ladies was long enough to reach below my calves. These French were so incredibly tiny. Kate, who was my height, proved to be my salvation. She arrived in the afternoon with her own crimson gauze ball gown and one for me. In the shoulders and hips the shimmering blue-violet gown was a fair fit. We merely took it up in the waist, and I was provided with an exquisite gown of that straight-skirted, high-waisted style which was in fashion five years ago at the court of Napoleon. It was far too low in the neck, and to keep myself respectable I wore over it a dainty little shawl of lace. Kate seemed to think it a pity, and made all manner of fun and idle flattery about my throat, etc., but I knew myself better than she and we went downstairs together most amiably, with Kate perfectly content to outshine me.

I felt rewarded by the expressions of Eustace and old Monsieur Trevain, who was huddled by the fire.

"*Nom de Dieu!*" said Eustace, his black eyes snapping. "Is this our little lady?"

"Ladies," Kate corrected him with a big grin on her generous red lips. She went to him and they embraced in the French fashion. I was embarrassed to see that he looked over his cousin's shoulder at me and winked. I pretended not to notice and went to inquire after Monsieur Trevain's health.

The solicitor looked more wizened than ever after his sad loss of blood and the dreadful shock of his encounter. But he was adamant against remaining longer unattended in his bedchamber. His dry, brittle fingers picked at the lace of my shawl, and his watery eyes flickered over me hopefully.

"How pretty you are tonight, mademoiselle! And a gown the color of your eyes. Come closer. Come, come, come – I want to tell you something. In confidence. You will believe me, mademoiselle, for I shall prove it to you. You will not laugh. You eyes are too kind. I saw that at once." He spoke in English, pronouncing badly, but quick, nervous, anxious to blurt it out.

"Believe you, sir? Why shouldn't I believe you?"

He glanced around. Kate was chatting with Eustace, questioning him about his years as an *émigré* in Coblenz and Vienna and London. The old gentleman motioned me closer. I leaned over him.

"I saw it again, you know. Just a moment since. As I saw it last night. I swear to you, I actually saw the Moura apparition in my room last night. It was after I heard the wolves howling below my window. Monsieur Eustace laughs at me, but I think Monsieur Edmond believes, though he will not say so. It came with its creatures, the wolves. There! Scoff at me, mademoiselle. But I shall show her to you, even so. At this moment, if you wish. I tell you this place is evil. Get out of it while you can. I shall leave the moment a carriage arrives from the village. It is promised for tomorrow – yet, I dread the night to come."

"I don't scoff, sir," I said quietly, aware of a coldness through my limbs. "There is evil in this place. I know that. But is it Edmond Moura?"

"Edmond! Mademoiselle, you still do not understand. It is a ghost, I tell you! And Edmond is as much a victim as you or I – come. Let me show you what I have seen."

His clawlike hands beckoned and I followed them. He tottered to the windows of the hall and pushed aside the great portieres so that I might see the East Tower.

I did not really care what his object was, or if he had seen anything. All I could think was that his had been the first reassuring word of Edmond Moura I had heard since entering this accursed place. I could have loved little Monsieur Trevain for it, even though it did not resolve my doubts.

"Now, mademoiselle, observe well the turret – do you see her?"

I confess I saw nothing at first but the turret opening, which was in deep shadow.

"I fear my eyes do not quite . . . " I began, when Eustace's thick, oily voice intruded.

"At it again, eh, my poor fellow? More Combing Ladies in the turret? I thought you had your fill of 'em right here in the main building."

The longer I looked at the turret, however, the more I fancied I could see something, perhaps only a strip of cloth shimmering in the faint and early starlight. Still, one could not be sure. At Moura.

Kate was annoyed at all this talk, annoyed and, I think, a trifle uneasy.

"Eustace, don't you start the wretched business. Next thing you know you'll have us rushing up to the tower in all our finery. And that I shouldn't like at all. Besides, I'm in no mood to tumble down as Laly did."

"Come now," said Eustace, "to tumble down as Laly did you would have to be pushed by her murderer. Now, who among us would push you? My dear Kate, my love, we

161

are blood cousins. Can you imagine one of us destroying our good Kate?"

"Nevertheless," she returned sharply, "I'll thank you to stop talking of it."

Eustace frowned up at the tower. I was sure something unpleasant was revolving inside his head.

"Yes – by Gad, you're right, Trevain. I do believe there is something up there."

"You see it?" asked Trevain anxiously. "You really see it?"

Eustace hesitated. He was most judicial. "I see it and yet – I do not see it. I think it requires examination. Indeed, I should say a personal examination by the master and by – witnesses . . . "

"Witnesses?" Kate demanded. "What the devil for? Let Edmond go up and find his old Combing Lady. The place is his anyway; so I suppose the ghost belongs to him also. I'm sure he's welcome to her."

"He'd never go alone," Eustace went on reasonably. "I'll wager he fears the tower. And even so, I should not trust his word. Not quite. Our brave Edmond has much to answer for."

I heard Monsieur Moura's footstep upon the bare floor at the door. "Indeed?" he asked laconically. "And what have I to answer for now?"

"For one thing," Kate put in, apparently fearing a breach between the two cousins, "Eustace and Monsieur Trevain here think they have seen a ghost in the tower. It would make them most frightfully happy if you'd go up and exorcize the damned thing!"

"But before witnesses," put in Eustace. "Say, Kate or our charming young – I believe you called her your housekeeper, did you not, dear boy?"

Monsieur Moura glanced at me. But Kate ran to him,

all red gauze and ribbons, to thank him for what she called "the ball." He nodded to her absently. I could see his face. There was a curious kind of blankness in his expression. I couldn't understand it.

Kate said, "And come see what I have done for our Irish lass."

It was generous of her. Edmond crossed the room rather slowly while I waited, nervous, wondering if I looked correct. Was my hair in place, no wisps flying out of the intricate Grecian style that Kate and Clou had worked so hard to achieve? Was my gown too sheer? I felt only half clad, under his intent, unsmiling gaze. Was he angry?

He came to me and took my hand and kissed it.

Eustace boomed out, "Edmond, you dog! What do you think of her?"

With that sardonic humor which was so natural to him Monsieur Moura asked, "Of mademoiselle, or of the ghost you have conjured up in the tower?"

Eustace ventured offhandedly, "Ah . . . the Combing Lady, too, of course. But I was speaking of mademoiselle."

Monsieur Moura said abruptly, "I am sure mademoiselle knows what I think of her."

He was sadly awry on that, for I hadn't the least notion of what he thought of me, or of anything else. He was being most mysterious. I wished he would give some attention to that business in the tower. I should like to have known if we only fancied we saw something up there. Or – if the Combing Lady actually existed and was wandering around in that turret. I should much have preferred meeting her face to face in that habitat to wondering when she would appear elsewhere.

"That's enthusiasm," said Kate. "You might at least have said our Anne was pretty."

"At least," he murmured, and offered me his arm.

We went in to dinner, Kate on his left, I in the place at his right that he had given me the first night I dined here. Eustace and Monsieur Trevain sat at the lower end of the table. Matilde had two husky young maids from the local peasant families to help serve, and the great dining hall was festive with lights and ancient hangings, some of which Clou and I had rescued yesterday from unused rooms.

I had imagined I should enjoy dressing up, masquerading as a lady in Monsieur Edmond's company. In my vanity, I even hoped that he would be pleased at my appearance, but he showed no evidence of it. It was much like that other night, after all. I was uneasy at his strange manner, unsure of myself. As a housekeeper I should have been so much more myself, confident, with my head high, knowing myself efficient and quite correct in my behavior. Now I kept wondering what he thought, whether I looked well, ate properly, drank moderately . . . All this nervousness made me pick up my wine glass at rather too frequent intervals. Did he truly like me tonight? If so, why was he so strange to me?

All through the interminable meal Kate chattered away. Even Trevain was moved to smile at her. Under cover of Kate's voice I said to Edmond in a low tone, "You are silent, monsieur. If I have displeased you, I am heartily sorry."

"Kate always irritates me," he said, not even bothering to look at me as he spoke. "It has nothing to do with you."

His quiet voice cut me deeply and I felt the proud, stupid tears sting my eyes. I said unsteadily, "As soon as we are done with dinner, I will make my excuses, sir. I have no wish to displease you. It would be better so."

He looked at me, frowning. "Sometimes you can be infernally stupid!"

I was of two minds whether to cry or to let him feel the good, hearty sting of an Irish palm across his face, but fortunately Kate's booming rich laughter as she regaled Monsieur Trevain brought me to my senses. I must behave like a lady at all costs, and I had noticed that under insult a true lady remained calm and unruffled; so I ignored him, turning to his cousin with a smile to inquire how he found his native land after so long a separation.

Monsieur Eustace licked his lips with the churning of a thick pink tongue, and I was reminded of the Moura wolves we saw last night after someone in this house had fed them.

"It grows more charming with each moment, mademoiselle. I should not have guessed that the presence of a new – er – housekeeper could make such an improvement in the old château."

I did not appreciate this nauseatingly insincere compliment, but I tried not to let him guess it and merely remarked that Clou and I had tried to clear away the rubble of a decade.

"Rubble, indeed, mademoiselle. I shouldn't be surprised to find that the Moura ghost herself had disappeared in all this cleanliness." He raised his voice. "She has gone to more suitable surroundings. I'll wager – yes – ten louis says she is in the East Tower at this moment . . . Wait! Let me be sure."

He asked pardon, arose from the table and left the room.

All conversation at the table ceased.

Kate and Monsieur Trevain glanced at Edmond. It was only by exercising the tightest rein on my muscles that I did not do likewise.

No one spoke, so I said as pleasantly as I might, "I should not think Monsieur Eustace is right; for I am told the Combing Lady liked pretty things, and I have seen the tower. It is overlaid with dust and filth. Not her sort at all."

I could almost feel the tension release. At my left Edmond laughed; and as Achille brought in a fresh bottle of wine, Edmond broached it.

Eustace returned to the dining hall as Edmond was pouring the bright, glowing wine; and although Eustace's fat countenance was unwontedly grave, I felt the nasty little gleam of excitement behind his comber mien. He addressed the solicitor.

"She is still there – or something is. I'm sure I saw a flutter of garments . . . "

I caught an odd, swift glance exchanged between Monsieur Moura and Achille, who shook his head ever so faintly.

"Will no one investigate?" asked Trevain plaintively.

"It is nothing," said Edmond. "The place is deserted."

"On the contrary. Ghosts always reappear when there has been foul play. They return to the place of their demise. But, of course, only their murderer would fear to encounter them."

Unexpectedly, the little solicitor would not give up. "I believe, Monsieur Moura, with respect, that there was something in the tower not an hour ago, and it is very likely still there. I would feel safer if you could determine what it is."

"I tell you nothing is up there. Nothing whatever. No ghosts, no hidden prisoners, no one." Nevertheless, I was not the only one who noticed that Edmond's voice was a little too sharp, too cutting.

I wondered.

Kate said calmly, "It's always been my opinion that our precious Laly fell quite by accident. Probably drunk. I shouldn't put it beyond her."

"Ah, my dear Kate, but Trevain here has seen her, you know. She would scarcely turn up if her death had been accidental." And Eustace tittered behind his lace-edged handkerchief.

"What is it you want to say?" asked Edmond.

"He's drunk," Kate put in.

But Eustace denied this indignantly. "Not so. What I want to say is that it would put a proper fillip to the meal if we adjourned to the tower like the Mouras of old, to test whether Edmond is hiding some secret there, or to disprove, once and for all, the mystery of our Combing Lady."

"I do not know what you expect to find. Footprints? She will be an unusual ghost to leave tracks," I reminded them.

Eustace merely grinned. "I have heard that people revert to type upon visiting the scene of the crime. If Laly's murderer is among us – "

"Oh, stuff!" said Kate.

But I had been thinking it over, and said suddenly – doubtless with the courage of too much wine – "No. He is right. Let us go up into the tower, all of us." I looked at Edmond directly. "After we have satisfied Monsieur Eustace, we are done with such talk forever."

Edmond's hand closed upon mine. "You are in the right, of course. It is an idiotic notion, but if it will silence this fool – "

Kate seemed reluctant. "This is absurd. I am in my new gown. It may tear. But – I suppose if we wait, Eustace will accuse us of smuggling out his Combing Lady."

She and I went upstairs and got our cloaks, while she

confided to me that she did not like to see Eustace tantalizing his cousin.

"Edmond is in a bad humor tonight. I was mistaken to let you wear that gown."

"But why? He asked me to dress. What have I done?"

"My dear Anne, you are naïve. It was a mistake because you are a temptation. I am sure that when you are wearing your dreadful little day gowns he reminds himself that you are an innocent young miss, under his protection in a sense. But when you dress like this, he is tempted to forget all that nonsense. My dear child, he loves you."

I felt this disclosure was hardly an occasion for a scene; quite the contrary. But I did not tell Kate so. She was a bit of a chatterbox. I would have liked to ask her why if he loved me he did not declare himself. But I knew the answer. He realized, as I did, the enormous degree of difference in our stations.

Poor little Monsieur Trevain managed to accompany the party as far as the lowest flight of steps in the East Tower. We left him there sitting disconsolately on one step, wrapped in an extra cloak. Edmond suggested that he wait in comfort with the comfort of Achille and the servants, but the solicitor whispered to me he would certainly not trust his life to that cutthroat Achille. I thought I should remain with him, for he really looked quite ill, but Edmond disagreed.

"It will only be a matter of minutes. Meanwhile, Trevain is as safe here from his ghosts as he would be anywhere."

As we mounted the circling, wedge-shaped steps of the tower, I said, "You are not very sympathetic to his illness."

Eustace, climbing the steps two by two ahead of us, heard this. "His illness! You want to make jokes, I think. Say rather, his ghosts and fancies."

Kate groaned and told us to stop arguing and go to climbing. When we reached the alcove at which I had heard the harmless footsteps of Charles Armitage above me, for the first time I began to feel the sinister atmosphere of this night journey.

Kate whispered, and I lagged back to wait for her. Panting, she clutched at my arm and almost staggered into the alcove.

"Name of ten thousand galloping saints! I have never been so tired!" And then she said to me, much lower, "Do not remain alone up there with Edmond."

I was irritated. I hadn't quite got round to being afraid yet.

Edmond came back down a few steps.

"Are you tired?"

I said I was not but that the view was exceptional. Below us the Moura woods shimmered under the rising moon.

"You will find it much superior from the turret, and really astounding from the archer's platform."

On my first day I had noticed that tiny platform about six feet below the turret embrasure, and did not intend to venture out upon it. Surely it would be unnerving even for a man to lower himself from the embrasure to the tiny ledge.

Kate came up behind me and whispered, "That is where *she* was – when she fell."

Now what could Lady Florin have been doing out on that tiny archer's platform? Seeing the famous Moura view? Well, I should not be such a fool.

We climbed higher and higher winding around and around until I was dizzy. Edmond took my arm and would have assisted me, but I had a prickling, uneasy sensation that I did not want him to touch me until I had seen just where Laly Florin fell. He read my reaction and although he did not grow angry, I could see that it overset him. As I drew away, I saw the hand I had refused tighten into a fist that was whiteknuckled with emotion.

The higher we climbed, the more glorious the moonlight view became. The beauty that revealed itself at each alcove made me lose all fear. However, I did not like the change in Edmond; for that I blamed myself. He had grown much more tense now, and began to have that bleak, coldly cruel look that I remembered seeing whenever I had mentioned persons he did not like.

At long last we heard Eustace cry out in triumph, "We arrive! The summit is ours! What a view!" As we came out into the open turret with its six-foot embrasure, he added, "What a place to die, eh, dear cousin?"

I do not know what made me look at the floor instead of the view – perhaps it was my nature as a housekeeper. But I remembered having said the stone floor of the turret would be a foot deep in dust. Sure enough, I was right. Not only that, but in the coating of dust over the uneven stones there were footprints after all. I glanced at Eustace's thick short foot in its evening pumps and knew that he had never made those footprints, nor would Charles have made the marks with his broad, large feet of the inveterate walker. These were the heels of top boots, just such as I had seen Edmond wear. So Edmond came up here alone, and often. I wondered why.

He stood now, paying no attention to the view or to Eustace's antics.

He is watching me, I thought, and tried to think how I should behave.

Eustace boomed out of the somber silence. "Well, then, it seems I was wrong. How disappointed poor old Trevain will be! Really, I quite sympathize with him. Not a sign of our precious ghost. Then I have brought you up this tiresome way to no purpose."

"Was there no purpose?" Edmond asked in his hard, sardonic voice.

Eustace shrugged. "You do me an injustice. What else should I have in mind? . . . But no matter, you must show mademoiselle just where Laly fell. She will be interested." As Edmond did not rise to the bait, he went on, "Come, tell us, cousin, how did it happen? Where precisely was Laly standing, and how did she fall?"

"How would I know?" asked Edmond. "I have not been up here since before she died. Reconstruct her death; it is your affair. You thought this would be amusing."

Eustace persisted with his taunts. "You always hated Laly; didn't you, cousin?"

Edmond said indifferently, "Nonsense, I despised her while she lived. It is only recently I have come to hate her!"

Kate laughed, but nervously, I thought, and went over to an embrasure to stare downward. I could not resist my curiosity any longer, and followed her.

After peering out at the exquisite softness of the moonlit Moura woods, the treetops of which formed a green carpet soft as velvet, it was shocking to look straight down into the courtyard. The stones gleamed in the night light, as brutal as they must have been to the body of Laly Florin. Kate and I looked at each other. She pointed a trifle to the left, at the little archer's platform which was about six feet below us and scarcely wide enough for two men to stand on even if they pressed close, side by side. How they could possibly get the leverage to draw back for a shot was more than I could imagine.

Kate pulled her head in from the turret embrasure and stepped back from the ledge. There was no protection

171

here. The embrasure was cut from the floor to half a foot over my head. It would be so easy for a murderer to stand behind one and just gently – push.

Eustace had already started down the steps around the first turn, and now he called to Kate to come down, claiming he had seen a dagger of some sort shining there in the semi-dark.

To confess the truth, I scarcely heard him; for he was a dreadful rattle, and I was much more interested in imagining just how Laly Florin had fallen. I saw that it was perfectly possible for one to lean out too far, lose one's balance, and go tumbling down into space, perhaps striking the edge of the archer's platform on the terrible journey down to those grey stones.

All at once I became aware of Edmond Moura behind me in the shadows. In spite of the October night and my none too warm cloak, I felt suddenly hot with expectancy. In a moment I should know one way or other whether Edmond Moura was a killer. For in despite of all Kate's warnings and Eustace's fatuous hints, I realized I had come up here tonight to prove one thing – that Edmond would not harm me.

I waited. He was so close I could hear the faint sound of the crushing of his coat sleeve against the cheap fustian of my cloak. Slowly, I turned around and looked up into his eyes. I could not read them. They were shadowed by his lashes, but I could feel the burning in me they always caused, and knew that even if he destroyed me now, I should be helpless to hate him.

"Are you so very frightened of me?" he asked. There was no softness in his voice.

"Should I be?"

"Eustace expects me to kill you as I killed Laly."

My fingertips began to turn cold and I hid them in my cloak.

"One more accident here, and Moura will belong to him. Shall I make my cousin happy?"

"If that is your wish in life."

He smiled and I knew I was safe.

"I have but one wish in life and have had it since that night in Miss Nutting's bookroom."

I knew then what I feared was not death but my own weakness. He took my head between his hands and kissed me. In confusion, I tried to pull away, for I knew I was out of my depth; but he held me and then his hands went down to my shoulders, slipped aside my cloak, closing upon my flesh bared by the low-cut gown, and drew me to him and kissed me again. I was more helpless than I should have been against my murderer. I had never been truly kissed before and was in panic not to show how I liked this smothering, pulse-pounding sensation or the wondrous sweetness of finding myself so close a part of his body, his lips warm upon mine and draining me of strength and will. I struggled, and shifted backward.

Suddenly, my foot encountered only space. I was half over the edge. I screamed, feeling my body entirely dependent upon his grip, and in that moment Kate came running up the steps and into the turret.

"Edmond! What the devil!"

He had a tight hold upon me, and as I felt the stone floor beneath me once again I was sure that he would not have let me go. Nonetheless, I was overjoyed to see Kate.

As Edmond released me, I said quickly, out of breath, "It's quite all right, Kate. I didn't mean to startle you, but I stepped back too far. Monsieur Edmond caught me."

She looked at both of us searchingly, as though she suspected me of lying to save him. Behind her came

173

Eustace, holding the rusty, ancient table knife whose discovery had drawn Kate away from the turret. He threw away the knife and it fell into a corner, ringing against the stones.

He smirked. "Lucky Anne. I suppose that is how it was done to Laly Florin."

Edmond reached past my face, so close I felt the heel of his hand against my cheek, and then, before any of us could stop him, he gave his cousin such a resounding blow across the head that it would have felled a man less stout. As it was, Eustace staggered against Kate, who got between her two cousins, crying for calm.

"Stop it, Edmond! Eustace, you fool! You started this. He saved the girl's life, if you've the wit to see it. Isn't it so, Anne?"

I got hold of myself and managed to agree, adding that I thought Monsieur Trevain must be disturbed at our long absence.

"Always so sensible, so unimaginative, our little Anne," Eustace murmured, grinning.

I ignored this and started quickly down the spiral steps. Kate joined me, and then Eustace. I did not hear Edmond. He was still standing where we had been, alone in the tower.

14

We went to our bedchambers quite late for Moura; it was just on nine. Kate turned to me with an awkward shyness I would never have credited in her. "You've a pretty grand bed, Anne. Big enough for six. What do you say to my sharing it tonight?"

As I hesitated in surprise, she went on roughly, "But if you'd rather not, it's all one to me. I'd as soon sleep anywhere. On top of our damned Laly Florin's ghostly comb, if it comes to that."

"No. No. Of course not! What am I about, to be so rude? You must share my room. Bring your things now." I almost stammered in my eagerness to assure her welcome. Dear Kate! The only person at Moura one could wholly trust. We stood in the doorway of my bedchamber, and I went on explaining hurriedly, "I was thinking of – "

Kate laughed. "No need to tell me. Do you suppose, like all of the ancient Mouras, he is still standing up there in the tower?"

She went to fetch her night robes from the room assigned to her and I began to undress, remembering in every detail the sensations I underwent in that East Tower. Edmond had kissed me for the whole world to see – the whole world of Moura. I had never thought too much about the fulfillment of love, but now I understood something of its fierce sensory power. If she existed at all, I hoped the Combing Lady had seen us. I could not forgive her for having known my Edmond first.

In a short time, silent wraithlike little Clou came by with a pannikin of warm water which was very welcome to me, for my hands and face still seemed grimy from our nearly disastrous tower visit.

There was a muddy spot on the shawl I had worn in the afternoon, and I shook my head over it as I began to wash my hands. Clou examined the spot on the shawl and then pointed proudly to herself.

"There now," I said. "You're a good, kind girl but I'll be cleaning it myself."

But she took the shawl off the table and after a shy glance at me swept it over her hand and around her shoulders. It was oddly becoming to her, the grass-green designs lending life to her pale face. She pulled the shawl forward. One could scarcely see her face now, but within that shawl I knew she was happy. She caressed the cashmere, pointed to the stain, and made motions that she would clean and return it.

She went off down the hall happy as a princess. Bless the childish sweet soul!

Kate passed her in the corridor, staring after her in surprise and then coming on into my room with a handful of sheer garments which were evidently all she slept in – and very little more they were, if the truth be told, than the total garments she had worn tonight at dinner.

I asked her if she ever got cold at night and she looked at me slyly. "Not when I can find a two legged warming pan."

I couldn't help laughing, hoping she did not suspect she had shocked me a little by her frankness.

She made no effort to wash before bed but simply dropped her clothing in pools on the floor, hung her shift around the bedposts, and draped herself in her very inadequate night robes. Occupying half the great bed – the center half – she watched me comb my hair out loose and remarked on its length.

"I should think Edmond would adore it like that. Why not wear it so one of these days?"

Without thinking, I confessed that he already had seen it like this.

She pricked up her ears. "When was this?"

"The other night. I – "

"Ah – ha!" She sat up, grinning her big – red-lipped smile. "I knew it. Miss Sly Boots! You'd have fooled me."

I explained hurriedly and a little crossly that it was not at all what she thought, that I had been disturbed by the Moura wolves and had gone out to investigate the trouble. But Kate was bound to believe the worst and refused to be disappointed.

"I know, darling. I know. Say no more. I envy you. By heaven, I do; he's that attractive! Moura wolves, indeed!"

I threw one of my hair bodkins at her and then came to bed. As I was about to snuff the candle, she stayed me, no longer amused and teasing. Again I noticed the tension in her that had surprised me a short time ago when she asked if she might share my room tonight. She tried to make light of it, but it was there all the same.

"Can you sleep with the candle burning? Makes it more cozy, somehow."

"Kate, I believe you are looking out for the Combing Lady."

"Don't joke." She peered beyond the open bed curtains, as if she would examine minutely every dark corner of the gloomy room.

177

I stared at her.

"Are you really frightened? But you knew Laly Florin. I should think that in itself would prevent you from imagining her a ghost."

She was studying the shadow made by the great armoire which was large enough to hide half a dozen Combing Ladies, and the casement windows which, after all, could not be kept closed against a phantom.

"You didn't know Laly. She used to do – things, just out of sheer evil."

"What things?"

"Oh – things. She killed animals. I've seen her. She liked to watch them die – very slowly. All but the wolves in the woods hereabouts. I'd swear they liked her. Children have seen her recently in the woods, when the moon is up, romping with those devilish playmates – or at least, that's the tale that's told. Perhaps the Moura wolves feel she is one of them. No. There's a matter for laughing!"

"Not at all," I said. "I've heard tales of people like that. In Ireland – "

"Oh well, that superstitious island! Everyone knows how ignorant they are. Like our peasants." I was bridling as she added, "But when intelligent, educated French people begin to see ghosts – "

I left the matter there, more interested in lying with my eyes closed, and reliving those moments I had known tonight in Edmond's arms. I wished that I had returned his embrace with the passion that now warmed me; but I had been uneasy over the revelation of my own feelings, and had been in the grip of that stupid embarrassment which every woman feels at her very first passionate kiss. If he were only teasing me, for example, if he felt nothing for me but was playing with me – then I should have revealed myself so transparently, and would be bitterly hurt. It was a lesson drilled into me long ago in Dublin when I was a scullery girl and was sent to scrub the public buildings and the old castle. How the good priests warned me on the score of wicked men who trifled with young serving girls!

Kate was chattering on about Combing Ladies. "Gad's life, but I have a thirst!" she cried suddenly.

I sighed. "There is water in a carafe that Clou left this afternoon."

"Water? To drink? What do these foreigners think of!" She turned over in bed with a great heave, dragging off half the covers. She lay there a few minutes and then flopped over on her back again and, moving her head, gazed at me while I pretended to sleep.

"Anne, *ma petite!* Are you asleep?"

I did not open my eyes.

"Anne – " She shook me.

"Well?"

"Anne, you are the housekeeper, after all's said. And I am so thirsty I could perish before morning. I give you my word."

"Where would I get wine at this hour?"

"There's a decanter of brandy in the withdrawing room downstairs."

I remembered that room very well and had no mind to venture down there at this hour.

"That is where your Laly Florin was seen the other day."

She stiffened. "By whom?"

"Jehan saw her. We finally discovered it was the wind in the great chimney."

Kate thought this over. "Yes. Laly was fond of that room. Had it done over in green velvet to suit her,

179

very like her bed-chamber – the one poor old Trevain is sleeping in. Imagine the old man seeing her as she would look now after her fall. She fell face down, you know. That lovely, lovely, evil face, with its wolfish little teeth and big, moist lips . . . Think of seeing that face as it must look after all these years."

I tried not to listen.

"Still, I don't see why Laly would hurt you. She never knew you. In my case, she hated me. We quarreled over too many men." Kate shook me. "That is all the more reason why you should go down instead of me."

"Good night," I said firmly, and closed my eyes.

She lay there, uncertain, her thirst warring with her fear of ghosts and the dark halls of Moura. I was almost asleep when I felt the weight on the mattresses lift, and Kate was out of bed.

"Can't stand it any longer. I'm going to get that decanter. May I take your candle?"

"This one is pretty far gone down. There is an extra candle on a shelf in the armoire."

She found it and after lighting it at my candle, opened the door, peering out into the pitch-black passage for all the world like a child on the watch for goblins. Once she looked back at me. There was desperation in her appeal.

"You – you wouldn't care to go with me?"

I could not help laughing at her lugubrious face. "If you don't return within the hour, I'll organize parties to search for you."

"Such funny jokes!" muttered Kate.

The door closed and she was gone. For a minute or two I heard her footsteps in her leather-soled evening shoes, and then the house was silent. It seemed abnormally so after the vigorous rattle of Kate's voice and I began to

180

be sorry that I had put her to such panic and fear. But I was feeling cross with her for disturbing my sleep – or more especially, my dreams, and this was my shoddy revenge.

Now that I could go back to my dreams, I found myself listening instead for her returning footsteps. I calculated the time it would take her to walk to the end of the passage, to the broken parapet, and then down the steps to the ground floor and along the passage to the withdrawing room where Jehan had heard his Combing Lady. She must be there by this time. I waited, picturing in my mind Kate in her thin nightrobes, picking up the decanter, walking across the room to the door, and starting her return trip through the black halls.

She would be nearing the broken parapet by this time.

I heard nothing, not a sound. Even the distant wolves were silent.

I counted off the minutes. Surely by this time she would be in the passage outside my door. Still no sound. I revised my picture, saw her take a drink from the decanter, perhaps using a dusty glass from the table in the green-shrouded room. But it was unlikely; for she might pour and begin to drink, then, as the glass was lifted to her lips, she might hear that faint, crisp sound – the combing of long, fine, silky hair that would gleam gold in her candlelight when she turned around and faced her old enemy, Laly Florin . . . Laly swaying there in the half-shadows, the lovely Laly who had fallen hundreds of feet to smash her body and her exquisite face upon the fierce stones of Moura! What would it be to see those broken hideous features tonight, and know that they were dead and yet – undead?

Poor Kate! I had been cruel to let her go down alone.

I got out of bed, still listening for her. I slipped off my

181

nightgown and put on my day dress, all within a minute or two. Then I snatched up my candle and went to escort Kate back to safety.

In the passage there was no sound of footsteps, nothing but the occasional creak of rotting wood, and now and then the slight but companionable scrabble of mice in the rafters. I went along to the steps, where I glanced out over the broken parapet but saw no terrible ring of wolves near the moat bridge below. I hurried down the steps to the ground floor. The closer I came to the withdrawing room, the more I was convinced that all I would find would be Kate guzzling brandy from the open decanter.

I opened the door to the green-velvet room and smelled its thick mustiness. It looked quiet and harmless. Beyond the soft flame of my candle, the green velvet hangings looked rich and glowed like emeralds in a pale light. I saw the decanter on the table by that high-backed chair which Jehan had pointed out as Laly Florin's favorite. Beside the decanter was the gauzy overwrap Kate had worn downstairs. It was neatly folded upon the table. There was no evidence of a hasty departure, and only Kate's candle was gone. Obviously, she had stepped into another room for something and would return for her precious decanter and the overwrap shortly. I leaned against the table, waiting; I thought of sitting in Laly Florin's chair, but something – not fright, but a curious kind of respect for the property of the dead – made me cross the room instead and seat myself in the deep, soft-cushioned chair in the opposite corner.

I made myself comfortable, perhaps too comfortable; I could drop off to sleep so easily in this chair. Who had sat here before, what great ladies? Had they been as fascinated by the Mouras as I was by one of them?

Surely not. Surely, no one else could make anyone feel quite as I felt now, reliving the sensations I had known in Edmond Moura's arms.

How silent the house was! I was dreaming, and in my dream I was combing my hair and Kate said, "Edmond should see your hair now." But even in my dream, I knew this had all happened before, and then I had put down my comb because the room grew darker and darker, and I could scarcely see.

I had stopped combing, and yet I could still hear the faint echo of those sounds.

I came so slowly out of my dream that for a few moments I could not tell what was dream and what reality. The candle I had set upon the table beside me had flickered out, burnt down to its socket. I was not surprised; it was very short. But there was something strange about the way it had died. I turned to stare at it and saw the faint trail of smoke floating toward the window, as though a breath had blown across it. As the last glow was gone, a faint light drifted through the room from between the great green velvet drapes over the windows facing on the courtyard.

It was extraordinarily cold.

I sat up, intending to rescue my candle and discover why it had blown out of its own accord. There must be a heavy draft through the room. I had not noticed it when I entered.

My dream haunted me still, the sound of my comb snapping through the strands of my hair. I even touched my hair to be quite sure there was no comb. In the shadowy room, with only that one streak of light cutting across the center of the floor, I heard the sound again, quite audibly. The chimney, of course! I had made Jehan's mistake. It was in almost the exact spot where Jehan had

183

heard the soot rustling down. I listened again. Between me and the great hearth at the other end of the room was the high-backed chair which had been Laly Florin's favorite. The sound came from within that chair. As I listened I saw something move above the arm of the chair, something that gleamed pale as marble in the streak of light from the courtyard. It appeared, disappeared, with the regularity of a woman combing out long, glowing strands of hair. What I had seen was a woman's slim fingers wielding a diamond-studded comb as it came with each stroke to the ends of the hair. I heard the resilient snap of the hair now very plainly, and softer, the sound of the comb at the scalp as it started on its long sweep.

I was dreaming still, either that or this was no phantom but a woman of flesh and blood, mad or trying to frighten me for some obscure reason of her own.

I got up, my mouth dry as a bone, and took a step forward. In that instant, the creature too became visible above the chairback. It was rising, very tiny, in flowing garments that seemed to let the light pass through them, and I saw the long, long golden hair above the great back of the chair. The creature was staring at me over the top of the chair through the half-dark. As I studied it, with my hand to my mouth, the great, glistening mane of hair was tossed back. I saw the face, and was paralyzed in frozen horror.

There were dark blotches where the face should have been. There seemed to be no face. Only something mangled and hideous – as if caused by a great fall.

I covered my own face and breathed the close, confining air between my hands while I counted to myself. If I am sane and awake, I thought, it will vanish when I look up again.

A slight sound of movement made me raise my head.

The door into the passage had opened and was closing very slowly. I rushed to the table and felt around for the candle, but there was no way of lighting whatever remained of the tallow. I leaned there a minute, swaying and getting hold of myself. Then I followed the Thing to the passage. I seemed to hear it faintly at the far end, and called out for help as I hurried after the sounds that told of its passing. There was a candle burning at the foot of the great staircase, and when I reached this hall, I was just able to see something entering the kitchen quarters beyond. I saw quite plainly the floating funeral draperies as they were swept in before the door closed.

It is real, I kept telling myself as I followed. Whatever this monster may be, it is flesh and blood and no wraith. It was a great comfort to me. Thus far, I had heard nothing in the house to indicate that anyone noted my screams for help, and by the time help reached this part of the building the "wraith" would be securely hidden. I went into the kitchen, and heard ahead of me the rustle and scurry of its garments as it descended the stone steps to the wine cellars.

There was a candle in the pantry, and I lit it quickly by a spill from the smouldering kitchen fireplace before I followed down those steps to the wine cellar. It was always ahead of me. I could hear that telltale rustle of the garments every now and then, and though I was still cold and shaking, my deep fear of the unnatural had turned to hatred for this creature, whatever it was. I remembered the deaths here at Moura. I remembered Palla and the golden little Caroline Durand; and if this monster should prove to be a Laly Florin very much alive in spite of her terrible fall, I knew it was time she was found out. *He* had been sheltering her. In all likelihood I should get no help there. But from a distance she appeared small, no

185

bigger than a wraith, and I was quite sure that I could manage her.

I tried to remember exactly which passages Clou and I had taken through these dungeons the other day, but I was also ready for my wraith if she leaped out upon me from any of these dark little alleys underground. I snatched up a bottle from the wine cellar as I passed. A good sound blow with this eighty-year-old brandy should be enough to sober any ghost.

It was a long pursuit. The damp and mould of centuries assailed me, and my skirts were snatched a dozen times by sharp stones and hooks in the walls. Once my foot slipped in a coating of slime on stones worn smooth with age, and it was only by a great pull upon all my muscles that I caught myself before falling. By the time I passed the place where Clou and I had found Caroline Durand's hair ribbon, I could no longer hear the Combing Lady ahead of me. I stopped and shaded my candle. Then I listened, and peered into the dark distance. Was it possible she had escaped me? There was not a sound.

I went on farther. I was very close now to the steps which led up into that curious exit in the center of the Moura woods. As a gust of wind blew down from the night-shrouded woods overhead, blowing out my candle, the glow was replaced by moonlight filtering down through that wretched hole. Streaks of moonlight glanced off a heap of dirty rags at the foot of the steps by which one ascended a ladder to the ground level, and I saw that my own green shawl lay over the heap. Amazed that my shawl should be here, I reached for it, and in doing so I saw a thin, wasted human hand fall away. I scrambled the shawl off the heap, and found Clou, her faded little gown drenched in blood from a deep, narrow-lipped wound at her breast.

The bottle of brandy dropped from my nerveless hand, strewing the stones with broken glass and a strong odor of spirits.

Clou was dead, but not yet stiff as corpses are. It must have happened in the last hour. This helpless, goodhearted little creature had seen it all – the plunging knife or dagger, the monstrous face of her murderer – and yet had been unable to hear a thing, or to utter a sound to bring help. And whom had she recognized in that murderer's face to give her own blank little features such a look of unbelieving horror?

I looked around into the two dark passages behind me. In one of them lurked the Combing Lady, I had no doubt. I was no longer brave. I felt nothing but terror and sickness. I was shivering, and my throat hurt with pity for Clou and fear for myself. My head whirled.

There was no safety at Moura, no corner where there was peace.

If I wanted justice for Clou and Palla and all those who had been murdered here, there was no help for it but in Moura village. Charles must surely have reached there this afternoon. I would fetch him and the villagers themselves. They would come. They hated Moura.

Behind me was the labyrinthine way back to my room, but I knew that I could never return through those passages tonight with no candle and nothing but the slithering, rustling sound of the Combing Lady at my heels.

I went up the stone steps as fast as I could, and when I reached the ladder, I climbed that too. I was not nearly so afraid of the Moura wolves as I was of Moura itself.

15

If I was cold in the forest, where moonlight dappled the treetops, making weird and terrible shapes out of the low thickets, it was not because of autumn. My flesh was still frozen with the terror of those underground passages at Moura. I ran down the path until I thought I should die of the fierce thudding at my heart and the sharp, cutting pains in my chest. But nothing came at me out of those dreadful woods. Where the wolves were, I know not. Watching me from those dark places at either side of the path, most likely. Perhaps they had already been fed tonight by their mistress, the Combing Lady.

Poor little Clou! I could not stop thinking of the dreadful things she must have suffered in her small world of silence during those last moments of her life. And Clou's murderer – or murderess – was shielded by Edmond Moura.

Why? Was she, perhaps, his wife in secret? Or a relation of some kind?

I ran on and on until – I never knew quite how – I found myself on the main path to the highroad, and it must have lacked only an hour of midnight when I reached the highroad itself. I paused before the darkened lodge where Kate lived, wondering for the first time what had happened to her tonight. Her pony cart was in its usual place, but otherwise the lodge had the look of the rest of Moura, as though nothing human had touched it in a decade.

Now it began to be chill in earnest. The road was wider and there was less protection against the wind; the sky overhead with the radiant moon seemed terribly cold. But at least I was out of the Moura woods, out of the evil, fetid atmosphere of Moura itself. Much as I loved Edmond, I knew I could never again return there except to end the terrors that lurked in the dungeons below the château, in the East Tower, and – not least – the Thing that had the power to summon the Moura wolves to their dinner by the old moat bridge.

The moon, moving slowly across the sky, lengthened the shadows bordering the road until I imagined every long, black branch of a tree was a finger stretching out before me. How cold it was! I hurried on, stumbling occasionally over a crisp, rotten branch, and picking myself up heedless of bruised elbows and knees, only to find eyes burning at me from the confines of the woods. When I had gone some distance and felt that my journey was at least half over, I stopped and stared into the shadowed woods, to satisfy myself that those burning eyes were imaginary. I made out the grey shape of an animal, and another, and another, some little distance within the woods; yet nothing moved except their eyes, which caught the flicker of moonlight and glowed like marsh; fire as they followed me with motionless heads.

At last, I gratefully heard the tired clip-clop of a horse's hooves behind me. It was one of the local peasants. He arose in the saddle, staring at my figure. His horse too behaved oddly, balking and skittish. I waved again and came further into the road. To my amazement he leaned forward in the saddle and, plunging his heels into the flanks of his tired old horse, galloped past.

189

I realized then that with my clinging skirts, no petticoats, and my hair flying out around me, I had been taken for the Combing Lady. I could have laughed if it were not such a hideous thought.

I was alone again, and getting a good deal tireder than I had ever thought possible when I came to a stone bridge arching high over a river in a gorge so far below it was impossible to see, even in the moonlight. I stopped on the bridge and sat down on the ancient stone wall. It was the first time I had rested since my sight of the Combing Lady in the green-velvet room. I was in such a turmoil that I could not think properly, but only breathe deep of the sharp night air, rich with late autumn fragrance from the nearby woods. Somewhere in the Moura woods behind me came the weird, lonely howl of a wolf, and then the quick, senseless chatter of a big night bird.

I looked ahead at what lay beyond. The chasm of the river gorge was so deep that on the farther side of the bridge a wholly new landscape appeared to my tired eyes, made up of great stony hillocks, as though nature had turned this part of the world upside down. I could faintly see the road twisting around the shoulder of one of these hills, which, before it wound out of sight, picked up the Moura look.

Without realizing it, I must have been aware of faint hoofbeats and the squeak and rattle of wheels in the direction from which I had come. I looked back, wondering if it were any use to try again for a ride into the village. As quickly as possible, I wound my hair into a temporary braid down my back and tried to make myself look less like a phantom. By the time the pony and cart came into sight, I looked at least human, though scarcely prepossessing.

The cart was rather like the one Kate was in the habit

of riding in to the village, but the driver appeared to be a peasant in stocking cap and short jacket. As the pony trotted onto the bridge I stood up and waved, and although he gave signs of skittishness, the driver controlled him with complete ease by only a slight operation of the reins. I saw that they were going to stop for me and went out into the center of the bridge to speak to the driver. I saw then the striped sailor's shirt beneath the jacket. He leaned down from the pony cart, and I looked up into the face of Edmond Moura.

All my terror and weariness and cold came back over me in a rush, and I saw Clou's blood and all the horrors of Moura in his eyes.

"Come," he said, and put out his hand.

"No. No!" I managed to whisper. "Go away!" I turned to run, but before I could reach the stone wall of the bridge, he was down from the cart and had me around the waist. While I struggled, all arms and legs like a caught crab, he lifted me across the road and dumped me into the cart, then mounted and took the reins again. I scrambled up to jump out of the cart and with one arm he caught me to him in a smothering grip, my face pressed against his jacket, so that I could scarcely breathe.

"Sooner or later you are going to listen to me," he said when I calmed down, although I was still breathing with some difficulty.

Half stifled, I muttered, "You let her murder poor little Clou?"

"Who?" He raised my head by the nape of the neck with his hand under my wildly tousled hair, rather like a cat holding a kitten.

"You know who. Your hideous Combing Lady. I saw her."

He looked down at me and in his eyes I saw that

expression of tenderness and concern that could destroy all my resolve to hate him. While I was trying to persuade myself that it was only a trick, that he was actually the master of that dreadful fiend at Moura, he lowered his head and his lips were warm and comforting upon my forehead.

"I know. When I heard your scream outside the velvet room, I came after you. But by the time I discovered Clou, you were gone. It was Kate who saw you running down the path to the highroad."

"Kate! Where was she?"

"In Eustace's room. He found her wandering in the hall, complaining of ghosts. He and Kate are old – friends."

I might have known! Kate and her two-legged warming pans.

"But why Clou?" I asked. "Why poor little deaf-and-dumb Clou who never hurt anyone?"

He paused and seemed intent upon the reins and the growing gloom of the forest as we rounded a turn on the rocky hillside. When he spoke, his quiet voice was terrible.

"Clou was not meant to die. Clou was wearing your green shawl. The blow was meant for you."

Coldness smote me like ice. He took a robe from the back of the little seat and wrapped me in it, for which I was grateful, though my brain whirled with these new terrors.

"Why was I to die?"

His arm tightened around me.

"I cannot tell you that. Not yet. Perhaps in a few days. In the meanwhile, you must stay at the village where you are safe, and I will come for you when it is all over."

I did not know what he intended by me when he "came for me," whether he assumed I would marry him, or had something else in mind. I did not like to ask, so I got on with the matter of poor Clou. "Have you notified the authorities about Clou?"

"I am the authority at Moura."

I looked up at him, very direct. I had to know this one thing.

"Was the Combing Lady a relation of yours? Your wife, perhaps?"

He laughed shortly and harshly.

"Good God, no! Never in a thousand years."

"But she does exist."

He did not answer. He kissed me again and I tried to think of how I had wanted him to kiss me earlier tonight, when I lay in bed waiting for Kate to go to sleep. But now I felt none of that earlier burning and a kind of shameful desire. He was different, comforting as a father or a brother, someone who would love and protect me, if I could only believe in him.

He surprised me by asking suddenly, "How well do you know this Monsieur Armitage?"

"Charles?"

"Oh. It's Charles now. I had forgotten."

I ignored this, which I set down to a Frenchman's natural pique against an honest, sturdy Englishman.

"I know him to be an honorable man of good family."

"But of course." Now he was being sarcastic. "And do you love him?"

"No!" I said it very shortly. I did not know why I was so angry.

He smiled.

*   *   *

193

Moura village appeared in a hollow of cleared land just beyond the forest. At its back were great grey boulders of volcanic origin, and before it, of course, lay the forest. It was very small and reminded me a little of the Irish villages of my childhood. One thing surprised me. I was not used to seeing a village at an hour past midnight alight from one end to the other, with gaily decked lanterns, candles, and steamers and colored ribbons. Then I remembered the fair that Charles had mentioned; and I remembered too, that several months ago there had been just such a fair which my poor Palla desired to see. The houses on the dusty main street must have been built not long after the Third Crusade, weathered and crooked, with secretive windows that could shed very little light upon the interiors. The roofs were all pointed and severe, like sharply cut bonnets around sly, disreputable old faces.

Edmond frowned at the commotion in the village, the general look of a witches' dance that it presented at this hour of the morning, lighted only by lanterns and the waning moonlight.

"I had forgotten about the fair. What a time for celebration!"

As we drove along a winding side street, more like an alley, we could hear the dance music in the village square, and its discordant counterpart in the streets shooting off from the square, which were lined with noisy puppet shows and vendors of apples and candies and all sorts of trifles. Strong men were balancing half a dozen village youngsters pyramid fashion, higher and higher overhead; and there were fire-eaters with barbaric faces and black mustaches that stood out from their lips like broom straws. Everyone was masked and in costume; and although none of the costumes seemed to match by period or color, in the aggregate they made a beautiful

194

picture, like a collection of little colored glasses in a kaleidoscope.

After a struggle to get the attention of the youth at the small stable on the outskirts of the village, Edmond put up the pony and cart, and considered the shortest way to the village inn without passing through the carnival.

"Wear a mask, monseigneur," suggested the stable boy. "See? So cheap, too. I will sell you two little ones, just for the eyes."

"We are in no mood for carnivals and street dancing," said Edmond brusquely. "Perhaps if we – "

"Monseigneur cannot avoid the carnival," the boy pursued, holding out two masks. "The three streets by which you reach the one inn, they are all very gay."

Edmond looked at me. I remembered Charles' remark that the villagers hated Edmond and thought the mask would make him safer. I smiled and said it would be simpler to go through the crowds in masks, and he bought the two from the boy. He adjusted one over my eyes and tied the strings in a knot under my hair. His hands in my hair gave me an odd but highly pleasant sensation and seemed to please him too, for he kissed the nape of my neck and I pretended not to notice, for fear the boy might think me too free in my ways.

We walked rapidly through the street crowd, smiling now and then at each other as we passed the ridiculous animal masks that must surely reflect something of the faces beneath. I shivered when we passed the shows where one puppet invariably slapped and beat the other over the head. Even in my childhood I felt every blow that was struck between those wooden-heads, and they still sickened me; for I remembered seeing many a mother or father sling a great fish in a child's face in just such a way, and my own head had often rung with the tempestuous

195

(though not intentionally cruel) blow of some woman for whom I worked.

Edmond hurried me on, but our progress was delayed time and again by other sights: a fantastically fat woman wearing a huge headdress in the style of the late French queen, Marie Antoinette. The fat woman was having a grand time, surrounded as she was by several dancing, skipping admirers, some of whom had hold of the silken streamers of her wig, like children at a Maypole. Below her mask, one could see the great dewlaps of her jaws and double chin all jiggling with laughter. Edmond and I laughed heartily at her as we passed. It was good to hear him laugh. He swung my hand as though he were truly a young sailor and I his sweetheart. And so did we come into the village square, like two happy countryfolk enjoying the great event of our year – instead of two people between whom lay the memory of murder.

A swarthy fire-eater thrust a burning faggot into my face and I ducked as Edmond pushed him aside. The center of the square had been cleared of all but dancers, and in some corner, hidden by the watchers who had gathered, a little country group of musicians with gay violins, a drum, a gypsy tambourine, and an assortment of instruments I could not recognize, were striking up a country dance that was very like one of my own native Irish jigs. My feet went tapping to the music in spite of myself.

We paused for an absurd knight riding a very uncertain, four-legged dragon to pass through the milling throng. I had to laugh at the ridiculous, cross-gartered legs of the dragon, which were reacting very drunkenly. Edmond looked like a boy, with that crisp hair of his curling around the old stocking cap, his mouth softened in a laugh that showed his white teeth, and his eyes gentle and merry behind the mask. In figure, especially in the jacket

196

and sailor's pantaloons, he was lithe as a stripling. Then I remembered where, in all likelihood, he had known such clothing, and winced at the thought of Edmond Moura hired out by the State to work in the chain gang on the docks.

The music struck up louder, and at the same time the drunken dragon reared up and unseated the knight, who crashed against Edmond and me, thrusting us out into the square. I felt my waist encircled by a passing dancer, Edmond was seized upon by two prettily shaped females, and we were soon separated in the dance. I tried for a few steps to break away, but it seemed pointless; besides, the progress of the dance brought us closer to the northwest corner of the square, which Edmond pointed to, apparently as nearest the inn.

I do not know why I should have been so surprised that Edmond was an excellent dancer and as rhythmic on his feet as though he had been born in my own green island, but so it was, as I watched him in the dance.

Though I was ashamed of my own gaiety after the nightmarish hours, I felt a peculiar nervous reaction, as though I must go on dancing to the end of time. I had never been so tired, and yet I wanted to go on and on, not thinking of Moura; in all the long years since, I have never forgotten that dance. It was like a tiny clearing in the dreadful Moura forest.

And then another masquerader joined the reel. At first I saw her only faintly across the square as she made her way forward, but soon she was within our own figure, as unearthly as the fading moonlight, wearing white draperies, a white mask, and long, terrible, flowing golden hair. Some village had chosen her costume with more imagination than the general run. Tonight she was the Moura ghost.

I lost my step; I could not bear to touch her as we came together. Her fingers brushed mine. To my overwrought imagination they were like ice. Now that she was close to me, I could see the scarlet mouth, all glittering in the moonlight, and fancied I caught the rank breath of the dead as we passed each other. There were comments in the group, several pointing her out, whispering and buzzing. Pinned to her funeral draperies she wore a green ribbon, and I heard whispers that she had won the contest for the best costume of the night. Perhaps she was only a village girl, but I remembered Clou's body and the bloody face of the ghost in the velvet room, and I could not have torn the mask off the face of this Combing Lady – possibly to see the other, hideous thing behind it – if my life were at stake.

Edmond then came to me again, and as we spun around in the turn, he saw her. I was shocked at his expression. In that instant, his eyes glittered behind his mask, his mouth was hard and set. I think he would have gone after her, but the music stopped then, and as we made our way through the laughing crowd toward the northeast corner of the square, we could no longer see the village girl in her prize costume.

"What masquerade will they be thinking of next?" I said quickly. "That girl looked like an apparition."

I think he was relieved. We had almost reached the dark alley that led to the inn when an old crone of a gypsy, squatting on a tuffet before a tent, screeched at us: "Come, let me tell the fair lady's fortune."

She seemed to shine with the cheap, imitation gold pieces that threaded her headdress. Edmond did not hear her at first, and I pretended to ignore her, but eventually I realized that we must pass close by to escape into that alley at her back. My eyes wandered to her; for such things as

198

fortune-tellers and dealers in black magic were to me on a par with ghosts and apparitions, impossible but true. I never could resist them, even when I jeered at my own gullibility. Well do I remember the last gypsy who told my fortune at a Sussex fair a year or two before I went to France. Most particularly she warned me against a voyage on the waters, a very unlikely event, in any case. "There is horror and death in it," she had predicted. It occurred to me tonight that her prediction had been fulfilled.

As we tried to make our way between the gypsy and the crowd, she reached out and fastened a clawlike hand upon my wrist.

"Pretty lady's fortune, eh, monseigneur?"

It was a strange title she gave Edmond; for it was not likely that anyone in the village would ever be addressed so distinctively except the master of Moura. But Edmond did not notice, perhaps because he was so used to the title. I could not help wondering if she had penetrated his mask.

"They are all thieves and liars, you know," he told me with a smile, but mistaking my puzzlement for disagreement, he gave in and stopped for a minute or two. The rays of a gay-colored lantern hanging from the peak of the opening in her tent glinted off the gold pieces that bedecked the gypsy's headdress.

I saw then in surprise that they were real golden louis. Probably her life savings (or stealings) which she wore on her person instead of leaving them to idle in a bank.

The wrinkled old woman peered up at us through muddy brown eyes, the shape of which had been obliterated by the folds of age until they had the blank, slitted look of a serpent. Edmond seemed to interest her; she studied him from his stocking cap to his boots before turning to me.

"Pretty lady has a fortune – such exciting fortune. Cross my palm."

Edmond threw onto her dry and withered hand a silver piece, and she bit it with two yellowing, decayed stumpteeth before slipping it into her shrunken bosom. Then she bent over my palm, glancing now and then up into my face as though she saw the continuation of my life line in my lineaments below the eye-mask.

"Ah! I see great splotches . . . They gleam in the starlight. They are crimson. I see – death!"

"To me?" I asked.

She shrugged.

"To you, or one you love. That will depend. Let me see the hand of monsieur."

Edmond drew back a little, but I was watching, and finally, when her sharp claws seized on his palm, he did not withdraw it. She sucked in her breath and studied it briefly. Then she looked up into his face, as though her evil little eyes saw through the mask and knew every feature.

"It is so. There is death in you. *You* are Death – Monsieur Moura . . . " Her voice rose. Around us, people in masks and costumes turned as she uttered his name. Still she raised her voice, until half the square must have heard her. Her long, bony forefinger pointed at him.

"*Le Maître de Moura . . . Le Monstre!* How did you find the galleys? Evil One!"

There was a general withdrawal away from us, slow, with something of terror in it and more of revulsion. Among these village watchers, a woman cried out: "What have you done with the dead at Moura, monsieur?"

Edmond had snatched his hand away from the old gypsy. His fingers worked nervously, like a strangler's hand. He reached for the nearest miscreant, a stout man who had been muttering, "Fiend! Monster!" Edmond seized upon the fellow's seventeenth-century doublet and shook him like a terrier shaking a rat.

"Begone, you fool! What do you know of Moura? Begone!"

No one cared to remain within reach of his hands, least of all the stout man, who, upon his release, burst out of the crowd and ran for his life. Others on the outskirts of the gathering circle around us muttered insults and threats.

The old gypsy wrapped her hideous bony form in a glittering golden scarf and, taking up a lighted pipe, started smoking. She had done her mischief.

I could feel that Edmond was torn between the natural desire to break a few heads and the knowledge that at all costs he must remain calm so that there would be no riot or trouble here of major proportions. It was obvious to me that this crowd would never have dared to raise its voice against its magistrate if it were not masked in the anonymity of night and costume.

"Assassin of children!"

It was all disgusting, and frightening, too. I wished with all my heart that I and not Edmond had been the target. I would have walloped a few faces and stalked out. But Edmond was different; I was not at all sure of his control upon his temper.

More alarming sounds were spreading through the crowd, which grew thicker every minute, cutting us off from the obscurity of the tiny street behind the gypsy's tent. They were the human equivalent of the growling wolves safely hidden in a wolf pack. The wrong word, the wrong act, and they would leap upon Edmond Moura and rend him.

A stone, aimed from the rear of the crowd, struck

Edmond on the cheek. He put his hand up, took it away. I saw blood on his fingers.

"Murderer of maidens!" cried some anonymous voice. There were murmurs of assent.

Edmond turned to face them, slowly removing his mask. He stared at them, his eyes seeming to penetrate the masks of all who faced him. His eyes were terrifying in the starlight. The crowd moved back a step or two under his gaze, drifting like an outgoing tide.

"The evil eye!" someone murmured.

There were many who made the sign of the cross.

Edmond took me by the hand and started forward, taking long, slow strides directly toward the crowd. As he advanced, they retreated. We passed through them without a finger laid upon him.

Five minutes later, we were alone in a small street off the square, where the houses leaning drunkenly out over the street enclosed us in darkness.

"Is there more than one inn?" I asked him, remembering that I must be making a call upon Charles very soon.

There was only one. That made it simpler. As soon as Edmond had gone, I would ask for the English monsieur and tell him the grim events that had occurred at Moura tonight.

We came shortly upon a comfortable old tavern with two stories and a high attic. The innkeeper bowed and scraped before Edmond; yet I was sure he bore no affection for the magistrate of his village. All the politeness and courtesy was on the surface. He showed us upstairs to a large, warm old room on the front of the first floor, where a fire burned pleasantly at the big hearth. Edmond agreed that it was satisfactory, paid the innkeeper, and then said good night to me while I was embarrassedly explaining to him that I would repay him once I had my

202

own purse in hand. The innkeeper was all eyes watching us – as who can blame him, what with Edmond paying my score; so Edmond merely kissed my hand and looked at me searchingly as he asked, "Did those superstitious fools frighten you tonight?"

"No," I said. It was far from the first street riot I had witnessed. What would my native town be without them? I added honestly, "I was only afraid for you."

"God keep you," he said, looking gentler, and went away.

No talk of seeing me later in the week, or indeed, at all ever again. I turned to the fire, then recalled the innkeeper's presence.

"Would you ask Monsieur Charles Armitage to wait upon me in the morning, if you please?"

"Monsieur Armi-tage? I do not understand, madame."

I thought my French was at fault and repeated my words. This time there could be no mistake.

"But does not Madame know? Monsieur Armi-tage went to Moura Castle yesterday morning. He has not returned."

16

I was unnerved by this news and wondered briefly if Edmond had lied to me after all about Charles' safety. But then I recalled Charles' anxiety to get to the king's attorney and thought it likely that he had not returned to this inn but started out on the highroad to meet him. It was like Charles. I was sure he would walk to China on a whim.

It may have been my extreme weariness that made me dismiss this non-arrival of Charles, but the truth is, I found it restful to go to sleep in a room without having to carefully search it before closing my eyes. I was awakened briefly an hour or two later by the drunken, laughing and singing groups dancing home from the fair; but it was a pleasant sound in spite of what I had seen them capable of tonight. The thing I really despised in these villagers was their cowardice in hiding behind masks. How much braver Edmond had been to tear his off and face them down!

When I opened my door the next morning to an imperious knock, I half expected to see my breakfast on a tray, so much the lady had I become after supping in a dining hall twice in my life. I was surprised and not a little unnerved to see a brutish-looking man in a uniform of the French Imperial Army, hastily redecorated with the cockade of the new royalist regime.

"Madame Wicklow?"

I replied that was I, and asked what was desired of me.

"You are wanted by the police, madame."

I remembered all at once the plenitude of stories we had heard in England of the imperial police force, of mysterious arrests and shootings at dawn, all without trial. I had been assured that these were mere propaganda tales and that the Code instituted by the Emperor had, on the contrary, done away with these mysterious dawn visits and deaths without trial. But at the moment it was hard to believe.

"What have I done? What am I accused of?"

The officer shrugged. He looked me up and down insultingly, as though aware that I had slept in my gown.

"It is no concern of mine, madame. A matter of murder, I believe. Come!"

I snatched up the little robe Edmond had loaned me last night in the pony cart, and stepped into my shoes. Then I followed him into the passage. He took my arm in a strong grip.

There was no protesting my innocence. It must be something to do with Clou's murder, I thought, and wondered how I had become the culprit. Not that I believed myself in much danger. No. Surely they would know I had no motive. I liked Clou. I had shown her kindness.

Ah, but one heard of women alone in foreign countries, mistreated, disappearing from sight. I was frightened, but in the way one is frightened in a dream, knowing all the time that one will awaken to sanity and morning light.

Alas! The morning was everywhere about me, an

exquisite late autumn day full of sunlight and flaky clouds, casting a soft patina over the pointed roof and winding little streets of the aged village.

I was amazed to see the village (so busy at midnight) going about its usual work, the tiny shops open, a lone glazier wandering across the square with a piece of opaque glass slung from his shoulders, for all the world like the glass-peddlers in the great cities of France. And here, throwing slops into the gutter at my feet, was a harridan of a woman with deep red hair under a mob-cap, looking as much a part of the Revolutionary Tribunal as though the Empire and the new royalist regime had never come. She reminded me very forcibly of my old enemy, Matilde, at Moura.

It was wracking to the nerves to hear the babble of French all about me, and to understand so little of it. There is some mistake, I kept telling myself.

We came at last to a shop that had once been a milliner's. The old swinging sign, beaten and faded by the elements, still hung out over the street by one hook. The shop adjoined a wretched little building of great antiquity, with a high, pointed roof and windows no bigger than slits up near the roof. This, I guessed, was the local jail. Inside the milliner's shop I could see a number of faces, and was vastly relieved to recognize one of them as belonging to Kate Moura. My escort brought me into the shop, and I saw that it had been roughly adapted to a kind of inquiring room for the village police. Kate came forward solicitously.

"My dear, we need you. Don't frown so."

"Then I am not under arrest?" I asked flatly, quite furious at the fright I had taken.

"Good Lord, no! Why should you be? It is about

poor little Clou's death. Eustace, speak up, you fool. Reassure her."

I saw then that stout Eustace, still looking like a dandy in his lace ruffles and fine breeches, was seated as became the future owner of Moura, next to a somber-looking pale-eyed man of forty or so.

"But of course. Anne, may I present Monsieur le Capitaine Etienne Gerard, late of the Imperial Guard, and prior to that a member of the Revolutionary Committee of Public Safety."

I did not like the sound of this, and I stared at the lean, hardfaced man at Eustace's right hand; for I had heard something of the workings of those terrible French committees during their Revolution. They were implacable foes of the aristocrats and would sooner send a man – or a woman – to the guillotine than invite him to tea. Still, this Captain Gerard looked sternly honest, and his pale eyes and hard, thin mouth appeared to be intelligent too. He bowed stiffly.

"It is concerning the recent mysterious deaths at Moura, madame. I have watched Monsieur Moura dispense justice here and have admired him for it; but I cannot condone murder, if such is the case."

As is so often the case when great tension is suddenly relaxed, the mind seeks refuge in the safety of trivialities. Instead of answering him I turned to Kate.

"Did you find the decanter safely?"

Kate was worthy of the Comédie-Française, at once all breathless with excitement. "My dear, believe me, it was dreadful. I had the most excellent reasons for not returning to you last night. I saw *her*. Right in the velvet room, in that high-backed chair I had just reached for the decanter – believe me, I needed it! And there she was! Well – I ran. And whom should

207

I meet in the passage but this good old Eustace who offered me a brandy in his room. Of course, tiresome fellow, he insists it was all my imagination. Claims we found no Combing Lady in the tower, so she doesn't exist."

"Madame," said the stern captain to me, cutting off Kate without seeming to. "Our concern is not with a ghost, but with the reality of two mysterious deaths at Moura recently; one – the death of the serving girl – is most certainly murder. It is highly likely that Monsieur Moura is in some way concerned with these deaths. He must be brought to an investigation."

"After all is said, he has killed before."

We looked at Eustace as though he had used an obscenity, but he stared at us blandly and blew on his lace cuffs.

"That is beside the point," said the captain. "He has paid for that crime. However, it makes him vulnerable to new accusations. Yes, madame, we need your help. Can you tell us of any evidence against Monsieur Moura?"

I hesitated. Here it was, my test. I thought of Palla Florin lying there so still in death, and of Clou, in her terrible world of silence, watching the knife fall. I must go warily; I must report only what I knew to be true.

"There is an Englishman, Charles Armitage. He believes a young lady of his acquaintance was murdered at Moura. We found her portmanteau in the cellars. She has disappeared. He thought – that is, he said it was strange she should vanish without a trace, leaving all her garments behind her. But this is only supposition. He did not know of a certainty."

"Ah," murmured Eustace. "How naïve we are today!"

"If only Edmond did not behave so awkwardly," Kate

said. "But no. He must have poor little Clou put away without ceremony, and he keeps telling us to wait and be silent."

"By that time," Eustace took up the refrain, "the good God knows we may all have been put away, also without ceremony."

"Madame," said the captain, "will you accompany us back to Moura to make search of the place, and help us find whatever evidence your English friend knows to exist?"

I began to protest. I did not want ever to set foot in Moura again. I knew not whether Edmond was concealing the murderer of Clou, but of one thing I felt sure. The actual killer was the Combing Lady. There was one place at Moura – and Charles had guessed it long before I – where the truth might be known: the Moura burial vault. If the body of Laly Florin was not in its coffin, then she was the murderess. How she had escaped death, and how Edmond had been sentenced for the killing of a woman who still lived, I did not know. It was a thought so frightful that I stammered in telling the captain about the vault. He seemed to think it less important, however, to solve the mystery of the Combing Lady than to locate the clothing that had belonged to the missing Caroline Durand. Eustace, however, was all for searching the vault, to prove once and for all, as he put it, that there was no Combing Lady and that Laly Florin was still in her tomb.

And so, at last, I agreed to accompany them, more especially to prove Eustace wrong. But I vowed it would be the last time I journeyed to Moura.

Or anywhere else, as it almost turned out.

*   *   *

How different the road to Moura looked by day! The terrible haunts of ghosts and watchful night creatures I had known a few hours ago had disappeared with the warm sun, and yet I recalled all too vividly when we passed the old Roman stone bridge where Edmond snatched me up so unceremoniously. Had that glorious sensation been awakened in me by a man with the blood of two, and perhaps more, women on his hands? I have seen more of the world now and know that all things – even love, that dearest affection – can be destroyed, but on that last journey into the horror of Moura, I was still young and told myself that whatever befell me my deep affection would never swerve.

The soldier, Corporal Joubainbert, suggested that we approach in a straightforward fashion, himself holding Monsieur Edmond at pistol-point if he refused to cooperate, while I led the captain to such evidence as I knew existed. But Eustace had a better idea. Having discovered that there was a circuitous entrance into Moura through the well in the woods, he directed that we find the evidence first, and afterward put it to Edmond.

Abandoning the carriage behind Kate's lodging, we walked up through the woods to the well and descended to the passage under Moura where I had last seen poor little Clou.

Again I felt the creeping cold, the hideous sensation of nightmare that had come over me when I knew that somewhere in the dark passages behind me the Combing Lady was waiting. Eustace pointed out clues ages old which he considered clear proof of his cousin's guilt. I ventured once to protest that the Combing Lady could scarcely be the tall and virile Edmond Moura, but I was quickly silenced by Eustace's contempt.

"How would you know, *ma chère?* You were in terror

for your life. You might have seen anything. A woman's figure had been planted in your mind and when you saw the murderer, you thought at once of our local ghost, no?"

I glanced at Captain Gerard who seemed so level-headed, too levelheaded, perhaps, for Edmond's safety.

"It is possible, mademoiselle."

I shuddered. How hideous if it had actually been Edmond whom I followed, whose presence in the darkness while I examined Clou had so terrified me! Was my whole observation of that awful hour at fault? The Combing Lady had seemed small, but then my mind was full of Kate's stories of Lady Florin's wickedness.

Gradually, I was able to bring them to the old storage room where Charles Armitage had discovered the portmanteau of his young friend, Caroline Durand. By the aid of the hooded lantern Captain Gerard had brought, I pointed out the location of Mademoiselle Durand's portmanteau. It was not in sight.

Corporal Joubainbert climbed up and looked. He found nothing.

The captain sighed. "I am very much afraid, mademoiselle, that Monsieur Moura has beaten us to this evidence."

I looked myself, but he was right. I was torn between relief and the strong prick of my conscience – and a moment later, anger. Who but Edmond had waited for Charles and me that morning as we emerged from this place? Who but Edmond could have given the order to destroy those last vestiges of Caroline Durand's presence?

Kate looked at me sharply. "Are you ill?"

I said that I was not; for I still wanted to be quite sure that Laly Florin's body was in the burial vault before I made my final assessment of Edmond Moura.

211

We left the storage room after a thorough search. Once we just missed Achille, who came along an outer passage with that serpent way of his, making almost no sound. We remained perfectly still, the corporal with his hand ominously on his sword, while Achille looked around as though even in the silence his animal instincts heard us and knew of our presence. But after a moment he shrugged and went on.

Then it was that Kate remembered an old fireplace at one end of the cellars and remarked that it had often been used to burn trash. The men examined it, and almost at once found scraps of clothing still warm from the ashes of a recent fire. While the corporal stood guard, Captain Gerard combed the charred rubbish for evidence.

"What is this? Does anyone recognize it?" asked the captain. He turned around to show us a badly scorched tasseled end of cashmere. I recognized it at once.

Kate did too. "Yes. I saw that little blond governess wearing a shawl of this kind. Very like."

It was the same shawl that Charles had pointed out to me yesterday, a part of Caroline Durand's wardrobe. Captain Gerard then drew out a stiff piece of embroidered damask cloth that had resisted the fire.

"It was Miss Durand's portmanteau," I said with a kind of numbness.

Gerard took a black-bound book from his pocket and pressed into the pages the two pieces of evidence. Then he slapped his sooty hands clean, and I wondered what Edmond and Achille and the others were doing over our heads. Had they heard nothing?

"Now for the burial vault," Eustace cried, his little eyes glistening with triumph. "When we uncover Laly's corpse, Edmond will have no occasion to blame this business on her ghost."

"I am not concerned with ghosts and corpses long buried, monsieur," the captain said. "Only with presenting these facts to your cousin. Are you coming up with me to confront him?"

"Yes, yes. But first give me a few minutes in that vault."

"I will go with you," I said, remembering my last hope, that Laly Florin should not be buried there.

Somewhat to my surprise, Eustace seemed glad of my company and asked Kate as well. She agreed with the proviso that she remain outside the vault; and so we left the corporal and Captain Gerard, who had drawn a tiny pistol of the Spanish type, nearly small enough to fit in the palm, yet with a bore that looked deadly and well-used.

Hurrying back through the passages to the wine cellars, Eustace armed himself with a meat ax. I found on the great ring of keys hanging from a peg halfway up the kitchen steps the key to the burial vault. Then I followed the two Mouras to our old method of egress, the ladder in the ancient well. As earlier, we saw no signs of those bad-tempered guardians of the woods, the Moura wolves. Eustace looked about apprehensively, fingering that butcher's weapon so unfamiliar to his stubby hand, and even Kate went cautiously, even though she was often in these woods and had never been attacked.

"They are used to me," she laughed, but with a glance over her shoulder. "Perhaps I am like the Combing Lady. They think I am one of them."

I looked at her. "Do you feed them?"

"I have been known to do so. Poor devils! They're a good deal like dogs, you know. Nasty teeth, rather blunted here and there. But pathetic, too. Not that I am fond of them. They give me a chill. But I never make the mistake of running from them. I imagine that was Trevain's downfall."

I said without inflection, "The Combing Lady feeds them."

Eustace laughed, but she did not seem to hear me.

The afternoon sun was out in all its late autumn splendor when we reached the burial vault, and it cast a smoky, dusty pall over the ancient vines and thick walls of the tomb. No one was around. We could hear the faint chirruping of insects in the underbrush, and occasionally the hum of small flying things – sounds that go pleasantly with a day's outing but which for me will always hereafter be the harbingers of decay and death.

Eustace fitted the rusty key into the lock, then looked puzzled. "It is unlocked."

Kate did not seem surprised. "Probably Achille has set the workers to preparing the place for Clou. They've gone home for the day and forgotten to lock up."

Eustace thought this the probable explanation and pulled the thick stone door wider so that we might enter.

"No one in here, in any case," he said, "if we except the delightful heap of coffins back there."

Kate held back. "It smells so – musty."

I did not like to confess that it would take a good deal of filth to overset my stomach, so I merely nodded and watched Eustace squeeze his bulk in through the narrow opening. I would have joined him, but he suggested that we both wait outside, to prevent the great door from closing suddenly and trapping him.

It had an ominous sound. I should not like to be in that vault with the great door blown shut, to have for companions the terrible Moura dead.

"All is well," he called to us from within. "Only do not go away, whatever happens."

"Trust us," said Kate, with a relieved sigh. She preferred the open danger of the Moura woods.

Through the partially opened door I watched Eustace roll up his fine lawn sleeves, the coat sleeves as well. It was amazing to what an extent this effete fellow would go to prove his cousin a murderer. He set to work examining the ancient wooden coffins stacked in the back of the vault. There was not too much light, but enough from the doorway so that he could find the two wooden coffins on top with the name FLORIN carved at the foot of each.

He shoved aside the poor, wretched coffin I remembered as Palla Florin's resting place, and went to work on the other coffin, which should have been the last home of Palla's mother, that enchanting little witch, Laly Florin.

With the blade of the ax, Eustace tried to prize up the coffin lid. This was not too difficult, because it was only pegged down to make headway. The lid was coming apart from the box itself, and I saw him fling his head back as though overwhelmed by the deadly odor of sweet oils and other preservatives.

I was suddenly terrified. I had not expected to find a body within. If, as I suspected, Laly was not dead, why should there be any odor of the dead? If she were dead, then there was no last tiny hope for Edmond Moura.

As Eustace prized open the lid, which fell behind the other coffins with a horrid clatter, Kate called to me in a strange, frightened voice that I scarcely recognized. I removed my foot, which had served as a doorstop, and stepped around the side of the burial vault. Then I saw what had alarmed her.

Standing in the shadow of the woods beyond the tiny clearing was a great grey wolf. Lean and dusty, his opaque eyes staring at us without the slightest movement, he was

215

so still that he might have been a stone guardian of the woods. He did not stand at point, like hunting dogs I have seen, but rather in the fashion of a dog awaiting his master, alert to the sound and smell of that one loved person.

Kate said quietly, "There is another one behind you, across the clearing."

Gazing slowly over my shoulder I saw that one too, hardly larger than a fair-sized hound, his coarse fur a peculiar dun color that blended with the dying autumn landscape. I saw then that there must be half a dozen of the creatures at intervals ringed around the clearing, some almost out of sight under thickets, and all of them silent as death.

"They are waiting for someone," I said. "Devil-a-doubt they even see us."

"Yes, but who . . . or *what* are they waiting for?"

"Probably they know their good friend the Combing Lady is somewhere in these woods," I said. "And it proves to me that Mister Eustace will not find her body in that tomb."

Kate moved very slowly toward me, eying the silent guardians of the glade as she did so.

"No, Anne. It is worse than that. It proves they know she is buried here. And perhaps" – she looked up at the slanting rays of the afternoon sun – "perhaps they know she comes out at sunset. I have always had a terror of Moura after the sun goes down."

What was I doing here in this place listening to such nonsense? I should be home in my narrow bed at Miss Nutting's, busy with my nightmares after chastising mischievous young Palla and her friends.

"A ghost," Kate insisted. "I saw her last night and so did you – in the velvet room."

"No! She was real. Remember Clou. She was struck down by a human hand."

"My poor child, it was Edmond's hand. Whose else?"

Forgetting the ring of silent wolves, I ran to the door of the vault. "I'll prove to you Laly Florin's body is not here. I'll show you."

But the great, thick door had fallen shut.

The watchers behind me did not stir. They waited. For what? My back was cold with the sensation of their strange, fathomless eyes upon me.

Kate said nervously, "What's happened to the door?"

Meanwhile from within, Eustace was calling to us. We could hear him dimly, muffled, as we worked to prize open the door. "Help me. I can't see a thing in here. Do you hear me out there?"

"Yes, Eustace," Kate called, "We'll have it opened in a trice. It's stuck on some stones. Are you all right?"

"Of course I am all right. But this miserable place is dark as – "

He broke off. We were pulling at the door, Kate scraping stones out from under it, when we heard a scream from within the vault. A ghastly scream of unbelief and terror and madness.

Kate herself cried out. "What is it, Eustace?"

We heard him now, right behind the great door, his bare hands clawing at the stone. Together we managed to move the door so that a sliver of light showed within, and we could see an inch of his face, grey as death. He was whining at us.

"Let me out. Let me out!"

A sudden panic, nothing more, I tried to assure myself. He is frightened at being sealed in with the dead. Who would not be?

"These damned stones!" Kate murmured. She looked

217

up at me from the ground where she was kneeling at her work. "What do you think he has seen, Anne? What can it be?"

"Hurry! Don't talk."

But her words affected me like an echo of that awful scream with which he had pierced us a moment ago.

"Shall we go for help?" she asked then.

"No, no!" screamed Eustace. I could see one of his little eyes glinting through the crack in the door. The pupil was dilated. He looked like a madman. "Don't leave me. In God's name, don't leave me!"

"Holy Saints!" whispered Kate. "And he is the unbeliever."

I put my strength to the door, pulling hard. As I did so, I saw that he was no longer pressed against the door. I heard strange sounds within, like a puppy whimpering in fright, and then there were disjointed sounds and phrases.

"Please! Leave me . . . go away . . . I have not hurt you, Laly . . . Laly! Oh, I can't bear it! Is it you, Laly . . . "

What is it? I asked myself over and over. What is in there with him?

Kate and I gave a mighty heave, and the door swung open again, gritting loudly over the rocks and dirt. We found Eustace on the stone floor of the tomb, crouched with his knees drawn up hard into his breast, and his arms huddled in. So I had huddled many years ago, on bitterly cold nights when there were no covers.

I thought for an instant that he was dead, but he looked up as we took him and tried to get him to his feet. His supercilious face with its flaccid mouth and ugly little eyes was a pitiful, wrinkled thing. His nerves had betrayed him so that he could not recover himself. He twitched convulsively and there was a froth upon his lips.

"Please . . . " he begged us. "Please . . . "

Kate kept whispering, "God of heaven! What has happened to him?"

We dragged him out into the sunlight and around the side of the tomb. It was an effort. While we were ministering to him, I heard the faintest sound of rustling leaves behind us and, looking around, saw that the silent guardians of the glade had vanished.

"He is better now," said Kate. She was wiping his face with his handkerchief, and he had a little color. But still he twitched and babbled to her, pinching nervously at her hands.

"Help me – help me to go. Just to go!"

"Yes, cousin. We will go. Can you walk?"

I was deeply shocked at the physical deterioration in this stout, lascivious man; his face looked suddenly ancient and shriveled. I had never before realized how grey his dark hair was.

I stood up, seeing that Kate could manage him. I knew that whatever we were going to find in that tomb would have to be found now. Whatever had driven Eustace into this pitiable state must still be there.

The vault did not seem so deadly with the door swung wide, and putting many stones around to keep it so I felt that I could venture inside for at least long enough to find out the truth, before, as so often in the past at Moura, it was obliterated by the Thing that haunted this evil country.

Kate looked at me as though I too had gone mad.

"Are you going inside?"

"Stay here," I said. "No matter what happens around you. Stay here by the door. Eustace has already opened the coffin. It won't take a minute."

I went inside, not feeling safe until I had picked up the ax dropped near the door by Eustace. But aside from the ugly, fetid, sick-sweet odor of the place, I could see nothing that might have driven Eustace into such a condition. The square vault was empty of everything but coffins. The old, ornate boxes to the left must have been here for hundreds of years. Those in the center would be within the memory of living man, and of course, to the right, were the recent coffins, on top of which was the box containing the remains of Laly Florin or whatever was buried in her place.

I mounted the coffins and looked into the open box on the top. My stomach began to act queerly and I restrained myself with great effort. Something was in that coffin. I could see the winding sheet, and when I had turned away and taken a deep breath, I carefully unwrapped a few inches of the sheet.

I saw then what must have driven Eustace into that frenzy of terror (though how he had managed it pursuing him to the very door of the vault, I could not say). It was the discolored remains of a young face, too young and too ingenuous for Laly Florin. The lovely blonde hair was unnaturally long and ragged, apparently having grown since the body was laid here to rest. But the silken strands were tied, heartbreakingly, with a pale blue ribbon such as young Caroline Durand had favored.

I hesitated, then moved the head ever so slightly, grateful that the eyes were closed. I knew then how she had died. Though the head had been carefully washed, nothing could completely hide the wound at the base of the skull between the flesh and sinews. Once again, as with Clou, I guessed that a sharp blade of some kind had done this foul thing.

This was no body dead ten years, but fresh, done to death within a few weeks at the most.

And then, as I laid this poor child to rest again, my

hand encountered something else beneath it. The light from the doorway fell directly across those remains, the delicate bone structure, the sharp little teeth that both Kate and Jehan had mentioned. And at last I knew why Laly Florin could not be the live and deadly murderess of Moura; for what was left of her lay beneath Caroline Durand. Quite dead – and for many years.

I was sick.

I made my way down from those coffins of dead Mouras and stumbled out into the blessed sunlight.

17

Within the smoked-stained ancient Great Hall of the château, Edmond Moura was dressed for the road, in boots and a caped greatcoat, and was calmly putting on his gloves as Captain Gerard and the big corporal questioned the wretched Eustace.

"What did you see? What frightened you, monsieur?"

"He cannot tell you," Kate shouted as though they were all deaf. "Don't you see? He's lost his wits. He saw Laly Florin and no one will believe him."

I poured a goblet of brandy for Eustace and he took it with hands that shook pitifully. He drank with long, guzzling sounds, unlike his well-mannered self. Then he looked up over the rim of the goblet.

"She was behind me . . . I felt her tiny hand, her wet mouth upon the nape of my neck, as in the old days . . . I felt her, I tell you, didn't I, Anne? You went in. You know."

They looked at me. I did not mind. I felt only one overwhelming sickness that numbed me to every thing else. Edmond Moura was guilty of all the foulness that had occurred in this house, and in my innocence I thought nothing could have greater horror than that knowledge.

"No, Monsieur Eustace. You could not have felt Laly Florin behind you. She was safe in her last bed. I saw her myself – beneath the body of that blonde child who was murdered." And this time I looked directly at Edmond, trying to keep on my face nothing but the blank indifference of a stranger. His eyelids flickered as though he had not quite expected this blow from me, but he smiled a little. It was not a gay smile.

"Yes. That would be Caroline Durand, the governess to my niece . . . Well, messieurs, I think the game is nearly played out. A day or two more, and all should have been explained. But I see you are determined."

I said quietly, "Another day or two might bring more murders, monsieur. No one – not even those who care most – can chance that."

He looked at me across the room as though we two were alone. "And do you believe I would have murdered you?"

I felt, clear to my heart, the terrible sweetness of that assurance; for I knew that, with all his crimes upon his hands, still he would not have killed me. I knew even that he loved me. But now it was nothing. I had had one friend in all my life, his niece; and one lover, himself. And he destroyed both.

"No, monsieur," I said. "But I wonder if anyone will ever see Charles Armitage again."

I had pricked him there. "That bungling, miserable fool!" he exclaimed, his gloved hand slapping the other in anger.

"Come, come, monsieur, no threats," cut in the corporal abruptly.

Captain Gerard silenced him. "That will do. We are late now. If you will be so kind, Monsieur Moura, as to precede me."

"But of course," said Edmond with arctic politeness.

They arranged that the captain should go into the village with his prisoner and with Kate who would care for Eustace at the inn.

"There must be some way in which mademoiselle may also come with us," Edmond said, disturbed for the first time.

"I shall send soldiers back to give her safe conduct and to uncover the matter of Mademoiselle Durand. Meanwhile, the corporal is here. It will be his task to begin the search of this place."

"May I speak to my servants?"

The captain made a sign and Joubainbert went out for Achille and Matilde. We were all a good deal surprised at the anxiety shown by the huge Matilde who came bustling in from the kitchen, wiping her flour-stained hands on the front of her gown.

"You will not leave us alone, monseigneur. No! You cannot."

We looked in astonishment as Achille too displayed this singular fear of the house in which he had lived since childhood. His long, silvery hair was flung back and he looked like a youth again. He had been running.

"Monsieur, do not leave us here. Not yet. Not today."

"Be calm," said Edmond, taking him by his slim shoulders. "The corporal will be here. He will see to things."

Achille turned to Captain Gerard in great distress.

"But Monsieur le Capitaine is so very wrong. If Monsieur will listen – "

Edmond cut him short. "We have all heard enough about ghosts and phantoms, Achille. Now, you must set a good example and go about your work, and if you see any ghosts, then exorcize them."

The mere mention brought Eustace to attention.

"Yes . . . I felt her. Her wet, cold lips touched my throat. Kate! Kate! Don't let her come near me."

Edmond shuddered at his words, and we all felt the cold breath of fear that the picture he described brought into

224

the room. Kate, bundling him into his greatcoat, soothed him as though he were a child.

"It is all right, Eustace. We are leaving. She cannot hurt you now."

As they were about to depart, Edmond turned to me. I would have avoided him, but he took my hands and I could not refuse this last good-by. He looked tired and ill, but it seemed to me that in his strange and terrible mind, he cared more for my coldness than for what lay ahead of him.

"Anne, be my brave girl and you will soon be out of this."

"It makes no matter now," I said.

"Promise me something."

"If I can."

"Promise to remain perfectly quiet here, and to obey Achille. Will you promise?"

It was such an odd thing, the last in the world that I would ever have imagined, and I could only nod, to please him. I had no faith whatever in the protection of that sinuous little man who was no bigger, and probably no stronger than I.

He kissed my hands, first one and then the other while I stood there frozen in grief and horror at the truth about him that I had evaded so long. He left me and went out with Kate and his cousin, giving his strong arm to assist the trembling Eustace. The captain thanked me for yielding my place to Eustace, and promised that he would return with soldiers some time in the night or early morning at the latest.

It did not matter. The Criminal of Moura was departing with him. There was no terror left in Moura now. Only an awful loneliness for what might have been . . .

I walked across the old moat bridge and watched them

drive away, down through the dust toward the highroad. When I turned back toward the great ugly stone house, the light of day was waning behind the battlements, and the East Tower loomed in all its shadowy splendor, the blood-red rim of the fallen sun around its ancient turret.

It was the time Kate always dreaded. It was the beginning of twilight.

The next two hours were a strange, silent ordeal, in the lonely Great Hall. If I stood up, even to rekindle Achille's miserly fire, he would come hurrying into the room from nowhere as though I must be kept under constant surveillance. This reminder of the general terror in the household was unnerving to say the least. I even thought it a little silly.

At sight of Laly Florin's corpse this afternoon, I lost my last fear of creeping Combing Ladies. Laly was dead. And it was all too horribly plain that the murders at Moura had been committed by a human hand, a hand that I had loved.

Why then were Achille and Matilde so terrified of this evil old house when the master, its true villain, was gone?

Corporal Joubainbert came in from the burial vault while I was having a glass of wine, some bread, and my evening porridge – for we were back to porridge again. He declined the porridge but toasted me very prettily in a goblet of wine the size of which staggered me, though it had only the effect of mellowing the big, brutal-looking soldier. In his other hand he carried a spyglass unfolded to its full length.

I was so lonely I welcomed the corporal. "Well, sir, and what'll you be finding with a spyglass so far from the sea?"

"Many things, madame. Thought I saw a ghost in the East Tower when I was down at the vault. Mere stuff, though."

"Are you satisfied with the evidence in the vault?"

He grimaced over the wine goblet but quaffed it like water before replying.

"It is enough to send him to the National Razor. Interesting spectacle, madame, have you ever seen it in action? The sharp, triangle blade, the little window where goes the head . . . So?" He enacted the whole execution so vividly that I thought I should never be able to see any other image again in my life.

I got up and walked away, hoping he would take my meaning, but he did not cease his rambling horror until he took another drink.

"Foul stuff. Ah, but I've seen other casks in the cellar, madame. There's an opened bottle out in the kitchens. Smelled the right age, too."

"How would you be knowing that?" I asked, because he antagonized me, not because I cared.

"But it is so simple. I began my search in the kitchens. And up here" – he tapped what I felt sure must be the hollow cavity of his head – "up here I have noted this bottle hidden away. When the servants hide a bottle away; this means it is the best."

He strode away swinging his spyglass, on his search for the hidden bottle, while I went to the curtained windows overlooking the courtyard, which was just beginning to gleam in the first rays of the moon.

Up there in the turret of the East Tower, Edmond had kissed me, and I remembered vividly the feel of his warm hands upon my shoulders; those same hands which were within an hour of doing that bloody deed to little Clou.

Why all of this blood lust? Was it his revenge upon

womankind for what he had suffered in the galleys? Was he truly a madman? And yet he had spared me.

My head ached in a dull, monotonous way. It felt cooler against the leaded window panes.

I thought: This is my last night at Moura . . . I hated and feared the place, and yet, within these somber walls, I had known the only real happiness in my life, a happiness I should never know again.

The candlelight behind me glittered on the dregs of wine in my glass, and I put the ruby stuff to my lips, hoping it would give me peace, at any rate.

All of a sudden the glass was dashed from my hand, and I was thunderstruck to see its contents fast trickling over the stone floor. Achille was taking me by the arms and shaking me. I was sure he had run mad and in the mixup of my thoughts, I assumed he must be the actual murderer of Moura. Well then, he would have quite an armful if he meant to subdue me!

I twisted in his grasp and gave him a resounding hard clop across the side of the head that almost hurtled him to the floor.

"Is it drunk you are, or mad?" I demanded, forgetting all my French.

"No, mademoiselle, no! You don't understand. The wine – did you drink any?"

"Of course I have. And for an hour past."

He was pale as ashes, and shaking a little. His silvery eyes had terror in them.

"But – you feel – How do you feel?"

"Well enough until this senseless attack."

"Where did you get the wine?"

How tiresome he was! "But from the decanter there on the sideboard."

He relaxed, seeming to recover slowly. "Then you are

safe, but there is another wine in the house that you must not drink. Monsieur would strangle me with his bare hands – if you drank that and came to harm."

"What made you think I had drunk it?" (Why should there be a wine in the house that would bring me, or anyone else, to "harm"?)

"Because someone has taken it from the place we have hidden it. Behind some pots in the stillroom. How can it have disappeared, unless . . . "

I realized what must have happened. "Corporal Joubainbert told me had located some hidden wine. He seemed to think it an excellent vintage. He must have it now."

Achille raised his head. "But this is terrible! What will they do to us? We must save him. Where did he go, this corporal?"

I did not know. He had gone towards the kitchens, although after that I had not seen him.

"Will it help you if I search too? He cannot be far from here."

"No, no mademoiselle." He stood me against the window unceremoniously. "You will stay here, just so! Do not move from this place. I will make search for him. Yes . . . " And he hurried away, leaving me the prey to all sorts of uneasy fantasies.

The wine was poisoned. So much seemed evident. Yet, why would there be a bottle of poisoned wine on hand? Would I never be done with these insane mysteries at Moura?

A few minutes later I heard Achille's voice calling to Matilde from far off upstairs somewhere, and presently she answered. I took my handkerchief and tried to soak up the spilled wine. Then I went back to the window, wiping my hands upon each other. I became aware of a big man crossing the courtyard toward the East Tower. He passed through a streak of moonlight, reeling drunkenly, and I saw that he was Corporal Joubainbert.

I ran to the doorway and called to Achille. There was no answer. I crossed the larger corridor between the Great Hall and the dining quarters, hoping to find Matilde in the kitchen, but she was gone too, apparently having answered Achille's summons ten minutes before.

I went back into the Great Hall and ran to the windows, trying to call to the corporal, but he was just vanishing up the stone steps that wound their way to the turret of the East Tower.

There was no help for it. I looked around for a weapon (one never know when such an item might be of use at Moura) and finding the knife with which I had cut my bread for supper, I went out and entered upon the moonlit courtyard. This time when I called to the corporal he appeared suddenly at an embrasure in the tower, about thirty feet above, and waved his spyglass at me: then he made idiotic faces not the least of which was a huge gesture of one finger at his mouth, as though cautioning me to silence. He pointed upward to the turret of the tower far above him. I supposed this was some drunken prank, as if he intended to prove that he could climb so far. I realized that the poison – if it was poison – in the wine had not thus far effected any serious damage to him, and he might yet be saved. But I would have to fetch him myself.

It was really most provoking, if it had not been so serious. As I mounted the first step inside that ancient tower, I wished myself a thousand miles away. I had seen enough. I wanted to go home. But much as I disliked the corporal, I did not wish him dead.

It was black as the grave inside the tower, and I was grateful, as I had been that first day at Moura, when I reached an embrasure and saw the moonlight pouring in. I kept calling to the corporal every few minutes, hoping at least that my voice would prevent his falling into a stupor; for I had heard it was easier to administer to a poisoned man if he were still conscious.

The more tired my limbs became, and the more the muscles pulled at the back of my knees and thighs, the more I was determined to wrest this last life from the deadly claws of Moura.

At first I had heard the corporal's shuffling tread high above me. But now it became fainter, and at last was silent. I must be very near the turret. How black it was in the damp cold where no light ever intruded!

I came around the final sharp wedge-shaped steps to the turret itself, wreathed in darkness except for one patch of moonlight at the east embrasure. I hesitated before stepping out into the turret; for it seemed to my uneasy fancy that I had heard a small shuffling sound up here in the darkness. Then my foot stumbled over an object, and when I felt around on the stone floor, I found the corporal lying sprawled, half on the top step, and half on the floor of the turret. He was breathing heavily but without pain, as though merely drugged.

Then again I heard that peculiar, light scuffling . . . as though someone or some Thing had moved in haste.

I peered around vainly. The darkness was Stygian. A rat, probably. Nevertheless, I kept the bread knife in my right hand, at the ready. I could do nothing with the unfortunate soldier in the darkness, and without letting go the knife I pulled him toward the open embrasure and the light, careful not to retreat any further myself. Even now my heels were at the outer edge, and a sliver of stone dropped over the side, a moment later striking the narrow archer's platform, six feet below the embrasure.

I looked behind me, aware of the great space between me and the rest of the world. So conscious was I of the eery night that for a moment I thought I saw tiny dark figures far off. I waved vigorously, imagining it must be the captain and his soldiers returning. But then the vision evaporated in the moonlight, and I returned to care for the corporal.

Curious, the fancies one has at such times. It seemed to me as I looked back across the turret, staring hard into the darkness, that two eyes gleamed at me like a cat's eyes, with golden, slitted pupils.

My patient did not seem so very ill. It was true that Achille had said nothing about poison. Perhaps the wine was merely drugged. I set the knife down and raised the corporal's head with one hand, slapping the poor fellow's cheeks with the other.

"Come, sir, wake up. Come!"

He obliged me by fluttering his eyelids and opening them to gaze at me in a drunken way, and muttered thickly, "All right with me. Never fear . . . "

The corporal plucked at my sleeve insistently. "The ghost of Moura, madame! Almost had it . . . You see it?"

I said I had seen nothing. He fumbled around blindly and I, after ascertaining that he wanted his spyglass, found it for him. With my help he sat up and tried in vain to focus it to his eye. He handed it to me finally.

"Must have escaped before you came. It was up here. Almost had it in my hands, then – too much wine. I fell – listen! You hear that?"

Surely it was our imagination, but it did seem that there were faint sounds somewhere in the courtyard below us now. Was someone coming up to help me with the corporal?

Or was it . . . something else?

The corporal took up the spyglass again and focused it straight down to the foot of the tower.

"Damn! Can't see a thing. Too much wine."

I took the spyglass from his slack fingers and focused it myself. Then I saw it.

A running thing, slight, in draperies that looked white and transparent in the moonlight, with silvery golden hair streaming down behind. Whatever was in the burial vault, it was not the Combing Lady; for this was Laly Florin herself.

"Yes," I said to the corporal. "It is your ghost. It is the Combing Lady, but very much in the flesh. What shall I do?"

"Get me on my feet. Here. Damned business . . . try again."

I used every ounce of energy and finally got the big fellow up, but he was still wavering. Achille's secret store of drugged wine was most potent.

"Wasting time. See where it goes – so you can tell the others."

I took back the spyglass and followed the fleeing figure. Suddenly, it stopped and turned, as though I myself were as clearly seen by it, and stared up at me. It was too far to make out the bloody features I remembered so well from that horrible night in the velvet room; and yet, an old, half-forgotten memory haunted me. . . .

Where had I seen this, upon awakening from sleep, this fancy of a shrouded figure in the moonlight?

I could see the figure drift away then and almost vanish in the components of the moonlight. I shivered and put down the spyglass.

At last, I remembered. That apparition on the circle drive at Miss Nutting's, the night I met Edmond Moura.

The phantom thing that had no face. It had been a warning of this.

I said with a briskness I was far from feeling, "Come now. We must go down and get help. Whatever it is, Achille must know. He can attend to it."

Together we got down the winding steps to the court-yard, though it required a good deal of effort and fierce determination on the part of the corporal who applied to my shoulder as to a crutch through most of the journey. But by the time we reached the Great Hall, he was too dazed to do more than fall into a high-backed chair and snore.

Somewhere in the front of the house I heard Achille calling. It sounded as though it came from the moat bridge; still armed with the corporal's spyglass I hurried out to tell him what we had found.

The moat bridge gleamed in the moonlight, but its shadow cast all the dying vegetation and stagnant stream of water beneath into deepest shade. I stood on the bridge getting my bearings. I called to Achille, using my full lung power, but heard for answer only the deathlike silence of the Moura woods. They were all about me. At my back was the solid stone of the château itself. I dared not go further. I knew the sick fancies that would take hold of my mind if I ventured into the woods, to be stalked by those softpadding sentinels, playmates of the Combing Lady, the Moura wolves.

I called again, and this time I thought I made out an answering hail from far inside the woods. I stood there, wondering if I should go on; then I ventured off the bridge and onto the dusty path that led by circuitous routes to the highroad. I was careful to stay near the old moat, so that the woods would not enclose me on all sides, and I did not walk far.

I was still well within sight of the moat bridge when I became aware of faint, moving shadows at the edge of the woods. At once, I turned in order to retreat to the bridge; for I recognized the gathering of the Moura wolves. They came out into the moonlight, one by one, slinking along as unwanted dogs will do, and out of the corner of my eye I could see the dull coats falsely bright in the moonlight. I felt I should be safe once I reached the bridge, for the main door of the château was only a few yards beyond, and I did not believe they would attack me unless I ran.

Then I looked ahead. On the bridge, my haven, I saw the Combing Lady.

She stood there in the moonlight, her funeral draperies fluttering around and behind her like the white plumage of a bird. Her bright, spun-gold hair flowed below her shoulders, and she was smiling. Her red lips gleamed in the brightness of the night. I could see the two canine teeth that everyone had mentioned, just at the sides of her mouth. She was beckoning to me.

I stood there a moment, wanting to shrink away, hating it – or her – at the same time pitying it, but with a horrible revulsion lest it should touch me with its cold little decaying hand. The good, solid substance of my spyglass gave me courage, and I beat it against my other palm to feel the sting and know whatever stood before me, I was alive and strong.

She beckoned again and I came on; for I meant to have it out with her this night. I was two hands taller than she. I was more than her match, if she was indeed human and alive. Behind me, the soft padding of the wolves came to my ears.

As I reached the bridge, she moved toward me, seeming to flow in those white cerements. Before I could stop her, she had taken something bloody, some slab of meat, and hurled it across my face and throat. I dashed it away instantly, and saw that she was waving to that wolf pack that stood now in a semi-circle at the edge of the bridge. Then she retreated, stepping slowly backward, until she was in the center of the bridge again.

I understood then what she had been up to; for the wolves smelled the blood upon me, and the foremost of them would have leaped but with my spy-glass I beat off the closest animal by a hard whack over the head.

They went to slavering over the piece of meat she had hurled at me, and I, wasting no time, hurried across the bridge. There she stood in the center, the Combing Lady, in all her foulness. She stank of the meat she had been carrying. Her dainty little hands were still bloody. Into her golden eyes now came a look of unbelievable hatred, and her tongue churned fiercely over her young lips.

I looked down into her eyes.

It must be a ghost, the horror of Moura; for this Combing Lady was a week dead. I had seen her sealed in her coffin.

"Palla . . . " I whispered. "Is it you, then?"

In the bright glare of moonlight her little face seemed enormous with her fury. It was puffed and white and gloating. She whispered in a terrible voice I would never have known.

"I wanted you when I was ill, Anne Wicklow. I wrote, I begged you for help. Where were you then? Now you come when it is too late. Why don't you die? Mama died easier. Just a push. That was all . . . Silly thing!"

"Why?" I asked, shaken with horror at this parody of my little friend.

"Why did you have to come at all when you were too late? I could have had Uncle and the estate. How I would have laughed at Mama then! Pretty Mama! Jealous of me.

236

Everyone said so. When people talked to me and admired me, she called them away. Did you know that? Whenever I wanted something my way, she would not have it so. It must be her way." She leaned toward me, the white cerements reeking with the acrid stench of blood. "I told you once I could have given Count Montoni a nasty game of it. You didn't know what I meant. They were all so stupid at that school. It was great fun. I remember their silly little sad faces when they saw the dogs that died. You see, dear Anne, it's so easy to get rid of someone . . . There was Mama, standing on the edge of the turret, pretending she would jump, ordering me to run down and fetch Uncle to stop her. But Uncle knew she was just pretending, and he wouldn't come. So there was only Mama and me. One little push – that was all. I knew if I pushed her, she'd never again be pretty as I, nor have her way when I wanted mine."

"And so you pushed her." I was appalled at my own calmness now that I understood. Palla was no more murderess than the wolves she fed in the night. She was one of those monstrous growths that must be kept away from the world because they are abnormal. "But I was your friend, Palla. I am now. Let me . . . "

It was no use. In her eyes was that yellow glitter one sees in an unreasoning animal.

"And that stupid governess, spying, talebearing, interfering like Mama . . . "

Oh God, I thought, my poor Palla! You spare me nothing.

"She was the easiest of all," said this wraith before me, smiling.

She put out her hands, and I perceived that she would thrust me into the path of those beasts beyond the bridge.

Behind me I heard the even pad of the wolves as they trooped up onto the wooden timbers. I knew what I must do, and I did it. I flung this bloodstained witch, this poor, evil little monster, into their path, all bloody as she was, and ran for the door of Moura.

I heard her scream as she fell among them, a hideous, gurgling noise, and then other sounds, the ravenous animals snarling and rending. Then there were shots, three or four.

Thanking God, I turned and saw figures hurrying along the path from the lodge. I recognized Achille and one or two others, including Charles Armitage, but I was too stunned to wonder what he was doing here.

I do not even remember whether he caught me as I fainted – for the first time in my life.

18

I think that, between them, Achille and Charles must have given me a sip or two of that wine which had proved so disastrous to Corporal Joubainbert, for I slept the night through and did not open my eyes until the late autumn sun was well over the sill of my window. I lay there, trying to remember what was nightmare and what real last night. But it was all fuzzy and vague.

Matilde came into the room, quite as usual, carrying a tray of breakfast and set it down on my knees, smack in the middle of the bed. I tried to thank her, but it was plain that whatever upheavals had occurred at Moura, she was in no way changed by them.

"Matilde, when will Monsieur Moura be free?"

"Three, four days. Who knows? No thanks to you, Mademoiselle Anglaise."

I could not be angry with her. She was right, of course.

"Is Mr. Armitage here? May I speak with him? I must know what has happened."

"Happen? Nothing happen," Matilde grumbled. "We have a wicked one. She is gone. Now it is necessary to wait upon another such. It is necessary to carry trays and feed and care for her" – she turned and looked at me squarely – "maybe you too murder us in our beds, eh?" With that parting shot, she slammed the

239

door and I heard her sabots noisily stalking down the corridor.

I was still picking over the food, for I was rather too nervous and my spirits too low to enjoy the meal, when Charles Armitage scratched on the door and opened it, as usual, without a by-your-leave. He came toward my bed looking very fit, with his customary walker's stride.

"My dear Anne, what a brave girl you are! Upon my life, I know few more brave! Facing down a little fiend like that, and not going clear off your head."

For some reason, his words annoyed me, and I snatched my hand away from him before he could take it in his. I said crossly, "Don't! She was once my friend." Then I remembered. "Is – is she dead?"

"Nothing to worry about on that score," he reassured me heartily. "Quite dead. Almost before we reached her. Little monster, you know. Think of it! She stabbed poor Caroline in the back."

"Yes. She told me." Suddenly I thought of that dreadful night in the velvet room. "I saw her two nights ago. I think it was Palla – but there was blood on her face."

Charles sat down on the bed and pushed away my tray. "That would be the night the servant girl, Clou, was killed. It must have been her blood you saw on this Palla's face."

I could believe that. Clou must have died less than an hour before I encountered the Combing Lady and pursued her through those underground chambers. Poor Clou! She had been wearing my shawl. Just as Edmond said, she had been murdered in mistake for me.

I had always known Palla must have her own way, must get what she wanted. I had seen her use her devious methods to subdue the girls at Miss Nutting's school. Yes, but these fiendish murders!

"And I thought she was playing when she said she loved those bloodthirsty old romances she was always reading. Curious! But did she actually feel that I was such a menace to her happiness? I stood her friend long ago, and would have last night."

Charles smiled. "Yet Achille says the girl saw Moura kiss you two nights since, in that obnoxious tower. You see, Edmond Moura was one of those things she wanted, probably because she couldn't have him. Can't think of any other reason."

"Can't you?" I asked tartly, and then, at his amused look, I went on more calmly, "In any case, she need not have been jealous. Monsieur Moura will never look at me again."

"Oh, indeed? May one ask why?"

"I betrayed him yesterday when he needed me."

"Nonsense. How could you know?"

"But I should have had faith in him. All along I ought to have believed in my own instincts." I added half defiantly, "Besides, it was not so much that Palla was jealous. She knew that if Monsieur – "

"If he married, she would lose Moura. Come, out with it. You are going to marry a Frenchy. Really, Anne!" But he was smiling, and I had to pretend not to be hurt by this impossible dream he had conjured up.

"I fear not. There are many reasons why it would be out of the question."

"Well!" He shrugged. "What a pother about nothing, a mere kiss! My dear Anne, you and he would never go on well at all. How different to the comradeship between us!"

"Very different!" I decided it was time to be up and about my work; for I had been determining during these past moments to leave Moura clean and decent for

Monsieur Edmond to come home to after his terrible ordeal. But it must be done rapidly. There was no question of my waiting for him. I was much too ashamed; even if he forgave me, I could not forgive myself.

"Now, if you will excuse me, I have much to do. Where have you put the other gentlemen who came with you last night?"

He stood up and politely averted his head as I got out of the great bed and reached for my shawl to use as a robe while I dressed. He felt me so little to be feminine that it did not surprise me when he remained now. I knew the type he considered feminine. A blonde little ninny, of course!

"That would be the king's attorney, the Comte de Varennes. He came to Moura thinking to take away his daughter. He's gone – an hour since."

"His daughter!" I nearly dropped the shawl in my astonishment. "Not Palla! But what of Edmond's brother the invalid Pierre Moura?"

"Humbug, my dear Anne, pure fustian." He turned around to me to explain himself, and finding me in deshabille hastily looked back out the window. "I imagine the invalid thought he was the father of that pretty child, but according to the tale the Comte de Varennes told me, Laly Florin had been his mistress when she was an opera dancer in Paris. Varennes already had a wife – you know these Frenchies, my dear – as Laly Florin was with child, he arranged a meeting with Pierre, who was so overcome by the fawning attentions of this notorious woman that when Palla arrived on the scene, he convinced himself rather naïvely that the child was his."

"Good God!" I exclaimed, only half believing. "Is that why Palla has been kept here in seclusion? Of course.

242

They must wait until her true father could arrange to commit her to . . . But this is dreadful! Abandoned by her father – disliked by her jealous mother! Small wonder poor Palla became what she was."

Charles lost his temper, but in that polite way which still remembered that he was a gentleman.

"I wish you will not speak of a fiendish murderess as 'poor Palla.' "

"Oh, stuff!" I said. "Will you help me with my gown? I cannot fasten it there in the back. It is caught on the shawl."

He came over and obeyed me, his cool fingers fumbling clumsily until he had untangled the hooks from the shawl. When he had completed this task, he bent his head rather close over me. I was almost afraid he would kiss me – but one simply does not kiss a brave squire, a fine, reliable companion-at-arms.

"We deal remarkably well together, Anne. You see? I am even equipped to play the domesticated husband."

I tried to pass this off as a small jest on his part. "What, sir? A gentleman and a housekeeper? What would the Prince Regent say? Come now, let us be practical."

He grinned and sighed a little. Almost I could have thought it was a sigh of relief. "You are so sensible, my dear. It is one of your greatest virtues. But it will be a lucky man who wins you."

I wrinkled my nose at this approbation. Who wants to be "sensible" in love, indeed?

"I am resigned to living my life out alone," I told him calmly. "With a position of responsibility somewhere, and perhaps a dog and cat for company."

"But may I escort you back to London? Now that the little fiend is buried, I shall be leaving myself in the morning."

"She is buried then?"

"This morning," he said briefly. "Shortly after dawn. Varennes wanted no talk of it, no witnesses except the two physicians he had brought with him. Achille and Jehan attended to it. It was better so. Varennes tells me he and Edmond Moura had searched over the half of France during this past month to find an asylum in which to place the child, but conditions were so frightful. Constant beatings, torture – hideous places. It is better that she is dead and buried than to be locked away in such a place."

I was glad, too. The child was safe from her own nature and from the wickedness of others who had brought her to this pass; for I would always believe, in despite of everything that Charles and the others told me, that in different circumstances Palla might have been a different girl, or at least one not driven to such dreadful excesses. I could see now that her insanity was her refuge from a world that offered her not one shred of love.

Perhaps she was born with the taint of murder, as her mother had been born with the taint of selfishness and vanity, but in a world where no one felt for her any bond of communion – not even Edmond Moura who had been so gentle to me – then surely it was inevitable that Palla should turn inward and live only for her own dreadful little pleasures.

I spent that day, as I promised myself, thoroughly cleaning all of the inhabitable rooms, with the assistance of that good Jehan whom I suspected, for a brief few hours yesterday, of having led Charles into some trap and murdered him. But I might have known my assessment of Charles was right. Nothing less than an Act of God would stop him from reaching the king's attorney, and he had indeed not returned to the inn before finding him.

244

While I worked, I thought now and again of Palla's first crime. What misery it must have meant to Edmond to be falsely accused of murdering Laly Florin, to know the ignominy of the galleys, while little Palla, too childish to be suspected of anything more than a mischievous smile, played happily at school, having accomplished what she set out to do – the simple act of pushing "Mama" so she would no longer be so pretty. For even if Edmond had suspected that it was the child who pushed Laly out of that turret, who would have believed him?

Charles Armitage rode away the following morning with my blessing. He was a fine, handsome fellow and would make some young woman of good family an excellent husband. At the last, we shook hands gravely, as between knight and squire, and once more he gave me his highest benediction, pronouncing me "as brave as a lion." Really, for one instant as he rode away, I was hard put to it not to throw rocks at his fine, straight back!

On the day the diligence was due to pass the Moura gates, I packed my few belongings and, wearing my workaday shawl and bonnet and older gown, I walked down the steps from the broken parapet where long ago, or so it seemed, Palla must have stood in the moonlit night and thrown pieces of meat to those wretched Moura wolves. As I went along the ground-floor passage, Achille came out of his room, as slippery and honey-mouthed as ever. He offered to take my small portmanteau, but I did not relinquish it and he did not insist.

As he opened the great door for me, however, he surprised me by saying suddenly, "Monsieur will expect to find mademoiselle here when he returns."

"I think not," I told him honestly. I remembered too well that look of pain and disappointment when I denied

245

Monsieur Edmond the day he was taken under custody to the village.

He took it that I knew his master's mind better than he. "Mademoiselle had a fondness for that poor Palla Florin? Isn't it so?"

I said that it was true.

"Yes. Even as a child she was – adorable, so long as she had her way. Then, when she did not – " He threw up his hands.

I ignored this. We all knew what Palla had done. There was no point in our laboring over it now. I turned away, saying stiffly, "Then perhaps it was something in her treatment here; for I assure you, she committed no such crimes in England."

"Ah, but mademoiselle," he ventured softly, putting out one of his smooth hands to detain me, "it was her behavior at that school for young ladies that caused Monsieur Moura to send for her."

I set my bag down and faced him.

"What'll you be telling me now? That she went about murdering people at Miss Nutting's? I know that for a lie."

"I beg you, listen to me. There are other crimes that point the way, that give a terrible light upon the events here of late at Moura. Palla was born to reign wherever she lived. She boasted of her domination of the English young ladies in those letters she wrote home upon occasion. But she must command other things as well. She had a taste for inflicting pain, as her mother had before her. She would take a club to a helpless little mongrel dog. She would drown a cat. These accidents frightened the other young ladies and made them fearful or sad, she said. They admired Palla because she could stand the sight of such poor, dumb creatures and not shudder or faint. Her mother was used to do such things at Moura. Some sort of strange satisfaction in watching an animal die. But no matter. In short, it was when we received one of Palla's communications to this effect – for she was frank with me and, as in the old days, loved to speak of her pranks – that we knew Palla must be brought back under our eyes before her lust for cruelty turned itself upon human beings.

"At first, at Moura, all went well. She had no rivals. She got on so well Monsieur Moura employed a Mademoiselle Caroline Durand to complete her education. Then, the jealousy – the tempers. Mademoiselle Durand carried tales to me and to Monsieur Moura. It was enough. Palla awaited the moment, and struck her down."

I understood a great deal now, more especially why it had been so necessary to keep Palla under drugs, during which time Edmond had been searching over France, trying to determine, perhaps with Palla's true father, what should be done with her. Edmond and the Comte de Varennes had been right. An asylum of the kind that existed in my girlhood was no place for Palla, or, indeed, for any human being, sane or otherwise. But what a frightful dilemma! And yet, during that same period, Palla, genuinely terrified, had smuggled out her letter to me – her one true friend, she thought!

"I wonder, mademoiselle, can you forgive us now?" The sweetness of his voice still cloyed, but once in a while during my dealings with Achille I had surprised just the sort of deep sincerity that I read in his eyes now.

"It is you and your master who should forgive me for my suspicions. When I saw the child lying on that bed – dead, as I thought . . . "

"Drugged. Thoroughly drugged. It was necessary to present such an illusion of death, for she had to "die" before we could place her in confinement in one of the west chambers. Otherwise, the whole world should know of her infamy, and then there would be a cry to send her to an asylum. But even so, she escaped. A tiny window, so tiny only a child could get through, but she managed. And in doing so, she was seen, and the stories of the Combing Lady came to life again and spread."

"She must have been wandering in the glade the day Monsieur Eustace and Kate and I examined the burial vault. Perhaps she hid inside, and so frightened poor Monsieur Eustace almost to death."

I remembered the slight rustling as we cared for Eustace – the noise made by Palla leaving the vault and retreating in the company of the wolves.

"That is how we see it," said Achille. "And later that night, Monsieur Moura tells me he saw something from the tower that may have been Palla running through the courtyard below. Perhaps she saw, as – forgive me – I saw, monsieur embrace you, mademoiselle. She would then have determined to kill you. After all she never knew the true story of her parentage. She would have thought if you were to marry monsieur, then where would her inheritance be?"

I took up my portmanteau and frowned into the pale noon sunlight. It was coming on for winter. I could feel it in the still and solitary air.

"Good-by, Achille," I said, and offered him my hand.

He took it in surprise, offering a faint, damp pressure of his boneless fingers. And yet, I thought, for all his weakness, it must have taken a special courage to live in the same house with the real Palla Florin!

It was a sad and lonely leave-taking. I left my little friend dead, in circumstances of peculiar horror, and I left behind me the one man in the all the world whom I loved.

As I crossed the moat bridge I almost missed my footing,

for there before me was the rusty spatter of something I knew must be Palla's blood. I walked around the stain, holding tight to my emotions, endeavoring not to think.

I looked back at the dark grey stone rectangle that was Moura, saw Achille wave to me in a friendly way, and I waved back. Then I walked briskly down the path to the lodge.

The diligence was just lumbering into sight as I reached the great arch with its deep-cut lettering that had first chilled me. The fat little coachman pulled up before me and I was about to throw my bag into the opening doorway when someone stepped out of the coach, and I made way for him.

It was Edmond Moura, looking dusty and travel-stained as I first remembered him. His face was tired and stern, but that dear, tender expression that I had occasionally seen was in his eyes.

"Please to make time," bellowed the coachman.

Edmond looked from him to me. Then he took my bag and set it down in the dusty road, and as the coachman shrugged and cracked his whip explosively over the heads of his team, Edmond drew me to his side, and I was warm and safe as I had never been warm and safe or loved in all my years.

THE BECKONING

For
Donnie Coffman Micciche
with deepest love

I

ALONG THE WILD, fog-hung westerly headlands of the Irish Coast there are still, as there were in my girlhood, lonely villages tugged between the gray Atlantic roaring at their front, and the emerald green bottomless bogs pulling stealthily at their back. Such appeared my birthplace upon my return to it in 1819, as a young widow of twenty-two. Rude and grim it was, a place to form a corpse—or a man. No timid boys, no fragile, wispy females educated above their stations were to be found there.

As the Ballyglen mail coach jogged across the countryside, I watched the lovely open weather of Waterford and Limerick give way now to the misty fog of my mother's birthplace, and I told myself that for the first time since my childhood I would be among a people and a race who saw me as one of them, not the foreign-born young housekeeper in an English academy for young females, or the loving, untutored wife of a French aristocrat. I was to be myself again, Anne Wicklow, one among my own kind. Or so I thought.

My parents had met on this coast twenty-five years before, as servants in Conor House, which was now crumbling away on Kelper Head, a ragged finger of land that groped daringly out into the Atlantic mists. The headland was named for the Kelp Gatherers, half real, half phantom, who plied their trade along the coasts of Galway and County Mayo, and even as an infant I have a memory of my mother telling Papa and me how, in her youth, she had seen the ghostly Kelp Gatherers drifting along the headland, enchained by their long ropes of shining, jellylike kelp, and beckoning to her. An eerie thing it was, and chilling, to see the Kelp Gatherers; for they foretold of death to come, perhaps one's own. I was like my Irish mother in that the dangers of the high road and the filthy warrens of a great city held for me fewer terrors than the possible sight of a floating apparition.

On that late November day in 1819 when the Ballyglen stage set me down at the crossroads, I was minded of my mother's visions as I gazed about me, quite alone in the clammy sheet of fog. A moment later I smiled at my own gullibility. Here before me was the road to Kelper Head, no King's Highway to ring with the sound of horses' hooves, but rather a series of muddy wagon ruts, mired by the footsteps of men and dog carts. Not a phantom within leagues on this God-forsaken place. What respectable ghost would lurk among such untidy scenes? Myself, I would prefer to haunt a salt-rimed beach, in the invigorating fury of an Atlantic gale.

With these wry thoughts for company I started off along the bumpy, rutted path that would bring me to the sea, and to the village where I imagined my life would take the quiet turn that must come to a woman who is not like to meet a second great love in one lifetime.

Something that occurred earlier today had been so curious I was beset by doubts that "a quiet turn" would come to me when I took this position as housekeeper at Conor House.

Only this morning, shortly before my departure in the mail coach from Carrickmore to the Crossroads Gibbet, a sealed missive from my recent employer, Miss Nutting, had been put in my hand, and to my astonishment I read the brief letter, forwarded and franked by Miss Nutting from

6

London, which told me my services were not required at Conor House after all, and that my long journey across England and Ireland had been for nothing.

A change of plans, said the letter, *due to the invalidism of the Master of the Household.*

I took out the letter and re-read it now as I walked, for my own intuition was shared by Miss Nutting who had added a footnote. She believed, as I did upon reflection, that the original summons to me was genuine, and only this second one, for some curious reason—perhaps a silly jest—was false:

> *Miss Anne Wicklow is advised that, due to the invalidism of the Master of Conor House, her services will not be required at this time. I regret that I may have put you to some trouble, but am happy that this missive arrives in time to forestall what must, in such case, have been an intolerable and futile journey for you.* And the signature, as in the first letter which hired me, was the large, flourishing, Maeve Conor.

Obviously, the message had not arrived in time to forestall my "intolerable and futile" journey, and Miss Nutting had sent it on to me, hoping to catch me on my journey, but with the addition which was so like the direct and ever honest Honoria Nutting:

> *What do you make of this, Anne? The signature is Maeve to the last swirl. But I'll go bail it is not Maeve's letter. Keep to your present journey. It's my belief someone is having a private joke, either at Maeve's expense or your own. Have you made any enemies recently? Someone who wishes to keep you from Conor House? Watch yourself, my girl! Look behind you. The enemy lurks, and danger is afoot at every turn!*

The latter was Miss Nutting's notion of humor. It was a silly form of humor, but the warning itself was foolish, if it was meant to be a joke. Who would wish to keep me from Conor House? I suspected it might be someone trying to cause difficulties for Lady Maeve Conor herself. It might even be her husband who was, as I had heard from Miss Nutting, an invalid. Perhaps he was in desperate mental straits and had sent me this note over his wife's signature, out of some strange insanity of his own.

In any case, I had come too far to return to England now, without hearing from Lady Maeve Conor's own lips that she wished me gone from Conor House. But it was an uneasy thing to happen, all the same.

Was it possible to have an enemy, and not to know it?

I savored the feel of the mist pricking my face and sparkling my hair with droplets. I carried a bandbox and a portmanteau, some of whose contents I could never wear at Kelper Head. They had been chosen by my husband for my use in France, and I could not bear to part with them. But I did not find my baggage heavy. I had been orphaned at an early age, and hard, healthy work soon taught me I was not like to become a vaporish creature at twenty-two. If my husband had admired my form rather too extravagantly for truth, there was that unforgotten girlhood to thank for it, and for my excellent health.

A crossroads gibbet, happily free of its swinging company, bore the weatherstained information that it was less than two leagues to Kelper Head, and not so far by half to the Ballyglen Bog, a dank and unpleasant fact that I would rather not know.

My morocco slippers which had served me faithfully in my journey across France and England after my husband's death in a Bonapartist uprising, now sank with each step into the ooze of the cart tracks, and I prudently shifted over to the shoulder of the road where dark hummocks of turf-cuttings lined the path, feeling spongy underfoot. The fog had turned to a stubborn mizzle which an occasional blade of light from the late afternoon sky seemed to pierce as if it cut through a shimmering curtain. The earth was now almost dark, but by the curious gleam of the rain and the light from the heavens, gigantic shadows huddled against the blue-black sky ahead and seemed to bend over me, as though peering down to read my face.

I walked with greater care now, knowing from childhood memory what must appear along this road presently, after the green turf changed to little pools reflecting these odd sky shapes that hovered over the solitary walker. How often my mother had recounted tales of Ballyglen Bog! Beyond the pools I would soon be treading a pitifully narrow thread of highway, careful to avoid either side.

The man-killing Bog of Ballyglen soon crept around me. At this time of evening a stranger might suppose the bog to be a great stretch of muddy turf with a frequent pool to give it variety, but sorry was the man or beast who ventured to cross Ballyglen Bog on that assumption. He was heard of no more save, of course, for his last stifled cries as the vile sucking thing drew its victim down to devour it.

I had just entered onto the Bog region when I began to be aware of the difference in the sounds of the landscape. Before, there had been the light speckle of mist, the soughing of the wind. Now all this was gone, drowned in the repeated digesting of the sand, bubbling and sucking through each reedy mere. I peered ahead into the overcast and saw that I had come but half my way toward Kelper Head. There was no mistaking my fatigue at this moment. But something else to the right of me and across the Bog took my attention and my thoughts. Among the great, hunchbacked shadows that overhung the Bog, there was one in particular, smaller than its fellows, and quite unlike the clouds which formed the greater shadows. It appeared on the edge of my limited horizon, advancing toward the road like a loosely wrapped man walking over the Bog towards me, a feat manifestly impossible.

My pace faltered an instant, then picked up. Whatever the creature was—and I confess my first thought was of my mother's phantom Kelp Gatherers—I meant to attract no undue attention. But my hands were icily stiff within the shelter of my cloak and the shawl that partially covered my head and shoulders. I felt sick with apprehension yet ashamed at being so. The great Ballyglen Bog was silent as a tomb for several minutes. Then the familiar bubbling, sucking sounds began again, now hard by the road. Despite myself, I started in fright and ran a few steps, trying not to hear that faint, greedy sound as the Bog devoured some hapless creature close enough for me to touch.

By this time the evening had advanced so that I could barely see the Bog. It seemed part of the general darkness until I became aware that the shadow crossing the Bog in a Kelper's fringed cloak was almost upon me. I stopped straight in my tracks and demanded as crisply and defiantly as my icy fright would allow:

"What is it then? What do you want of me?"

Phantoms, even Irish phantoms, are not the most garrulous of creatures, and I could not have been more surprised when a woman's voice called out to me, "If you please . . . are you for Ballyglen?"

I could have given her a slap for frightening me so, and a sound kick to myself for letting her frighten me; yet it was passing strange, this pretty, young female drifting across the Bog and onto the road, quite as though used to such goings-on. A gust of wind blew open the great red cloak which was too big for her, and she shivered. She was dressed in the height of Dublin fashion, obviously a lady, and her presence out here was nearly as mysterious as if she had, indeed, been a phantom Kelper.

"No, miss," I said, more gently than at first. "I have a post to take at Kelper Head. The Ballyglen Road is more than a league behind me. Too far for you to be walking this night."

"I know where it is—nearly," she surprised me by saying. For then, why had she spoken to me, unless for the company of my voice. "You see, I come from Kelper Head."

She made her way to me across the mire of the road, careless of what it did to her dainty slippers and stockings. Close up to her like this, I saw that her face was older than her voice. She was very possibly older than I, in her middle or late twenties, but something about her, an extraordinary childish sweetness in her voice, restored to me my first uneasiness. Was she, perhaps, a Natural? One of those unlucky creatures born mindless? A pity, for she appeared kind and gentle, and would have been a beauty had her manner and voice matched her face in maturity.

"Is all well with you, miss?" I asked, supposing there must be a reasonable explanation for her appearance out here in the center of the infamous Bog. "How did you come upon me? You must know the Bog very well to avoid the potholes and all the dangers."

She said wisely, "Oh no. There is a path to the east and north, if you read it right. But you have to be clever."

She must be extraordinarily clever. I should not have chanced it myself. When in England I had been offered the position at Kelper Head in the very house where my mother and father once served, I was warned most strongly about the danger of the Bog and its many deceptive paths. I still carried Lady Maeve Conor's first letter in which Her Ladyship advised me to be at the expense of hiring a dog cart in Ballyglen in order to avoid the Bog. Although I should not be my father's frugal daughter if I paid out good coin for such luxuries as a dog cart, I had been sensible enough to keep to the road.

"Will you walk with me, miss?" I ventured then. "You may hire a cart tomorrow and get to Ballyglen in as great a hurry as you could wish."

She wrapped the coarse wool cloak around her and hugged it tight, to warm herself. She appeared to be studying me.

"I lied to you. It was not Ballyglen Town I started for, but the Bog itself." An odd statement, surely, and at this hour of the afternoon. "They talked of a housekeeper. Are you the woman Wicklow?"

"I am for Conor House."

She smiled again. It was not a happy smile, and it ill-suited her sweet, heart-shaped face. Once more I felt uneasy and almost wished I had not encountered her at all.

"I am from Conor House, Miss Wicklow. I was Maureen Conor, before my marriage."

"But then—" I began.

She interrupted sweetly. "You still do not see. I like to run from Conor House, and from—them." When I stared at her, she added, "You see, I must."

What nonsense was this? We could not stand here the entire night, encompassed by the Bog, and our shoes sinking further into the mud every minute. I spoke roughly, hoping it would have a healthy effect upon her.

"I'll be on my way, then, Miss. I have my work to do, my post to take from Lady Maeve. You had best come with me."

She hesitated, saw me step onward with a vigor that let her know I was not joking. Then she hurried after me.

"I'll stay the night, if you will. I always come back. But I am not mad, truly not. And I won't be treated like a murderess; for I am not. It was the Kelper! They'll be sorry, right enough. One day I will not come back." She took hold of my shawl and her fingers dug sharply into my forearm. "Promise me, Miss Wicklow, you will not listen to them. You will believe me, won't you?"

I could not but feel that "they"—whoever they might be—had reason on their side. Miss Maureen was not behaving like a rational creature. Nevertheless, her plea could scarcely be denied. My heart went out to the poor lady.

"Come along," said I as cheerfully as may be. "We are two against Them. And they shan't make us believe anything we don't wish to believe about each other." It was in my thoughts that if Miss Maureen could stand up to the great Ballyglen Bog without a shudder, she could scarcely be in danger from the dwellers in Conor House.

We walked on rapidly. Miss Maureen surprised me by her swift movements, her ease in finding the best path through the muddy morass of the road. She did not seem in the least afraid of phantoms and ghosts and the general debilitation of the area. Perhaps she often took these late afternoon strolls over the Bog. But she was nervous. And I set this to her mental state. To be afraid of fellow human beings and yet not to be afraid of the netherworld was a thing I would never understand. One can stand up to one's fellow men, but it is difficult to stand up to a floating apparition, and this was a wonderously perfect region for such folk tales.

I fancy we must have been three-quarters of the way to Kelper Head when I began to hear sounds on the road ahead of us that did not come from the greedy digestion of the swamp. The squeak and rattle of badly fastened wheels, and then the snorting of an animal, probably a pony, relieved me of any apprehension that the sounds were ghostly. There came further proof in the storm lantern swinging from a hook above the right wheel, the light within casting a cheerful, blushing glow upon the immediate scene.

I said aloud, "Now, here's luck, indeed, ma'am. Perhaps we can beg a ride back to the Head. Will the rider turn about, do you think?"

Miss Maureen clutched my arm again.

"Let them go by," she murmured in a hushed voice. "They try to hide things from me. They speak in whispers when they think I do not hear. But it is about me. Always my name is in it."

I began to understand better the "persecution" that this poor lady fancied herself suffering.

"But, miss, they are not truly cruel, not by deed, surely?"

She wrinkled her nose and raised her voice as though no longer caring that the approaching driver might hear. "They were horrid cruel. No one would take me to the Fair at Carrickmore, and there was to be a high walker and dancing tinkers and a puppet show. So I said I should make them sorry." She pulled me closer. "Will they be sorry if I do it?"

This was foolish beyond permission. We could not help being seen. We were the only two creatures on the road and in a region where everyone must know everyone else by the very nature of its isolation. I did not want to make an enemy of one of the Conor House ladies, but this seemed a moment for common sense. As it happened there was no need of a choice between pleasing Miss Maureen and accosting the lone pony cart and rider. The squeaky cart slowed at the moment we came into sight, and the man on the rough board seat leaned forward and called to us: "Is it you, Maury? What a-devil will you be doing here? Are you all right then?"

Despite the brusque words his voice attacted the hearer by its peculiar timbre and a kind of musical quality not quite Gaelic yet neither was it the flat, broadly anglicized accent of my school employer. One felt concern behind his brief question, and Miss Maureen rushed forward to the man and the pony, obviously delighted to see them. The little pony pawed the mud tracks and made sounds of uneasiness in the midst of this great dark that looked even darker beyond the circle of lantern light. I felt heartily in sympathy with the poor animal's feelings. The man at the reins, however, was competent to meet the situation.

"There, there, Boru. Quiet now. It's only the bog. There's the good lad you are." He swung down from the cart and opened his arms wide, receiving Miss Maureen in a warm embrace. He soothed her much as he had the pony.

"Maury, love! You had us upon the rack, girl. Nurse Kellinch is gone up the headlands making search."

"Oh, bother Miss Kellinch!" Maureen cried in the querulous, childish voice of irresponsibility. "Everyone's been out of reason cross the whole day. And I'll not be treated so. There's a thing I can do, and hurt them all."

I had walked up to the cart by this time and saw a sturdy young man of middle height and a Celtic look about him that was more grim and rugged than the Gaelic Irish with which I was familiar. He caressed her ruffled dark curls as he said calmly, with good sense, "It's for home like a good child. There'll be hot tea and supper. What do you say? Hmm?"

He gazed over her lowered head at me. I liked his tender solicitude for her, which was a happy mingling of common sense and devotion. An odd combination of traits to find in a face like his, with its look of passions leashed, and his curious eyes, now a lively green, now brown and fathomless as a peat bog. Nor was I made more secure by my awareness that those expressive eyes studied my person from head to foot, their somber depths scarcely lighted by his smile.

"Thanks be to you, ma'am, for your help. My wife has not been well of late."

Before I could respond, his wife raised her head with an abruptness that shook his hand off her.

"I'm quite well. I walked halfway to the crossroads gibbet." Then her rainbow of moods changed and she was all smiles. "Be kind to her, for my sake, Jonathan. She's the new housekeeper Maeve sent to England for."

The man, not a gentleman perhaps, but a very masculine man surely, reached out one hand and took mine in a warm, gloved grasp, preventing me from an awkward curtsey that would have dipped my skirts in the mud.

"I am Dr. Jonathan Trumble, ma'am. You must be Miss Wicklow."

Maureen said suddenly, "Isn't it odd, Maeve employing a pretty woman? Maeve will dislike it excessively when she spies you, Miss Wicklow."

"What a little silly you are!" said the doctor with a directness that seemed to react favorably upon his childish wife. "Lady Maeve is very like to be as pleased as you and me."

"You and I," said Miss Maureen complacently.

This rude and public correction did not appear to disturb the rugged young doctor whose defense of me was pleasant to my ears. He was apparently well used to his wife's whims and regarded this whole odd encounter as something in the everyday line. He swung her up onto the seat of the cart with great ease, offered me a place, and then, after a brisk liftup to me, he walked beside the nervous little pony, turning the equipage around on the narrow road to face the coast and Kelper Head. As he did so, one of the rackety wheels only just missed a nasty sucking pothold that bordered the road. After that, we bobbed along in a fair style with Dr. Trumble walking beside us.

I could not help wondering if Lady Maeve Conor would dislike my appearance excessively, as Maureen Trumble predicted. Unless, of course, she had actually written that strange second note, advising me not to come. I felt sure that my former employer, Miss Nutting, had said nothing to my disadvantage; for she was as near a mother to me as makes no matter. Nor did she speak out against the Irish offer of employment when I returned so suddenly from France. Lady Maeve had been one of her pupils twenty years gone and Miss Nutting had spoken about Lady Maeve's offer with more than usual warmth. I decided that Miss Maureen's remarks were but a symptom of an obvious mental state.

I said to Dr. Trumble, "A curious thing happened, sir. After I had departed for Ireland, another message came from Lady Maeve, asking me not to come. I received it only this morning. My late employer had the goodness to frank the letter as far as Carrickmore. It awaited me there. I have been visiting the coteen where I was born near Dublin Town, or I should have received it sooner."

He raised his eyebrows. "An odd thing, certainly. I expect it was a joke of some sort. Only last evening Maeve was deep in the frets for want of the new housekeeper. Our last one tipped the bottle."

Maureen giggled. "It was too funny. We never truly saw Mrs. Fergus tippling. She was a sly one. But we were forever finding her empty bottles and whisky mugs."

"Then perhaps she is my enemy," I suggested.

"That's as may be," said the doctor indifferently. "Fergus is in the North of Scotland and like to remain there."

"But why should it be anyone else?" I asked. "A silly, pointless joke, cheating me of a position and perhaps putting Her Ladyship to the trouble of hiring another woman in my place."

Maureen looked wise.

"It's very like Theo. He is my brother, Miss Anne. Theo might do something as deliciously absurd."

"Delicious, maybe," said Dr. Trumble, with a sardonic edge to his voice that made me suspect no love was lost between himself and his brother-in-law. "But absurd, surely. It is apparent Miss Wicklow, you are not wanted at Conor House—by someone. Is it, I wonder, because you'll be proving too efficient? I only hope no further jests are played in that line, or you will be peeping about in dark places and starting at the drop of a pin."

"Good heavens!" I said. "You think there may be danger to me?"

For the barest fraction of time he hesitated. The lantern light showed me his face in quick-changing lights and shadows, illuminating several pock marks on his cheek that, curiously enough, gave his face one of its rugged attractions. "Not if you are resolute," he replied.

I did not like the reply.

"Perhaps someone thinks you will see too much of our lives, of what goes on at Conor," Maureen suggested surprisingly.

"That'll be enough, love," her husband silenced her. I recognized then his use of the endearment which I had thought effusive for such a man. But though he gave it the same casual use I had often heard between Yorkshiremen of both sexes, it was lovely to see his wife's flowering under his voice, even when he issued orders.

"Then you think I may safely apply tonight to Lady Maeve?" I asked.

"Miss Wicklow, if you did not, it would be a sorry state altogether, and that's my thought on it."

Maureen raised her chin.

"I don't know, Jono. It might be very amusing to think someone does not want Anne at Conor. Things are tiresome enough this past month."

He reached over and took her hand. For an instant she looked at him with her heart in her eyes, as the saying is. Then he let her hand go, and she was very silent. He seemed to know exactly how to deal with her.

Presently, when I thought the Bog must go on forever, we began to hear a great, distant roaring, and Dr. Trumble looked up at us and smiled, the expression of his face softening perceptibly.

"The sea will make you forget the ugly neighbor at our back. I'll say the truth: I prefer it to the swamp and bogland."

"Not I," Maureen burst out. "The sea hurts. The sea is bad. It doesn't warm you and cover you with a nice thick blanket, like the Bog. . . . And Wicklow, did you know? The Kelper Ghosts come out of the sea, all dripping slime and brine and seaweed. But with the Bog, it is different."

It was that, right enough! I swallowed hard and with great effort only just kept from shuddering at her extraordinary words. To me, her love of Ballyglen Bog was like an affection for the grave, fitting only to one already dead.

Her husband, however, wisely paid no heed to her rambling. "You'll soon be sitting down to tea and forget all about ghostly kelpers and the Bog and the like."

"Are there buns, with sugar?" Maureen wanted to know.

I honored Dr. Trumble for his perfectly natural reply.

"Sugar buns, and the current scones that cut such a dash with you. A very nice tea."

He glanced at me for a bare second and then looked away. I stared down at my fingers and plucked uneasily on a loose thread of my shawl. By that swift glance I had surprised in his eyes such turbulence and bitterness as was almost a silent outcry against his wife's condition.

The pounding of the Atlantic combers blotted out all other sounds, and I was tremendously impressed by my first sight of the gray, forbidding beach, swept by the sea spray and looking desolate as a landscape on the deserts of Cathay.

"What are those dark patches scattered about the beach?" I asked Dr. Trumble, and laughed to show that I was only joking. "They look for all the world like human beings, lying on the sand."

He said, "They are the usual debris that washes up after a wreck. A pair of fishermen in corraghs were lost off Lough Head in the south last night. There be— There are the remains."

"Remains?" I echoed faintly.

"Of one corragh and its catch of fish."

"Were the fishermen found?"

"Not likely! When they are lost off those headlands they

go for to be banged about and don't wash ashore until a deal of time after."

A cheerful thought. I began to understand, in slight part, Miss Maureen's preference for the Bog.

The pony differed with us, however. It was plain that he loved the salt smell of the air, and the sight of the low-slanting dunes with their weedy crop, as the road turned, and became little more than a sandy path, cut deep with wagon ruts and footprints. Behind us, I barely made out a scramble of thatched and white-washed cottages, or "co-teens" which must be the village of Kelper Head. Ahead of us, at the end of the beach, was a rocky eminence stretching out into the sea like a bony finger. Along this rock the road climbed a trifle, to the foot of what I took to be Conor House, a white Palladian building of four storeys facing on the sea, with an enormous escarpment and limewashed stone wall raising it above the wild combers off Kelper Head.

"You can see the whirlpool a little further on," said Maureen helpfully. "Just below the escarpment. My kitten fell over into the pool there last month and I cried all evening, even though he had scratched me and deserved to die. Didn't I cry, Jono?"

"That you did, love, and if you'd please me, you'll not be playing with any more creatures so close to the edge of the terrace. It is cruel of you. A thing I don't like to see in my girl."

"What is the whirlpool?" I asked the doctor, partly in my dismay, and partly to forestall Miss Maureen's revelations of her character.

Dr. Trumble explained, "Just a churning of two currents at the south foot of the escarpment. We've some fierce tides through this region, and a deal of them meet at Kelper Head. But there'll be no danger to Conor House. Although" —he seemed to be expending effort to ease my mind by making light of it— "I don't advise you do a bit of knitting out on the edge of the terrace. The females of Conor House are forever losing skeins of wool and the like over the edge."

"I hope Nurse Kellinch loses a skein of wool—and herself too—over the edge, when she is horrid to me," said Maureen pleasantly.

THE BECKONING

Neither the doctor nor I said anything. I do not know which of us was the more relieved when the little pony cart began to mount the headland toward the foot of the great white stone building that was Conor House.

II

IT WAS IN my thoughts that Conor House, which presented
a noble prospect from the sea, should have an impressive
entrance, but this was not the case. As we jogged under
the shadow of the great rectangular escarpment upon which
the house was built, I saw an unprepossessing door no bigger
than a postern gate in that side of the wall which formed
a right angle to the foaming waves below. The Conors
made themselves inaccessible to the world, from every reach
save only the gray harpies of the Atlantic. The combers
flung themselves against the broad western face of the
escarpment, sending up a vicious spray, but even they were
helpless to reach the terrace that ran along the top of the
great stone barrier.

Before Mrs. Trumble and I were got down from the cart
I was surprised to see that someone from Conor House stood
on the high terrace, peering out at the ill-tempered sea.
Whether the windblown watcher was a tall woman, or a
man of middle height I could not make out. The flapping garments were long, probably a greatcoat, and the face turned
intently seaward. Dr. Trumble, having lifted his wife down,
saw my gaze and followed it.

"Maeve," he called to the lone figure, his distinctive voice
audible even above the clamor of the sea. "We have
her safe."

The woman turned and came over to the edge of the
terrace above us, away from the sea spray. By the glimmer of the lantern I saw a slender, beautiful creature peering
down at us, a woman in her thirties, perhaps a trifle older,
as poised as a ship's figurehead, with masses of astonishing
hair which had partially blown out of its confines and was
hammered by the wind and sea until the wild, coppery
strands seemed to light everything about her. She nodded
to us and smiled. She had excellent teeth that gleamed

20

noticeably in the offshoots of lantern light. I looked at Dr. Trumble in surprise. As he reached up to lift me down he guessed what puzzled me.

"My wife's stepmother, Lady Maeve Conor."

My employer. The woman to whom I should be answerable, and whose conduct to me would make my life either bearable or otherwise. I looked up again. She had left the terrace and was probably going inside the house like a sensible woman.

If first impressions counted for anything, I felt that in Lady Maeve I found a lively, charming, and perhaps unusual employer.

But what a curious pastime, to be staring at the sea in weather like this; and on such a dangerous walkway! What did the woman think about during these hours? Was she troubled by something? Or was it merely an old habit of hers?

Maureen Trumble had gone ahead of me, rushing to the door as though delighted to be home. And after all her tall tales to me about fleeing from Conor house!

"Come along, Wicklow," she bade me as the door opened inward. A shaded candle flashed in her face. She did not even blink, though I did, instinctively. A burly dark man stood there looking gigantic until I realized that the door opened onto a steep flight of stone stairs, and this giant was standing before us on the bottom step. There was nothing else behind or around him but the bare stone walls of the staircase, sweating faintly with seepage. A curious entrance hall for such a palatial home. There was, in fact, not even a passage, merely the steps, spiraling upward.

"O'Glaney, I'm home," Maureen said cheerfully.

"Och, ye're found then, Missus!" he said, looking not quite so brutal. "There's a good lass it is! And is himself with you? If ye'll be takin' the light I'll stable the beast."

I assumed the beast he referred to was the little pony, but something in his manner as he said "himself" when referring to Dr. Trumble, made me suspect he was not overfond of Maureen Conor's young and vigorous husband.

He stepped down to our level and Maureen took the candlestick with its metal hood that made dancing lights flick over the narrow, confining flight of steps. When he passed me and went out to join Dr. Trumble at the cart,

I saw that he was not quite so enormous. But his clothing added to the illusion—thick, padded garments, a jacket fit for service in the farthest reaches of the Orkneys, heavy breeches, and his legs were wound over and over with thick strips of wool.

"Poor O'Glaney. He cannot like Jonathan," Maureen confided. "You see, my Jono was once very poor, but he is so clever he learned to be a surgeon and very nearly a gentleman." She mounted the first step, looking upward into the murky dark beyond the candlelight. "Still, he is not a Conor like my brother and me." She paused, as though recalling an addendum. "And father, of course. We are all that is left of the Conors."

"Except for Lady Maeve, who is a Conor by marriage," I added, remembering my sight of that extraordinary red-haired beauty.

"How funny you are, Wicklow! We are Conors by birth. Maeve was only a Loughrea." Maureen's light, girlish trill of laughter wafted down to me out of the darkness above. It gave me an eerie little chill, as though a bird's wings fluttered by my cheek. Nor did I understand her amusement. I knew, from the description of my former employer, Miss Nutting, that Lady Maeve was the daughter of an Irish earl, one of the peers of the realm, who had, alas! beggared himself in trying to keep company with our expensive Prince Regent. But though the father was a suicide, his title was honorably come by. Sure, it was an overweening pride in these Conors to put themselves above an earl's daughter. They seemed never to forget, as Miss Nutting had reminded me, the Conors were as ancient as Ireland's Christianity.

But it was no concern of mine. I must be guarding myself against the expression of opinions which did not befit my station as housekeeper. How disappointed my beloved husband would have been! He had taken great pains to tear away my "servile" ideas like cobwebs, and to assure me that I was the equal of duchesses and queens.

At the top of the steps I saw Maureen Trumble open a door and immediately we were in a parlor whose cheerfulness, comfort and excellent taste were so unexpected it took my breath for a moment. A great fire roared in the Tudor fireplace, and all the portieres, of warm red velvet, closed out the cold night, though not, unfortunately, the roar of the sea. I guessed that beyond the portieres were windows which gave upon the open terrace atop the escarpment, but I was more concerned with the cheerful warmth of the rest of the room which beckoned to us. Miss Maureen had gone directly to a worn but still beautiful wing chair with its rich gold-threaded crimson brocade covering, and curled up in the chair like a child, warming herself before the fire.

"Come to the fire before we introduce you," she said and I did so, but hesitantly, not quite at ease.

"Shall I be meeting Lady Maeve and Mr. Conor presently?" I asked as I rubbed my numbed hands together and held them, rather gingerly, toward the fire. I did not want the family to think I presumed on our accidental meeting at Ballyglen Bog.

"Yes, yes, presently. But not in here, of course. Maeve never comes in the Kelper Room."

It wasn't my business to ask, "Whyever not?" but the question haunted me for the next few minutes as Maureen chattered on.

"Always remember, Wicklow, you must see to it that the fires in the house are never let die. The peat fires burn always. That is frightfully important. Father used to give us a great scold for it, Theo and me. He said that we must learn to manage the servants. But that was before Father married Maeve, of course."

I made a mental note of this instruction.

"Is is because of the dampness?" I asked.

"Oh, no one cares for that in itself. It is only that where the rooms are damp the servants believe the Kelpers may be attracted. Of course, ghosts are only for little sillies like the parlormaid Rosaleen."

I thought severely, *Only for little sillies, is it? Well then, I could be telling you a tale or two, my fine young scoffer!*

"There it is. To keep the family peace we have the peat fires burning all the year in the rooms. As for the damp, Father used to say it was what made our whisky good, the dampness seeping down the walls and into the casks. Father was a knowing one."

I was a trifle unnerved by her repeated use of the past tense in speaking of her father, Mr. Conor.

"I was told that a Mr. Aengus Conor would be my employer, though Lady Maeve, his wife, would give me my orders. Mr. Conor has not died, surely?"

She shook her head and beckoned to me. I came closer and she started to whisper something. Her dark curls partly muffled her words, and I did not understand. I was about to ask her to repeat, when I was badly shaken by the swift change in her face. She went livid with terror. She was staring at something behind my back. I swung around, fully expecting to be confronted by a ghostly kelp gatherer, at the very least.

"Maury, love," said Dr. Trumble briskly, "you ramble prodigiously. You'll be tiring Miss Wicklow who's been good enough to hear you out."

"Oh, bother!" said Maureen, soon normal again. "It was only that, for a moment, I remembered something I . . . might have done today. I'm glad I did not."

The doctor had come up the steps and into the room so silently that I too might have shared Maureen's fright, though not for the same reason. I could not imagine what she had meant to do today that would produce this curious terror in her. The doctor closed the staircase door behind him and I wondered how long he had been listening to us. It was disconcerting to realize that anyone from the sandy road at the foot of the embankment could come up those steps and into this room without being seen or heard.

"Poor Jono!" Maureen scolded in her little girl way. "You might at least wear squeaking boots." She had changed her mood swiftly again, and confirmed my suspicions that one could not rely upon her for anything in the way of commonsense. I could only admire Dr. Trumble, however; for now he showed no embarrassment or other signs of the natural uneasiness he must feel over his wife. Yet, when he went to the fire, I saw him touch the mantel carving thoughtfully, with the forefingers of both hands, and they shook just a trifle. He rested his forehead upon his arms and gazed down into the leaping flames. I pitied him as I pitied his wife, and I resolved to be at my ease with Miss Maureen, just as he was. But it would help me if I knew the extent of her lunacy, its cause, and the other odd things that seemed to creep out every few minutes about Conor House and its occupants. I began to surmise

24

that Miss Nutting had either been deliberately mendacious in describing my post here, or Lady Maeve had not told Miss Nutting all that should be known.

I said, "If Her Ladyship is expecting me, sir, I had best not be waiting about in the family quarters."

The doctor smiled. "You'll find no London ways hereabouts, Miss Wicklow. All the same, there's some'ut—something in what you say. Maeve is keen to see you." He added after a pause, "You'll be muchly welcomed and that if only for Miss Nutting's praise of you."

He seemed to appreciate the delicacy of my position, perhaps because he himself must be on his preferment in Conor House. If the Conors considered themselves lowered by the addition to the family of a belted earl's daughter in the person of Lady Maeve, Miss Maureen had certainly stepped down in marrying Jonathan Trumble, whatever his mental attainments. He was, after all, only a surgeon, one of those persons like myself on the social fringe, halfway between the backstairs of the servant class and the drawing rooms of the gentlefolk. Except for my husband, I was never at ease with the Quality, deeming myself as superior to them in competence as I was inferior in breeding and station, and I felt in Jonathan Trumble that I might find an understanding ally, should the Conors prove inordinately proud or arbitrary.

Dr. Trumble caught my arm now above the wrist in one of his sturdy brown hands, and I winced at the force of the contact. He did not notice, but led me companionably out of the room and into a gloomy, damp passage which, being unheated and with door open at the far end upon a balcony, caught the roar of the sea and seemed to reecho it in these narrow confines.

Glad I was when I found myself being shown into a room off the end of the passage, next to the open balcony which ended the passage itself. I saw at once that it must be the morning room of the house, and undoubtedly the office of the lady who ran the household. It was a room done in new white and gold draperies and carpeting, at variance with the worn but serviceable furnishings of the parlor I had seen. There was great elegance here, and money. The great windows were closed, but one could almost feel the cold miasma of spray and fog which pressed against the windows as if almost humanly curious to watch the inhabitants within.

Interesting as was this room, more interesting still was the lady who sat at the desk with her back exposed to the prowling fog and the terrace. She was quite as beautiful as I had supposed her to be upon that first view of her on the high walkway of the terrace, though she was older than I had thought her. Probably forty. Her red hair was now more or less neatly confined in a Grecian style popular a few years previous, but even so, the wisps of that fine-spun hair were still uncontrolled and made me think suddenly and absurdly of a tale told me by my husband. It happened long ago in a far country that a sorceress had hair like this, and when one came close, one saw that it was many writhing, poisonous vipers, and to look upon this sorceress was to die.

Absurd, indeed. I was ashamed for thinking of it. The lady smiled charmingly and held out her hand to me as I curtseyed, and Dr. Trumble introduced me.

"How good of you to come so promptly, my dear. I am Maeve Conor. I hope it has not put you to too much trouble. I have sent for Mrs. O'Glaney, who is our cook. She will show you about and see to it that a hot supper is prepared for you. Then, if you are not too tired, we will talk later. But now, I can see you are fairly shivering with the cold."

The thought of a hot supper put me into an excellent state. It is not often that the comforts of a new housekeeper in a household are seen to so quickly.

Dr. Trumble said, "The lass tells a tale of a second letter from you, dismissing her before ever she could begin her duties here."

"Not 'lass,' Jono. She is no milkmaid. She is Mrs.—or shall we say Miss Wicklow," Lady Maeve corrected him, as though out of long habit.

" 'Miss' Wicklow would be most satisfactory," I put in, hoping to make him forget the little snub. "My husband's political activities in France were against the present regime, and for that reason Miss Nutting and I felt that it would be more discreet if I retained the name by which I formerly served her."

"Just so," said Lady Maeve and a silence fell between the three of us. Why did she not either tell me she was aware of the "joke," if joke the letter was, or express astonishment? She passed her hands over some papers on the desk and took up one.

"Did you write this, Miss Wicklow?"

I looked at it. The paper was smudged, the seal broken, of course, and it showed every sign of having travelled a distance, but what amazed me was the writing, which was, I confess, very similar to mine in answering the application Lady Maeve had made to Miss Nutting for a housekeeper. It said simply: *Begging Your Ladyship's pardon, but a matter has come up that carries me to the North Counties, and I am obliged to say I cannot take the position offered me.*

"No, ma'am," I said, and curtseyed. "I did not write it. Nor then, I take it, did Your Ladyship write to Miss Nutting requesting her to withdraw your offer."

Lady Maeve looked over my head at the doctor. She smiled.

"Well, Jonathan, I fear Kelper Head has a troublemaker. You had best inquire which of the servants has learned to write . . . and to ferret among my correspondence."

"Excuse me," I said, "but why would anyone do such a thing?"

Dr. Trumble laughed shortly. "There's a question for you! Servants hate masters. It's the way of things. And Miss—er—Nutting—gave you a good character, or so Maeve says."

"Exceptional," Her Ladyship agreed, to my pleasure. She looked as though she would return to the matter of the "joke" played by someone among the servants. Extraordinary servants, I thought, if they could not only read but write in disguise so well. But then she thrust the paper back among her correspondence. "No matter. I knew it must be a trick of some kind. So Maureen is back, Jono. Where did you find her?"

"To state it flat out," said the doctor, "she found me. She and Miss Wicklow stumbled upon each other on the Bog Road."

These last words gave Lady Maeve a small start. She pretended not to be moved, but I saw her fingers tremble and her mouth betray her by a tightening of the lips. I did not know why, but I felt undercurrents here. Neither the doctor nor Lady Maeve had said nor looked anything but the civilities that I here record; yet when they spoke to each other, I seemed to feel things unsaid.

"That was unfortunate," said Her Ladyship. "My husband's daughter, as you may have perceived, Miss Wicklow, is a very dear little person, but sometimes she commits foolish acts which in this desolate country might endanger her. So we give her our best care. Ah, but here is Mrs. O'Glaney now. Sara dear, will you be good enough to take our Miss Wicklow in hand. Something in the nature of a hot supper would be most welcome, I am sure."

I turned and put out my hand which was not received. Mrs. O'Glaney was a solidly built person with a square face and direct gaze. No fal-lals and furbelows for Sara O'Glaney, nor warmth for me until I had earned it. When my hand was ignored I tried a smile, but she did not yield.

Lady Maeve chided her in a way that I wished had not been done.

"Come, Sara, be friends. Miss Wicklow, though very young for the post, is a most accomplished person. And it would be politic of you to go warily with her, since you will henceforth take your orders from her."

"Oh, will I so?" said Sara O'Glaney with a martial light in her blue-gray eyes. I recognized the spirit, as I sympathized with her manner, but I felt that she was not a woman who would accept sniveling attempts to ingratiate oneself with her. I wondered an instant if she had written the two forged letters. It seemed extraordinary that Lady Maeve should dismiss such a thing so lightly. It was almost as though she knew who to blame.

"If we may be excused," I said to Lady Maeve and when she nodded, accepting our curtseys and dismissing us, I walked out firmly with Mrs. O'Glaney, but was not able to escape before I heard the unexpectedly cool, flat comment by Her Ladyship: "Not quite what we expected, eh, Jono?"

"What, love? Were you out to have another gangling Mrs. Fergus then?"

"I see you find her attractive," said Lady Maeve dryly.

My cheeks burned with this discussion of me, and to hide it I quickly spoke to the cook as we made our way back down the passage in the cold half-dark. "I wonder if you knew my mother. She was in service here before she married Padraic Wicklow, my father."

"Well now," said Mrs. O'Glaney, pushing open a door which gave onto a downward thrust of stone steps. "That I do, and more. So you're Katie O'Fierna's wee one. You've shot up a mite, so you have. She was a good one, a stout worker, for all her pretty figure. Never one to be above herself, neither."

"And I am Katie's daughter," I said again, hoping she would understand without more explanation.

She nodded, picking up a lighted candle from the freezing stone floor at the head of the narrowest, most villainous twisting flight of steps I ever encountered. At first glance I felt that they must lead downward to the devil's quarters. But even the devil could not live down there with such a racketing noise as that pounding sea. I might have expected the servants' stairs to be so; for I remembered the steep, ancient steps I had already mounted leading up to the family's quarters.

"Let us hope you'll suit," Mrs. O'Glaney said stiffly. I asked no more than that, and wondered if our conversation had wiped out the memory of Lady Maeve's ill-advised words to her.

We descended carefully, circling round and round in a way to make one dizzy before we came hard up against a door at the foot of the steps. Mrs. O'Glaney pushed it open with one sturdy elbow and forearm. I found myself in a kind of military guardroom which appeared to occupy the same dimensions as the terrace that served as its roof. This big, hollow, windswept guardroom, open to the night air at the south end, extended to the wall of the escarpment which separated us from the thunder of the Atlantic, and we were, in fact, at sea level. Not a pretty prospect in a high tide; for I could make out the scummed and stagnant ocean water which had seeped in all along the base of the guardroom's westerly wall.

I began to understand my unusually quick acceptance by the Conors. My qualifications were probably less important than the unpopularity of the Conor House servants' quarters. Living down there in what should be the cellars of an English mansion would take a bit of doing.

As we turned our backs to the guardroom and the earth-shaking sea beyond, I discovered that the quarters under the main portion of the house itself were a maze of box-like rooms opening off a tiny corridor that emptied into the guardroom beside the staircase door.

"Me and O'Glaney has the sitting room there off the left hand of you." said the cook. "And the bedchamber beyond."

"And these other doors? Are they pantries and closets?" I asked, noting the dour cubicles that faced on the corridor.

The woman made a scornful motion which accorded well with her faint, derisive smile.

"That, no. They're what ye might be callin' "let by the fortnight," to our parlormaids and pantrymen, and the footman and ladies' maids what we had formerly when things was in a better way, afore Mister Aengus's accident. The maids and the lot was forever coming and going, so that it's no use nor even taking down their names. The dainty lasses and lads don't take to Conor House for long, even in the good times. Too drear by half for the little darlin's. It's the goings on in Dublin Town and the like that they'll be praying for."

"You yourself have been here for long, ma'am?"

She noted the "ma'am" and was pleased. "None longer. Not even O'Glaney, him that come to Conor House forty years gone, for to cut peat in Ballyglen Bog. But myself now, I come into the world not an arm's length from where you stand, miss." At the end of the little passage, with the wind whistling behind us every step of the way, Mrs. O'Glaney pushed open a door. I was relieved to see that the mite of a room contained a window facing east, which was pleasantly curtained now and shut out the view. There was a comfortable deep chair, a rough deal table covered in the same pretty green material as the curtains, and a cupboard very like a French armoire, for my possessions which had been set on the old drugget carpeting to await me. There was also, I was pleased to observe, a little fireplace with a low peat fire glowing, and a kettle steaming on a hook over the fire; so the hot tea that I was craving would be no problem. This little sitting room had a door ajar, which opened into my bedchamber behind it, a room even tinier, but blessed with two windows, one facing east and the other facing the south, both curtained in green homespun material that would have done nicely for a summer frock. A clothespress and a narrow bed with a green-trimmed white tester overhead but no curtains at the side, nearly completed the furnishings, save for a candlestand by the bed, and a little prayer stand across the room. Even the roaring sea was muffled here, and except for the seepage and dampness of the walls, I thought I might be content in these quarters. If I missed the presence of my husband, I must become used to that.

Nevertheless, I astonished myself by the sudden recollection of Lady Maeve's last remark about me after she had supposed the corridor door closed behind us. It is shocking what the experience of love will do to a person! Before I met my husband I did not give thought to such matters from one day's end to the next. But now that I had lost him, even a small and indirect compliment seemed to me something to be cherished. In order to change the direction of my thoughts, I stepped over to the south window and drew aside the curtains by an inch or two. The view that met my eyes was astonishing.

"What is that beneath the window, Mrs. O'Glaney? A great pile of rubble—rocks overturned, sand everywhere . . . At high tide the sea must pour over it nearly to this window."

"So it was, ma'am," said the cook phlegmatically. "After the Frenchies come. Two years ago, it was. Some Frenchies was to join us in the West of Ireland for the grand war upon England. But it come to nothing. There was cannonading right on Kelper Head when the Redbellies fought 'em off."

"But why had nothing been done to clear away the rubble? The cannonading, or whatever, has even cracked off bits of the escarpment."

"That's as may be," she said, bustling around as though very busy indeed. "There was high plans for the clearing of it. But then the Master was took bad, and all was set at an end." She paused, looked at me in a sidelong way, not like the broad-faced, honest woman I had encountered until now. "They're good husbandmen, be the Conors. They've the care of this country to heart. But 'tis said they've no money now, what with Mister Aengus's accident, and that. Still and all," she looked upward as though through the ceiling to the Conors above us. "They'd the—what's called income—of Miss Maury and Master Theo that come from their mother, the first Mrs. Conor. The first mistress was very well breeched. But the story is, Master Theo went and spent his on high bobbery in Dublin Town and such like."

"Do you mean," I asked, startled, "that the first Mrs. Conor left her money, or even the income of her fortune, to Miss Maureen? The young lady seems hardly capable of the conduct of great sums." Then I wished that I had not said this; for it was no concern of mine, but the story of poverty at Conor House seemed curiously false in certain details.

"Well, miss, the income . . . that be the money what is paid by the muckers in great banks for the use of Miss Maureen's fortune. The income was to be paid to Miss Maury's husband for the care of her, upon the young lady's finding a suitable gentleman. But as ye may see, upon Miss Maury's wedding with Dr. Jono, which the Master did not think suitable, no income was paid out to them. A bad business was made of it all around; for there be hard feelings in that quarter, mark me!"

Where was this money, this income, I thought. If Mr. Conor still receives it, why was it not, at the last, used to improve the house, remove the rubble on the headland, and the rest. I remembered the damp, dark passages, the unhealthy atmosphere of so much of the house, all except the rooms Lady Maeve had assigned to herself. I thought I knew then, where the money went and continued to go.

"Did Lady Maeve bring no money to the family?" I asked.

"Contrarily, miss. The Earl, her father, died with his pockets to let, and when she wed Mr. Aengus, three years gone, there was a settlement made on her, so she could pay the Earl's debts. Or so 'tis said." This last was added in a tone I could not mistake, one of incredulity, typical of the way in which so many servants implied their disbelief in something by the master.

"A settlement taken from Mister Aengus's children," I murmured.

She shrugged but looked wise. "Ivy Kellinch, that's the long-nosed, sharp-eyed baggage what sees to Miss Maureen's wants, she says Mister Aengus settled a part of his own fortune on Lady Maeve, nor ever touched his children's estate. But Ivy's bound for to see Her Ladyship's side of it."

"If Miss Maury had not married, her income would remain in her father's hands?" I asked." And I almost added, *Then where is it now?*

"That's the way of it. And on Mr. Aengus's death, her brother, Master Theo, would be set to guarding her, and her fortune," finished the cook, triumphantly, as though she herself had worked out this intricate needlework.

"Good God!" I said. "Is it possible her spendthrift brother can be called a better manager of her affairs than Dr. Trumble?"

The cook sniffed. "You do be forgetting, ma'am. Dr. Jono was the son of a mere land agent, and that a wicked creature from York or some such heathen place in England. Lady Maeve's papa, the Earl, paid wages to the wretched heathen, and when he come to get himself killed collecting the rents in a famine time, the Earl took up the boy, our Dr. Jono, and sent him off to the Sisters to have his letters and numbers. Later, he saw to the lad's teaching for to be a surgeon. The Earl was like that, forever doing a good turn. But I swear he never thought to see his miserable land agent's son marry into the Conor family."

I could not help saying, "Dr. Trumble seems very skillful. Certainly he knows how to care for Miss Maureen."

"Well then. But who would not? The dear soul. And to waste herself on a common orphan that owed the very breeches on his bottom to the charity of Her Ladyship's father. . . ."

I looked out again and watched the stealthy creep of the fog toward me.

"Is there nothing that can be done to remove even a small portion of that rubble?"

She said briskly, "We had the hire of some peat-cutters and bogmen, and a kelper or two. But Mr. Aengus got himself hurt. The doctor talks of it now and again, and I've seen him out throwing bits of rubbish here and there, but cormorants and gulls nest on the rubble betimes, and Miss Maury is taken with birds. She's a great fancy to all flying creatures. I'll be saying one thing for Dr. Jono: He do pay the feeding of his wife and himself in this house, even when it's hard come by. The folks hereabouts that he treats being poor and not always paying their debts."

I thought of the Trumble and Conor problems while I stared out the window, and thought how odd that Dr. Jonathan should be reared by Lady Maeve's father, and yet he should be so resented by the Conors, and presumably by Lady Maeve as well. Snobbery was a strange illness, indeed! Mrs. O'Glaney came over behind me and looked out around my shoulder.

"Will you be seeing that now! How the kelp shines in the fog! Never saw the like, I do swear!"

I looked out again. It was true. High tides had left the seaweed and shore vegetation trailing over the ruins, and there just at the side of my window a long rope of kelp hung down the rocks, its loathesome jelly mass gleaming in the peculiar white light of the fog. I closed the curtain quickly, almost in the cook's face. She did not take offense.

"Ay," she said with a grim smile. "Ye're human, after all."

I followed Mrs. O'Glaney into the little sitting room where she prepared strong tea, took off the coals a pannikan of sweet spiced cakes, pleasantly scorched around the edges, and inquired whether I took sugar. I replied in the negative, with cool politeness.

The tea was dark, as I liked it, and with a faint flavor of peat, so that it brought to memory the scent of tea in my parents' small white-washed coteen, and for the first time since the news of my husband's death was brought to me, I felt the prick of tears behind my lids. I looked down into the fire quickly, willing myself to banish the pain of old memories. Mrs. O'Glaney's matter-of-fact manner went far to help me.

"Someone is coming down to the quarters, I think. Will you see them, miss?"

My ears, generally sharp enough, were not yet so attuned to the roar of the surf that I could hear lesser sounds, and I looked up with a trifle uneasiness, wondering aloud if this might be the master of the house, Mr. Aengus Conor himself.

"Faith, that would be a miracle indeed, miss. The master does not walk about. Haven't ye been told? He lies abed. An invalid, so he is. More work for us, but then, it's the will of God."

We waited. It was only now that I could hear the faint shuffle of footsteps on the cold stone outside my sitting room door, and then the door was pushed open and it was only my poor little friend, Miss Maureen, in bed slippers below her day dress, smiling her eager, childish smile, and sniffing the air as she joined us.

"Ah! It is perfume, the smell of good Irish-brewed tea. Let me have some, Sara, do! There's a fair good one you are." I saw that in spite of her education, Miss Maureen was teasing the cook with a thick brogue. But Mrs. O'Glaney took no offense.

"Now, Miss Maury, you're not dressed proper for coming down here, and well you know it. Do you want to be laid on your bed all the day, like your dear father?" As she scolded, she bustled around fetching a teacup for the young lady. I always thought of Miss Maureen as young, though I later learned she was several years my senior. She dropped down beside the miniature hearth in a graceful heap of silk skirts and petticoats, and stared up at me in my chair, as though I were her teacher or her mother.

"I'm glad you are here. Truly, I am; for when I am down here they do not like to fetch me, and so I can do as I like. Up there it's eyes forever watching me, everywhere, from every cupboard, from the pantry closet and every door that's ajar. And she's the worst of them."

I did not pry into this. Whether Miss Maureen was put upon, as she indicated, or whether it was all a parcel with her mental state, I could not guess at this early date. She was charming and as friendly as a puppy. Yet being in her company was a strain. One never knew when she would go off into some jumbled dark world of her own, leaving one hanging on her words as on a cliff's edge.

The cook did not share my uneasiness. That was evident.

"Well then, Miss Maury, there's none wishes you harm, nor spies on you. It is wicked to talk so. You will have Miss Wicklow to be taking herself off like Mrs. Fergus."

"Bother Mrs. Fergus!" This set her off seeking another scattered thought. "Isn't it strange, O'Glaney, that we never truly saw her drunk? Only the bottles and things."

What might she be meaning by that? I said, "But did she not drink?"

The cook said severely, "Someone wanted her gone,

and she is gone. The O'Glaney and I have our thoughts on it."

"Oh, Sara, tell. Do tell!"

Mrs. O'Glaney, plainly flattered by this plea, scolded her favorite, but I thought, with tongue in cheek.

"Miss Maury, don't you be talking of it. It's not for your innocence." _

"Yet—" I ventured.

There was no stopping her. She knew she had the interest of her audience. She leaned nearer to us and spoke softly so that we heard the wind howling out-of-doors as she said, "Mrs. Fergus saw things 'tis best not to see. And so the bottles were put about, and the poor woman went off with a flea in her ear and a "bad character," beside."

I began to see certain hitherto concealed perils in my position. I had best not be spying upon my betters, asking questions on their finances and the like. During these few moments Maureen sat there sipping tea and smiling, and perhaps speculating, as I was, upon what secrets Mrs. Fergus could have discovered. We did not talk then for a short space. The thunder of the waves against the escarpment echoed through the walls at intervals. I looked around, aware that no matter how high the little fire in my grate, the walls dripped incessantly from the wetness of the foundations, and I felt sure that not even the excellence of their Irish whisky was worth this eternal damp. I studied the opposite wall, wondering if the dark shadow I saw crawling down the stones was an insect of some kind. Then, studying it more carefully, I made out the soft, deep emerald green of moss in spreading patches down the wall.

"I must visit you often, Wicklow," said Maureen presently. "If I want to hide from them and their scoldings I shall come here. . . . And be scolded properly by my own dear Sara."

"Out upon you, girl!" The cook roughly disclaimed any softness, but her cheeks had a warm pink glow of pleasure.

"And for you to tell us tales of mystery," Maureen added, and then turned swiftly to me. "Why are you called Wicklow? Jonathan says you were married to a Frenchie."

"My husband was a Bonapartist. He was—" It was hard to think it now, and harder to say, so I said it flatly, boldly,

as though out of long custom. "He was killed in the attempt
to return the Emperor's son from Vienna to Paris. My
married name is on the roll of those proscribed in France."

"Proscribed? But that means—why, how savage! They
could have you executed, Wicklow."

"But only in France, miss, isn't it so?" the cook asked
with some curiosity.

"Very true. I am quite safe in England, I believe. But
as you know," I reminded her, "in Ireland there are those
who might want to oblige the French, if only to disoblige
the English."

Before I had finished speaking I saw that both women
were listening to something else, and no longer atten-
tive to my explanation. They exchanged glances and their
mood darkened. In the sudden fall of silence I too heard a
female voice in the distance, dimmed by the masonry of the
enclosed stone staircase, yet forceful and hard in its enuncia-
tion.

"Mrs. Trumble! I know you are down there. Don't make
me fetch you. Mrs. Trumble. . . ! Very well. Pleasure first.
And then punishment. You know what to expect."

It seemed to me an incredible outburst against the only
daughter of Conor House, but neither Miss Maureen nor
the cook appeared in the least surprised. The young lady
lowered her head. Absently, her fingers groped over the
hearth until they fastened on the fire tongs almost as if
they did so of their own volition. The pale fingers raised
the blackened, well-used tongs and shoved them repeatedly
into the coals while her face kept its absent, haunting smile.
The whole gesture was vaguely reminiscent of something
troubling. While I tried to recall the memory, I asked Mrs.
O'Glaney, "Who called just now?"

"That'll be Nurse Kellinch, miss."

The cook sniffed and said abruptly, "She takes her orders, that one. Same as all of us. The punishment is no
sugar buns."

Maureen appeared to be listening again. Then she looked up.

"That's the sea rushing at Kelper Head. How it smashes
against us! And all that's resting here! Poor Father!"

I looked at Mrs. O'Glaney who shrugged, but I saw her
eyeing Maureen in a puzzled way. We both watched the

young lady who seemed oblivious to us. After a moment I realized what Maureen's swift, ruthless gestures with the fire tongs brought to my mind, and I wondered if Mrs. O'Glaney thought, as I did, how very like they were to the short jabs of a dagger into quivering flesh.

III

GRADUALLY, I began to suspect that my two guests did not intend to leave my little sitting room until I entered the family fray on the side of Miss Maureen, but I did not like to become a partisan quite so early. Miss Maureen kept stirring up the fire and Mrs. O'Glaney poured more tea and passed around her delicious spice cakes.

"I wonder now," said the cook at last, "if My Lady might be waiting for to give the morrow's orders to you, miss. Not but what it's no place of mine to be making suggestions, I'm sure. Her Ladyship set that to rights straightaway."

Catching the echo of a very understandable pride in her, I assured her calmly, without making a great show of my friendship, "I am sure, Mrs. O'Glaney, that between us we shall make a satisfactory thing of it; don't you agree?"

Her heavy, worn features lightened a trifle.

"That's as may be," she said with a prim pursing of her lips, and then added, as though dropping an extra raisin in the cake, "If you're anything of your sainted mother, miss, we'll jog along very well, I'm thinking."

Maureen Trumble spoke suddenly, "If you are for Maeve, I believe I shall go along—to show the way."

I was sure now that she had been passing the time here for this very purpose, to be sure she returned to the family quarters accompanied by a friend. The thought that she must stoop to such strategems was a moving one to me. I determined on the instant to stand between her and Nurse Kellinch, who must be an old hedgehog, from the sound of her.

"I should be happy of your company, ma'am."

As I went into the tiny bedchamber and took up my everyday shawl, Miss Maureen and the cook spoke rapidly to each other, in low tones. I confess to a strong curiosity about that conversation. But outside, in the rubble under my win-

39

dow, the thunderous roar at the base of Conor House drowned out all other sounds. When I returned to the sitting room the two women were silent, staring rather self-consciously into the fire.

I went to the door, dreading the drafty dampness that would meet me as I stepped out into the stone passage, but as I was about to go, I saw that Miss Maureen still knelt by the fire, absently sipping the dregs of her tea.

"Ma'am?" I hinted, making a sound with the iron bolt on the door. The cook gave me some aid, passing a hooded candle to me, the while she said to Mrs. Trumble, "You'll be safe going along of Miss here. Go now. There's a dear you are, Miss Maury."

I held out my free hand and the young woman took it as a child takes the hand of a games mistress, and we stepped into the blowing darkness of the passage. It was only by great maneuvering that I was able to keep the candle from blowing out, despite its metal hood. Underfoot the salty rime scrunched and crackled, seeming louder than when I had come through here before, probably because at that time I had been deafened by the waves beating against the front wall of the guardroom.

We found our way easily enough to the stone-enclosed staircase, and started up. I had the singularly unpleasant notion that Nurse Kellinch might be waiting for us in these narrow confines, perhaps around the next turn, or the next. She was rapidly developing into a ghoul, who put poor Miss Maureen and the strong-minded cook into a freezing terror. But whatever her ghoulish qualities, Nurse Kellinch was not waiting for us in such uncomfortable confines. We came out into the hall of the family quarters, found that a door onto the little balcony had been shut, so that the hall was not quite so windswept as the servants' quarters.

"I wonder," I said aloud, not expecting much in the way of sense from my companion. "Would Lady Maeve await me in the morning room, or elsewhere? One of the parlors, perhaps?"

Miss Maureen smiled.

"Not that parlor. I told you. She never goes in the Kelper Room."

My curiosity got the better of my training.

"Whyever not?"

"But, silly, that's where Father got hurt, and bled and bled . . . all over the pretty carpet."

This was startling enough, even in view of the other odd happenings in the household.

"I knew he was an invalid, but I supposed it was for some chronic cause."

"Oh no," she said airily. "He was right as a trivet before the Kelper got im."

It sounded to me like some sort of dispute between the gentry and the local peasants, which had grown into a fantasy about Kelpers and the like.

"Now, Miss Maureen, I do believe it must have been some human agency, not a phantom at all."

She was leading the way to the morning room, but turned and frowned crossly at me.

"It was not what you think. Nor what they think. No. It was not. And only I saw it." Swift as a summer shower, her face clouded from the querulous, cross look to a sharpening of the features, the lines drawn, older. I recognized this change as the mirror of similar moments in my own life—for it was fear. "You see, Wicklow, I was the only one who saw it. But some day they will say I did it and am mad, and they will hang me at the crossroads gibbet or put me to Bedlam Asylum, which is a horrid place."

I dismissed this ghastly fear as a figment of her brain, along with the Kelper business.

"What did you see, precisely?"

She looked at me, over her shoulder.

"I saw a kelper. He came through the terrace behind Father, all dripping and slimy with nasty kelp, and afterward, the water dripped on the carpet and ran into the blood."

"Yes, but who—?"

She put her finger to her lips and then pushed open the door of the morning room. A sharp burst of cold air struck me, which was surprising because I remembered how cozy it had been an hour or two before. Then I saw what had caused this draft. The long window facing on the terrace stood open. It was a door, after all. There was no one in the room but Miss Maureen and me; yet it was clear someone had only just left it; for the lamp was burning on the white and gold desk, and the glowing lights of the wall sconce made long flickering tongues as their flames swayed in the draft. Instinctively, I crossed the room to close the door and in doing so, saw two figures standing far out on the terrace, their garments flying and snapping around them, loud as a whip's crack. I knew one of the two. It was Lady Maeve Conor; for I recognized the coppery hair. The other, somewhat obscured beyond her, was a man. I could make out nothing more about him, except that he and Lady Maeve were talking or arguing. I felt it wiser to leave the door as I had found it, and stepped back into the room, but as I did so, the two on the terrace moved, and the dark silhouette of the male figure stood facing me. In that instant I must have been plainly seen, outlined as I was against the candlelight from the morning room. It was an awkward moment, but I could not stop myself. I took another step backward into the room without looking behind me, until I was out of view of Lady Maeve's companion. As I turned around I asked, "Who is that man?"

But when I faced the morning room I found myself alone. Miss Maureen was nowhere in sight. It was annoying. I felt much as I might have in playing a game with a too-frisky pup, who ran and hid and expected me to chase him, just once too often. I remained where I was, standing respectfully before the desk, my arms folded, my gaze fixed upon the ornate inkstand. But the hairs on my neck crawled a little; for I half expected Maureen to come playfully up behind me, just to see me jump.

She did not do so, however, and I was forced to wait in my submissive position for some minutes before Lady Maeve came in through the terrace door busily putting up her windblown hair. She saw me at once, but even her poise was not proof against the movement of surprise, and the quick glance she gave behind her as she closed the door. Evidently her companion had not mentioned to her that he saw me eavesdropping. I was relieved, but at the same time puzzled. Why had he not told her?

Lady Maeve sat down at the desk, looking at me pleasantly as she threw back a man's greatcoat.

"How good of you to come, Anne! I had forgotten that we were to speak about household matters this evening. I hope you will allow me to call you Anne. What do you think of Conor House?"

The abruptness of the question took me aback.

"It is very large," I said.

The leanness of my answer must have been unexpected, or perhaps my expressionless tone. If I told her what I really thought of Conor House, my answer would have been comprehensive enough to occupy us several minutes.

She lowered her green-eyed gaze to the desk and played with a gold-plated letter opener.

"That is all you have to say of a mansion, a fortress, that has stood since time out of mind?"

"It is all that concerns the housekeeper of Conor House."

She smiled faintly. "Just so. Admirably put. You are everything that Miss Nutting promised, and above all, you are discreet. We were not always so fortunate with the persons employed here. Mrs. O'Glaney, for instance, feels very strongly on matters that in no way concern her."

So! I thought. You are warning me against a sympathy for your stepdaughter. I am to remain neutral. We shall see.

"You will take the day's orders directly from me, as you know, Anne. And I must say, I like your quick understanding of this. In the general way, I think we may establish a rule that you will speak with me in this room every evening before ten o'clock. You will have determined previously, each night, what foodstuffs Mrs. O'Glaney is prepared to serve, and what the conditions are in the household. We are planning to refurbish the upper floors of the house, particularly at the south end where some of the little rooms may do very well for the servants. It seems they object to their present quarters."

"Faith! Is that the truth now?" I exclaimed innocently.

Again I had the strong suspicion that she was testing me, and I flattered myself that I passed inspection. She would not drag any opinions out of me until I was more mistress of the situation.

Her eyes searched my face carefully. I saw that although her eyes were beautiful, they were by no means gentle, and they saw a great deal.

"Aengus, my husband, is an invalid, confined to his room. The rest of the family takes its meals in the small breakfast parlor two doors from this room. You will find we have a unique system invented by my stepson, that allows the food to arrive reasonably warm from the kitchen which is in a corner of the guardroom directly below. You must go and examine this arrangement when we are done here."

"May I know how many are to be served?"

"Only four, in general. My husband has his special diet, since he has no exercise and requires little food. You will find the doctor, my stepdaughter, Ivy Kellinch and myself to be your chief concern."

I was surprised that Nurse Kellinch took her meals with the family. But it seemed to me that one other had been omitted, and I reviewed them in my mind.

"You did not mention your stepson."

"Dear me. Did I forget poor Theo?" She rustled some papers together on the desk, and ripped the seal of an unopened letter. The silence in the room made the breaking waves beyond the terrace sound the louder by contrast. Presently, she tossed the letter aside with an impatient movement and looked up at me. She seemed surprised to see me standing there.

"Well, Anne?"

"Ma'am—Mr. Theo Conor. Does he dine with you?"

She frowned. "On occasion. We do not count upon him in the general way. He and his father quarreled a year ago, before Maureen's marriage. In fact, at the time of Aengus's accident. Theo spends most of his time embarrassing the family name. His latest venture is the collecting and sale of wreckage washed ashore, and now and again a few pence on the sale of kelp, for use in the fields, you know. You will find him wandering the coast, living squalidly in the village. Though he sometimes sleeps in his chamber on the floor above."

A Wrecker? I asked myself uneasily.

"Which rooms would Your Ladyship like renovated?"

She shrugged.

"You will have the cleaning of all our apartments in your charge, except those of my husband. The slightest untoward sounds set his nerves atremble, so I find it more merciful to take his room in my own care. Mrs. O'Glaney will help you in these little decisions. How do you go on with her?"

"Very well, ma'am."

THE BECKONING

She studied her letter opener.

"Excellent. And so it will be, for you are aware, as Sara does not seem to be, that Mr. Aengus Conor has delegated to me the powers of Conor House, and one expects to be obeyed."

"Quite so, ma'am." I dropped a brief curtsey and left the room almost before she dismissed me. I felt more and more uneasy, even hostile, in her presence.

Before returning to my quarters, I remembered Lady Maeve's words about Master Theo's invention connecting the breakfast parlor to the kitchen on the floor below. I went along the passage, holding my candlestick fairly close, so no draft would blow it out, and opened the second door. The room was barely relieved from a thick and cloying dark by the coals still smouldering in the fireplace. It was not an unattractive room and, like the others on this side of the house, it opened on the terrace which was hidden behind heavy layers of scarlet portieres. The furnishings were old-fashioned and heavy of the Jacobean period. The table and chairs and sideboard were shockingly coated with dust, and I resolved that my first duty in the morning would be the thorough cleaning of this room. I found a door about half my height, let into the wall at a level with my waist. Upon opening it I saw nothing but black space and felt a surprising gush of warmth come up to meet me. I thrust the candle into the recess and by its illumination saw a deep stone well upon whose base, far below, rested a silver tray and some obviously unclean dishes. Small wonder that a housekeeper was needed here! Two lengths of chain and a kind of wheel apparently operated this affair. With my free hand I pulled on the chain and saw the base below, about twice the dimensions of the tray, start to rise, joggling the dirty dishes and causing a plaintive groan and creak of machinery. I released the chain and closed the door. I had heard of such arrangements before but was a little surprised that Miss Maureen's rascally brother, Theo, had the ingenuity to install this food shaft.

Out in the hall once more I realized I was not far from the "Kelper" room as Miss Maureen called the comfortable little parlor which had been my first view of the Conor House interior. Expecting it to be deserted, and curious about the "accident" which had befallen Aengus Conor there, I went into the room directly, and was startled to see it occupied by three persons. I recognized Jonathan Trumble who looked up from a chess board and gave me the first warm and welcoming smile since my arrival. His wife, kneeling before the fire, stared at the glowing coals. She gave me no heed. Nor was my attention caught by her at the moment; for the room's third occupant I had not seen before.

A woman sat opposite the doctor at the chess board, with her back to me, and she turned now, slowly, her slim, strong fingers tightening on the arms of her chair as she observed me.

Dr. Trumble arose and said to her, "Ivy, you'll be wanting to make the acquaintance of Miss Wicklow, our new housekeeper. Matters should be a deal more comfortable about Conor House."

Ivy Kellinch was as far from my picture of the harsh-voiced ghoul as I could have imagined; yet, I found myself wondering if the exterior of her was quite genuine? If so, where was the creature who had bellowed threats down the stairs at her charge, and inspired such fear and dislike both in Maureen and Mrs. O'Glaney? She was trim and blond, and very nearly beautiful. But the hardness was in her light eyes, in her sullen mouth, in her air of power and command, and most of all, in her obvious physical strength. Her wrists and hands, the way she carried herself, all suggested muscular power.

She apparently saved the courtesies of an introduction for those who were my social betters. I curtseyed, wishing I had not met this woman for the first time under conditions that put me clearly at fault.

"I beg pardon. Her Ladyship has been giving me my orders, and suggested I look at the breakfast parlor. I am afraid I—"

"Rubbish," said Jonathan Trumble abruptly. His manner, or lack of it, merely made me smile. "Your company's more wanted than your absence. I daresay my wife will agree. She finds chess boring. Shall we be asking Miss Anne to join us, love?"

The young woman looked up vaguely, first at him and then at me. It hurt me a trifle, or perhaps only annoyed me, when she said sulkily, "Oh, do go away. You are all so tiresome. Jono, I want to go to bed."

The doctor's face colored and it was plain to be seen that he kept from exploding into North Country wrath only by great effort. He turned from his wife to me. "The boot's on the other foot now. You'll do us the favor to pardon us, Miss Wicklow?"

Maureen repeated a little louder, "Take me to bed, Jono. I'm tired. All that wretched walking today. And not a bit of use." She glanced at Ivy Kellinch and I was surprised to see that there was no fear nor animosity in her regard, only a touching eagerness such as she had revealed to me upon occasion. "Ivy, won't you show Wicklow back to her quarters? My husband will care for me; won't you, Jono?"

For the briefest time doctor tried to catch my eye. I avoided him but it was a curious sensation, as though we shared an understanding. His apology and my acceptance were wordlessly understood. I started to leave without further hesitation but was not quick enough to prevent Nurse Kellinch from accompanying me down the corridor. Perhaps she wanted to be sure I really went.

"It is quite unnecessary," I told her frankly. "I know the way, and I think I may rely upon this candle."

She wasted no words nor courtesy. We were like two enemies in the zone of truce.

"No matter. It is simpler so. I can tell you the truth. It seems no one else will."

"The truth?" I repeated with an ironical edge to the words.

She opened the door to the winding stone staircase and watched me take the first careful steps.

"The parlor where you found us—it saw murder attempted."

I was pleased that I could say very coolly, "I know that."

"Oh, did you now? And did you know it is what they call an attempted parricide?"

That stopped me.

"And what'll that be?"

"Parricide. A young woman wishing to marry and when forbidden, attempts the murder of her father."

I began to see certain murky aspects emerging into the light.

"Mrs. Trumble—?"

"—stabbed Aengus Conor, and almost did for him entirely. A near thing it was. But she won her way and married Dr. Trumble. I bid you good night, Miss Wicklow."

IV

I WOULD have liked a confirmation or denial by Mrs. O'Glaney of the truth of the nurse's nasty gossip before I slept that night, but it was not to be. The cook had gone to her rooms, and the clammy passage outside my own little spartment was deserted. I felt that I owed it to my own courage to walk sedately down that ink-black passage, once I had conquered the enormous emptiness of the guardroom, but I confess it was good to be in the tiny sitting room assigned to me, to throw the bolt on the door, to take off my shawl and stand before the dying coals and the snapping of driftwood, which drove away the chill that clung to me from the dampness in the corridors of the great house.

I drew up the chair and took off my best black morocco walking slippers, and began to undress piecemeal before the fire. Remembering the bestial cold and the nearness of the sea, I laid on more peat, another branch or two of driftwood, and when I was satisfied that it would last the night, by judicious piling and arrangement, I hurried into my nightrobe, brushed my hair out for a good twenty minutes while thinking over the day's happenings, and then, leaving the door open between my two rooms, I went to bed. It was surprisingly comfortable. The sheets, while old and soft, seemed well aired, and the room was surprisingly free from drafts, though if I chose to, I found I might reach out one hand and touch the thick stone slabs on the wall.

The tide was going out, and once I had made my devotions, I snuggled down under the covers and was soon asleep. A fortnight of travel, snatches of sleep in jolting carriages, bad, ill-aired rooms in country lodgings, and the rest of the problems of crossing three countries, served me well now, for I did not open my eyes until deep in the night, but the aftermath of a disturbance shook me considerably more than its cause.

The occasion of the disturbance came sometime before dawn, when there was a heavy thud, followed by some choice Irish curses, in the passage outside my rooms. I sat up and listened, and presently heard the irritated but very competent voice of Mrs. O'Glaney.

"Come away, man. Will you raise the house then? A swallow of the Good Irish, indeed! Bedad, a cask-full! Young Miss won't be wanting your halloos 'til the daylight. Nor your jug of the Good Irish. And then to fall over your feet like the oaf you are! Come away now, indeed!"

I smiled and reflecting that all marriages had not been so happy as mine, I lay down again and closed my eyes.

Scarcely a moment later I heard the distinct sound of kelp or other weeds brushing against my window. Behind all the odd little sounds in a house to which I was unaccustomed, the soughing of the wind was present, and to this I laid the sounds made at my window. But it was passing strange that the sounds should be similar to those made by the prying open of my windows, the creak of shutters being forced. And I think one thing affected me more than all the rest. I began to feel, unmistakably, the icy, salt tang of fresh air upon my face.

I sat up rapidly, staring into the darkness toward the window. The fire in the sitting room blazed up fitfully and shot little gleams of light into my bedchamber. You may conceive my horror at the sight of a dark and slimy rope, slithering across the carpet toward my bed. Its back glistened in the single shaft of light of fire afforded me from the other room and I sprang out of bed on the opposite side and ran, or stumbled into the sitting room. I knew the candles must be about somewhere, but I could not remember where I had set them, so I snatched a smouldering brand of driftwood out of the fire and rushed back into my bedchamber with it, knowing full well, as I did so, that I was in grave danger of setting fire, not only to myself, but to the house. Yet it seemed to me that the smoking brand was my sole weapon against this crawling, slithering horrible thing that came from the window toward me.

The burning driftwood sputtered in the draft, and then I saw at my bare feet what I had mistaken for a serpent. It was, of course, the very thing I might have suspected, a long, sticky, prickling rope of kelp. I laughed at my own cowardice, my stupid imagination. Then I paused. How had this kelp entered my room? I knew perfectly well it had not been there earlier in the night, when I came to bed. I raised the brand, and the action made its smouldering embers catch the current of air which came, as I soon saw, from my partially opened windows. With the brand now flaming, I held it high and made out a sight that set my shivering, fearful body suddenly hot with indignation and fury. I have said before, that there was in me far more terror of the unnatural than of the crimes of quite human hands. And what I saw was a pair of gloved, human hands, pulling the window outward, toward the wretch himself. Obviously, he hoped to break into my bedchamber.

I made no doubt it was that insufferable O'Glaney, trying, after all, to approach me and offer me a glass of the Good Irish, as he had boasted to his wife.

"At your peril, man!" I shouted, pouring all my now stifled fears into that angry command. "I'll be toasting those hands of yours! How'll you like this? And this?" I swung the fiery stake at the hands, saw them snatched back, but not before I made out the red fringe of a kelp gatherer's cloak behind those gloves. I ran to the window with my torch, but the furious wind, beating in from the headland, blew out the flaring light by which I had seen this astonishing thing, and I could see nothing out on the headland but the faint glimmer of the crawling seaweed. I threw the stake out onto the headland, and brought in the window, slammed it shut. So much for O'Glaney and his precious offer of a drink of whisky!

I would certainly tell Sara O'Glaney on the morrow that she had best keep her hulking husband to herself.

When I laid myself down upon my bed, I was still shaking, though with rage, not with fear. Once I discovered the intruder was human, I was not only intensely relieved, but felt all the righteous indignation of anyone unnecessarily disturbed in his slumber.

I now found it exceedingly difficult to sleep. The tension of the last few minutes, the slight searing of my fingers where the burning brand had sputtered and flared, and most of all, the curious events of the day, kept me from closing my eyes. What an odd thing it had been, that letter to

Lady Maeve, signed with my name, and very nearly in my writing, and conversely, the letter to me, which was not written in Lady Maeve's hand either! The work of some servant, said Her Ladyship, or was it Dr. Trumble who had suggested it? Either way, it seemed obvious to me now that O'Glaney might be in it somewhere. But could he write?

Yet . . . why should he try to break into my room to offer me a drink, if he did not want me at Conor House? Or had he been merely trying to frighten me away, in a further effort begun by those two forged letters?

I closed my eyes and counted backward in French, as my husband had taught me when I was under tension. But it was no use. I kept seeing the kelper's red fringe, the black-gloved hands, the slimy kelp slithering across the floor toward me. I remembered O'Glaney's loud-voiced colloquy with his wife, in the corridor outside my sitting room. What a noisy fellow he was!

And then an ugly little thought began to nibble at my brain: How could O'Glaney have sped down the corridor and through the guardroom and out upon Kelper Head, in time to force my window, only a minute or two after he had spoken with his wife? Obviously, it was impossible. He could not be in two places at once. And if he had run madly through the halls in the dark in order to accomplish this curious effort, why had not Mrs. O'Glaney stopped him?

So noisy he was! He must have been heard had he attempted that mad dash. And then, curiously enough, at my window he had not uttered a sound. One would have expected him to make his drunken proposal that I share his jug. And when I thrust the burning driftwood at him, surely he would have exclaimed, or cursed, and made protests that he only wanted to offer me a sociable drink. But not a sound! Only that fast retreat, the eerie silence.

Had the creature at my window not been O'Glaney, after all?

I sat up again, shivering. I listened. The night wind roared through the ancient structure. It was impossible to hear anything outside my window, even if I fancied I did so.

I jumped out of bed again, set my bare foot immediately upon the horrid prickling kelp that trailed across the floor, and kicked it from me in a panic. My bare foot still felt its imprint, the slime-covered, salty feel of the seaweed, but I had more serious things to think of. I dragged a chair from the sitting room into my bedchamber and placed its great back against the window. Then I fumbled around until I found my bed candle, lighted it, and set it on the chair. I should not only see but hear anything that attempted to annoy me later in the night.

After that, and considerable palpitations that I recognized angrily as the remnants of my fear, I crawled back into bed, and eventually to an undisturbed sleep.

I woke much later than my habit, and removed the chair and pool of melted wax from beneath the window. I peered out and was refreshed at the sight of blue skies coming to light over the sea whose great, foaming waves sparkled now as the morning progressed and the sun shone upon the rocky headland of Conor House. Someone tapped on my outer door as I finished dressing, and when I threw back the latch I saw a young woman with an Irish bloom upon her small, round face, and the air of one who knew her worth with the gentlemen. She bobbed a curtsey to me and offered me a blackened silver tray with tea and welcome porridge. I took the tray, thanking her, and inquiring her name. She bobbed again, tossing ringlets of hair in a saucy way.

"Rosaleen, Miss. From the coteens, I am. Lady Maeve is after training me. A nice cosy castle outside Dublin Town, is my hope. And I'm fair eager to go to service for you, seeing as Master Theo says you're Ireland's own Dark Eva come to life."

I was completely bereft of my tongue at this bit of pretty speaking, which is not uncommon among those who wish to curry favor, and for a moment I felt inadequate to reply.

"Ay," said Rosaleen, "and more's the pity I cannot learn from Miss to be the very image of her. That's what Master Theo says of me when I spill his breakfast meat."

"But I do not know Master Theo Conor," I said quickly, trying not to be amused at the picture of breakfast calamity she presented.

She giggled as though I had said something excruciatingly funny, lighting up dimples in her face. Master Theo must be teasing her if he pretended to mislike such a pretty creature. I racked my brain, meanwhile, trying to imagine where he had seen me, or if the whole speech was merely spoken to make pretty Rosaleen jealous. I confess the words, though, heard in this absurd fashion, had an effect upon me like strong spirits. But I shocked myself immediately after by wondering what Dr. Jonathan thought of me, in comparison to the smooth compliments of a rascal, and perhaps a Wrecker, like Theo Conor.

Forbidden ground! Dr. Jonathan Trumble's feelings, his compliments and thoughts belonged to another, and that other a helpless creature who, anyone could see, adored her husband.

The matter of Theo Conor's easy tongue was not important, but rather, the fact that he knew me at all . . . if he did. Where had we met? Where had he seen me? Perhaps the whole thing was a bit of nonsense, and he'd never cast eyes upon me.

By the time I joined Mrs. O'Glaney in the ancient, smoke-blackened kitchen that smelled of peat and mutton and—surprisingly—of whisky, I was determined to forget both the light words of Theo Conor and the possible thoughts of Miss Maureen's husband.

"Well now, Miss," said the cook upon looking up from the firehooks and espying me. "And how would you be sleeping the night, then?" As was her habit, she looked severe, square-faced, with sweat beading her upper lip and a sooty streak across her brow. She was admirable in her indifference to the small amenities.

I spoke to her then of my night intruder.

"Mrs. O'Glaney, did your husband, by chance, wish to give me a drink of whisky last night at my window?"

She was astonished.

"Saints, now! What'll you be thinking of himself? 'Twas in the passage, and a wee bit under the influence he was, as you might say. But at your window, miss, no, thanks be! He is not a man for chasing after every skirt that may brush him by."

I ignored this for the more important aspect of the matter.

"But someone tried to get in. I saw his gloved hands, and the kelper's cloak he wore."

Mrs. O'Glaney's frown cleared. She slapped a pan with her cloth.

"Och, ay! 'Tis the hungry ones. Now and again, when it's thought the rooms are empty, there'll be a breaking in, and mayhap a bit of food stolen. It's all they have, sometimes, to keep the wee ones from starving flat out. But you'll not be troubled again. I'd lay my life to it.'Tis only a surprise the man had gloves. But maybe Her Ladyship gave some of the worn clothing away. She often does."

It was shocking, but not so shocking as it might have been, had I not seen something of this poverty as I crossed Ireland. My adoptive country across the Irish Sea had done none so well for my native land, since the Act of Union twenty years before. But the realization that there was a natural cause for those hands I had seen, and the forced window, gave me relief. The gloves had looked sturdy and expensive. Still, they might be a gift from Conor House. A pity the fellow tried to steal from his benefactress. But hunger knows no ethics.

"Perhaps we might help them in some way," I suggested.

" 'Tis not for us to say. Mr. Aengus was always one to care for the peasantry. Afore he was took with the accident, he was ever and always out upon the lands, seeing to the fields, the bogs, the tenantry. There's none in these parts can say the Conors have not done their share. And for proper wages, too, when all's said. But it's them others, the absent owners. Them as cavorts at Brighton and London and Carlton House when they'd ought to be doing their duty by their lands and people here at home!"

This sounded like a slap at the late Earl, Lady Maeve's father, but for all that, it was probably true. And she had opened a subject that interested me excessively.

"Nurse Kellinch told me a tale about Miss Maureen. Is it true that she tried to kill her father? Is this the cause of his invalid condition?"

Mrs. O'Glaney shook kettles and firehooks and made a furious rackety noise.

"I'd as lief believe the devil as Nurse Kellinch! Wicked one that she is, to be spreading such tales."

"But is it true?"

She ceased the noise and shrugged.

"Well then, who is to say? Miss Maury was the only

one that saw—whatever happened. And it was known all about the village that Miss Maury threatened her father when he forbade her marrying the doctor." She shook a spoon at me. "But that's not to say Nurse Kellinch is in the right of it. . . . Now is there aught else you'd be wanting to know, Miss?"

"Yes," I said. "How may I help you?"

Her pale eyebrows went up.

"So it's help you'll be giving! Faith! It was in my mind you'd be abovestairs, skittering with that she-devil, and eating off fine plate with your betters."

I smiled and took the carefully wrapped pan of smoking breakfast meats from her hands. It was almost a forceful taking. Obviously, she still did not believe my protestations.

"Which she-devil is in your mind, Mrs. O'Glaney?" I asked, and something in my face made her grin.

"There be more than one, and no mistake. But it's Miss Maureen's precious guardian I'm thinking of, that big-voiced witch, Ivy Kellinch." She reached for the kettle, then slapped it back as it scorched through her covering cloth. "I do believe you're not so blind at all, miss."

"Nor am I," I echoed her briskly, as we worked to get the food into its covered dishes and over on the floor of the food shaft. High above my head, in the breakfast parlor, a snub-nosed, freckled boy about fifteen peered down.

"Ye be at the ready now, ma'am?" he called to me in something between a hoarse whisper and a shout, that must have been audible to everyone on that floor.

"Pull up."

He did so. I never heard such caterwauling as the squeaks and squeals of the machinery that followed, but the family breakfast rose before my eyes, and passed above my head.

"I wonder now," said Mrs. O'Glaney, "will himself be eating a bit of breakfast? And will Her Ladyship be taking it to him? It's an odd one, is Mr. Aengus. As if he half made out we was trying to poison him. All his food prepared and served so careful-like."

I could not blame Mr. Aengus Conor for this. He had, after all, been the victim of an attempt on his life. And by his own daughter. Incredible thing for the sweet-faced Maureen to do.

I earnestly desired to know the straight of this crime and wondered if the cook would be in position to tell me more, but as we busied ourselves with the housework and she showed me around the stillroom, pantries and various storage quarters, the pretty young housemaid, Rosaleen, was often present, and I never quite found the moment to ask point-blank: "Did Miss Maureen stab her father in a quarrel over her desire to marry Dr. Trumble?"

By noontime, so busy were we that we had not ventured up to the family quarters, nor yet the disorganized rooms on the upper floor which Lady Maeve mentioned to me.

I paused late in the morning by the archway which led out of the guardroom onto the rocks and rubble beside Conor House. The air at the side of the building was still salty and sprayed by the pounding of the sea against the front ramparts of Conor House. Two currents met before the escarpment, and hence the boiling turmoil there. But the south bounds of the headland were quite different. Below the rubble and stretching out over the ocean, it was neither fearful nor tumultuous, just a gentle tilting of the rocky land shelf down into and under the sea. I stepped out over the slabs of broken rock and rotted wood, and trailing kelp, thinking with a certain pleasant sense of accomplishment, that I would be having this whole headland cleared in a short time. It would not cost overmuch, and a pair of good lads with sturdy shoulders would get it done without any difficulty from Her Ladyship.

"Very likely I could get that cleared away myself with some small aid from local lads," I said to Mrs. O'Glaney. "It is one of the first things that should be done. The clearing of the rubble and all this growth of seaweed. A wretched sight entirely."

She had a bundle of broomsticks in her hands and set up a great cloud of dust and beach sand as I finished speaking.

"Now, Miss, I'd not be moving too fast in those quarters. Dr. Jono had a notion the kelp and what-not was bad for the lungs, but though he tried to remove it, Miss Maury was forever complaining that he disturbed the gulls and such, and Her Ladyship says Miss Maury shall be humored. And who is to say no? Like Her Ladyship says, there be matters that take the—the precedence."

Perhaps she was right. I did not understand the delay and the efforts to keep Dr. Jonathan from upsetting Miss Maureen's precious birds but I supposed that, like most ladies of the manor, Aengus Conor's wife preferred the improvements made to the rooms in which she and the family were occupied, rather than out on the headland under the housekeeper's quarters. Still and all, it was a strange business.

"Your pardon . . . sir," said Mrs. O'Glaney behind me. I felt her move away from me, and looked around. Jonathan Trumble had come through the guardroom looking exceedingly natural in fisherman's garments, breeches rather than his gentlemanly English pantaloons, boots rather than the more modern shoes, and a heavy short jacket with a thick collar of some kind of dark fur. He smiled at me and while I was reflecting that his eyes, lively and green this morning, made one feel welcome, he explained his different appearance.

"There's talk of sighting a fisherman whose corragh was swamped nearest the headland two days gone. He may have clung to some wreckage, his lobster bales, belike. Not that there'll be much hope, but it's that or flat despair in the families. It's my guess he's long since gone to the bottom . . . . Miss Anne?"

"Yes, sir."

"My wife is resting. When she's about, would you tell her where I've gone?"

I curtseyed and assured him I would do so. He put out his hand, rather to my surprise, and took mine.

"I know I can count on you. Mrs. Trumble has times, as you've seen, more's the pity, when no one is her friend. It is part of her illness. And Nurse Kellinch makes herself disliked in this house. If I could know you would overlook Maureen's ways now and again. . . . She is but a child, you know. All smiles, then cross as two sticks. But she likes you, no matter how she went on last night."

His hand closed, hard as a lobsterman's clasp, upon mine, and I looked away from him to hide my self-consciousness, reflecting that this welcome handclasp should not be so welcome to me. Yet it was the first genuine affection for me since my husband's political murder, and so I excused what was inexcusable, the fact that Dr. Trumble's kindness moved me deeply, and said as calmly as may be, "Mrs. Trumble was my first friend at Ballyglen. She may count upon me at any hour. I pledge you that, sir."

The doctor studied me while I was torn between a strong desire to prolong this moment, and an even greater sense of my own iniquity. My opinion of myself was not raised by the sudden awareness that another person had' come upon the scene. The massive form of Mrs. O'Glaney's husband loomed behind me and the smell of whisky upon his person put an end to an impossible, yet exciting moment.

I realized suddenly that it was a fancied resemblance between Jonathan Trumble and my late husband which had produced in me an entirely unaccustomed warmth toward another woman's husband. I resolved to banish the sensation upon that instant.

"Good day to you, O'Glaney," said the doctor.

The lumbering fellow touched his forelock in a surly but respectful reply. The doctor then glanced at me again.

"Thank you, Miss Anne. I'll be counting on your . . . loyalty."

It was an innocuous word but made me flinch at the lie that O'Glaney must read into it, having seen my hand in that of the doctor. I was relieved after all, when the doctor left me. He walked out upon the rubble with his firm, forceful stride, seized a long, sticky strand of kelp that lay in his path, and broke it off impatiently, tossing it aside.

"Perhaps, sir," I called to him, "there'll be cleaning and the like to clear away that wreckage. Then Conor House would have a fine spot to sit and watch the sea, and sheltered too, by the house walls."

He frowned, raising the back of his hand to his eyes to shade them from the combined glare of sun and sea-fog.

"Sure, you'll have a time of it. I've tried. And I'll be that surprised if Maeve agrees."

He went down over the rocks as surefooted as the native fishermen. He was headed for the gray shingle that stretched southward into a protected cove. Presently, his figure was gone from my sight.

"Meddler, I'll be bound," said O'Glaney, surprisingly.

Mrs. O'Glaney called to him out of the dim recesses of the guardroom: "O'Glaney! None of that, man!"

She seemed to have extraordinary control over so large and overpowering a hulk as her husband; for he sniffed mightily, swiped his sleeve over his nose, and muttered, "Acts as how he is master of Conor House." He added with grim emphasis, "Not quite yet, I'm thinking. Not . . . quite . . . yet."

Mrs. O'Glaney plucked at my arm.

"It's for you to say, Miss, but if there be truth in what you were swearing to himself, you'll go and see to Miss Maureen before that Bog-face nurse comes at her today again."

"Yes, of course." I hurried through the guardroom and up the winding steps, anxious to show the cook that I had, indeed, meant what I promised Dr. Trumble. I met Rosaleen in the corridor which held the Kelper Room and the morning room, and inquired as to Mrs. Trumble's bedchamber. It proved to be across from Lady Maeve's morning room, and I knocked, surprised and a trifle anxious when Ivy Kellinch's voice responded hoarsely, "Well, then!"

I called out my name and she opened the door to me. She was alone in the room which had much the look of a man's den or bookroom with only a small dressing room opening off one side of the room suggesting Maureen's preferences. The chamber she shared with the onetime land agent's son seemed to be entirely his. It was what might be expected of a union between the masterful, perhaps selfish surgeon, and the adoring wife with her almost excessive affection and dependence centered in him.

"I had a message from Dr. Trumble for Miss Maureen," I explained. "Where may I find her?"

Nurse Kellinch went on picking up breakfast dishes from a breakfront secretary and placing them on a tray. She looked exceedingly efficient, her blond hair tightly knotted on the nape of her neck, and her gown high-collared, with a meager ruffle about the throat and wrists; yet her movements, exhibiting her highly curved form to its best advantage, suggested that Ivy Kellinch was not what she appeared to be at first glance. Her voice was brittle with scorn, and suggested to me that what it said, and what it concealed were not always ideally mated.

"Very likely, I'm sure. You'll find Mrs. Trumble in the Kelper Room. That is, if you really want her!"

I did not even trouble to thank her. Her malice was so palpable.

By daylight the cozy, scarlet curtained room which had seen an attempted murder appeared stuffy. The fire roaring on one side of the room at midday and the portieres drawn back so that the sun glinted on the dusty furnishings, made everything look dismal and drab. Maureen Trumble was not in the room. The door to the terrace swung back and forth and I went over and looked upon that wind-swept expanse. Out at the very edge of the terrace, staring down at the straight face of the escarpment beneath her, was the girl. Unlike her Lady Maeve, who appeared to dote on the wind streaming through her red hair, Maureen was tightly wrapped in a beautifully woven black shawl heavily fringed, which concealed her hair and most of her body. As I stepped out on the terrace I saw that she was not alone. Further along the top of the escarpment was Lady Maeve herself, with her back to Maureen. She was looking southward, leaning over the low wall which rose hardly above the hems of her skirts. I suspected she was interested in the progress of Dr. Trumble and the other men who must be combing the south coast below the headland for the lost fisherman. I made no effort to conceal the sound of my approach but the brisk wind and the roar of the waves beating up against the escarpment drowned all other sounds and I supposed it was this sense of solitude that made me move as I did. I went over to Lady Maeve before speaking to Maureen. Her Ladyship turned at my approach. She did not seem to observe her stepdaughter, even yet.

"Ah, Anne, how is the household running under your care?"

"Everyone has been most kind and helpful," I said, still with an eye upon Maureen who seemed to be extraordinarily secretive in her manner. "Dr. Trumble has gone to search the beaches in case one of the fishermen should have survived, as Your Ladyship probably knows."

"Of course. My father taught him to be ever the humanitarian," she said, not without malice. "But if the fisherman is dead, it will take more than Jono's influence to bring him ashore. I know these superstitious lads."

I did not understand this reference and soon forgot it in

the ensuing excitement; for I caught a movement from Maureen, just at the edge of my vision. She began to move toward us, slowly, sliding one foot at a time, with great stealth. It was this stealth, rather than anything in her childishly flushed face, that made me stiffen with intuition of danger. Even as I turned my head, aghast, the young woman reached out toward either Lady Maeve or me, I could not tell which, and put the flat of her hands toward us, gaining momentum, seeming about to push one of us.

Without thinking, I thrust Lady Maeve aside. It may have been my own furious rush, or my shout that was half-drowned by the wind, but in any case, Lady Maeve turned as her shoulders and mine were brushed by Maureen's suddenly curling fingers. I caught Maureen, stopping her from a now unimpeded plunge over the side of the escarpment. While I set Maureen firmly at arm's length after her narrow escape, Her Ladyship said calmly, "Take her inside, Anne. She has fretted for nothing. Jonathan has gone to do his duty like the humane lad that he is. Go in the house with Anne now, Maury, and brush yourself off. This terrace is full of sand and a lair for the gulls. You are filthy, child, and it is too chill out here for you."

Maureen clapped her hands. Her gay laugh lighted the pretty, young face. "Oh, I shan't mind. I love the gulls out here. It is the only thing I do love about the sea. I would not have come out if I had known the gulls were gone. And I do hate being alone out here."

I was speechless. She took my arm and obediently walked into the Kelper Room with me. I looked back once. Lady Maeve was staring after us, her eyes narrowed and speculative. As I glanced around, she smiled ever so faintly. Her red hair snapped and blew around her beautiful head like the flick of many whips.

"Her Ladyship is fond of the wind and spray, is she not?" I asked my companion, trying to arrive subtly at my point.

Miss Maureen leaned close to me, sharing a secret. "You fancied you saw her, too, didn't you?"

"She spoke to us," I reminded her.

"But she can do that. She can do anything. Make things disappear, like Father when he was hurt by the Kelper ghost, and like herself. You thought she was really out on the terrace today. But maybe it was only the shade of her."

"The shade!"

"Ay. There are times she stands there by the hour, watching . . . watching . . . I have thought she is beckoning to Them."

It was true that Lady Maeve had a strong affinity for the wind-swept terrace, as even I had noticed in my brief stay at Conor House.

"What do you think she is watching for?" I asked, half believing the young lady.

"But for Them, of course, the Kelp Gatherers that haunt these shores in the night and the fog." She paused as we came inside the stifling scarlet parlor. "She is one of Them, you know."

"Nonsense," I said before I thought. "You must not be talking like this about Her Ladyship."

Maureen smiled wisely. "Go and look. You will not see her. She is a phantom. A ghost, like the Kelpers. She does not really exist."

I would soon be correcting this illusion. I turned and with my eyes still on my charge, I pushed open the terrace door and motioned back to her.

"Come now, Miss Maureen. Look for yourself."

She came at my bidding and looked out. I was studying her face, and until I saw her simple, triumphant smile, I did not guess the truth. Then I looked out. She was right. Lady Maeve was not on the terrace.

"Don't you see?" asked Maureen. "It's not I who am addled. It's Them. A Kelper, one of her own kind, tried to kill Father. Right before my eyes it was. And I cried and cried but he wouldn't come alive. And then he came alive, but only because Maeve willed it to be so. . . .You see, Anne Wicklow, that woman is not human!"

V

I was beginning to wonder if poor simple-minded Maureen Conor Trumble was quite as simple-minded as others would have me believe. In point of fact, I no longer knew whom or what to trust. Even my old friend, Miss Nutting, had neglected to tell me some urgently necessary details.

I stepped out on the terrace and looked along its full length, getting badly blown by the wind in the bargain. The fog was beginning to roll in, mingling with the sunlight so that everything had the hazy obscurity of impure and dusty air. Either I had shared Miss Maureen's fantasy of Lady Maeve, or the mistress of Conor House had hurried in through one of the other rooms.

Maureen watched me, cat-and-mouse fashion. Even now I did not quite like to have my back exposed to her. I could not forget that when she made that grand push toward us this morning, she may have had me as her target, rather than her stepmother. It all added to the curious threats I had received so far, and totally without reason. The two forged letters, attempting to keep me from Conor House, the attempt to frighten me last night at my window, and now this attack—if it was an attack—by Maureen.

Maureen said, "You see? That is why I tried to touch her out there, when you screamed. I wanted to be sure she really existed."

This explanation of her homicidal movement seemed almost reasonable, and besides, I wanted to believe it.

"Well now, ma'am," I said. "I'm sure it's no matter, since she has gone about her business. I came to say that the doctor went down the beach to aid in the search for the fisherman. Or his body."

Her dark eyes got round and huge.

"His body!"

I was vexed at my clumsiness.

64

"I mean the body of one of those fishermen who were lost."

She had begun to shake, but at my words, she relaxed a trifle.

"I shall feel better if you take me down there, Wicklow. Away from this house and the wickedness in it."

I felt that it might do her good to get out in the freshening air of the seashore, and since she was warmly dressed, I agreed. As we went down the corridor, I remembered something, a small puzzling item that fitted into the general weirdness of Conor House.

"Why does not Lady Maeve come into the parlor we have just quitted?"

"Because Father was killed there, and she brought him to life again. And she said that she still sees the blood upon the carpet."

I shuddered and did not go on with this line of questioning. I could see that for Miss Maureen, her stepmother was both alive and dead. She spoke of Lady Maeve as one of the ghostly kelp gatherers, beckoning to her fellow ghosts from the terrace. But she also spoke of the lady as very much alive, a frightened woman who would not enter the scarlet parlor because of her horrid memories of it. This contradiction in Miss Maureen's head appeared to justify the family's belief in her mental sickness. But was the girl truly dangerous? Dangerous enough to need Ivy Kellinch as a guardian? If I could believe my eyes, out on the terrace a few minutes ago, she may have attempted murder. Or . . . was she, as she claimed, merely trying to prove the solid reality of Lady Maeve?

And what of Lady Maeve Conor herself? Even I did not feel quite my natural self in her presence. Was there something about her, some fancied quirk of character, or physical oddity that made her seem a little unreal, a ghost, in fact, who dwelt among the living?

What preposterous notions were these? I should be bound for Bedlam if such thoughts continued.

We went speedily down to the guardroom where I stopped in my own quarters for a wrap. Maureen watched me with great interest.

"I should like to be you, Anne Wicklow. To look like you

and to be as free as you, and to stand before Maeve and look her in the eye."

"It is easier for me," I said, smiling at her wistful eagerness. "I have done for myself most of my life."

"I should like to be you, and have Jonathan look at me as he looks at you."

I felt the red suffuse my face, and could not have chided my secret self more sternly if I had been Judas. Had I done anything amiss to provoke this terrible little confession of hers? To have done Maureen ill would be like striking a defenseless child. I resolved firmly to have as little to do with her husband as was possible in this strange household.

"Miss Maureen, you are not fair to yourself. Come—let me show you."

I stood her before the small oval mirror in my sitting room and let her see herself. She preened a bit in her little-girl way, studied her reflection, full face and profile, and smiled with satisfaction.

"I am pretty, aren't I, Anne?"

"It's a beauty you are entirely," I told her with perfect truth.

It was a wondrous thing to see her now so quickly at ease and playful again. We went out upon the overturned rocks, the stony chips and ruins where a portion of the cliff had been cannonaded, and she became excited.

"Where is he gone? Where is he?"

I pointed in the proper direction, down over the rubble of the cliff, and into the distant cove. We could see vague figures milling about on the foamy shingle. She started to run and I tried to stop her; for it seemed to me very easy to slip on the heavy growth of weeds and kelp that had been washed up around the westerly slopes of the headland. Maureen jerked her arm away from my detaining hand, and went on. Over her shoulder she cried to me, "You'd like to stop me; wouldn't you, Anne? But you shan't. You'll not keep us apart."

I let her go, feeling not so much chagrin as a sudden impatience, and self-justification. After all, I reasoned to myself, I had done nothing amiss. And truly, this woman was the outside of enough!

"You'll have it just as I do," said Ivy Kellinch's hard

voice as she came up from the south corner of the escarpment. She walked over the rubble with long strides, careless of her skirt hems, already showing waterstains and signs of the ocean spray.

"And what'll you mean by that?"

She laughed shortly. "Merely that I began as you have, with her all smiles, and soon, very soon, there were hints, then suspicions, then cries to heaven of how I persecuted her. She has the entire household by the thumb, let me tell you. Except for the doctor. Only he knows better."

"She is ill," I said, turning away and moving over the kelp to the edge of the cliff.

"Ill, is she! She is as near a murderess as makes no matter! But you'll learn . . . if she lets you live long enough, that is." And she went into the house.

The sun had now melted into the thick gobbets of fog, making the whole of it one dirty yellow curtain through which I peered at the angry sea and tried to calm myself. I welcomed the chill wet wind that beat against my cheeks, for it invigorated me and fought the depression that had me in its grip. From the ocean itself I looked back northward at the fury beneath the escarpment of Conor House, and then my eyes wandered along the coast beneath my present position. It was hardly wide enough to provide a beach, only a thin strand washed by the tide when it was in, and now damp and littered with the debris of the deadly currents. Long snakes of kelp quivered in each wave as more debris was washed up. One great mass of litter, more dark and solid than the rest, fascinated me, so like a body it was.

I stared at it, wondering what it could be. Perhaps some form of animal life common to the sea? I did not like what lay there in the shallows, swaying with each rising wave, never quite coming to rest on the little strand of shoreline. There was but one way to reassure myself. I made my way down the side of the cliff, holding my skirts with one hand to avoid the black and white spottings of many seabirds, while the other hand supported me down the face of the low abutment. In no time I was upon the shore, my shoes sinking into the wet sand and clearly marking my passage as I went over to the debris that had troubled me.

I could not reach it; for the waves shifted it back and

forth in ankle deep water, outlining it in foam. Unquestionably that sad bundle looked like a human form. I waded out, and reached down in a gingerly way, touching soggy cloth that tore in my fingers. What it revealed sickened me. I closed my eyes an instant, but was aroused by the shock of the next wave washing around my feet. The sodden cloth covered a human body, that of the lost fisherman, probably. One of the boots was gone, but there was no mistaking those garments common to the villagers that I had glimpsed this morning in the cove with Dr. Trumble. I steeled myself to look for the face, and saw what remained of rugged, hard features, partly gone. . . . For the rest, the hands bore the callus marks of the men who ventured out of these coasts in their small corraghs.

I swallowed rapidly several times, and while conquering my sickness and pity for the man, I wondered how I might get him ashore for burial. If I left him here, he might very well float out to sea and be gone forever, despite those who said all fishermen came home to their coasts in death.

I strengthened myself for the ordeal of dragging him a-shore, but the thought of taking a firm hold of the dead man was extremely repugnant to me.

Biting my lips to keep from trembling like a frightened child, I reached for the poor sodden mass, and in doing so, happened to look toward the south end of Conor House. The dirty yellow fog enshrouded the house itself, and made everything dim and hazy. I felt a shock of fear. A kelp gatherer was standing on the terrace in the great flying red cloak of that odd profession, the cloak fringe bobbing like skeletal fingers in the early afternoon wind. I could not make out the head because of the kelper's billed and peaked hat pulled forward over the eyes. In my panic I dropped the sleeve of the unfortunate fisherman and involuntarily stumbled backward, into the deeper water. The undertow around my feet almost overturned me.

I did not have quite the nerve to beckon to my phantom on the terrace, but instead tried to drag the fisherman's body toward shore, much handicapped by the rising tide. When I had taken several laborious steps, dragging not only the dead man but my waterladen skirts as well, I glanced up at the terrace. I did not know whether to be glad or sorry to see it empty once more. The body had become wedged by some debris left from the bombardment of the headland, and I was still working to untangle the clothing from a rocky snag when I heard a whistle behind me on the shore and looked around without letting go my burden. It was my phantom kelper in his flying red cloak, not so very phantom after all, if I could judge by the agile speed of his long legs as he strode over my footprints on the sand, and splashed through the water toward me.

The insufferable creature was grinning, a big, young, toothy, handsome grin; for I could see now at close range that he was one of those fellows far too well-favored for his own good. He was in his late twenties, perhaps, and had something of the look of Miss Maureen, except that in my kelper phantom, Miss Maureen's childishness was a perverse and wholly masculine charm.

"Nymph in thy ablutions," he misquoted as he joined me, "how lovely thou art!"

"Don't be impertinent," I said sharply. "This is a dead man."

"Yes. I knew Sean Flaherty. It's like the dear old rascal to come to rest at the foot of loveliness."

The bad taste of his banter at this time gave me just the authority I needed.

"I take it you are Master Theodore Conor. Will you be so kind as to rescue this poor creature?"

He had leaned over and was investigating the snag upon which the body was fastened. While he worked, swiftly and with a precision I envied, he corrected me.

"Theobald Conor, Anne. Not Theodore. Set the blame at my mother's door for that. Come, help me untangle this skein."

I went to helping him as I was bidden, almost forgiving his flippancy for his quick and masculine command of the situation. While we worked, for the body was entangled in several places, the narrow strand of beach slowly became populated by searchers and fishermen from the neighboring cove. Among them I observed the roughly clad figure of Dr. Trumble. He came toward us calmly, but with purpose. At almost the same time Theo Conor saw him too. He looked up from his work to say maliciously, "Faith, now! The good doctor. Here's one patient who's after escaping you."

The doctor paid this no heed except with a sudden tightening of the muscles about his jaws, and when we were about to be joined by other fishermen, he motioned them back.

"Let us get him ashore. One of you there, on the beach, go for a cart and bring it to the cliff's edge."

There were murmurs among the crowd, which puzzled and made me uneasy. We had the dead man free now, and I expected Theo Conor to go on with the work of bringing the body ashore. I was thunderstruck when he said with the greatest goodwill, "Dear Doctor! One would think a near lifetime on this coast would teach you something of us. We do not subscribe to your modern burial notions. It's the sea for Sean Flaherty. Back into the sea with him until he finds his rest on the ocean floor."

I cried out impulsively, "No, no! What are you thinking of?" But several on the beach joined Master Conor in this primitive notion.

Dr. Trumble said briefly, "I am not superstitious. If you will not do so, then let me bring him ashore."

Theo Conor turned to me. "He knows better and is a fool, but you, Anne, are excused. You see, it is bad luck to bring a body ashore; for then you rob the sea gods and they will take you or one of your loved ones to feed their altars."

"Pagan!" I uttered, horrified at this blasphemy. But Theo Conor only smiled. His every word was echoed by a chorus of grunts of "That be the way of it" from the shore. I could hardly conceive of such savagery in our enlightened year of 1819. Dr. Trumble was apparently familiar with this monstrous superstition and could be oblivious to it. He pushed Theo Conor aside and went about getting the body ashore. The men separated into two files, no one touching the body, so that if it had not been for me, Dr. Trumble would have had to handle the entire business himself. We had laid the poor creature on the strand when Theo Conor suddenly surprised me by saying, "Well, if you will have it so, there's a cart just behind the brow of the headland. I left it there. One never knows when it might be of use. I'll fetch it."

With a lift of the eyebrows and a brief look at my disheveled form, he left us.

"He must be mad," I said to Dr. Trumble just as Miss Maureen came through the group to join us. She had heard my last words, to my embarrassment, and said seriously, "Oh no, Anne. Theo intended to help all along. Only . . . he is such a tease."

It was not the word I would have used, but I said nothing more after Dr. Jonathan's brief, succinct agreement with his wife, "He has his own humor."

We were removing the fisherman's body to higher ground, with no help from the fishermen gathered on the shore, when one or two newcomers arrived and with muttered comments about the bad luck that would ensue, took over my task and left me to accompany Miss Maureen who wanted to cling to her husband's arm and thus slow the ascent of the men with their burden, up over the low cliff on the southerly side of Kelper Head.

"Go with Miss Wicklow, love," said her husband, briskly, and the good creature did so without more ado.

She stepped just behind me as we also ascended, and once when I slipped on a hard, moist prickle of seaweed, it was Maureen who put her strong little hands out and caught me, saving me from a bad tumble.

I had surely misjudged her out on the terrace earlier today. Miss Maureen with her sweet smile and the candid, childish wondering of her eyes, was a most unlikely candidate to push either me or her stepmother over the terrace into the foaming cauldron below. I would sooner have suspected Lady Maeve, or Nurse Kellinch of such an act.

"Look!" whispered Maureen at my ear. "How she watches us!"

Already I had enough of "watchers" in this stony old house, and could scarcely believe I had only arrived last evening. I looked up expectantly at the terrace but saw no one, though I was fully prepared for the usual phantom kelper, since there seemed to be a conspiracy to frighten me with these legendary horrors. Then I looked higher, and saw a figure at a window on the top floor just under what I assumed must be the attic and eaves of Conor House. I would not have said that what I saw was a woman. It seemed shadowy, but almost certainly masculine, to judge by the height, standing there behind curtains. How long had he been watching us?

VI

"Who is it?" I asked.

"Maeve, of course. She knows everything. Nothing escapes her."

I could believe that, for the strange mistress of Conor House seemed capable of being in many places at once; yet I was sure it was a man at the upper window.

"Whose quarters are those?"

"Papa's. The north room beside his bedchamber is shared by Papa and Maeve. It a sort of parlor. But that room—that is Papa's."

I frowned upward, shading my eyes against the dirty yellow glare of the sun through the fog. "Are you sure that was not your father at the window, Miss Maureen? Faith! I'd have sworn—"

She giggled merrily. "What a silly you are, Anne! Father cannot walk. He is an invalid. He does not stand. It happened when the Kelper came behind him that night, and stabbed him."

I looked at her carefully. "The night you saw your father injured in the red parlor?"

She put one hand out to me, experimentally, almost like a blind person feeling her way. And her eyes filled with the quick tears of a child.

"Oh, Anne! Not you too. Not like Ivy and Maeve and Jonathan."

To my shame and distress she had seen in my casual words a suspicion of her. I backtracked hastily.

"No, no, Miss Maureen. You must not think they believe. . ."

Her small pointed chin went up.

"I know what they believe. You need not be treating me like a child, as though I must be humored."

We were at the guardroom and Mrs. O'Glaney had come out, wiping her hands on her food-stained skirts.

72

THE BECKONING

"There, there, Miss Maury," she soothed her, putting an arm around the young lady's neck. "There's them that believes in you, and never you mind the others." Mrs. O'Glaney looked up at me. "Why do you think Dr. Jonathan was about the hiring of that wench, that Ivy Kellinch?"

"No, Sara," Maureen murmured through tears and sniffs. "Don't. It was Maeve that hired Ivy, in any case."

"All the same it's true, my lamb. True as true. Your precious doctor don't take no mind of your word, no more than the word of some bog-trotter. And Her Precious Ladyship's no better when it comes to that."

"Not Jono," protested Maureen, while I wished myself a thousand leagues from here. "He loves me. He does!"

I could see that the cook was going to encourage Maureen's doubts, and I interrupted briskly, "Dr. Trumble loves you very much, ma'am, and you are a grown girl now, and can love him and not believe bad things. It is wicked for folks to feed you on such bad thoughts."

"Hoity-toity, miss!" exclaimed Mrs. O'Glaney to me over Maureen's bowed head, and then, perhaps seeing the sense of my words, she changed her mood. "There'll be bad cess to bad thoughts, and no mistake!" I was relieved at this end to what had seemed an unnecessary harrowing of Miss Maureen's nerves. Sara O'Glaney finished sternly, "There's one as will take the part of you, Miss Maury. One you can be counting on to believe you."

Maureen raised her head, curious as a child. "You, Sara?"

"That rapscallion rogue, your brother. Master Theo, it is. You'll never be finding him at Lady Maeve's side, to be sure. No-account and kelp-gathering rascal that he is, Master Theo won't be going behind you and treating with the enemy."

It was at this precise moment that I realized I had seen Theo Conor before our meeting on the beach today. It was Master Conor, faithful believer in his sister, the man who would never be found at Lady Maeve's side, whom I had seen last night, in very close and secret conversation with Maeve Conor on the terrace. And now where was he? Not down there where he had ought to be, helping Dr. Trumble and the others, but off some place and up to mischief, I was sure.

Naturally, I said nothing of my suspicions about his friendship with Lady Maeve to these two who believed in him. But I wondered. . . .

By natural process of thought, I turned from this question to the matter of Lady Maeve's watching the beach from her husband's room on the top floor, if indeed it was she.

It was time I paid a visit to that floor, and upon the suggestion of Lady Maeve herself; for had she not mentioned it to me last night when giving me my orders? There was definite talk of my refurbishing the rooms on the top floor. Ah! And the curious warning: I was not to interfere with her husband's room. The Master of Conor House was apparently waited upon only by his wife and . . . who else? Or did the elegant Maeve Conor attend to all the menial tasks of the sickroom?

"Where are you going, Anne?" Maureen asked abruptly. She always surprised me by the suddenness of her changes in mood. It seemed to me now that she was sharp, quick, on guard.

"I promised Lady Maeve I should inspect the empty apartments on the top floor and see to their renovation. I fear the discovery of the poor fisherman's body has delayed me. I hope she will not be angry."

Sara O'Glaney and Maureen exchanged glances. The cook said significantly, "If you've failed to please Her Ladyship, miss, you'll be hearing of it, and in a way that puts the sharpest needle to shame, I'm thinking."

Maureen grinned. "It is true, Anne. Maeve is a witch when she is crossed. Not slam-bang like Sara here. But sly. . . . You'll find out."

Happy thought.

I went swiftly to my room, changed to a clean dress and petticoats, left my sodden ones where Rosaleen would fetch them, and brushed my shoes carefully. I ran my hands over my hair to smooth down the flying wisps.

I left my room and hurried up the winding stone staircase. I confess to a certain irritation of the nerves. I did not know what I should find on the half-deserted top floor, and was a trifle shaken by my absurd and apparently unquenchable idea that a man, and not Lady Maeve, had look-

ed down at the sea not fifteen minutes since, from Aengus
Conor's bedchamber.

On the main floor of the building I came upon Rosaleen
and the pantry boy in the corridor outside Lady Maeve's
morning room, busily arguing while the shards of a broken
crystal decanter lay between them, still aglitter under a
sea of Irish spirits. The aroma of the disaster was almost
enough to make one's head swim.

"Her did it! Her be at pushing me!" cried the pantry
boy, shrilly, and wiped his knobby young nose on his
jacket sleeve. I could see that the enormity of the crime
had quite unmanned him, and we should have him blub-
bering with the next cross word.

"Boy," I said to him, not mincing matters. "Go and fetch
water from the kitchen."

He would have been off like a streak but Rosaleen grab-
bed his shirt-tail.

"Begging your pardon, I'm sure, m'um," she said to me,
"but it's not time for the water man just yet. He comes
late in the day. We buy it by the barrel. Begging your
pardon."

Faith now, I should have guessed. Here in the great
house that fairly oozed dampness from the very walls, a
house so wet one felt the lung sickness must carry off
all who dwelt in it, there would, naturally, be no access to
fresh water except by purchase!

"Well then, we will make do with sea water," said I, nothing daunted. "Go now, boy!"

He made a face at Rosaleen, tore himself from her grasp,
and raced down the steps up which I had come.

"Miss," said Rosaleen, anxious to get her case before the
bar of justice, "you'll not be thinking I overturned the
pretty glass pitcher. No more did I! 'Twas that clumsy
spalpeen, Padraic, so it was! Stopped dead in his tracks, and
me but a step behind."

"Fetch me some scrubbing cloths," I told her, trying not
to let my voice show my impatience.

"Ay, m'um." She curtseyed and started away, but looked
over her shoulder at me. She seemed bursting with some
sort of news. "You might be wonderin' now, what'll be
making the boy stop so sudden-like, making me for to run
onto him."

I could not help smiling. "I see you wish to tell me."

She smirked. I felt sure her expression was not deliberate, but merely the natural desire to be the center of attention.

"Padraic is a clumsy lad, and no mistake. But now and again he sees things."

I was not surprised. My mother "saw things" and the half of Ireland also "saw things." The thought annoyed me always, by the very fact that, despite myself, I share the general Irish belief in them.

"He saw a phantom, right in the middle of the corridor," I guessed.

"Now, that I never said, miss!" She looked shocked. "That be wrong and wicked. Father MacMonigle says there be no phantasms. But what Paddy saw, or so he thought—was Mr. Aengus on the stair to the upper quarters."

"Nonsense. Mr. Aengus does not walk."

"No, no, and it is all in that flyaway Paddy's stupid head, surely. For it became to be not Mr. Aengus, at all, but Her La'ship carrying freshly ironed bed clothes for the master, on her arm."

"Well then—" I began, shrugging my shoulders at this long-winded and pointless tale.

"But don't you see, Miss, how passing strange it is! Her Ladyship heard the pretty pitcher break, and did not stop, nor even give us one of her freezing scolds."

"In a hurry, no doubt." I dismissed the matter from our conversation, and sent Rosaleen to bring me a bundle of dusty cloths from the bottom shelf of a linen press nearby. Nonetheless, I was surprised by her tale, and as she and I knelt at work, sopping up the whisky from the strip of carpet and the cold stone floor beyond, my thoughts reverted to this unlikely picture of Lady Maeve, so busy bringing garments to her invalid husband that she could not stop to attend to an accident done by her servants, involving a valuable piece of glass.

When the boy, Padraic, returned, I set him and Rosaleen to work on the carpet knowing full well that the salt water would leave its own stains, but at least it would remove the stench of spirits.

I went up the narrow, straight staircase to the top floor, espied what I took to be the empty rooms mentioned last night by Lady Maeve, and had just put my hand to the latch when I heard a door open down the dark and narrow hall. I looked in that direction, which is to say northward, and discerned the floating garments and the red tresses of the mistress of Conor House as she moved along the corridor to me. I could see how an impressionable servant, or Miss Maureen, with her arrested mental development, might fancy this odd woman to be a ghostly creature. Even I, standing dutifully in my place, felt a cold chill up my spine, as she moved toward me.

"Good afternoon, Miss Wicklow," she said, in her tinkling silvery voice that did not allow contradiction. "My husband has expressed a desire to see you. I think now would be a good time. Before his afternoon nap. Come this way."

She fastened her long, slim fingers on my wrist and I wondered at the iciness of her flesh. In spite of her tall, slender form, I felt a steel strength in her that was almost alarming.

With one of those contradictory impulses that a strong opponent often instills in me, I said calmly, "When I was upon the headland with Miss Maureen some moments ago I believe I saw you at the window of Mister Aengus's apartments."

She turned her head and stared at me. I could feel the stabbing gaze of her strange eyes.

"Impossible. I was . . ."

I did not allow myself to smile, but I knew I had caught her fairly and was not surprised when she changed her statement as one changes the course of a journey in midhighroad.

". . . but yes. I believe it was I. I wondered at the crowds this side of the cove, and so I glanced out."

I knew as surely as I knew the angry pressure of her fingers on my wrist that she was lying. For what reason I could not fathom. Besides, the figure at the window had been watching for some moments. It was no mere "glance" that Miss Maureen and I had intercepted. Was someone else up here on this floor today, besides Lady Maeve, her invalid husband, and perhaps, Ivy Kellinch? No. It could not be Nurse Kellinch we had surprised at the window. It had been a man.

"I wonder, ma'am," I ventured at hazard. "Are there any servants up in these quarters now?"

"Not yet. No. However, that will be one of your tasks, Miss Wicklow. To supervise the refurbishing of these empty rooms . . . . Now, these are my husband's quarters. You will remember what I told you. You will not disturb him upon any account except when instructed to. His nerves are quite undone. Quite undone. I could not answer for it if you were to come in upon him unexpectedly."

She ushered me in. Gently pushed me, I may say. As I stepped into the shadowy room, wondering that the invalid should prefer this gloomy solitude, Lady Maeve left me, and though I was often uneasy in her presence, I found her absence at this moment a severe test of my own nerves. The prospect of meeting my true employer, the master of Conor House, alone in these dour surroundings put me in mind of hobgoblins and other fancies.

I assumed he must be lying in the great canopied bed whose curtains were drawn tightly against draft and light; so I stood respectfully, waiting to be acknowledged. I did not like to cough or otherwise call attention to my presence, but was glad I stood on the floor beyond the carpet's edge, where my day slippers made a faint, gritting shuffle now and then upon the stony surface, for having been wet, they were stiffer than was usual.

There was a door ajar this side of the canopied bed, which probably opened into the north parlor shared by the master and mistress of Conor House. Expecting as I did, some sign from the deeply shrouded bed, I was surprised to hear a voice with the musical lilt of my ancestors, call to me through the door which stood ajar.

"What a comely wench it is, to be sure! Ah! I have startled you, Miss Wexford. Does it set you in a quake to be stared at without your knowledge?"

"Set me in a quake" was a mild way of expressing it. I very nearly handed in my notice as of that instant, for the wretched creature had been watching me from a hidden place. After whirling around in confusion, I finally discovered a baleful eye staring at me from the north parlor, in that space only an inch or two wide, between the hinged door and the wall. The man must be mad, to hide himself behind doors and stare at housekeepers! A very curious amusement, indeed! And all of a piece with the rest of the household.

"You will be taking your death of the cold, hiding behind doors, sir," I said calmly, and awaited a truly Irish explosion of wrath at my impudence.

There was a little pause. Then my peeping employer roared with laughter and I will confess I was relieved.

"Come in, girl. Come in where I can get my view of the whole of you."

I walked into the north parlor, pushing open the door a trifle more, and having the strong inclination to slam it against the wall and Mister Aengus. Somehow, he had contrived to place most of his weight at the head of a chaise longue which had been fitted with small wheels by some mechanical genius, probably his son. He was half-reclining in this odd way, and apparently had watched me during the time I stood at a loss in his bedchamber. He turned now and signaled to me with one finger. I came to him. In spite of the tasseled night cap that all but concealed his gray locks and gave him a ludicrously jaunty look, I should have known him anywhere, for he was very like his two children, with the gentle, facial features of Miss Maureen rubbed off slightly by the mischievous, sharp Conor eyes. He appeared to be in his mid-forties and very nearly handsome —if one admired the mercurial, quick and moody type of the Conors. He did not look to be a man that a woman might trust, either in the matter of fidelity or to earn a livelihood. I found myself misliking him heartily for that sparkle of malicious amusement in his eyes now. I have an abhorrence of being made a figure of fun.

"Lift me down into the chaise," he bade me, and with his not inconsiderable aid, I did so. I felt his body beneath the gaudy, green-striped silk dressing robe he affected, and thought it a pity that so hard and lean a body should have been cut down in this brutal fashion.

"Ah, that is more like. Now, let us talk before my beloved spouse returns with her long and pointed pretty ears."

I had not expected this, and pretended not to notice. He looked me up and down, and said, "Be at ease, Miss Wexford. I assure you I can do nothing to harm you in my present state."

"No, sir," I said; and could not but add, "Nor am I a-fraid of you, sir."

"Then why the frown on that—if I may say—alabaster brow?"

"My name is Wicklow, not Wexford."

He laughed.

"But I'll wager it won't be Wicklow either, for very long, once our Irish lads catch a look at you. Beware of them, Anne. They are said to charm the birds out of the trees."

His words were not amusing and his sharp eyes saw the change in my expression.

"Come, I have offended you. I had forgotten. Maeve tells me you are a widow, and Wicklow is the name you bore in maidenhood. How came this to be, and you so young?"

"My husband was killed in an attempt to restore the Emperor Napoleon's son to his rightful heritage. It was thought best that I retain my own name, since Ireland has some ties with France and there might be Bourbon sympathizers here."

He grunted. "Most unlikely. We are a poor country. We should be better occupied with our own affairs. . . . Still . . ."

"There is the rubble on the south portion of Kelper Head," I reminded him. "That was made in a French attempt to land forces here to fight the English, I am told."

He raised his eyebrows, and started to say something. But I pursued the subject that had been troubling me since I looked out of my bedchamber window last night.

"That rubble would be better removed, sir. If I may suggest . . ."

"We can't afford it," he said abruptly.

"But if I myself—"

"That will do. . . . I have called you in to discuss quite another matter. What are you looking at?"

I did not reply, and he looked down his lean, acquiline nose and discovered that he had somehow uncovered the hem of his nightgown which was ruffled. His face looked slightly flushed as he raised his head, but it may have been the remnants of the late afternoon sun from the west windows which made him appear so.

"My wife's taste, not mine," he explained, and I was pleased to have caught him at a disadvantage for the first time. He covered up his lean and disused feet hastily with the skirt of his striped robe, and the very swiftness of the gesture was so like a little boy that I had a deplorable desire to laugh, but I presented him as sober a face as may be.

"You say you have a commission for me, sir?"

"Yes." He was obviously relieved at the change of subject. "I am told that you are a good sturdy walker."

I said nothing to this. He looked me up and down, doubtless trying to pay me back for his own embarrassment a moment before.

"I should imagine you'll do. I am in need of someone who can walk a good pace without resorting to carts and vehicles that can tell a tale."

"Tell a tale?" I repeated, all bewildered.

He continued to stare at me in a way that made me blush and be at odds with myself because I had done so. "I daresay those long, pretty Irish limbs of yours will be hiding beneath a thousand skirts. But they'll be there."

"I can walk," I said, ignoring the rest, for what should he know of any long limbs of mine, pretty or otherwise? "I walked from the gallows on Ballyglen Highroad to Kelper Head. Will that be walking enough for you, sir?"

"Just so. Well then." He looked around. I followed his glance, seeing nothing out of the ordinary except the peculiar, sly man himself. "See to the door, Anne Wexford. Is it bolted?" I started out through the bedchamber when he stopped me. "No, no! The parlor door into my son's room. It is at the opposite end of this room."

The east end of the room had been in such heavy shadow I hadn't noticed the door similar to the one through which he had been peeping, and which apparently opened into Theo Conor's bedchamber. I went to that door, opened it and peered into the empty room beyond. It looked as one might have expected, rather helterskelter, amusingly jumbled, yet with an artistic touch here and there in the unusual drawings affixed to the walls, mostly French in taste and design. I shot the bolt. Mr. Aengus Conor asked impatiently, "Well? Well?"

"Locked, sir."

"Very good. I want no one to hear us. No one to know."

"But Lady Maeve brought me to you."

81

"That's as may be. But no one else. Do you understand me?" His voice had raised in tone, though it was more of a harsh whisper now, and would be quite unheard beyond this room. He beckoned to me to sit on the edge of his chaise, but that was rather too much, and too close. Either he wished to embarrass me, or he wished to exercise some familiarity. He was a nasty creature entirely, for all his Irish charm. I remained where I was, and he smiled. In that instant he looked endearingly young and very like his two children.

"I fear you are too great a lady for the raucous Conors. No matter. My son will soon be giving me his report upon your unassailable virtue. Lock the door into my chamber."

I did so, more and more mystified. If he had been capable of walking I should be already in flight. I did not like the notion of being locked in with the odd creature.

"You are quite sure we are alone, and none can hear us?"

"Quite, sir."

"Nor see us?"

I could not resist saying, "I know only one person who watches from cracks in doors, sir."

"Ah. You can smile, Anne Wexford. Enchanting. Put your head nearer. I would whisper my instructions."

I had long since given up on my name, and put my head forward rather gingerly but he appeared satisfied, though my careful propriety seemed to amuse him.

"Now, then. You'll be finding a sealed paper placed between two pages of the Book of Common Prayer upon my desk yonder. You will take the entire book, not merely the paper, and the other two books you see on the desk, and replace them in the bookroom on the lower floor. But before you do so, and when you are quite alone, you will extract the note you find."

It was very puzzling.

"I don't think I understand, Mister Conor."

His snub was deliberate and malicious. "You are not meant to. But do you understand what I require of you?"

"Yes, sir."

"Excellent. You will then take this sealed paper, which has no superscription and put it safely among your things, in your reticule, or whatever. And tomorrow, at two in the

afternoon, or as near as you can, I want you to deliver it
to the person who asks for it in Ballyglen Town. You
will have walked there meanwhile."

"Walk to Ballyglen! But that is—"

"Quite beyond your powers? A mere two hour walk?
Come now, Miss Wexford!"

"Wicklow!" I said furiously.

"Yes, well, no matter. You can surely walk to the gallows on the High Road, and someone will take you up in
a cart. All I ask is that no one know to whom you deliver the paper in Ballyglen."

"And who is this person?"

He beckoned to me. I leaned nearer. By this time, I was
overcome with curiosity.

"Never you mind. You will go in to Ballyglen, to the
churchyard, and you will put a few leafy twigs upon the
Gaelic gravestone with the name of Fergan O'Carty. You
will stay in an attitude of prayer for some ten minutes. If
no one approaches you or asks you if you have anything
for them, you will return to Kelper."

I drew away from him. I wanted to refuse. I was, in fact,
upon the very brink of refusing but something held me
from it. Either the strange, intent look in his expressive eyes,
or perhaps only my own curiosity.

"And where shall I be finding the leafy twigs?" I inquired
calmly.

He relaxed. Almost, I could fancy, his whole body, even
the paralyzed part of him, relaxed. He made a carefree
gesture.

"From the Bog, most probably. Just snatch up a handful as you pass."

"I shall not report back to you at night, and that you
may wager on," I assured him, not mincing matters.

His smile illuminated his face more than the dying sun.
Some women would have thought these Conors excessively handsome, I reflected severely.

"No, nor would I have you do so; for you are quite the
most likely thing that has happened to Conor House in
many a year."

I did not know how to accept this dubious remark, and
to avoid more of it I went instantly to the desk and took
up the books he had mentioned. He said no more to me

and when I looked around, awaiting my dismissal, I saw that his eyes were closed, and he frowned, as though in pain.

Nonetheless, when I paused to throw back the bolt of the door through which I had entered the parlor, I looked back at him and caught an expression quite different upon his face. He was watching me, and very much awake.

"One more thing, Anne. Let no one who resides in this house, know what you have done when your mission is completed. That is to include my children, my son-in-law, my daughter's nurse, and the servants."

"And Mrs. Conor?"

Was I mistaken or had there been the briefest pause here?

"And Mrs. Conor. Remember this. If, by some mischance, you should encounter any of them upon the Bog road or elsewhere while you are doing me this service, you will use your wits. It is even possible someone may follow you, but I think you can deal with that. Not that anyone is likely to harm you, of course."

"Of course," I agreed ironically.

"Promise me you will trust no one in this house except myself."

"Certainly, sir. I promise." He was my employer, after all. I could do no other.

I would have gone but he said suddenly, "You do not ask me why these things are necessary?"

"I am not paid to ask, Mr. Conor. Good day to you, sir." I curtseyed and swung around and left the room.

Yet, as I carried the books out into the dark, damp-smelling hall, I could not rid myself of the fear that behind every door in this house Mr. Aengus Conor's expressive eyes were watching me. And did he not know that the quickest and easiest way to have someone follow me on my secret journey was to have me make the journey on foot?

VII

It MAY have been an irritation of the nerves that caused my hands to tremble as I prepared the tea service that afternoon, caused by Mister Aengus's instructions to me for the morrow. Mrs. O'Glaney, busied with the sillabub that was favored by the ladies of the household for a supper sweet, eyed me curiously. I fancied that her shrewd eyes saw through me and guessed I was thinking of Mister Aengus's books which I had temporarily laid in my sitting room. It was teatime and I had still not found the time to return them to the bookroom after extracting the messages to be delivered to the unnamed person in Ballyglen Town. The small, loosely sealed missive they had contained now lay heavy beneath the bodice of my gown.

Suppose, I thought, someone is in my room at this instant, seizing those books, searching for the message Mr. Aengus was so mysterious about. Could it be O'Glaney? Or Theo Conor? Or any of the others, for that matter?

Mrs. O'Glaney could not possibly know I was thinking these things. Yet the fact that she noted my nervous preoccupation, was annoying.

"Would aught be troubling you, miss?" she inquired, when I very nearly dropped the jam tarts off Miss Maureen's tea tray.

"Not in the least," I replied rather more sharply than was my habit. And looking for a scapegoat by which to change the subject, I hit upon the helpless wife of Dr. Jonathan. "But, in fact, I do think Miss Maureen eats too many sweets."

"How, now! Sits the wind in that direction, is it?" The cook flew up into the boughs, metaphorically, and went on with heat in defense of her favorite. "If you were plagued as that poor child, sure, you'd be nibbling the sweetmeats as well. Ay, and more!"

I took shame at her words, but did not let her guess as much. With Rosaleen waiting upstairs in the dining parlor, I sent up the trays by the mechanical contrivance which was, so far as I could see, the sole contribution of Master Theo Conor to this house. I watched the tea service I had polished this afternoon as it rose in the semi-dark, now and again catching the faint shafts of light from the candle sconces in the dining parlor above, and I observed the richness of the chinaware as well. Strange, all this wealth, in a family too poor to remove the debris of wartime from its doorstep.

I questioned the cook upon this matter now. "One would imagine the Conors still lived in some luxury, to judge by many things. Yet there is all the talk of their poverty."

"So they say, now," Mrs. O'Glaney assured me, yet her meaning seemed precisely the opposite. "But was never so you'd notice, until the Master was laid by the heels a year gone by. Then, of a sudden, Her Ladyship announces to one and all that the Conors are paupers. And all the time, herself with her grand marriage settlement afore she would ever have married Aengus Conor. 'Tis my thought the talk is only for to keep Miss Maury and her doctor from Miss Maury's income. The O'Glaney once, with a wee drop under his belt, flat out asked Her Ladyship why Miss Maury did not get her money, that is, why Dr. Jono should not have the use of it for Miss Maury. But Her Ladyship said some'ut we don't rightly take into our heads. She said the money was not bringing in the income that it should."

"Bad investments?" I suggested.

"Just so." She sniffed, quite patently not believing this.

Quite possibly Mrs. O'Glaney was right, but I had to take into account her natural affection for the family which had employed her during her lifetime, a family so different from the earl's daughter who had come upon the Conors as both a second wife, and a woman of authority, but with no fortune of her own. The household which had jogged along on what I could only regard as the lax way of life known to the Conors, found itself suddenly put into harness and a tight rein. Small wonder that Lady Maeve was resented and made the villain.

As soon as I decently could, I returned to my quarters

to get the books and follow Mr. Aengus's instructions with them. It was now coming on for dark and I began to have all my original dislike of those drafty passages on the lower level of the house, and I knew that if I looked out the window of my little bedchamber, I should see the obscene and prickly kelp beckoning to me in the wind.

The kitchen and stillroom were aglow with sturdy storm lamps that swung in the draft, and I touched the wick of a bed-candle to one of them and lighted my way through the great emptiness with it. Presently, I was in my own narrow passage and put my hand to the latch on the door. As I did so, I saw that the door stood ajar. I knew that I had closed it snugly, for I had ever the worry of Mister Aengus's books on my mind, and now with a chilling grue upon my senses, I became aware that someone was in my sitting room in the dark. I was not minded to stalk this intruder, nor to chance being attacked in the darkness; so I raised the candle high to get a better light and walked in to see Maureen Trumble kneeling on my hearth, warming her hands at the low peat fire.

"Hallo, Wicklow," she said cheerfully. "I am ever so glad you came. It is lonely here and I fancy things are trying to get in at me. Isn't it absurd?"

"Not at all, ma'am," said I, meaning every word of it. "And if I were permitted, I should remove all that kelp and seaweed and all such; for it breeds such unhealthy notions." I came in and while talking looked for the three books I remembered setting down on a little round tilt-top table in one corner of the room. It was dark in that corner and I walked over to it as I spoke. "Would you be knowing, now, Miss Maureen, why Her Ladyship does not desire me to have all that unpleasantness removed?"

"I daresay she has her reasons," Maureen said and giggled unexpectedly.

I was not thinking too much about our conversation, for the light of my candle just then illuminated the tilt-top table and shone on its fine-grained, but dusty surface. The dust was a reproach to me, but I did not have time to think about that more than briefly because the mere fact that I was staring at the grained surface rather than the three books was proof of what I had feared. The books had been removed.

Meanwhile, I became aware of the silence in the room behind me and could hear the stillness filled suddenly by the rush of waves against the escarpment beyond the passage and the guardroom. I turned to ask Maureen what she knew about the disappearance of the books and saw her listening, not to the noise of the roaring Atlantic, but to something at the back of the great old house, something I could not hear.

"What is it, Miss Maureen?"

"Hush," she murmured, putting one finger to her lips. Then she relaxed and smiled. "Now then, Anne, I've frightened you, and I never meant to at all. But it is easy to fancy there are prowlers about at night. The Kelp Gatherers . . ."

"Nonsense," I said, hoping my voice was salutary. But I fear even my own state was not the calmest. "If the Gatherers do their work at night, of course, we must hear them, or at the least, see them. But why should they be skulking about this house?"

"Perhaps—" she said slowly, teasing, yet with her head cocked on one side as though still listening. "Perhaps they are coming to fetch someone." She was still obsessed with her belief that the ordinary gatherers of seaweed were somehow phantomlike, unreal. Superstition died hard on these time-forgotten coasts.

"Then they will surely not be fetching you, Miss," I told her at once, "for I never saw a young lady less like to be called away by ghosts."

"I saw Father carried away by ghosts, as you say, Anne. And I was all-over blood. And I felt so sick. . . ."

"You must not be thinking on such matters. It is morbid and a bad thing entirely." I was looking around the room, all the while I approached her with an appearance of ease, but thus far, I saw no trace of Mr. Aengus's books.

"What are you looking for, Anne?"

"Nothing of consequence. Merely some books I had finished and meant to return to the bookroom."

"Oh, those tiresome things!" She sat up and drew her skirts more tightly against her thighs. I could see now that she had been sitting on the books, and I took them up, thanking her. She seemed to think their subject matter a trifle odd and asked with all the flat, bold curiosity of a child,

"Why do you read such fusty work, Wicklow? It is more to the taste of my father. I did not think you so wise by half."

"There are many things we do not suspect about others, Miss Maureen. No one is quite an open chart to another."

Maureen hugged her knees and rocked back and forth, leaning back further and further each time until I thought she would go into the fireplace, and was decidedly nervous for her safety. She seemed in excellent spirits and said in the singsong voice of childhood, half laughing, "Oh, it is true, so true, Anne. No one really knows about heaps of things except me. I know ever so many secrets, ever so many. Shall I tell you one?"

"Not if it is a secret, Miss. Now, be a good girl, do. You are liable to catch your hair on fire."

She flung herself away from the fire and said the most curious thing. "I know why Maeve refuses to have the ruins removed from the south spur of Kelper Head. I know, I know, I know."

"Well then, suppose you save your secret for Dr. Trumble. He will know what to do with it." I was going through Mr. Aengus's books, skimming the pages to see if anything else of a personal nature would fall out, and her chatter did not make much sense. And then too, I thought it unwise that one so unstable mentally should work herself up to this pitch of excitement. Miss Maureen laughed again so that it was difficult to understand her.

"Oh, you are so funny. . . .You cannot imagine. Why don't you ask me to tell Nurse Kellinch. Ivy is clever, you know. She has money. I saw it an hour ago. A great deal of money, and I suspect she got it from Conor House. And what do you think of *that* secret, Anne Wicklow!"

This was interesting, indeed. If it were true, where—and more to the point—*why* had Ivy Kellinch gotten money from this household which claimed to be poor as a kelper?

Speak of the Devil! At that precise moment, as though upon cue at Covent Garden, Nurse Kellinch's voice called down the stairs shrilly. "Miss Maury! You are wanted abovestairs. Come, at once. Do you hear me? At once!"

Maureen got up lightly, shook herself, and rumpled her hair, scratching her scalp.

"Old Monster!" she murmured to herself. "Hateful Old

Monster!" and stuck her tongue out at the ceiling of my room, presumably at Ivy Kellinch.

It made me want to smile, but ruefully, at her eternal youthfulness.

"You need not go if you do not choose," I reminded her. "I must return these books and I can tell Nurse Kellinch you will be along presently."

Maureen stopped playing the fool, and looked behind her on both sides. "Oh no, Wicklow. I wouldn't stay here alone now. It comes on for dark too soon down here."

She arose and followed me, not saying more, but pattering along behind me so that I had the odd sensation of being followed by a child, a child with an adult's power and an adult's weapons. . . . a push, a shove on the stairs, even a weapon hidden. . . . I was ashamed of my slight but ever-present suspicions, yet they were there all the same. I was fortunate to have her company, however, as I did not in the least know where to turn, to locate the bookroom, when we reached the upper floor. Maureen walked with me, pointed to a door halfway along the corridor and as I opened it, I half expected her to vanish as she had the previous night in the morning room, but she merely waved to me and went her own way.

The bookroom was lighted by one miserly candle which had been set carelessly upon a stack of books on a cumbersome Jacobean table. Already, the wax was spilling over upon the books. I wondered who had left it here, and was slightly uneasy at finding that I could not see all of the room at once. There was an ell at the east end of the room which, I guessed, cut into the bookroom in order to allow for the winding staircase on the other side of that wall. I could not see anything there except more book shelves; for the room was a dusty, mouldy cave lined in every direction with unused books. Part way down the room, and opposite to the nook formed by the ell, I saw that there were spaces among the books on the wall shelves, which must have been meant to accommodate the books in my hand; for there was a stool standing below the empty space. I stepped out of my shoes, to protect the petit-point cover on the stool, lifted my skirts and stepped up on it.

My candle which I had set down carefully on an ancient plate beside the melting tallow, glowed steadily and

I caught its reflection in the glass of the enclosed bookshelves beside me. The rest of the room, especially the narrow ell with its parallel walls choked by manuscripts, appeared dim and murky to my eyes. A nebulous little trail that appeared to be candle smoke floated upon the still air and dissolved as I watched its reflection in the glass of the book shelves. It puzzled me. My own candle still glowed straight upward in another part of the room. The elusive puff of smoke must have come from a candle snuffed out in the last few minutes, scarcely seconds before I entered the room. Whose hand had snuffed that candle?

I paused in the act of replacing one of Mr. Aengus's books, for I had the sudden knowledge that eyes were watching me out of the darkness of that ell-shaped cavern behind me. In my vulnerable position atop the footstool I experienced all the crawling chill of a child afraid of the dark. Why was I being silently watched, for what purpose? Did the person hiding in the shadow of those bookshelves hope to discover the secret of my visit to Mr. Aengus? If so, he was doomed to a sad setdown. Nothing would be learned from the books themselves. What my watcher obviously wanted was the message I carried in the bodice of my gown.

As my eyes grew more accustomed to the darkness of the room's far corners I made out, at last, the form of a man deep in the shadow of the ell, leaning back against what I took to be a tabletop, and watching me, for I was in the direct line of his vision. It was not difficult now to make out the lighter outline of his hands grasping the edge of the table on either side of him, and something of his facial features.

In my nervousness I thought it was Aengus Conor, whom I knew to be crippled and helpless in his darkened room upstairs. I nearly let one of the books fall from my hand, all the while trying to stifle a trembling in my body at my own impossible suspicions.

Whoever he was, would he attack me? But sure now, if he intended to do me physical violence, he would have acted during that first minute or two before I was aware of him.

There was a tremendous relief in me when a sudden current of air passed under the door from the corridor and sent the flame of my own candle rocketing high with a liberal shower of sparks. In the glow I made out the tousled hair and the lithe, flippant features of Theo Conor. So it was he who was curious about my mission. It should not have surprised me. I remembered how his father had asked that the door into Master Theo's chamber should be bolted before ever he confided in me. But the realization of my watcher's identity calmed my fears. He did not seem the sort to use violence upon a woman, except, perhaps in some amatory exploit. I smiled with contempt at his spying upon me and was pleased that he could have learned nothing. I hoped he would enjoy conjuring with the title of the last of my books: *A History of the Covenanters.* Much good it might do him!

Yet . . . was not this silence a trifle eerie? Did he not know that I could see his reflection? My eyes met his in the glass and we stared at each other. An emotion almost beyond fear gripped me in that moment, and when I tore my gaze from the glass with great effort, I knew that I had been mesmerized as a bird is mesmerized by the hawk that pounces.

The longer I stood there, perched on the stool, the more I became aware of the prickly paper which was inside my bodice. I wondered if Master Theo guessed after all, that those books had contained a sealed paper which might be of great interest to him? What had his father said of Theo? Something about not trusting anyone, even his own son.

In that shadowed room, I found it well nigh impossible to avoid touching the place at my bodice where Mr. Conor's message lay. I pretended to cough, touched my breast, assured myself of the safety of the paper, and made as if to step down. Behind me, I heard him move quickly, from the sound of the rubbing of the sleeves of the leathery fisherman's jacket that he affected. In a panic I stared at his reflection in the glass door, stiffening myself to beat off the attack of this man who may have guessed that his father's missive was secreted upon me.

Knowing that a few commonplace words had warded off attack before now in many a situation, I said sternly, "Sir, what might you be doing here in the darkness? Not reading, I'll be bound."

He paused, good humored as usual.

"Well now, the plain fact of the matter is, pretty Anne, I was reading in my own private angle-nook when I heard strange sounds, and wondering who might be tempted into these dusty archives, I watched. And lo! I was rewarded by the sight of our dark enchantress."

I could not but smile, after my recent fears.

"What an absurd thing to say, indeed, sir! I was replacing some books I found lying about. That is all."

He was rather closer behind me now but I went on talking, hoping to change the subject. "I shall be gone in short order and you may have your bookroom, sir."

"Nonsense, sweet Anne. No one in this house but me ever reads, with the dubious exception of our rough-hewn surgeon, and his tomes are not like to be found in a Conor collection. Let me see."

He reached past me, just touching the front of my gown, and I could not help the swift, panic-stricken breath I took, wondering what he suspected, and if he would actually take Mr. Aengus's paper from my own person. I had encountered many lovesick young squires in my previous household experience, several of whom had resorted to slight force, which I resisted by the easy method of teasing and smiling them out of their intention. If that failed, a sound slap across the cheek did wonders to cool their ardor. But I was not at all sure I could manage this devil-may-care Irish rogue, and watched nervously as he touched the last book I had replaced, then withdrew his hand, resting it for a moment upon my arm. As his hand moved again, to my surprise and self-disgust, I cried out like any school girl. I was exceedingly mortified to see him use my own trick and laugh at my panic, teasing me as I had teased others out of a bad situation.

"Come, Mavourneen, if it's a love tussle you're wanting, I'll oblige. What a sweet armful it is, indeed. Now, don't struggle. I won't hurt you."

He had seized me around the waist, and held me there absurdly on that footstool between his two hands, as though measuring my waist. He was so close I saw his eyes laughing and very Irish, with the candle flame reflected in their depths, not the least like a man who intended me great harm; yet perhaps the harm of such light-hearted, gay rascals was more damaging to the female heart, in the long view. I would not let it ruffle me though. I was still struggling, annoyed at my own helplessness when my humiliation was completed by the opening of the bookroom door from the corridor, and though Master Theo had my back to the door I recognized the voice of Jonathan Trumble saying, "What in the devil's name are you about, Theo!"

What a ridiculous thing to happen! Of course, Master Theo was only teasing. I knew that. Why then had I panicked in that absurd way? And in the sight of Dr. Trumble whose good opinion I valued so highly. He must think me no better than a parlormaid, to be pinched and fondled behind the parlor door. But I was reassured by the doctor's next words, "I heard the lass cry out. I might've guessed! Don't be struggling now, Miss Wicklow. He won't harm you. Good God, Theo! I've half a mind to rouse your father. He'll know how to deal with you."

Theo appeared taken aback, whether by this threat or something else, I did not know. Certainly the arrival of the doctor had upset his plans. Then, he appeared to have an idea and grinned suddenly, a crooked Gaelic grin, and politely set me down upon the worn drugget. I stepped into my flat-heeled work slippers again, horridly embarrassed and knowing full well my face must be flaming with color.

"Jonathan, old lad, you don't in the least understand. Pretty Anne has some secret with my father. She's been up to mischief. I can tell by her blush when I mention it. What were you hiding on those shelves, Miss Wicklow?"

I saw Jonathan give a quick glance at the shelves I had quitted. He was frowning, and I knew that he would make nothing of the book stack, but I was surprised when he moved nearer and stared at it silently, as Master Theo watched him with the most peculiar smile.

The sooner I left the room the better, and I was making for the open door as unobtrusively as my rustling skirts would permit when Theo said, "Anne . . ."

I stopped in mid-step, without looking back at the two men.

"Aye, sir."

"Do you have secrets with my father?"

I did not like the absolute stillness of my friend, Dr. Jonathan. Did he suspect me of something dishonorable as well?

"No, sir." It was a lie, but it was necessary.

"I mean to keep an eye upon you, Anne. A pleasant task, and I shan't mind. I mean to know where you go tonight, and tomorrow. Whenever you go off by yourself I shall say, pretty Anne is up to no good. She is buying love potions to win my father away from Maeve."

At this unlooked-for ending, I stifled a laugh at the absurdity of it. So all this frightening catechism was merely Master Theo's way of letting me know he suspected me of designs upon his father! It was absurd, although the older man did fascinate me in an odd way. But hardly in a way to play upon Lady Maeve's jealousy.

I turned around and said to him and to Dr. Jonathan who was listening with a scowl that surprised me, "You do well, sir, to be asking your father what proceeded between us today. And he will tell you he'd no notion the household cares were so complicated. He'd as lief captain a Ship of the Line, said Mr. Conor." It was lame, but I was so bold in this story that I was not surprised when the rascal waved me away, as pleasant and good-humored as you may please.

"Oh, Anne, Anne, what a one you are! I'd give ten guineas to hear Father's story of it. No matter. Go, now." As I turned away he had the impudence to give me a slap upon the back of my skirts and I felt strongly inclined to haul about and give him a ringing smack over the nasty cheerful face of him. But remembering the missive I must secrete from the view of those in the household, I accepted this dismissal and went with what dignity I could, from the book-room while Jonathan said roughly, "The noble Conors! The mannerly gentlefolk!"

"Come now, no hypocrisy," said Master Theo. "You only want her for yourself, so why these airs!"

I put my hands to my ears and almost ran into the hall.

Passing the dining parlor, I wondered if the tea trays had been removed and glanced in. Two trays remained, and as I stacked them together, I heard my name called in sepulchral tones from what seemed to me the bowels of the earth. It was too early for supper and I gazed around, wondering if I could have imagined the whole of that ghoulish sound. But not. There it came again.

"Miss Anne . . . Oh, Miss Anne!"

The call seemed to come from within the walls, but then I remembered the odd contrivance of Master Theo's and was vexed at my own stupidity. I went over to the lifting apparatus and peered down into the kitchen far below and saw Mrs. O'Glaney's commonplace and welcome face. How much more cheery it looked, that broad, strong face with its ruddy glow from the kitchen fires, than the secretive faces, the masks, of the Conors!

"Yes, Mrs. O'Glaney?"

"I thought it might be you, Miss. I heard the silver clinking as it were. Her high-and-mightiness, Miss Ivy, wants her supper served to her more earlylike. I've been and sent Paddy to fetch the laundress for tomorrow, and Rosaleen is off, with the divvil himself, for aught I know. Would you be—"

"Yes, of course," I replied. "Send her tray up if you like. I'll take it to Miss Ivy."

"Thanks be, Miss. If you'll take stout hold on the ropes and the chain, I'll be sending it up now."

"Why does she dine so early tonight?" I wondered aloud. "Is she ill, do you think?" For Ivy Kellinch struck me as the kind of pushing sort of person who would make it a point to be present at every family meal, thus becoming one with the Conors and very toplofty with the rest of us.

"A fit of the sullens, belike. Mind, now!"

The air was filled with groans and shrieks as the supper tray arose, and I was minded very forcefully of a sackful of cats, all loudly protesting their treatment. I took off the tray and bore it to Miss Ivy Kellinch's bedchamber where I propped the tray on one arm and one knee long enough to rap upon the door panel. There was a little silence. Then her hoarse, authoritative voice called out, "Ah! Is it you? Changed your mind, eh? Well, there'll be none of—"

She slung the door open and I nearly pitched into the room at her feet, tray and all.

While I was gathering a choice assortment of indignant epithets, I had no chance to use them. Ivy Kellinch, half dressed, said impatiently, "Well, well, so it's you! Come in. Come in." And she added with grudging good will, "Kind of you, I'm sure. I've—I've things to do tonight. Need a trifling of nourishment first."

"The servants were all occupied," I said.

Although she had ordered supper, it was plain to my first glance that she was not prepared to receive it or me, for either she was a disorderly woman or she was in a great hurry over something. The room was strewn with her belongings, lacings, mantles, petticoats, some spilled powder of various shades including the shade of a blush . . . so her vivid complexion was not her own, I thought smugly.

I found Nurse Kellinch odd in other ways that night. She seemed exhilarated, nervous. I wondered if she could be a trifle foxed, as the gentlemen used to say in England. There was an empty Irish whisky bottle on its side half under her bed.

"You are moving your things about?" I asked. "Would you like one of the servants sent to you when convenient?"

"One of the Conor servants," said Ivy Kellinch, rolling her full lips into a twist that threatened to blot out whatever good looks the young woman had. "Snooping, prowling, gossiping? No, I thank you, my efficient friend. I have plans, I have. And one day there'll be servants scraping and bowing to Ivy Kellinch, and there'll be no half-witted, simpering young wives to take my time from better things."

"Really?" I asked, burning secretly at this affront to the family that employed me. "Now then, we are to congratulate you upon the death of a rich uncle, I make no doubt."

"God!" said Ivy Kellinch profanely. "You are a stupid wench for one I suspect to be rather shrewd. Why does one come into a wretched house like this but to nose about like a good hunting hound, and see what refuse may be swept into a corner and which—if uncovered—will give you a deal more than you'll ever get nursing and housekeeping for these toffs."

She was drunk indeed. I could scarcely make out her words or their meaning. The words slurred, the meaning seemed horrid and unclean. I said as quietly as I could, "Let us hope you have all the fortune you deserve, Miss Kellinch," and I left the room while she was still talking, hurling after me the challenge, "I'll be nobbing with the toffs when you're six feet under the good old Irish sod, my girl. Mark you that!"

She was a disagreeable woman, but there was no denying her room aroused my curiosity. But for the difficulties of transportation, and the strong likelihood that Ivy Kellinch had no income of her own, I would have guessed she was departing this night. And good riddance, if it came to that! I did not by half like her treatment of and terrorizing of Mrs. O'Glaney and Miss Maury.

It was very nearly time to call upon Lady Maeve for tomorrow's orders, and I was about to go down the passage to the morning room when, in the darkness that was only fitfully lighted by one candle sconce at the far end, I came upon an obstruction of no mean proportions. O'Glaney was in my way, him and a monumental-sized armoire or wardrobe which he was trundling down the passage upon orders from Lady Maeve, as he explained it.

"Ye'll be making stout work of it, around this fusty monster, mum. Best go out across terrace yonder," he volunteered, upon my protest. " 'T'mornin' room's hard by terrace, as ye'll be finding. Her la'ship goes by terrace many's a time and oft."

He need not tell me of Her Ladyship's peculiar penchant for that vast, wind-swept, sea-girt terrace. I looked at him thoughtfully, remembering my suspicions of last night, and Mrs. O'Glaney's assurance that my intruder at the window must have been a starving kelper. She was undoubtedly right, yet I could not rid myself of the notion that the whole attempt was somehow connected to the substitute letters Lady Maeve and I received. I felt deeply that someone had deliberately tried to frighten me. But I could prove nothing and so I thanked him for his advice and went through the red parlor after knocking and hearing no response. I stepped out upon the terrace, and made my way in a gingerly fashion along it toward the morning room. There was a gust of pure salt spray so thick I tasted its rime upon my lips, and it blinded me as well. I staggered, eyes shut, and instantly imagined the whole terrace was alive with evil things, waiting to prey upon me. It was all nonsense, of course, and I tried to open my eyes, but the salt spray was so strong it stung, and I blinked repeatedly.

But there was something out here with me!

Leathery wings, the acrid, mephitic odor of a creature unknown to me. Despite the spray I opened my eyes and in that instant a great flying thing darted at me, its wings whirring past my brow, as it vanished out over the escarpment and into the wild Atlantic fog. I screamed, for the pain was severe, and putting my apron to my forehead, felt the warm wetness of it, and knew that those savage wings had dealt me a nasty and tainted blow. I fumbled for the nearest secure wall and my fingertips brushed something, a human form.

Blinking rapidly, painfully, I looked and saw a figure standing there before me in the mist. Like a statue, she seemed, this fine red-haired Lady Maeve Conor watching me, making no effort to save me, or so I thought. Were these horrid seabirds her own playthings that she stood here unhurt while they skirled their wicked tune and flew off into the hellish Atlantic night?

VIII

"Is it you, Miss Wicklow?" asked Lady Maeve in a puzzled voice. "What can you be about, walking the terrace in the dark? One step amiss and you might plunge over into— But there. You are hurt."

I might have fired back into her own teeth the question she asked me, but she added in her imperious way, "Come, Anne, come! We'll apply an excellent powder to that cut. These cormorants can be ugly when disturbed."

Vexed at my own panic over a bird that was excessively familiar to my parents, and all coastal dwellers, I let Lady Maeve usher me into the morning room which was bright and well-ordered in this great dark pile of a house.

I would have preferred treating myself, thus avoiding a scene of violent activity that often occurs at such moments, but I need not have troubled over that. Her Ladyship made no great pother about attending to my small but sanguinary wound. As she moved to her white and gilt desk, took out a packet from one of the drawers and asked me quietly to be seated in her own armchair, I marvelled at her control.

As she dusted the healing grains upon my forehead and I closed my eyes to hide the sting, I thought upon the odd events of recent days and reflected that Lady Maeve's capabilities knew no limit, an idea that gave me pause. I remember thinking as I opened my eyes, what strong wrists she had. One would not have thought so in a lady of the quality.

"How came you to be walking the terrace?" she asked me then. There was a little frown between her brows.

I hesitated before answering. "Upon advice of O'Glaney, ma'am. He was moving a great wardrobe and I could not pass him."

I half expected her to remark upon O'Glaney's advice and

was readying myself to defend him, when she surprised me by nodding, smiling ever so little.

"But of course. O'Glaney. I instructed him to remove the wardrobe to Ivy Kellinch's room. That room has always needed a clothespress."

I ventured then, treading softly with my words, "Is Nurse Kellinch happy here?"

Lady Maeve's eyebrows raised. Now, indeed, she had the look of an earl's daughter.

"She is amply paid. Her position is rather more than she might expect from such meager gifts of mind and person, if I may say so. Does she tell you she is unhappy?"

"Not precisely, ma'am. No. I only wondered if she might be intending a journey of sorts."

Lady Maeve put by the Basilicum Powders, dusted her hands and wiped them carefully upon an elegant lace handkerchief without replying. I was about to broach another matter when she said in an odd, breathless voice, quite unlike her, "Do you believe she is embarking upon a journey? Did she say anything of this to you? The causes, perhaps? The means? What has she said?"

"Nothing, ma'am, but that she intends to put by her money and became a toff, as she expresses it."

Lady Maeve's form seemed to relax, whether from relief or disappointment, it was hard to say.

"Yes, that would be like Ivy. By the by, Miss Wicklow, how did you go on with my husband today?"

"Very well, indeed, ma'am. A most unusual gentleman."

Again I had startled her, and me without a clue to the cause!

"How so? How do you mean? Did he perhaps suggest a flirt with you?"

I opened my mouth and, I regret to say, did not close it for an instant.

"No, ma'am. Only that he hides from people. He watches them from behind doors. At least . . . he watched me."

She laughed. "Oh, that. Yes. Being an invalid he has few interests, as you may perceive. His spine was injured, you know, in the attack which—Miss Maury witnessed. One of his joys is to watch people when they are unaware, much as though we were fish in a pool for his observance. A harmless diversion."

I was not so sure. I took in extreme dislike the thought of eyes watching me during my solitary moments.

To my surprise, Lady Maeve pursued the conversation, just as had Master Theo, hoping, as I began to suspect, that they would put me in the way of betraying a secret. But neither the wiles of young Theo, nor the real charm of Her Ladyship was going to woo me from my trust.

"There was very little to our business, ma'am. Merely, I think that the Master wanted to see what sort of housekeeper he had got."

"What else did Aengus say to you?"

I hesitated, without intending to, but I was not used to these subterfuges.

"N-Nothing, ma'am. Was there aught else you expected us to discuss?"

She blinked and began to riffle through some papers on her desk as I stood up, making way for her to resume her place at the desk.

"It does not matter. Except that the letters . . ."

Again it was in our midst, that later correspondence which was patently fase. For the first time I wondered if that someone who was guilty had been Lady Maeve, herself. Perhaps she did not wish an extra pair of eyes and an observing woman to peer about Conor House and its dark recesses.

While I was thinking these things, Lady Maeve gave me her instructions for the morrow.

"Anne, are you listening to me?" she asked me once, to my acute embarrassment.

Rising suddenly from the desk chair, I had an instant's dizziness from the blow of the cormorant, and seized upon that as an excuse for my inattention. Her Ladyship accepted this with a promptness and attention that made me heartily ashamed. She looked around, as though to offer me medicinal relief, then put her hand to a decanter of Irish Whisky at the corner of her desk. She poured a liberal dosage into a glass and offered it to me.

"Thank you, ma'am," I said. "But if it is all the same to you, I will drink it before sleep. I have had one or two unpleasantnesses just before sleep these nights, and perhaps the Good Irish will be more palatable then."

"As you choose," she said with a smile and an indifferent shrug. "That will be all for tonight, Anne."

As I curtseyed and turned away, she stopped me. "You have not taken the glass."

"No, ma'am. I thought I would collect Miss Ivy's tray first, and then pick up the whisky."

"That will make further steps. I shall be snuffing the candles in here when you leave; so you had best take the whisky with you and send Ivy's tray down by the food shaft in the dining parlor. It will save you some effort. In fact, Anne, I do not know why the servants could not have attended to these things. Has Mrs. O'Glaney been giving you difficulty?"

I said no hastily, explaining that Rosaleen and Paddy were both busy, and whatever other servants were hired by the day, I had not, as yet, seen them.

"Well, then, so long as you are satisfied. Good night, Anne."

I went out into the corridor, such a gloomy dark place after the bright, London-smartness of Lady Maeve's morning room! Her Ladyship puzzled me greatly. She seemed concerned for the welfare of those in her charge, servants as well as her husband . . . yet I suspected a streak of ruthlessness in her if ever she was crossed.

O'Glaney had gotten his burden out of the corridor and I went at once to the nurse's quarters and rapped on Ivy Kellinch's door. This time I was answered almost immediately. She opened the door and let me in herself. Again I noticed the dishevelled state of the room. I set this down to the fact that she was removing her things to the gigantic wardrobe which The O'Glaney was bringing to her, but I saw nothing of the wardrobe yet.

Ivy's tray bore the remains of her meal, but the wine glass was empty. I thought of the villagers eternally at their diet of potatoes, and wondered what they would have made of the food that Ivy Kellinch left upon her dishes.

Ivy went back to her work. She was busily engaged in sorting out petticoats. Probably for darning and other repairs, I thought.

"Wicklow," she said, in a voice conciliatory for Ivy. "Will you favor me?"

"If I can, miss."

"Fetch me down that bandbox on the high shelf. I think you may reach it better than I."

I set the whisky glass down on her tray beside her, and did as she asked. It was a fine, noble bandbox, with luscious-looking deep green ribbons. What on earth was she doing at this time of night with a bandbox? Well, it was no concern of mine.

As though reading my mind, Ivy said, "I'm putting by some summer things, as you may see, Wicklow. A pity, in a way. I had rather a good summer. But then"—her voice thickened a trifle, as though she might still be tipsy—"the winter promises well."

She thanked me for my efforts and I took away the tray, saying good night to her and leaving her surrounded by heaps of clothing, some of it new and expensive. Ivy Kellinch must receive a tidy payment for her work. But how could she, if the Conors were as poor as they made out to be? I supposed it must be the poverty of the quality, which is to say, they were too poor to have a hundred servants, and were reduced to ten or twenty! They had not forty ball gowns apiece, but only a score. They wore not rubies, but only diamonds. Such, in my experience, was the poverty of the rich.

I followed Lady Maeve's advice, putting the tray upon the food shaft and sending it below into the kitchen. Then I went down the winding steps, feeling my way in the dark. Presently, I was in the kitchen, and met by Mrs. O'Glaney who demanded to know what ailed my forehead. When I explained briefly, she asked what Ivy Kellinch's tray was doing with one of Her Ladyship's precious crystal glasses upon it.

"It is for me," I explained. "Her Ladyship thought it would make me sleep."

Mrs. O'Glaney sniffed. "Small likelihood, so long as you've been drinking it beforehand."

I did not at first take her meaning. Then I looked at the glass. It was empty. I remembered setting it down in Ivy Kellinch's room. How tiresome of her! She must have thought it was for her and drunk the whole of it! I did not envy her the headache she would have in the morning, for she had also indulged in a quantity of wine with her supper.

"Miss Kellinch must have drunk it, thinking I brought it for her," I explained.

Mrs. O'Glaney said stiffly, "Very like. A drinker of bloos and lees, that one. Mark me well."

I sat down to eat my own supper, and paused long enough to say, "I think if that rubble were removed, we should have less talk and less trouble. It breeds ghost tales, all that kelp growing over the broken stone and ruins. Are the Conors really so poor they cannot afford to remove it? I feel, at moments, that they are not so poor as they pretend."

Mrs. O'Glaney lighted her pipe by a spill in the fireplace, and thoughtfully puffed.

"Like as I was telling you this morning, they was rich as heathens afore Mr. Aengus had the thing happen. The Conors always did well, and did well by their tenants too, I may add. Even in conacre—them is the lease-holders, you know—even them had no complaints. Conor House was the only place hereabouts where the owners wa'n't absentee. Ay, the Conors be rich, right enough."

"But then—"

"Then suddenly, they are poor. Many's the time I've said to The O'Glaney, let us be putting by the rubbish and ruins on the headland. Let us make it look like the good Conor House of old. But himself, he won't touch it. Says the Kelpers will get him. For aught I know, mayhap they would. It's a strange place, the headland. Once it was fair and smooth. Now it's green as the sea-bottom, and treacherous with stones and weeds and what-not."

Rosaleen came in with one of Mrs. O'Glaney's day maids, and together they washed the dishes, so I went to my own rooms, and set my mind to enjoy the warmth of the fire and the good, thick comfort of my bed, which was a mockery on the face of it. There was no peace where that accursed headland crowded in at my bedchamber window. Even in my little sitting room I felt stifled, aware of the dark, slimy evil that wound its tentacles around the window, and had, that first night, reached into my very room for me.

Eventually, there was nothing for it but to go to bed, no matter what strange things might lie outside curling and twisting in the night air. I changed to my night clothes very much aware of the constant scratching sounds at the south window. I had determined not to give way to the ridiculous fear and superstition that was a kind of legacy to me, but presently, when I had brushed my hair and was ready for bed, I went to the window, despite myself, and thrusting the curtains aside, looked out. Just as on the first night, the horrid kelp pressed against the glass. Its opaque body, with the faint filtered moonlight flowing through it, looked for all the world like a floating ghostly creature, a lost soul, pressing to peer in at the world it had lost.

All the odd prickles along the length of the seaweed, its monstrous tumorous growths, appeared like eyes staring at me. Truly, I had had enough. I determined to remove this obscene growth before I ever slept in this room again. Strike with a hot iron, said I to myself in the voice I felt sure my mother would have used.

Upon the instant I changed my garments, put on my day dress, heavy slippers and my heaviest shawl which I arranged to cover my head and the greater part of my body, for it looked cold out upon those overturned rocks of the Kelper Head, and at the last minute had the problem of what sort of weapon would serve best against those toughened fibers. There was nothing in my warm little rooms that would serve, so I made my way toward the kitchen and by the light of the low-burning peat fire, I saw the head of an ax gleaming in one corner. I took it up and went directly down the main passage through the guardroom to the open headland. It might be best not to go contrary to the wishes of the Conors who seemed to prefer this rubble just as it was, but there could be no conceivable objection to my chopping away that growth which rapped and tapped and beckoned to me through my window.

The night was very still. Even the breakers at the escarpment seemed to have retreated, and the moon seeped through the fog so that the whole headland was cast in a peculiar, luminous glow. When I trod upon the slippery, sticky tendrils, they did not seem half so formidable as from my window; yet it eased my mind to employ this physical effort against them. I paused and glanced around at the opaque and frosty silver of the night.

A trim black corragh stood out to sea. I watched the little craft, remembering a tale told to me by my husband, of the dark God, Charon, ferrying the dead to the underworld. Surely, Charon must have poled just such a little black vessel!

What a thing to think of out here in the eerie night, vulnerable from almost every direction! I swung around, with my ax in the air, but found myself alone, as I had every reason to be. The ax whirred through the air, and when I brought it down, it very nearly lopped off one long tentacle of the obnoxious kelp. I kept to this sturdy work for several minutes while I became gradually conscious of an increase in the sounds around me. Subtly, mysteriously, the night sounds had come back.

It was as if they had waited, suspended in eternity, not stirring the air nor breathing, until they saw that I was no threat to them. Then they came back. . . .

The roar of the waves beating up the headland began to echo so that it seemed to come from the direction of the Ballyglen Bog, with all its night creatures astir. As I removed the longest tentacle of kelp from my bedchamber window, I had the strongest desire to look behind me, for the evil substance I had just handled seemed almost like a living, breathing creature, and I half expected to feel its tentacles winding insidiously around my throat.

It had taken me a scant ten minutes, and already the window was partially free of seaweed, although some of the overturned rocks would be less easy to remove. I would leave them until the morrow when, by daylight, perhaps I could persuade either the boy, Padraic, or O'Glaney to help me. I stepped back carefully, minding the sharp, jagged rocks, the slippery kelp-strewn ground, and was just chopping away what I thought might be my last bit of seaweed for the night, when a curtain was parted in a room on the Conor family's floor, and bright light pierced the scene, showing me absurdly armed with my ax, and heavily muffled in my shawl against the sea air.

I made out the figure of Dr. Jonathan looking down at me. Then the curtain closed. I wondered what he must think of this new housekeeper who had taken upon herself the forbidden task, the removal of some of this rubbish. Well, no matter! If he disapproved, so be it. I could sleep better tonight, knowing that accursed kelp was not spreading its feelers over my window.

I took up the heavy ax again, made one last tentative chop at a particularly tough specimen, and was about to give up for the night when the point of my ax caught in an old piece of decayed leather boot. I paused to extricate it.

A shadow crossed the headland, cast against Conor House, lengthening monstrously, like a creature hovering above me in the murky sky. It was an effect I had noticed in the Ballyglen Bog, but I liked it no better out here on the headland. The foggy moonlight gave the shadow a singular reality, rousing in me my first doubt that it was but a freak of fancy. I turned and looked over my shoulder.

The shadow had its source in a thing rising from the cove, first the head in the billed cap of the Kelp Gatherer, or so I fancied, then the familiar red fringed cloak. The creature advanced over the headland toward me, floating through the faint moon's rays, and dripping seaweed from head to toe. It was the seaweed, I think, that made the whole phantom seem transparent, for the light shown through those tentacles of kelp and appeared to emanate from the terrible figure.

I dropped the ax, and even above the echoing roar of the distant sea, I know that I made a sound which was half scream, half choked exclamation. I was stiff with terror.

The creature put out a hand, dripping kelp and gleaming in the moonlight, beckoning to me. The hand came closer and closer. At last, I knew that the beckoning was only a kind of groping . . . a terrible exhausted effort to touch me. Quite unable to contain myself, I turned to run toward the guardroom. Too late. The creature reached out. Ice-wet fingers caught in my shawl and clung there while I tried desperately to shake them off. I screamed, overcome by terror. The thing pressed against me, clinging, clinging, as the kelp sometimes did when it was especially sticky and full of prickles. Then, after my frantic struggle with the incubus, the fog cleared and the moon lighted the creature before me. The billed kelper's cap was only a cloak's hood, and the crimson wool cloak itself I had mistaken for a kelp gatherer's garments. The creature still groped to hold me, but its cold fingers were fast losing strength, and before I could tear away that covering hood, it fell with all its weight against me, knocking me down so that I struck the sharp, overturned rocks with a sickening blow that turned everything black for me momentarily.

Breathless, and with my head spinning, I opened my eyes a minute later to find myself looking into the stiffened features, the gleaming teeth, the staring eyes of Ivy Kellinch, her lips drawn back in agony, so that she looked for all the world like a dog about to snarl. But this poor creature would not snarl again. I had seen enough of death to recognize that Ivy Kellinch had staggered to me for help too late. I had let her die.

I felt her heart beneath the cloak and then her strong muscular wrist. There was no pulse. It was a particularly horrid sensation to see the whites of her eyes, gleaming in that awful blindness. By what means had she died? And how had she been able to stagger up from the cove to this spot to die? Drowning being thus out of the question, I could only assume that her heart had weakened, despite her fierce strength. I felt very deeply my own guilt in trying to run from her, but the red cloak, the hood, the entire figure, had seemed so like the kelper ghosts. . . .

It was my fault. I should have had the courage to save her. Poor Ivy Kellinch! I recalled those last seconds when she clung to me with all her waning strength, and I had run from her, a dying woman.

I heard a footstep crunch on the guardroom floor and looked up quickly, ready for almost anything. The ax I had dropped in my panic lay close to hand, and I felt for it. I made out the figure of Doctor Jonathan Trumble. He strode quickly from the guardroom to kneel beside me and my poor burden.

"Who is it? I see. How did it happen?"

"I don't know," I murmured hoarsely, having difficulty in finding my voice. "She just—died. Staggered up from the cove and . . . died."

He worked over her as he explained, "I saw you hacking at that seaweed and came down to help you. It should have been got away long ago."

His fingers, strong and rough, yet so expert, moved over Ivy's head and neck. He loosened the cloak, felt for her heart-beat, shook his head. His face was dark and a little glowering in the moonlight, but he so obviously knew what to do that I felt complete confidence in him.

"She does not seem to have been injured in any way."
He glanced up at me, his voice warmer, with a tenderness
that brought to mind my husband's voice upon occasion.
"But what's happened to you, Anne? You've a nasty cut over
your eye. Did it happen when Ivy fell against you?"

"No, no," I disclaimed quickly, anxious to banish the
painful memory of her dying moments that his words evok-
ed. "A cormorant, I think it was."

"Don't be touching it. You only worsen it," he said, but
I broke in to change his thoughts.

"Can it be her heart failed her?" I ventured timidly. It
was not my province, after all.

He had finished his examination of Ivy's head.

"That's as may be. I shouldn't have thought it, however."

Nor I.

As he turned to examining her hands that looked like
veined marble in the moonlight, I saw his fingers pause.
He had been so busy, so efficient, that this sudden stillness, the lack of movement, caught my attention. He glanced
at me, saw me watching. I said, "I believe something is
caught in her fingers, sir."

He opened the dead fingers. There was a twist of black
wool caught in Ivy Kellinch's death grip.

"No but a bit of string." He took it beween his own
fingers, rubbed the black yarn into a ball and would have
tossed it away but that I caught my breath sharply. "Why?
What is it?" he asked.

I pointed to it. "Don't you see, sir? Don't you recognize
it?"

He studied the telltale strands.

"Well then?"

"But sir, they are fringes from a lady's shawl." I looked
down at my own green shawl and showed him the fringed
ends. "Like this, you see."

He said at last, direct and flat out, "From my wife's black
shawl, you think. And it's a lie! I do not know how Ivy
came by this, but there's another reason."

"Very likely," I said because I wanted to believe it.

"It could have got into Ivy's hand a hundred ways. Besides, Maury is incapable of such a thing."

"What thing, sir?" I asked evenly.

He looked away from me, returned to his study of the

110

corpse. Salt water ran from around Ivy Kellinch's body. She must have fallen at the shore's edge, before she staggered to my side.

Jonathan studied her thoughtfully, saying to me, "What really matters is—why she was down there at the cove at all. You're certain you saw her come from there?"

"Quite certain, sir. She came up from the beach, it seems to me."

"Like as not she was meeting some local lad. A love-tryst. Still, it's not in the least like Ivy Kellinch."

I could only agree with him. I was beginning to have my own theory.

"I believe she was running away, sir. And then she had the heart attack, or whatever, and came back for help."

Dr. Jonathan's eyes opened a trifle wider. I had really astonished him.

"Good Lord, why? Why was she running away?"

"I think she expected to come into money. Or perhaps she already had it, and it was lost in the sea when she fell."

"Where would she get the money? We're all poor as Job hereabouts," he added with a grim laugh. He had finished his examination for the moment and looked around for some way to bear her inside without disturbing her more than was necessary. I started to guess again at the cause of her death, but he cut me short in his pleasant but efficient way. "Will you fetch O'Glaney and explain the difficulty? Ask him to bring blankets. . . . Ah! Here is Mrs. O'Glaney."

I looked up and saw the good woman standing in the guardroom doorway, hands on her hips, ready to demand what in the name of all the Saints we were doing out here at this hour, but one look from Dr. Jonathan silenced her.

"If you please, Sara. We're needing blankets and your husband. And Master Theo too, if he is at home."

She started to obey but could not forbear asking with a shyness unlike her: "Who—who is it, sir?"

"Nurse Kellinch," said the doctor briefly. "Please go."

I half expected her to sniff and make some remark about the wonderful workings of Providence, but she did not. She looked excessively pale in the moonlight, and almost tottered as she went to fetch her husband and Theo Conor.

Ivy seemed especially pitiable to me as I glanced at her still form again, for I noticed now the deep ragged wound that bled no longer, just under her left ear. I hoped the blow had occurred after her death, so she had not felt it. It seemed peculiarily my fault that I had not come to her assistance when she first clung to me in her death throes.

When I saw Theo Conor arrive almost immediately I knew that Mrs. O'Glaney's husband had proved too drunk for the task. Master Theo was unwontedly serious when told the news, and obeyed all of Dr. Jonathan's instructions very carefully. Between them, they soon had Ivy Kellinch's body removed to an empty room near mine on the ground floor. I could see that no one was anxious to sit up with the corpse, and feeling my own guilt in not having saved her, I volunteered to do so, though I confess the whole notion chilled me. I was relieved when Lady Maeve came down, said nothing surprised her that happened to Ivy Kellinch, and then told me it would not be necessary to sit with the corpse. Nurse Kellinch had not been Catholic; at least, no one remembered ever seeing her inside a church.

"About the magistrate, ma'am," I ventured. "Shouldn't the Lord Lieutenant's representatives in the County be informed, as well as the burial folk?"

"In due course," said Lady Maeve. "All in due course." But I had an idea my suggestion did not go down well, at all.

I wondered what would be done about the bits of black fringe which I had seen minutes ago in Dr. Trumble's hand. Presently, as Lady Maeve was warming her hands at my fire before retiring and I was in my bedchamber wardrobe, fetching a sheet to put over the dead woman, I saw Her Ladyship go to my passage door and beckon to someone. Then Theo Conor came in, and they whispered together. I saw that she had something in her hand and showed it to Theo. This time he was quite audible.

"Maury's, do you think?"

"Of course it is Maury's. We've seen the shawl often enough. The one she uses when she's feeding those tiresome gulls on the terrace."

"God in heaven!" Theo exclaimed. "What next, then?"

I called from my bedchamber, "Pardon, did you say something, Your Ladyship?"

There was a pause before Lady Maeve said, "No, Anne. I was only bidding Theo good night."

I came into the little sitting room with the sheet, and saw that Lady Maeve no longer had what must have been the shawl fringes in her hand. Had she given them to Theo to dispose of?

Dr. Jonathan called me, and I went down the passage to him. Together, we shrouded the dead woman as well as possible.

"Did you give the fringes to Lady Maeve?" I asked him point-blank.

He was looking more angry than I had ever seen him, and I wondered if this might be the cause.

"She saw me when I tried to burn them in the kitchen. I told her I found it on the guardroom floor. I shall be grateful if you'll tell her the same tale, Anne."

"Certainly, sir. Unless—"

"Yes?"

I was in difficulties. Loyalty was very well, but to connive against the law was another thing. I did not know quite what to do.

"The magistrates may never hear of it. In that case, I can promise you I will say nothing."

He took my hand a moment as we left the dreary little windowless room.

"I count upon you for that, Anne. Say what you will, if you are asked the direct question. But otherwise, I know you'll protect my poor lass. I have no one else I can trust."

I felt the warmth of pride at his words. "I hope you can always trust me, sir, and I hope Miss Maury can do the same."

He did not smile but his harsh features relaxed a little. I was glad I was responsible for that, at any rate.

Theo Conor called him then, and together they went down to the cove to see, as Theo put it, whether there were any signs of a partner in Ivy's rendezvous with death.

I went back to the kitchen and returned the ax I had borrowed. The faint light of the coals in the fireplace was reflected by myriad lights from the crystal glass Lady Maeve had given me.

It was, I thought, a pity that Ivy Kellinch drank all the contents. I was a good deal shaken by the night's events and felt the need of something to warm me.

It was very odd, Ivy's death. She had seemed healthy enough an hour or two gone by. Before, in fact, I brought the crystal glass of whisky and set it down within reach of her.

I examined the glass. It had been washed and polished. My mind was full of unaccustomed fears and suspicions. If there was anything foreign in the whisky, had it been meant for me . . . and not for Ivy Kellinch?

IX

I LAY DOWN upon my bed fully dressed save for my shoes, thinking to be ready, should I be needed. Every few minutes I touched Aengus Conor's letter at my bosom and wondered how I could wait until noon on the morrow to carry out his orders and start for Ballyglen. I would much prefer to have had the wracking matter ended as soon as possible.

It was with considerable relief that I heard Master Theo and the doctor some time later as they passed under my windows, and both seemed agreed that nothing more could be done that night. But my relief was shortlived. Theo, crying, "Oh, the devil!" caught his booted foot in some of the kelp I had cut down but neglected to remove, and he paused to extricate himself from the clinging stuff.

"Then you are determined upon this tale of heart seizure?" I heard Jonathan ask, as though this were an ultimatim.

"My dear Jono, your surgical abilities will hardly be considerable enough to route Maeve, if that is the story she and Aengus agree upon."

I could sense that this had cut Dr. Jonathan upon the raw, and I understood it, much as if my own housekeeping talents had been questioned.

"My abilities aren't in this business. I may not be gentleman enough to attend on Aengus, but I know a heart seizure when I see it. And if I do, another will. Ivy did not die by a heart seizure. The veriest butcher who examines her will give me the lie. And then they'll be asking why I lied."

How lordly were all the Conors, I thought. And how insignificant were mere mortals like Dr. Jonathan and myself! It was not fair, I told myself, as I listened.

"Until you think of some more reasonable—and safe—explanation of her death, it's a heart seizure! Now, I'll pose another for you," said Theo reasonably, having stilled Jona-

115

than's protests in an underhanded way. "The marks in the wet sand just below the Headland path. You will maintain they were only Ivy's footprints?"

I sat up in bed, suddenly alert. The men had paused by my window to finish their argument. I did not like the direction it was taking.

"Ivy's, certainly. Or at worst, a man's prints. But not another woman."

Maureen's shawl fringe. That was what they were coming to. And yet Theo laughed. There was in it some of the sarcasm as though other meanings were hidden behind that humor.

"Best keep to the heart seizure even if it does brand you a butcher of a surgeon, as you say. For it will be said by those who see the prints that another woman was there, and well you know it! I am not blind."

Jonathan's deeper voice cut him short.

"Your eyes were mistaken! Are you so greedy for my poor Maury's inheritance?"

"Good God! For pure audacity!" muttered Theo, not very coherently.

"Well then," said Jonathan. "Listen to me. Those were all Ivy's footprints. Or they were the prints of a man in town-shoes."

"Very likely," Theo jeered. "And how did he kill her? By frightening her to death? You don't frighten Ivy Kellinch easily."

He was moving beyond my window when Jonathan murmured suddenly,

"What of poison? There'll be a thing about the pupils of her eyes. . . . Maybe I am refining too much on it. But laudanum is a possibility."

Theo raised his voice. What a temper! He was angry again.

"Charming! She took some of my stepmother's laudanum, or some of yours, in order to put herself to sleep, and then went walking. Come now, Jono, you must do better than that."

"I will do better. I'll put whatever facts I have in the hands of the Lord Lieutenant's man. He'll fetch up the truth. Ivy Kellinch went to meet a man, not my wife!"

"You will put *all* facts in the hands of the authorities?

Including the damned black yarn from Maury's shawl, and the other footprints?" Theo asked.

"Ay! To include Ivy's footprints By day all footprints will have washed away, and God knows you'd best get your evidence straight with Maeve's and mine. Maureen never left our room all evening. And that I'll swear to at any Assizes! She was there five minutes before I went down to see what the prowler on the Headland was about. It was Miss Wicklow, of course, that I saw from the window, and doing what we should have done months ago, removing this filth that holds fast to Conor House. But believe me, Maureen was with me when Ivy staggered up the Headland to die. We can swear to that!"

"Ever the loyal husband," Theo said in a voice I could not acquit of sneering. "I suppose you have a neat explanation for the fringe, as well."

I moved to the window and unashamedly eavesdropped; for Jonathan's voice seemed further away as he apparently moved about, picking up kelp, or examining it.

"As to the fringe, it might prove something quite the other way round. That someone is wishing to destroy my wife. But it's no matter about the fringe now, since it is gone, and I'll deny its existence. I warn you to leave Maureen out of this, Theo."

"Oho!" cried Theo. "You warn me; do you? And shall I wake to find laudanum in my tea, my fine doctor?"

To this Jonathan answered coldly: "I've never known you to drink tea, my dear Theo. I'd do better to lace your whisky with it."

This caused Theo to laugh in earnest, and I was relieved when Dr. Jonathan bade him good night again, in a friendlier voice, and they separated, Jonathan going into the guardroom, and presently his footsteps sounded upon the winding steps. Master Theo wandered off toward the silent white coteens in the village.

Laudanum in the whisky! I sat in bed and pondered this, and shivered with the dampness of the night, and perhaps with my thoughts as well. If Ivy Kellinch had been poisoned by the crystal glass of whisky, it had been done in a singularly roundabout way. It was only by accident that Ivy drank it. But for her greed, or her thirst, as I had realized earlier tonight, I should have drunk the whisky.

But why was it necessary to poison me, a stranger to Conor House? I had no real bonds in this household. True, I admired Dr. Jonathan in many ways, not the least for the way he kept his dignity in the face of the Conor arrogance. How it must sear his very natural pride to know that intellect and professional skill meant nothing in the face of an earldom, or an ancient Irish name!

But was our common position of social inferiority enough to arouse someone's hatred of me? And if so, who else but Jonathan's wife?

I would not believe it. Besides, it was Lady Maeve who gave me the whisky glass. But then, perhaps Her Ladyship had not known the whisky was poisoned. An entire whisky decanter containing enough laudanum so that one glass would kill. . . . Surely that was a greater threat to Lady Maeve than to me.

And what of the footprints around the sand where Ivy Kellinch had been walking? Were they Ivy's own footprints? Surely, the men had found her double tracks, going and coming. And there were more footprints. Ivy's? Or another woman's? Or a man in town-shoes, as Jonathan tried to claim?

In those midnight hours my senses darted from suspicion to suspicion. It was quite conceivable that someone had put laudanum into Maeve Conor's decanter in the natural expectation that she herself would die of it.

In that case, she might drink of that decanter at any time.

I sighed and shivered, and finally threw off the coverlet, knowing I could not sleep until I had satisfied myself that no one else would drink from that decanter before morning. Probably an investigation would prove that the whisky was harmless; yet I could not gamble upon that. I was still dressed, but it took some time to gather up a cloak and my bedslippers. They would be quieter than shoes, and I did not wish to arouse the household again, after the recent calamitous events. The person to help me would be Mrs. O'Glaney. But could we trust Lady Maeve? She seemed the logical one for either the cook or myself to go to with our tale. I could not very well meet Dr. Jonathan at this time of night. Whatever the cause or justification, it would assuredly prey upon Miss Maureen's overwrought nerves. No. We must see Lady Maeve. If the entire decanter had been poisoned, and I saw her pour from it myself, the original threat was to her and not to me or to Ivy Kellinch.

By the light of a bed-candle I made my way through the drafty hall to the stillroom which joined the escarpment wall, and discovered a serviceable storm-lantern whose candle was well protected from sudden winds and the moist seepage of the walls and floors. With this I found my way along the passage into which Mr. and Mrs. O'Glaney's rooms opened. I rapped on the door, hearing furious snores within, from which I needed no one to tell me that O'Glaney was sleeping off a busy night of whisky drinking in the village. To make myself heard over this unmusical sound was an effort, but presently Mrs. O'Glaney came to the door and opened it just a crack. An incongruously frilled nightcap crowned her head, and her face looked very old and worn in the light of my lantern. I was sorry it had been necessary to disturb her.

"Oh, it's you, miss. Surely there'll be no more things happening this night?"

"No, no. I'm sorry to disturb you. It is only that someone may have put a drug into Lady Maeve's whisky decanter in the morning room. I wondered if you would go with me and remove the whisky."

"Now?" she asked, her pale blue eyes widening until you would have thought I was the Devil himself.

"But someone may drink of it at any time. . . ."

"Let them," she said firmly. "Good riddance to that wicked Kellinch woman. Treating my Miss Maury as if she was a prisoner, and ordering her about as though Miss Maury wasn't the lady of Conor House, indeed!"

Behind her, the O'Glaney snores took a turn for the worse, and she ducked around and yelled at him, "Now, will you be still then, man!" When she gave me her attention once again, she had a little more color in her face, but her attitude had in no way changed. "Lookee, miss, it's no call of us to stop their drinking. Her La'ship knows what she's about, and ye may lay a guinea to that!"

It was cold, and I was discouraged and not a little unnerved by the blackness beyond my lantern. I very nearly agreed with Sara O'Glaney, but the thought of another poisoning in the household was too great a risk.

"Very well. Then I must go. Do you think Lady Maeve may still be in the morning room?"

"I'd not be knowing. You may see the lights cast from the morning room on the terrace if you step out upon the headland. But you'll go alone, miss. I've no mind to be passing the shade of Ivy Kellinch. It'll be abroad this night, and no mistake. Ay! It's as if I saw her now, a-floating down the guardroom in all her evil ways. . . . Good night to you, miss." She backed away from the door to close it.

There was nothing for it but to walk back through the guardroom, past the little cubicle room where Ivy Kellinch lay. I liked the idea of Ivy's ghost no better than did Mrs. O'Glaney. I hurried along, fancying all sorts of odd noises behind me, and half expecting at any minute to be tapped on the shoulder by the floating apparition of the dead nurse. Her room was very silent. I had a notion to look in and assure myself that the shrouded body was still there. I resisted this appeal to my most childlike fears, and stepped boldly out upon the headland where she had died. As the cook said, I could make out a faint light through the half-open shutters at the south window of the morning room. It was a great relief to know that Lady Maeve was there, for it would mean no more prowling about this unhealthy house in the bad hours before dawn, the hours when the dead are said to walk.

I went back inside and swiftly ascended the winding steps and with intense relief, reached the door of the morning room. I tried the knob. It was warm, as though grasped only a moment before, but the door did not give. I rapped and when I got no reply, I pushed the door, first gently, then with all my strength. It was obviously locked. Lady Maeve must have left this room only seconds before I arrived, in which case she would still be near, in the hall or on the way upstairs.

I listened, but I heard nothing. Pretending that I still thought she was in the morning room, I called in a low voice, "Lady Maeve! May I speak to you?"

I was beginning to wonder if it had been Lady Maeve, after all, whose light I saw in the morning room when I looked up from the headland. I leaned against the door, wondering what on earth I should do.

It would be necessary to go up to the next floor and rap

on Lady Maeve's door. This presented difficulties. Did she, or did she not, share Mr. Aengus's bedchamber? I seemed to remember, from my conversation this afternoon with him, that his wife's apartment was at the end of the corridor, the north chamber, in fact.

I wrapped my cloak more securely around me, and started up the final flight of stairs. I fancied I heard something astir, either on the floor I had quitted, or on the winding stone steps leading up from the guardroom and my quarters, but no one else seemed to be about. I decided my imagination had outgrown my common sense, and proceeded up the stairs to the top floor. Surely, no one was abroad but me at this hour, unless, of course, it was the person who had just quitted the morning room. I chided myself severely for my fears. Ivy's astonishing death had shaken me so that even the slightest sound sent me into flutters quite unlike myself.

On the top floor as I walked along the corridor, I saw no tell-tale light beneath the doors to suggest that anyone else in the house was still awake. I began to wish I had never even seen that troublesome decanter.

At the far end of the corridor I paused before the door of the north chamber. It was not quite closed, caught by the bolt which was only half-shot. I rapped lightly. The sound seemed inordinately loud to my strained attention. There was no answer, but the door swung inward under my knock. Still there was no protest or response. I stepped inside, whispering, "Lady Maeve, it is Ann Wicklow. May I speak to you?"

Hearing nothing but the whistling wind and the muffled blows of the surf upon the escarpment far below, I raised the lantern and looked around the big room. It appeared very much as it had this afternoon (or was it now yesterday?) during my interview with Aengus Conor. Lady Maeve's bedgown and robe were laid over a chaise longue at the other end of the room, but she herself was nowhere to be seen.

Suddenly, I heard a heavy thump in Mr. Aengus's room, as though something had fallen upon the floor. I could not mistake the curse that followed. Mr. Aengus apparently had the quick, mercurial temper of the other Conors. I hesitated to disturb him in his present mood, but someone had to be warned and despite his condition he was, after all, the head of the household and should know what was happening under his very nose.

I went back into the corridor and rapped upon his door. "Well, well, don't be dallying! Come in!" commanded the voice I remembered so well from my visit yesterday afternoon. I tried the door, found it yielded, and went in, standing in the doorway waiting to be given further orders. The room was dark, and my lantern flickered fitfully over the distant, curtained bed. Presently, his lean, hard fingers closed upon the bed curtains, pulled them aside, and his face peered out at me. He was wearing a tasseled night cap which looked ludicrous against the fine, sculptured planes of his shadowy face. I started to raise the lantern, but he waved it aside and said curtly, "Now, see what you've done. Tallow upon the carpet. Set it down and come near me."

I did as I was bidden, wondering at his power to make me obey him so instantly, despite the rudeness of his orders.

"Well?" he prompted me as I approached the bed and saw him half-raised in bed, propped up by pillows behind him, and framed like a king at *Levée* by the ancient but elegant bed-curtains, that were only partially open.

"Sir, it is the whisky decanter in the morning room. After Miss Ivy's death, I heard the doctor and your son discussing the possibility of laudanum poisoning, and I remembered that decanter."

With the curious humor which lighted his eyes but not his sculptured mouth, he protested, "You'll not be telling me you fed laudanum to that creature!"

"No, sir. It is only that she drank from a glass poured for me by your wife. And after she died, I wondered . . ."

"It is my wife then that you accuse of Borgia tendencies?"

It was very tiresome to play games at this time of night with an invalid who probably did not have enough to amuse him during the day.

"I thought it might have been the whisky decanter. In which case, as you see, sir, the laudanum might have been meant for Lady Maeve . . . if there is any of it in that decanter at all."

He appeared to think this over, and eyed me with one brow cocked, as if trying to read my mind. The lantern across the room flickered and cast strange shadows on his face, so that I looked away from him uneasily.

"Nonsense," he said, at last, "Maeve takes laudanum to sleep, just as I do. It would be very unlikely to poison her if she drank the decanter dry. It might, however, have killed you. Or Nurse Kellinch. Where did you get this idea about laudanum?"

"Dr. Trumble mentioned it tonight."

After a pause he exclaimed impatiently, "That underbred rent-agent's brat! What a fool! Doesn't he know that it places him under gravest suspicion? He is, after all is said, a physician of sorts, and carries laudanum."

I felt a strong desire to defend Dr. Jonathan, but something in the shadowy recesses of Aengus Conor's face made me hesitate. He might guess, or suspect, that my feelings were not quite unprejudiced. I said instead, "There must be many easier ways for a doctor to kill a woman than by a drug which will point directly to him, sir."

"Possibly." He seemed to have his mind on something else.

I ventured, "Why do you mislike him, sir?"

He looked at me directly and laughed.

"Because, I suppose, Maeve rather despises him. It's habit, you see. She used to refine too much upon his background, or lack of one, and his language and habits which she is forever correcting. They grew up together, you know, the Earl's daughter and the son of a wretched little snirp who squeezed every farthing of rents out of our poor devils here so that the half of them were forever starving. And then, for such a creature's son to ask for my daughter's hand! The presumption of him! Good God! What next will these underbred commoners aspire to?"

One would have thought the daughter of the West County farmer, Aengus Conor, was a child of many kings. I very nearly made the tactical error of laughing at this pride of his.

"Perhaps if he were allowed to treat you, it might help."

"Rubbish! Won't have the fellow near me. Pock-marked Yorkshire pup! Did you know that I offered him money to break off with Maureen? Wouldn't take it, the fool. Very furious and waved his fists and talked of my insulting him; so nothing came of it. The fellow's an idiot!"

"Yet he has been good for Miss Maureen," I reminded him. He paused, seemed to regard this as a curious line of thought, as though either it was false, or it had never occurred to him before.

"That's as may be. Maury has always been weak in the head. It happens that way at birth, sometimes. But those of us who love her, love her the more for it."

I could understand that. Her very childlike qualities, her mercurial moods, the Conor temper made more mercurial by her mental weakness, were endearing to any who met her. But even so, I felt that Mr. Aengus was fortunate that Maureen had married a doctor, and not someone who knew nothing of proper treatment in such cases. She might even have married someone with the pride of her own father, who would, very likely, have despised her, not appreciating her qualities. I said no more on that score, however.

"And now about the whisky decanter," Aengus Conor said after a little silence during which he straightened his pillows and sighed. "You will find a key to the lock and bolt in that tabaret yonder. Take it, and go into the morning room, remove the decanter and bring it up to me. Do not look into it, or destroy it. You understand?"

"Quite. Thank you, sir." In great relief, I did as I was ordered, took my lantern, lighted a bed-candle for him on the table by the door, and left him quickly.

There were no sounds in the lower hall except the wind, now receding with the dawn, and I hurriedly opened the door, fetched the decanter and locked the door and returned to Mr. Aengus's room with the key and the beautiful glass container which gave off a thousand sparkles in the flickering light of my lantern.

"Now then," said Aengus, "you'll not have forgot tomorrow's errand?"

I put my hand self-consciously to my bosom, remembering the sealed paper there, and saw him smile at me, across the room, from behind the half-opened bed curtains.

"Good girl. Shall I be counting upon you?"

"Tomorrow, sir. As soon as the investigation into Miss Ivy's death is done."

"Excellent." I started to leave, and he added more sharply, "Do not mention this decanter at the investigation. It may have no bearing upon it whatsoever. You know nothing about it. Do you understand?"

"Yes, sir." I went out, puzzled and not a little disturbed by that parting admonition. I would have preferred that the entire story be told, and the truth revealed, all of it. It would seem that at Conor House all of the truth must never be known.

I returned to my rooms below in an uncertain state entirely. I should be hard put to remember what items I must forget when questioned today by the Lord Lieutenant's representative in the County.

Just before falling asleep I reflected how fortunate it was that Aengus Conor was still awake, so that I could tell him my tale without first rousing him from sleep. If it had been anyone but a crippled man, I should have thought he had only that instant come into his room. But that was patently impossible, and I went to sleep at last, still puzzling over it.

X

My NATURAL good health asserted itself during those hours of rest, so that I awoke refreshed shortly after the servants were up and about. After an all-over scrubbing from a large ewer of ice-crusted water, which did wonders to waken me, I dressed clean from the skin out, and felt ready to face Conors, laudanum, Lord-Lieutenants of Ireland, and the benighted Act of Union itself.

As I was hurrying through breakfast so as not to discommode the Conors who would be ringing at any moment, Miss Maureen came into the kitchen where Mrs. O'Glaney sat with me at the old, knife-scarred table. The cook was peeling potatoes for the early dinner, but brightened when she saw her favorite in the doorway.

"There's my little lady, and as fair to see as any in Ireland, it is."

Maureen gave us both a big smile, peculiarly childlike and guileless, so guileless that I wondered, as she kissed Mrs. O'Glaney's cheek, whether it was possible that she was, in fact, far more intelligent than she pretended to be. I had had experience of such matters in my life, and once almost died of a misplaced trust in guileless innocence. But there was no mistrusting Miss Maury. She turned to me and gave me her hand and said as if reciting a lesson, "Dear Anne, Jono says I am to look to you for protection now. Ivy is dead, and you are to take her place."

I could not help wishing that her news had been expressed in a different way for I saw Sara O'Glaney look at me with an odd expression, and then say gently to Maureen, "Let us no'be wishing Miss will take that creature's place in all ways, lamb. Only in the way of being companion to you, and looking out for you, so no harm will come."

Dimples appeared in Maureen's face as she giggled.

"Oh, I didn't mean she was to take Ivy's place in that

horrid graveyard. Poor Ivy. Buried so far from home."

"She is to be buried here?" I asked curiously.

"After the churching, and after there's been the talking and the keening and the things they do when people die. Theo's been out early to ask Sir Horace Pumbleby to sit and hear what's said about Ivy's death. Sir Horace is the magistrate for the County and a cousin to the Lord-Lieutenent of Ireland, you know."

"You'll be taking Miss Maury," the cook said briskly to me. "They'll meet for the talking down t'other end of the coteens. It's the building they use for the famine times and the Board of Works. You may even meet Sir Horace, Miss, so you'd best be gowned for it in whatever you may have in the way of being respectable but not forward."

I smiled. "I shall try to choose wisely."

Maureen broke off a piece of the potato I was about to eat, and popped it into her mouth.

"If I can't have Jono to take me, I'd as lief have you, Anne. But," she added importantly, "Jonathan is wanted today. They admire him in the village, whatever they may think of him at home. Only last week he cured an infant of the black leg. Horrid thing. Why should my Jono have to go near such things?"

I saw that Maureen had no more feeling for her fellow men than the rest of the Conors, and could not help telling her, "It is not the child's fault that it had the black leg, Miss Maureen. It may be, as my husband was used to say, that such diseases are brought by hunger and bad conditions. Perhaps your family should do a little more for the villagers and you would not be exposed to such 'horrid things."

She wrinkled her nose.

"You talk like Jonathan. It is all very well for men to think like that, but it is none of my doing. I didn't make them peasants."

Mrs. O'Glaney avoided my eyes when I looked at her, and I gave up any attempt to teach Maureen her duty to humanity.

As I got up to change my clothes for what Maureen and the cook conceived to be a Grand Occasion, Mrs. O'Glaney walked with me down the guardroom to my own passage.

"Ye musn't be thinking, miss, that all Conors is heartless. Maybe Mr. Aengus was, afore he was taken sick, even though he was good with the tenants and the conacrefolk. But Master Theo now and again does what he can, when he thinks upon it. Since his father's illness he's become a bit more of a rogue, I think, than afore, but he began as a good boy, and only seems to have turned wild with the attack upon his father."

"And Miss Maureen's husband?" I asked.

She shrugged. "He does well enough in the coteens. But he can't be too good, because Mr. Aengus won't have him near. Howsomever, I'll be saying this for Dr. Jonathan, it's a pity he's not Irish; for he may have the good making of one."

I laughed at this and left her.

As I came out of my sitting room a little later in what I hoped was the correct gown, my best cloak and bonnet, I was accosted by two burly men, each deferentially holding his stocking cap crushed in one great hand.

"Will ye be tellin' us, now, me darlin' miss, where's the corpse that's to be?" one of them asked.

I showed them the little room where poor Ivy Kellinch lay shrouded, and they went in and took up the terrible, sheeted bundle and carried it out between them, grinning at me in thanks, and the one telling the other a long, involved tale about a corpse he had brought to the church a year gone, and how it had not been properly dead, and moved and twitched and stiffened straightaway under his very eyes. I shuddered.

"Don't mind them," said Maureen cheerfully as she joined me. "It's talk like that, or weep. I know them. It was the same when my mother died many years ago. It keeps them hard, for the life."

I could not believe my ears. "But Miss Maury, I thought you did not care what became of the villagers?"

"Sometimes I do." She looked sober, adult, fully her true age. Then the other look came over her face, like a mask. "Sometimes I do not. I don't like to think about things like that. They make me sad because they put me in mind that I must soon go and—do the bad thing."

"What bad thing?"

"I must," she said, and then repeated in a sing-song

way as she straightened the collar of my gown over my cloak. "I must . . . must . . . must do it, because it is what is to happen to me. I mustn't tell you more. It is a secret. Come. I'll show you something. Would you like to know where I go when I want to be alone, a place nobody but me ever goes, away from everyone but God? Where I may talk to God?"

The back of my neck prickled.

"We must go to the village, Miss Maury," I reminded her, hoping to change the subject.

"Yes, yes. But later. Let me show you. It is very close. . . . Come." She led me along by the hand, and I followed reluctantly. I could not imagine what she had in mind. We went back through the house, and just beyond the kitchen in the darkest corner of the guardroom, she pointed out a door in the escarpment wall that I had not noticed before. Its ancient hinges were thick with rust and the seepage of endless salt sprays. Even before she touched the door I could tell that it must be difficult to move. But Maureen went over to the door and began to pull and push in such a way as to put the heavy stone door off its regular circumference. I did not quite see how she managed, but the door began to swing open very slowly where the stone floor beneath had been eaten away by the ages and the sea, and there was always a runnel of sea water. Presently, it was just wide enough for us to pass through. Still reluctant, I found myself pulled by her persistent hand, out onto a narrow sandy ledge where the tide had run out a foot or two below. I leaned back against the great escarpment wall and peered up. It seemed many kilometers to the top of the escarpment. I had never seen a wall so impressive as this great, stone barrier against which the sea, racing over our little ledge, beat so fiercely at high tide.

"We are alone with Things, out here," said Maureen, her eyes rapt and wondering as she stared at the sea creeping away from her feet, and then at the blue sky overhead. "I come out here very often when no one knows, when the tide is out. Some day I might stay here until the tide comes in."

I looked at her in horror. "Miss Maureen, what are you thinking of! Do you know how strong that tide would be? The fury of those breakers against the escarpment . . .

I could even feel the force shake the house last night in your father's apartments."

She said quietly, "What might you be doing in father's apartments last night?"

I reddened at the idiocy of the trap into which I had fallen. "He asked me to bring him a decanter of whisky."

"How did he ask you?" she went on in that expressionless voice. "Did he ring? But then, Maeve would have come. Did he call to you? But that would be difficult; wouldn't it? You being so far away, in your own room." All the time she spoke, she was looking at me in such an odd way, as though someone else were inside the girlish sweet face of her. Someone adult, someone frightening. I looked around, partly to avoid her strange look, and partly, also, to see if there was any way off this little pit of wet sand and stone besides the half-opened door in front of which she stood. But it was like a tiny island surrounded by the sea. It was an extraordinary thing to find myself physically afraid of her. She was the one person in the household that I had never feared in that way, until this moment.

"I came up to speak with Lady Maeve," I explained. "And your father heard me and asked me to do the errand for him."

"I wonder," she said brightly again, "if he could be like Maeve, both living and dead. Able to summon up people to do his bidding, as the dead can do."

"The dead are dead," I told her sharply and reached behind her for the door. "They do not come back."

She sighed like a child again. "Oh, I wish I could believe it. I shouldn't wish to come back physically. But when we are dead, we are sometimes better loved by those who remain. They belong to us and we belong to them, more than if we lived."

"You must not talk like this," I said, selfishly remembering my own terrible and aching loss, my love who was dead and would not come back to me.

She ignored me. "If I were gone, how sorry they would be, sorrier than now, and not so out of reason cross with me when I behave badly. . . . But if we stay here longer they will put Ivy in the ground without us."

"Very true," I said, and after the two of us had closed the escarpment door behind us we were only just in time to join Lady Maeve, who was waiting with the pony cart at the entrance to Conor House, and would have made room for both of us except that I could see it was a close fit. I decided to walk the distance. It would be the first time I had done so since the day I arrived. Then I remembered that this afternoon I would be walking to Ballyglen and was greatly relieved when Dr. Jonathan came up from the coteens on horseback and volunteered to take his wife up with him. This pleased Maureen immensely, and it was with the pleasure of an adult watching a child that I saw her seated with her husband's arms securely holding her, as he handled the reins. She waved at us from her high seat, very proud, and my heart gave a little tug of mingled jealousy and happiness for her, as I saw how she loved her husband's arms about her.

Dr. Jonathan looked down at me to say in his deep, remembered voice, "We give you a deal of trouble, don't we, Anne? But you know you have all my—gratitude."

I tried not to look the pleasure that his words gave me, but as I got into the pony cart beside Lady Maeve she said suddenly, "You find him attractive?"

"He is kind," I said.

"And rudely, roughly attractive," she agreed; and added lightly, "but for having his pockets to let, and that frightful Yorkshire twang, he should have been nearly exceptional."

"He may not always be poor," I reminded her.

"His kind? An interesting thought."

Glancing at her I wondered, too, if perhaps she did not regret her choice of the rich Conor rather than the boy who had been reared and educated by her father. It was true that Aengus Conor, in his strange devil's way, held a fascination for me. But what did Lady Maeve feel for the man she had married, thinking him rich, only to find that he also had "his pockets to let." It must have been a severe shock to her, despite the settlement Mr. Aengus made upon her at their marriage. Enough of a shock so that she might even destroy the Conors in the hope of salvaging something out of the ancient glories?

What a wicked thought! I had no proof of these suspicions; yet here was I, willing to believe the worst of a woman who had shown me nothing but kindness.

"Did Your Ladyship notice the removal of the decanter from the morning room?"

"Yes," she said, looking straight ahead as she maneuvered the reins and the little pony started down the slope off Kelper Head. "I believe we are to thank you for the thought."

"Did—" It was difficult to frame my question. "Did Mr. Aengus discover whether it had been poisoned?"

"It was not. However . . ."

I felt the most ridiculous disappointment. I had not wished that there should be laudanum in that whisky, and yet I felt a complete fool for having disturbed everyone over a harmless decanter of Irish whisky.

"Well then, ma'am, I am glad of that. Faith, it might have been meant for Your Ladyship."

"It might," she said, a trifle grimly, I thought; and added the crushing reminder, "Henceforth, it might be as well if we leave such spying for those properly suited to the task. Not that I mean to be unkind, my dear. But it is conceivable that you might interfere with . . ."

With someone else's death? I asked myself.

". . . with medicinal potions. That sort of thing. It isn't as though Ivy Kellinch died of poison."

"But she did die," I reminded Her Ladyship, still smarting over the setdown I had received.

"Heart seizure. That was what took her off. Why are you smiling?"

I would have thought I was wearing more nearly a "sardonic expression" than a smile, but I could not see my own face to judge.

"That is what Master Theo said it would be. I believe the doctor thought it highly unlikely."

"The doctor has nothing to say in the matter. It was a heart seizure, and I'll thank all the dependents of Conor House to remember that when questioned."

I said no more. We drove in silence along the coast and through the village which, at a distance had appeared deserted. I liked the smiles of the cottagers, the waves of the children as we went by. It was plain to me that these people, quite incapable of putting a good face upon someone they hated, still looked to the Conors as their own, one of the last of the true Irish landowning families that had not been converted to London ways and Whitehall absenteeism.

I could not but observe upon their affection for Lady Maeve.

"Your Ladyship has their esteem. It is not always so, in the West Counties."

"Why not? I was born in Castle MacCulsh. My grandfather and my uncles fought the House of Orange at the Boyne Water. I had a cousin who swung at Ballina Bridge for his Stuart loyalty."

As I looked at her in surprise, she said with grim humor, "It was only my father who sought to curry favor with the English. And you may know what came of that."

All the while she was acknowledging the waves of the villagers with a faint smile, and an occasional flick of the reins. There was no condescension in Lady Maeve today. The villagers felt she was one with them, more exalted, perhaps, but a kin to them all the same. And in many ways they were right. Her aloofness, her air of the Earl's daughter, were reserved for those closer to her. I could not decide whether I liked her or did not, but she was an absorbing subject to speculate about.

Perhaps Maureen had been right, I thought, smiling to myself. Lady Maeve was one of those Living Dead whom it is impossible to feel close to, yet who continue to attract —"interest" seemed hardly the word.

At the far end of the sandy, rutted path which served the village for a main street, stood a gloomy-looking building with one storey above the ground floor, and made of stone not ancient enough to be picturesque, and not new enough to be clean-lined. I assumed this must be the headquarters for the Relief Committees during times of famine, and for the Board of Works.

Lady Maeve tethered the pony and we went inside where the group from Conor House sat around a huge table, much too grand for the dank, barn-like interior of the building, which was lightened even on this unusually sunny day by several storm lanterns. A number of villagers, anxious to hear "good talk," were milling about behind the Conor House folk, hoping for a seat at the table, I daresay.

Several men whom I did not recognize were seated at the other end of the table and I took them, rightly, to be tenants of the Conor lands. A stout gentleman, dressed in the very height of fashion, with a high stock threatening to engulf his red, receding chin, presided over the group. Upon Lady Maeve's arrival he bounced up from a high-backed and very regal chair, to advance and kiss her hand.

"Dear Lady Maeve, good to see you again! Quite the beauty as ever graced His Highness's drawing rooms! We miss you, My Lady. Gad, but we do." She accepted his flutters and his tribute in the way I noticed so often at Conor House, that is to say, with much more condescension than she used toward the villagers. Her eyebrows arched a trifle, and she seemed to be laughing at him secretly. I could not blame her.

She said, "Good day, Sir Horace. I think you know all present. Except my housekeeper in whose arms the woman expired. She is named Wicklow. Sir Horace Pumbleby—Anne. Shall we be seated now?"

"To be sure. To be sure." He patted his not inconsequential stomach several times, as though to be certain it existed, and then after ushering Lady Maeve to her chair beside him with great ceremony, he seated himself, flipping out the wide skirt of his riding jacket.

I looked around from my place at the end of the little group and saw that I was seated next to Dr. Jonathan who smiled at me and told me, "Be easy, girl. I know these little dealings. None gives a tinker's farthing for the dead, and there's no help in them."

I said nothing, for Theo Conor, seated next to Lady Maeve, looked down the table at me, and then at Jonathan. His sister was between him and her husband and she created a diversion by saying loudly, "How funny, Sir Horace! You've got two clickers!"

I took this to mean that he had two fobs and two pocket timepieces, and while the rest of the table looked a trifle embarrassed, Sir Horace puffed out proudly as he said in a deprecating way, "It is the fashion now. So what can one do? One must be enslaved to the fashion. What?"

Jonathan was whispering to his wife who put her hand in his confidingly, but Theo Conor looked at me again and grinned. There was malice in his grin. Perhaps he had put his sister up to the observation.

After a few more throat-clearings, Sir Horace Pumbleby

asked how he might oblige the Conors in this purely routine death of their nurse.

Lady Maeve said simply, "There were so many whispers after the attack upon my husband, that Mr. Conor felt the death of Nurse Kellinch should be aired and then settled forever, before her burial."

"Precisely. Excellently put. 'Aired and settled forever.' My sentiments exactly . . . It is nothing but a routine death, due to a sudden seizure of the heart, I am given to understand, while the woman was walking on the beach in Kelper Head Cove."

There were murmurs behind us, among the villagers, and one of the rugged fellows stepped forward, putting two fingers to a long forelock of black hair, in rough salute. He broke into a torrent of the Irish tongue, confounding Sir Horace and even puzzling me; for it was many and many a year since my parents' native tongue had been spoken to me so rapidly.

Theo Conor put his arm out and slapped the fellow goodnaturedly on the arm.

"Cease your blather, man. There's no understanding you. He's an outlander and not of our tongue."

"Ay," said the villager, looking abashed. "So it be. What I said, y'er Worship—there'll be Master Theo will tell the outlander, isn't it?" He nudged Theo in the ribs, as one drinking friend to another, and indicated Sir Horace who could scarcely understand even the Irishman's English tongue.

"What-what-what, Mister Theo, how was that the fellow said?"

Lady Maeve suddenly sat up a little straighter. She said nothing, but I saw Theo glance at her and then, looking as bland as cream, he began what I knew by instinct was a lying translation of the villager's talk.

"He says he's seen Ivy Kellinch have these attacks before, and does not wonder at it."

"But, y'er Worship—" the Irishman began and then coughed into the cap in his hand, and rubbed the back of that same hand over his mouth.

Sir Horace nodded wisely. He leaned nearer Lady Maeve. "Is the fellow to be trusted?"

"Perfectly," said Her Ladyship. "It is true he holds a half-acre of Conor lands by conacre and has done so these many years, but his family have been Conor tenants since time out of mind."

"By—conacre?" the puzzled London gentleman repeated.

"A form of rent," Theo cut in. "By the term. There are some that merely hold contracts on a bit of Conor land. But more there are who hold it by tenantry."

"I see," said Sir Horace who obviously did not. "In any case, I see no reason why this meeting should be prolonged beyond the usual half hour. I had hoped"—he looked flirtatiously at Lady Maeve—"the barest hope, my dear lady, that in my journey through the West Counties, I might be invited to Conor House for tea?"

Lady Maeve gave him her sweetest smile.

"But of course, dear Sir Horace. And how very much we have to discuss about old days in London, at Carlton House, and at Brighton. You will, of course, do us the honor of staying the night."

A shadow crossed the doorway and we all looked around. The black robes of a priest surprised me. These rough and rugged coasts had seemed almost beyond the care of God's minions. Several villagers greeted him as Father MacMonigle, and he and the Conors seemed on fair terms, for Theo explained to him the nature of the business here.

"So it is," said the Father, in an accent nearly as thick as the Irish-spoken villager. "The poor creature, and to be buried without so much as the consolation of her religion. I have come to inquire about that."

"She had no religion, Father," Theo put in sardonically.

"Boy!" said Father MacMonigle. "Be not damning what remains of the poor creature's soul. Would a prayer be of service, I'm thinking?"

Jonathan spoke for the first time then, seeing that the others made no effort. "You will be doing a service, Father, to attend the woman's burial. Her death being so"—he looked at the Conors and added roughly, without mincing words—"unusual, not to say unexpected!"

"Nonsense," put in Sir Horace, wiping specks of Irish dust off the panels of his coat with a lace handkerchief. "My dear boy—and you, Father—nothing in the least unusual about the woman's death. It was long overdue."

To the incredulous horror of everyone in the room, Theo Conor laughed.

"Beautifully put, Pumbleby. Ivy's death was 'long overdue.' Now . . . I wonder why."

After that, so many people jumped into the embarrassing void that no one could hear anyone else for a few moments.

It all ended as I might have expected. Healthy, toughened Ivy Kellinch died of a heart seizure and would be missed no more than if she had quitted Conor House and gone her way . . . as I privately believed she was intending when she died. What of her talk to me about the future? What of her plans? Her packing. What of the possible use of laudanum? Or the small bleeding mark at the side of her head. . . ? Whatever she had died of, I would swear it was not of a heart seizure.

But like the others, I did not say this. When called upon I gave my plain story of her staggering up the Headland and dying at my feet. It changed nothing. The verdict was foreseen.

Although the group stayed for half an hour longer, the conversation was general, and dealt with the recent potato harvest, the possibilities of a good year to come, or otherwise, and some choice words of wisdom delivered by Sir Horace Pumbleby, in the name of his cousin, the almighty Lord-Lieutenant of Ireland, who knew even less of conditions in the West Country than did Sir Horace.

"I must return to my husband with the news," said Lady Maeve, giving the signal for a general departure.

As we all left at last, Jonathan and I arose together.

"What a farce!" he muttered to me, and then took Maureen's hand and led her gently out.

I watched them go. Lady Maeve's mention of her husband reminded me that I had promised Aengus Conor to make that journey to Ballyglen today and deliver the letter I carried. It lacked half an hour of noon, and the road through Ballyglen Bog lay to the south of the village, so I lingered, making the excuse to Lady Maeve that I was going to purchase cloth in the village and then—a lie of which I was ashamed—that I would visit Father MacMonigle.

She made no objections. She was obviously thinking of more important things. But Theo Conor watched me more carefully than I had counted upon. It was exactly noon when

THE BECKONING

I set foot upon the road through Ballyglen Bog, with my sealed letter and my determination to please Aengus Conor, no matter what I suspected his family of being party to.

XI

THE LAST little mud-daubed coteen of the village was built into the bog region itself, and as I passed abruptly from the bright, reflected whiteness of the beach at Kelper Head into the green shade and moist odor of turf and stagnant waters, I saw a turf cutter removing chunks of peat to a place beside his cottage. He looked up as I passed and touched two fingers to his brow in salute. I nodded and said, "Good day" and had gone a little way when I was surprised to see, on the side of his cottage nearest the bog, several children playing, only inches, it seemed, from a treacherous deep green patch of what appeared to be grass, but was very like to be a wretched scum-pool. I called to them without thinking, "Have a care. You may fall in."

The grubby children looked up, and as they separated and peered at me probably wondering what concern of mine it was, I realized that Maureen Trumble was kneeling there behind them, almost hidden from my view. She waved to me with a crumpled handkerchief, and I stepped off the path, carefully making my way over the springy ground toward her. The children scattered, not being used to strangers, and out of the corner of my eye I saw them go to their father, the turf cutter, and point me out.

"Miss Maury," I said, "what may you be doing here?"

I could see now that she had been weeping. Her clear, limpid eyes were rimmed with tears and she complained between sniffs, "Old Mulcahy's wife was taken sick, and Jono is inside the coteen attending her. Always it is some tiresome patient. He promised me faithfully he would be with me all day. And then, to have that woman come down all swollen and stupid with the fever, and turning black to boot!"

Horrors! I thought. Were we to have the typhus visited upon us at Kelper Head?

"Is it typhus?"

"No. Something tiresome about her not eating proper. Jono is having O'Glaney send down food from Conor House." She laughed suddenly "How cross O'Glaney will be! He hates to do Jono's bidding. But," she added calmly as may be, "we all have to do bad things, even if we do not wish to. Father said that. And Theo, and even Jono says we may not always do what we want."

"And they are right, Miss Maury. Don't you feel better here, caring for the poor woman's children as you are now?"

Maureen looked at me in astonishment.

"Oh, you are a silly! You see, Jono put me in their care, not they in mine. You have it all round-about."

It was not a thing for laughter, but I could not resist smiling, and after telling her to mind that she did not go over the edge of the swim-pool that lay so close and innocent looking, I went back to the road. She called to me triumphantly, "I know all of the Ballyglen Bog. It would be very hard for me to drown in it. I should have to work harder than I have ever done. But Jono would be sorry and love me more if I were dead even, for that is how I would love him. If he died, he would belong all to me, like my gulls and my cormorants."

"Yes, yes," I said, "but let us not talk of dying."

"Oh, I shan't," she said airily. "Only that it would make them ever so obliging to me afterward."

I shook my head at this naughty reasoning and walked on, aware as I did that it was very damp, very warm and sticky, here in the bog, and wishing I had not worn so heavy a cloak.

I hadn't taken many steps when I heard my name called, and had been so busy reflecting upon the many wonders of Ballyglen Bog, that at first I did not realize it was myself was wanted. I looked around and saw Jonathan, rolling down the sleeves of his shirt, and striding toward me with Maureen hard upon his heels I stopped uneasily, for I did not want these two entangled in the lies I must tell to please my employer. Maureen had snatched up Jonathan's coat and was trying to hang it from his shoulders. She finally succeeded as he reached me. She caressed his shoulders in a proprietary way, saying, "How nice this jacket is, Jono! It was me chose it, even though Maeve paid. It was spun specially from good wool. A fine brown the color of the bog."

I thought this a doubtful compliment and not really fair to the jacket which was a fine, rich brown that looked very well on the doctor with his changeful brown eyes. He patted her hand absently as he said to me, "Where are you bound, Anne? Maureen would like you not to go too far from her."

"I do not care in the least," said Maureen stoutly, to our surprise. We both looked at her. She went on after a slightly abashed look at her husband, "I mean—Jono will care for me, won't you?"

He looked at her fondly but I thought with a touch of amused impatience, and I wondered if this relationship was the strong tie that held them together, his sense of being needed by her.

"But Maury, love," he reminded her, "Father MacMonigle told you how bad it was with the Lochiel child over on the bohireen."

I smiled to see how he managed this woman; for she was instantly reminded to tell me, "And what a pretty creature it is, Anne! Eyes big and round like the bog-ponds when you see the heavens in them still as a mirror."

"Well then," Jonathan went on with an understanding look at me, "you see why Miss Anne must be with you, and not me? You wouldn't want the Lochiel baby to be put to the earth; would you, indeed?"

"I'm so sorry," I said, trying to stop this before I became forced into a permanent guardianship of Maureen Trumble, "but I have missed my walks since I left France. You see, I was used to walk three or four kilometers each day, and now, in this brisk climate, I feel the need for it." I knew I had promised her husband to look out for her, but I had also promised my employer; so the lie was the best I could produce at short notice.

Jonathan took my refusal in good part. He said pleasantly, although I thought he was disappointed, "You are in fine looks, Miss Wicklow, so this walking of yours must be a grand thing. She is a handsome one, is she not, Maury?"

Maureen looked at me from head to toe and appeared to think this over. I avoided her husband's eyes, wishing he had said nothing.

"Well then, Jono, I would not be rude, but Anne has the look of a person who has not had enough sleep, isn't it so? Your eyes are very dark beneath them, I think . . . Did you sleep well last night?"

For the first time I saw Jonathan Trumble nearly at loss for words.

"Good God, Maury! What a thing to say! And it is a lie on the face of it."

Maureen dimpled at both of us. The sun glistened through the overhung trees, across her innocent, unlined face.

"Then why, Jono, did you ask me last night whether I thought the footsteps we heard were Anne's outside our door, when all the household should have been in bed?"

"March along, love," he said hastily, not looking at me. "The Mulcahy children will be wondering what has come to you."

I laughed, assuring them, as Maureen obediently took his hand, "You are quite right to wonder, Dr. Trumble. I was upon an errand for Mr. Aengus Conor."

Jonathan raised his head, and this time looked me full in the eyes. I could guess that he was very angry. "Your pardon now, if I don't shed my tears for Aengus Conor. I have borne my bit and my woman's bit in his household for a year and more. I have done my possible for them that are Conor tenantry and them that are not. Yet he will not trust me to aid him. Nor even examine him. Nor trust my wife's income to her, nor me. Is he a thief then? Do not gaggle about Aengus Conor! Come, Maureen!"

"I'm sure I beg your pardon, sir," I said meekly, understanding what he conceived this blow both to his pride and his professional abilities.

He did not turn around but strode back to the coteen, almost dragging his wife along, the while she turned and waved to me, as though making amends for both of them. I watched them until they reached the coteen where Maureen whispered something to him, and he lowered his head and kissed her gently on the cheek. Embarrassed at witnessing this tender and private moment, I hurried on my way.

At high noon it was easy to see why Maureen preferred Ballyglen Bog to the wild, salty, sea-swept coast of her native Kelper Head. Among the deep, emerald green of the jungle growth, and the black of the peat beds, were little pools that seemed to twinkle at the blue sky overhead, and an occasional lone bird like a heron skimmed over the surface, vanishing into the darker, thicker glens and woods ahead of me. There was a stench about the peatbeds, but it was not entirely unpleasant, for it put me in mind of the earliest fuel in our coteen in the East of Ireland, and of happy moments with my parents before their fatal accident on the road to Dublin Fair.

I walked to the edge of the wagon-rutted, narrow road and peered down at the spongy green turf. So innocent it seemed, yet, further out, the same deep, rich spongy turf beyond the little pool seemed to breathe, as I watched it. I walked on, but kept an eye out for these dangerous patches, so near the road. By such brisk walking, I was half-way through the Bog almost before I was aware of having gotten out of the sight of the doctor and his wife.

I had heard the distant song of some birds, then a cawing sound of others, hoarse and ugly, most likely the cormorants, then a trill very like light human laughter. But the trill of what I took to be meadow birds began to change subtly to my listening ears. I stopped in the roadway suddenly, overwhelmed by the most eerie thought:

Could that trill really be laughter? Soulless, tinkling and metallic, like laughter I remembered hearing recently. . . ?

I looked all around me. The road had taken a bend shortly before, and a clump of knotty little bushes hid the way by which I had come. I could almost have sworn that someone was following me, staying just out of sight, laughing, as though to attract my attention, to play some silly joke upon me, like a child at hide-and-seek. If it was laughter, and not some meadow bird, then I had heard such sounds before, metallic, without feeling.

And then I remembered. Ivy Kellinch had laughed like that. . . .

I was seized with the impulse to run as hard as I could, but the wagon ruts with their muddy runnels gave me pause. I even ran a few steps before discovering that it took all my concentration to keep to the center of the road and not wander off to those tempting green cushions so close by the road. Out of the corner of my eye I watched the green tufts. Like the deep, bottomless dark patches further out, these tufts seemed to move ever so faintly. Perhaps it was the rising wind that swept all the grass to one side and made it seem so, but I fancied those green tufts were living creatures with some awful intelligence of their own. Otherwise, why should they appear so exactly as if they breathed—up and down, up and down. . . .

As I hurried on, I told myself that the reason for this odd phenomenon was the disturbed and bottomless mud underneath the green turf. Still, it was not a thought to make my journey easier. But for this I should have run much faster, for it was not easy to take quick steps through those muddy wagon runnels. Often, the viscous mud threatened to hold my shoe, and I had to pause and slip my heel back into the slipper before proceeding. Each time I looked back and never saw a sign of human life. But when I looked ahead and commenced my journey again, there was the tinkling metallic sound, now and then varied with the humming of insects. Once, I cried out myself, when the air was assailed by the hideous screech of a large winged bird as it landed on the bog and was trapped. I could hear the terrible flutter of its great wings, and the panic which I felt echoed in my own throat, before the great sucking sounds resumed. I ran and ran, and was amazed to find I had run right out of Ballyglen Bog and was approaching the gibbet which marked the turnoff from Kelper Head.

It was now after mid-day, and the first shadows of early afternoon caused a streak of darkness across my path. I paused to rest a moment, before I started along the Carrickmore-to-Ballyglen High Road.

When I had gone some distance I looked back to see if my phantasy of a following presence was still with me. I saw nothing, and now that I had reached the High Road, I could no longer hear that fancied trill of laughter. It must have been the bogland birds, after all.

I could laugh now at my own fears. Why should I have fancied that the dead Ivy Kellinch was following me? I had done her no harm. Ah, but was that entirely true? Had she not staggered to me for help, which I had unwittingly refused her? My common sense, and the bright sun overhead, did much to banish these morbid thoughts.

Presently, I made out the clip-clop of a pony upon the High Road behind me and stepped to the roadside so as not to be trodden underfoot. I smiled to see Sir Horace

Pumbleby, sitting up very straight, and handling the reins of a little pony cart much as he must have ridden to hounds, that is to say, pompously, but not unpleasantly. He had a very large smile for me, which was surprising, and paused at my side so suddenly that the pony made an audible protest and tossed his head.

"Well, well, well, what bonny beauties these wild counties do grow, lass! May I take you up?"

"I am going to the mercer's shop in Ballyglen," I explained, and added, amazed at my own ability to lie, "on an errand for Lady Maeve."

"Ah, just so." He got down with considerable trouble, puffing a little, and then lifted me up more skillfully than I should have imagined. "You are the housekeeper at Conor House, are you not, Miss—er—?"

"Wicklow," I said as he got up again and we jogged along very nicely; a great comfort to me, for my run had tired me more than I guessed. "You are very kind, sir, to be obliging in this way."

He waved away the obligation grandly. "Not at all. You'll find me excessively fond of—of the people, if I may say so. I am a Whig, you know."

I had not known, and did not quite see how this was to the point, but assumed that Whigs were expected to be kind to "the people." In any case I was obliged to him, and tried to be as agreeable as possible without overstepping what he must conceive to be my place. I asked him if it was not true that he was dining at Conor House, reminding him by this hint that I would not have expected to find him on the Carrickmore High Road.

"Very true. Her Ladyship is always everything one could wish the Quality to be. She has graciously invited me to stay the night, and so I shall. My nightgear being at a wretched inn at Ballyglen, and my man lying in Kelper Head, dead-drunk, I must fetch my own gear. Lucky for me," he added jovially. He gave me a look which I can only call "arch" and moved just a trifle closer to me on the narrow seat. I had learned to counter such behavior by remaining precisely as I had been, not moving, polite as may be, but giving not an inch. It served only indifferently well now; for Sir Horace was not a lightweight by any means and before long we were distinctly closer than I would have liked.

"What a pretty creature it is!" he murmured, looking at me out of the corner of his eyes.

"Splendid animal," I said calmly, gazing at the pony.

He looked surprised, was taken aback, and after coughing, agreed with me that the animal was. He ventured one or two other familiarities which I countered without giving offense, for he amused me by his obvious tactics, and I had no mind to make an enemy of him, nor to behave like a silly little gudgeon. Nonetheless, I confess I saw the outskirts on Ballyglen Town with relief and very soon I asked to be set down before the mercer's shop halfway along the street. He pulled up, leaped down gallantly, came around and lifted me down, lingering too long as he did so, until I reminded him, "How happy Lady Maeve will be to see you at Conor House, sir!" at which he let me go with almost insulting haste.

"To be sure. You do right to remind me, Pretty Anne . . . I shall call you that. Pretty Anne!"

"Not before Her Ladyship, I should hope, sir," said I politely.

"No, no. Certainly not. Gad, no! Well, now, Pretty Anne, shall I be taking you up on my return to Conor House?"

I did not fancy the long journey back alone through the Bog, but I thought I might handle the eerie noises of that landscape with less disgust than the familiarities of Sir Horrace Pumbleby, so I told him regretfully that I would be much too long at my purchases, and Lady Maeve would be no end cross if her guest did not soon arrive.

He agreed that I showed great wisdom in this, and started to say good-by. For one dreadful moment I thought he was going to kiss me, as though I were a buxom milkmaid, but he restrained himself and merely chucked me under the chin, almost untying the ribbons of my bonnet. Then he leaped up into his pony cart like a stripling, and was off down the street while I tried not to notice the curious stares of the townsfolk.

Ballyglen was much larger than I had supposed, being a market town of several cross-streets, kept reasonably free of wagon-ruts, with its own inn, one or two taverns, several shops, and the whole of it crowned by an ancient gray stone church at the end of the village, where the rolling landscape behind it looked blue-violet in the distance, and the sky was fleecing up with clouds. I could just make out the rounded tops of one or two odd-shaped monuments which I recognized as Gaelic stones, and the back of the church, and felt that I could carry out Aengus Conor's orders without too much marked attention from the townspeople. I would simply pretend to be visiting the church, then go around to the back, and so fulfill my curious mission, and at exactly the hour prescribed by Mr. Aengus.

First, however, I went into the mercer's shop and bought a quantity of excellently woven homespun—a mauve that was neither violet nor blue but which had been my husband's favorite color upon me. Armed with this I inquired of the shopkeep whether the church held masses this day. Upon being informed by him in the broadest of Irish tongue that I would be welcome, masses or no, I went my way. Almost immediately, the shopkeeper was out upon the street and gossiping to a passerby. When I looked around, conscious of being discussed, sure enough, he was pointing to me. I was glad now that I had prepared him with my story of visiting the church.

I walked the length of the town, trying to slow my steps, but yet anxious to have done with my business here. Presently, I came to the church and studied its front, a noble piece of work, in spite of its small size. The building had a very solid, thick, square look, nothing gothic about it, and it seemed to me more nearly what my husband, who was very knowledgeable, would have called "Roman." Perhaps, indeed, this church had first been built when the Romans were still in England. However, my business was with the churchyard, not the architecture.

No one was within the church, and I paid my devotions, offered a prayer for the memory of him I had loved, and made my way through the shadows to the back of the altar where I hoped to find a door into the churchyard. I could not find a door here, so I retraced my steps through the interior. The large bundle of mauve wool that I carried caught upon my cloak, and I stopped to release it for fear it might pull out the fringe of my sleeve. During that moment of absolute silence I heard a footstep in the darkest part of the nave. Could it be the priest? I had better explain my presence. I cleared my throat, preparatory to speak, a trifle nervous over my lie to the good Father, when I saw the silhouette of the person in the dark, just as he moved across the center of the nave toward me. The silhouette was a man in a stocking-cap, a jerkin, fisherman's breeches, and boots. Had I interrupted someone in prayer? Embarrassed, I stepped back. But still he came toward me. Now, his boots rang loudly through the interior.

"Well, Anne," said he in that voice that was, like all his family, half humorous, half sardonic, never revealing the true self. "How come you to be here? I did not know you had a turn for religion."

"Is it you, Master Theo?" I asked, peering hard through the dark.

"Myself, of course. Now, I wonder . . . what can you possibly be doing in Ballyglen Church and in the dark?"

"At least," I said tartly, "I do not sneak about frightening people and following them."

"What a temper! Come out here where I can see you. Ah, this is better."

He fumbled in the dark for my hand, found it and led me toward the front of the church. "Shall I buy you a bit of luncheon and see you safely home?"

"No," I said with haste. "I—there's something I must do."

"Really?" His eyebrows went up in that way which always made me think he was amusing himself with me. In the shadowy portal of the church, he shoved me out into the sunlight so that I could not hide my expression and must use all my wits to evade him. "What can it be?" he asked. "The Father is probably still in Kelper Head, but you know that. Ivy Kellinch's burial."

I seized upon the straw that Ivy's burial afforded me. "I—I had a relation buried in the churchyard here, and came to pay my respects."

"A relation? I had no notion. When was this?"

"When my father and mother served at Conor House." I felt rather proud of having thought of this, but Theo Conor, leaning back in the cool shadows of the doorway, studied me in a way I found anything but reassuring. I felt I could have lied much more skillfully if the sun were not illuminating every feature of my face for him to see while he stood in the shadow, getting the better of me.

"But this is exceedingly interesting. What is this relation's name, if I may ask?"

I remembered a detail. "It is surely no concern of yours, Master Theo. But he was buried beneath the Gaelic Cross, if that will satisfy you." There! I had explained what I would be doing at the Gaelic Cross, should he see me waiting for Mister Aengus's man to pick up the letter. I snatched my hand away from him and walked down the step and around the church where I saw the churchyard was open, and overgrown with weeds, at the back. Theo Conor followed me slowly. He stopped under a stunted tree at the entrance to the graveyard and saw me hesitate, for there were two Gaelic Crosses, one half sunk in the unkept and grassy earth, the other standing like a beacon further away. Between them were a number of small stones, crosses for the most part, and much newer. I knelt before the sunken cross, and remembered too late that I had forgotten to bring the flowers Aengus Conor suggested. No matter. I would put a good face upon it. I did not look around, but I heard Theo Conor's voice with its half-concealed laughter.

"What relation did you say, Anne?"

"My—my grand-uncle," I said impatiently. "Does it matter?"

"A great deal, I should think," he called to me, adding with what must have been great glee, "I had no notion you were so old, Anne."

"What'll you be meaning by that?" I asked, angry but wary.

"Your grand-uncle died in 1062, according to that marker!"

I looked up, rubbed away lichen and grass and crusts of mud from the marker. Theo was right. My 'uncle' was eight hundred years dead when my family lived at Conor House!

I could have hurled my package at Master Theo's head, I was that angry. Would he wait here the entire time I remained, putting limitless obstacles in the way of my carrying out his father's orders? I knelt there for what seemed a long time to me, but was probably only a matter of minutes, wondering what on earth I should do. Then I cried quickly, without turning around, "Why do you annoy me like this?

Why don't you go away? Must I tell your father how you behave?"

Hearing no reply to this tirade, I opened my eyes and looked around. He was nowhere in sight.

I stood up, shook myself, letting fly a deal of churchyard dust, and looked around. Out on the street I could just barely see a tall, broad-shouldered man all in black, Father MacMonigle, talking to someone, and gesticulating in the volatile fashion of my ancestors. I moved across the graves, careful not to tread precisely where the ground was sunk the size of a coffin, betraying what lay within, and I recognized young Theo Conor talking to the Father. I smiled to myself. He was in good hands, and could not tease me for the moment. I wandered back among the stones and found that the other Celtic Cross was the one Aengus Conor had specifically mentioned. Deep-carved below a little cut Roman Cross was the name of Fergan O'Carty, him whose grave I sought.

It grew tiring to kneel in one position for any length of time, and gradually I sank down until I was seated beside the cross, with my cheek against the roughness of it, and reflecting on all the centuries that it had stood here in fair weather and foul, in good times and worse, marking the age of Irish Christianity, older in many places than the Christianity of England.

The sun overhead was gradually thinned and shadowed by the fleecy clouds I had seen earlier so that I did not guess its strength and was very much surprised to find how sleepy I became. It was, perhaps, the lateness of the hour that I had gone to bed the night before, what with wandering over Conor House for decanters, and chopping down seaweed and all. I shook my head, opened my eyes, and tried to concentrate upon my mission here. I took from my bodice the letter Aengus Conor had ordered me to deliver, and sat looking at it. Once, I remember looking up and glancing around, wondering why the recipient of this letter had not shown himself—or was it, perhaps, herself? Possibly I was too early. Perhaps, also, I was not expected today but tomorrow, or some other time. Not a soul was in the churchyard but myself, and the sun beat down in a way I had not been used to in many weeks.

I stood up and stretched, staring out along the side of

the church to the street and saw that the priest and Theo Conor had gone their way. An occasional passerby was to be seen, but none came in my direction. I sat down again, conscious that either my hurry through the Bog, or the sun itself had given me the beginnings of a headache, which was very unusual to me. I was not a woman given to the vapors and other weaknesses of that sort. I smoothed my forehead with my fingers, closed my eyes momentarily, and found myself sleepy again. This would never do.

As I rubbed my eyes now, angry at my own weakness, I heard the merest rustling of the tall grass behind the great old cross. A meadow creature stirring, I thought, and was just twisting my neck a trifle, to look over my shoulder when I felt the most searing pain at the back of my head, as though the sunlight had exploded in my brain.

And then there was a roaring in my ears, and darkness and exquisite peace.

XII

I NOTICED first the slant of the sun upon the back of my hand. The early afternoon wind from the sea had come sweeping in, and now passed quickly over me in a ticklish fashion. The back of my head hurt, and when I felt of it, I could have sworn there was a lump there, but it was not too painful, and from the position in which I found myself, I supposed that I must have struck my head against the stone monument as I collapsed from the sun.

In any case, I had stayed quite long enough, being of no mind to cross Ballyglen Bog after dark. As to Aengus Conor and his precious letter that must be delivered, let him send someone more accustomed to old, forgotten graveyards. I felt for the letter in my bodice, then remembered that I had gotten it out a few minutes before I fainted, and now I had apparently dropped it during my collapse. I felt around under me, looked over the graveyard which was still deserted and quiet, with only the tall grass soughing under the impact of the wind. What had I done with that letter?

Presently, I saw, to my relief, that the wind had carried it across the ground to rest against another gravestone, and I got up with an effort, for I ached in all my bones, and stepped across the graves to pick up the letter. The wind must have been stronger than I thought, for that, or the flight of the letter itself, had ripped the old-fashioned Conor seal on the back and the letter was open to the world.

I picked up and felt, in the circumstances, entitled to glance at its contents. You may perceive my amazement to find the page was virgin white, without so much as Aengus Conor's signature. It was, in fact, completely blank. I wondered if this empty page had been substituted for another. It was, however, the same letter I had borne with me since yesterday. Even the slight scent of my own perfume was

152

upon the page, and the folds were such as I remembered from the hours they had rested upon my person.

Now, Badad! I thought. I'll have your scalp for this, my precious Mr. Aengus Conor! To be sending me on this long, tedious business, and for no reason, for only a blank page! How do I know but that anyone was ever intended to meet me here? Was it only to get me out of Conor House that I was sent?

But that was ridiculous. Mr. Aengus was master of that house. He had but to dismiss me if he chose.

It was a strange business. But then, the whole of my stay at Conor House was a strange business, entirely. I should think of returning to England before worse befell me. . . .

. . . Worse befell me?

For the first time, I wondered if it had been the sun that felled me today during those few minutes. Again I felt of the back of my head. It is true that such a blow might have been caused by my striking the great stone cross. But such blows, as well, might be caused by that creature who held Kelper Head in thrall to some subtle terror. Was my injury connected with what went on at Conor House?

I began to shake, partly due to the rising wind after the heat of midday, and partly also to the doubts and fears that nibbled at my nerves.

I straightened my garments, brushed myself off, and walked toward the church and the distant street. As I did so, I passed two small girls carrying bundles of weedy little yellow flowers, such as are found out of season at the skirt of Ballyglen Bog. They looked at me curiously and one of them said in broadest Irish, "Would ye be swimming in the head then, Miss? You nearly trod on the gravestone of Father O'Meara."

So I had, and for an instant, furious at my own weakness, the abominable headache, and the notice the children had taken of it, I very nearly said, "Be damned to Father O'Meara!"

Fortunately, I caught myself before uttering this blasphemy, and said glumly, "Ay. It was the sun, and I have far to go."

The little girls looked after me in great puzzlement as I walked past the church and down the street to the end of Ballyglen town. A brisk walk, the salty wind, and my usual resilience, soon made me more myself. When I saw a tiny grog shop at the far end of the town, in which two townswomen and several men were drinking at tables close by the open door, I felt that this was the very thing to make me quite well again, ready for the long walk ahead.

I went in and was nearly blinded by the cool dark with its thick smell of peat and age, before I found the innkeeper squatting at the low-burning fire and stirring a pannikan of what could only be, to judge by its odor, boiling whisky.

In the dialect of my childhood that was gradually returning to me with use, I inquired whether he might serve me tea. The good-humored fellow agreed, though with the roguish addendum, "Pure tea, my girl, is no-what for the like of you. Bad, my girl. I've seen 'un buried of too much tea."

I sat down on a hard, high-backed settle and watched him take the whisky off the fire and mingle any number of savory ingredients with it—a trifling pinch of tea as well, I hoped—and presently there it was before me, a steaming tankard in which my nose warned me that the "mellowing Good Irish" was considerably more prevalent than the pinch of tea. It was astonishing how quickly my headache was gone, and even the long walk through the Bog did not seem so dreadful to contemplate. It was still early in the afternoon. I could not have been unconscious more than a matter of minutes. As to the why of that attack, after all was said, who might wish to attack me? And if so, why not in the Bog? Why wait until I reached Ballyglen and that forlorn old churchyard?

I took another long drink which cheered me again, and with some regret, left the half of the tankard behind me and resumed the long walk to Conor House.

I started along the High Road toward Carrickmore in far better spirits. As the day wore on an occasional dog-cart or pony-cart and driver passed me, once a man on horse-back, but all going in the direction of Ballyglen Town, so that I was forced to pause and rest when I reached the gibbet that marked the narrow, rutted road to the coast and Kelper Head.

The chains, screeching and slashing in the wind, seemed to fling themselves after me, as I started along the road to Kelper Head.

THE BECKONING

I was aware of the change in mood and the lowering of the sun, as I ventured once more upon the fringes of Ballyglen Bog. At least, it would not be dark for several hours yet. It was only that the sun now took on that frosty glow, like a great fire consumed in its own smoke, which was the sign of the ever-present fog groping its way in over Kelper Head. I did not want to linger, but my ankles had begun to betray me by their weakness, I felt tiredness creeping over me. The back of my head hurt as well, in that one place when I touched it, and I wondered again if the winter sun could possibly have given me such a jolt into unconsciousness. If I had struck my head upon the stone monument, surely I would remember the blow. In point of fact, the blow seemed to have occurred before I lost consciousness.

I stopped at one hummock beside the road which did not seem quite as unsteady or given to "breathing" as most of the green patches of bogland. There I took off one shoe at a time and rubbed my foot. As I did so, I peered around, sniffing at the acrid peat-smell, observing the vistas of strange, desolate beauty, like a primeval swamp which had never known the tread of man.

Ahead of me was the thickness of tangled growth crowding upon the roadside, and I knew this part would be the hardest upon my impressionable nerves. I replaced my shoe and walked on, not so briskly as before, but determined to pass through this jumbled spinney, as I thought of it, without silly echoes of laughing dead women, or ghostly Kelp Gatherers beckoning to me across the bogland wastes.

It was several minutes after the road had turned and curved its way into this gigantic copse of oak intermingled with slender trees that I began to hear again that tiresome laughter floating to me just as I fancied I heard it earlier in the day. I looked around in every direction, quite sure that either my imagination was playing me absurd tricks again, or some bird was trilling its little song. A lane of strange, unknown trees, stunted and twisted by the great Atlantic gales, bordered the bog just here. I moved among them with care, staying to the deepest wagon rut with its slippery lining of grass; for the afternoon shadows fell particularly thick in such places. Unlike my experience early in the day, this laughter, feminine, tinkling as light glass prisms struck together, became louder, more distinguishable as I moved on. I listened very carefully, for as I began to identify each separate sound I discovered something even more disquieting than the thought of Ivy Kellinch's ghost, laughing at me. Sounds through the copse and growing nearer to me were those of weeping. I had mistaken them altogether.

I hurried now, noticing as I did so, that I came closer and closer to the sounds until, as I reached the outer edge of that particular copse and was surrounded again by the bubbling ponds of the bog, I made out the same figure that had astonished me on first traveling this road. Maureen Trumble was out upon the bog, standing there in mud-spattered cloak and hair streaming in the wind, arms pushing out into the empty air before her, each finger of her hands outspread. Like a child she made no attempt to conceal the wailing, breath-catching little sounds of her crying. I thought for a terrible moment that she was about to plunge into the dark and sinister patch of mud at her feet, but she only stood there with her eyes closed and sobbed. I feared to disturb her too suddenly, for her feet were very close upon the slippery green turf that bordered the evil place.

As softly as ever I could, I called to her. It took her a few seconds to understand that my voice and not an imaginary one, spoke to her, for she put her arms down, still without opening her eyes, and stood there as though listening, her feet slipping ever so slightly forward, over the wet and wind-trampled grass, into the muddy abyss. I called again, and this time she opened her eyes and saw me. She did not smile, as I expected her to do, but only looked at me, sadly, with what seemed to my view a singularly hopeless expression, far older than she normally appeared.

"I must," she said, in a voice still uneven with the tears that were in it, but firmer as she repeated, "I must—don't you see?"

"Not now, Miss Maury," I said, not knowing what she could possibly be talking of, unless it was the wickedness of suicide. "How did you get out there?"

She had begun to recover her normal demeanor now, and looked down at her feet, so close to death, and then around her at that tiny island of safety.

"I can't hear you, Anne."

I started to repeat my question and then stopped as I noticed the mischievous manner beginning to replace that hopelessness which had baffled me.

"Come nearer, Anne. I can't hear you."

This made me out-of-reason cross. I wanted no tricks of hers at this moment when her childlike impulses might be the death of her.

"Nonsense. You must come to me, just the way you got out there. Where is the path?"

She was apparently used to being scolded, either by her family or by Dr. Jonathan, for she reacted to this as a child to its governess.

"I shan't. You can't make me, you know, Anne. You must come and fetch me." And she added in that endearing way which doubtless won those whom she chose to woo to friendship, "There's a dear Anne . . . Do come. See? I'll show you the way. I know the way and no one else does. There's none knows as well. . . ."

"Yes, yes," I said, growing more and more angry by the minute, and not caring that I showed it. "You are a very knowing young lady. Now, do as you are told." To show that I meant what I said, I began to walk on toward Kelper Head, but I only got a few steps. I could not contain my imaginings. I thought of how Jonathan had placed her in my charge, and how I was deserting her. I thought how easily she could find the ground beneath her giving away, and she lost in that horrid, bottomless hell of the bog.

Behind me, I heard her call to me, her voice beginning like any worried young woman, but then rising to a wail, in fear and childish petulance, "Anne—dear Annie—dear, dear Annie—don't you be leaving me too. . . . Annie . . ."

I felt the stab of pity and alarm overwhelm me, and I turned. Just as I feared, she began to circle around on her little green mound of safety, crying, "I can't remember. . . . I can't remember how I came to this place. . . . I can't find it. . . ."

"Yes, you can," I said firmly, more firmly than I felt, and went back to the edge of the pool next the road. It was still as glass and at its far end I could see the shadow of Maureen Trumble reflected in it while all around her was

the brassy glow of the first rays of sunset. I was relieved that
she had stepped away from the patch of bog which was
nothing but bottomless mud, but I could not imagine how
I should reach her from the road. The pool intervened, and
then those emerald-green tuffets that bordered the pool.
The tuffets sheltered deadly reed-meres, which I knew, even
from my meager experien ~, were hard to recognize from
the innocent green patches. She appeared to be in panic, and
as she swung around, more and more quickly on her precious
island, it seemed, to my nervous imagining, that bits of
her island kept slipping down into the pool of viscous mud,
until she left herself less and less footing upon which to
stand. Trying to retain what measure of calm I might have
left, I called to her again.

"How shall I reach you, Maureen? How did you come to
that place?"

She stopped spinning in that wild way, and peered
down on all sides of her as though seeing her surroundings
for the first time.

"I can't remember," she murmured; and then repeated
louder, "I can't. Truly. I th nk it was—that way."

She pointed in the direction opposite to the road, across
a stretch of green bog which led into another copse such
as I had just come through. I could imagine how treacherous
would be the footing on slippery grass surrounded by the
roots of half-submerged trees. I began to study the grassy
mounds and tuffets that bordered the pond. I had an
idea which I had heard somewhere, probably from my
mother when she spoke of the life of the West Counties. Grass-
covered meres such as dotted the bog would be easy enough
to discover, if one tested them before stepping forward;
the problem would be the darker patches of mud which
would suck one down in those bubbling little hells. Along
the edge of the pond I could now make out these mud-
pools. In the piercing rays of sunset, there was no mistaking their deeper color, the occasional bubble, or the sucking
sound. I now remembered how my mother used the gorse
and saplings and whatever else she could find, to mark
the safe places.

I went back up the road while Maureen asked in fright,
"Are you leaving me, Anne? Dear Annie, please do not. . . ."

"I'm coming," I promised, as I set my packet of home-

spun upon a mound of grass, and picked up several likely
sticks and broke up a dead tree-limb into twigs at the edge
of the thicket through which I had come. I went back to the
place where I had left Maureen, and saw her gingerly trying one foot upon a rounded hump surrounded by grass,
which proved to be an outcropping of rock. Before I could
stop her, she took another step, this time upon a tuft of
green, and screaming, almost lost her balance, as her toe
dipped into stagnant water.

"Stay where you are," I commanded her, in a voice so
chilled with my fear for her that it sounded like a cavalry
command. She caught her balance and poised dangerously
on the rock, folding her arms, and now calmly awaiting salvation at the hands of a woman who by no means shared
her confidence.

I studied the grass at the edge of the pond, then put one
foot upon it tentatively. It held my weight. I stuck a
twig into the tuft, and made another tentative step, with
equal success. The third time, however, my foot went into
mud which lay just beneath the brown turf, and when I drew
it back with great care so as not to lose my balance, I found
I had lost my shoe. Well, no matter. We should be lucky
if we lost no more than a pair of shoes in this day's work.
After that, by marking the safe places, I managed to find
my way out to Maureen on her little rock, and we both
stepped to temporary safety on the island where first I had
found her. There was scarcely more than room for the two
of us, and my shoeless foot was growing colder by the
minute, encrusted with mud as it was.

I explained what Maureen must do in returning to the
road.

"You must step only where I have placed the twigs in
the ground. You must not step elsewhere."

She sighed and looked around her.

"But Anne, I know this bog so well. That is why it was
difficult to do what I must."

"What you must do is to return home," I said severely.
"Dr. Trumble will be ever so cross with you. Why did
you run away? How did you get out there?"

She looked very much concerned.

"Oh, he will be cross. He will. And with you too. He
set you to be with me, to be my friend and not leave

me. And you did leave. And Jono was busy with that old silly, Mary Mulcahy, and after we walked here on the road for a while, he went and left me alone."

"Never you mind that. Go now. One step. Now, the next." She succeeded so well, she was all eager to set out any way, in any direction, that I only just snatched at her arm in time to keep her from stepping full-tilt into an ugly mere that was scummed over with blown grass and dead insects. I followed her carefully, aware that where one body might hold, two could prove disastrous. Halfway to the road, she paused before me so suddenly I had to stiffen every bone and muscle to brace myself. Immediately before her, where I had lost my shoe, she pointed out something fluttering there like little blades of grass in the wind.

"Look! A tiny bird. It is caught. Don't you see?"

God of heaven! I thought. One second's ill-timed step and we shall follow the bird.

"Don't step there," I warned her. "To the other side. No . . . no! That other side!"

She moved in the wrong direction and knelt there on a tuffet no bigger than double the length of our feet.

"Come, little bird. . . . Don't flutter so. Oh, Anne! It is beyond my reach. Anne!"

"Yes! Yes! Let be," I said in despair, knowing full well what I would have to do. "I'll get it. The next twig. There. And the next . . ." She was safely past. I saw her eyes upon me, sorrowful, hounding me, reminding me of my promise. I knelt carefully, reached out over the mere, and scooped up the bird, its cluttering, mud-crusted wings, and a handful of thick slime as well. But at least the thing was done. I followed Maureen to the road, and felt strongly inclined to faint, but could not, for Maureen was staring at me with deep admiration.

"How clever you are to see one safe! But perhaps some won't thank you for it. See how happy the little bird is. He is trying to tell you so."

"Never mind that. He is only trying to tell me he wants to be free again to repeat his folly," said I, finding my hands could not contain the little creature. Off it flew, flapping its wings as freely as if it had never known such peril. "What did you mean, Miss Maury—that others won't be thankful to see you safe?"

She began to walk on quickly, entirely unmindful of me with my mud-soaked foot which I was rubbing while I tried to balance myself.

"Because," she said over her shoulder, as calm as may be, "at Conor House it will be ever so good for them all when I am gone."

"Whatever do you mean?" I asked, running after her, wincing as my foot seemed to find every pebble embedded in the muddy road.

"How silly you are, Anne, not to know. I am different."

"You are not different at all," I told her sternly. "What lying tongue told you that?"

"Ivy it was. And I am glad she is dead instead of me. Because she said it would be me. Only it wasn't. It was Ivy."

I thought the day had been quite enough for me without this. "Did you— How did Ivy die?" I asked.

Maureen smiled wisely. "She died because I wanted her to be gone. Did you see how she looked at Jono? I saw her. She thought I didn't. And now she is dead. It serves her proper."

We walked along together in what would have been a companionable silence but for the impact of her words upon me. It was as though she saw deep into my thoughts with that curious, childlike, yet so perceptive mind of hers. She said after a few minutes, as the late shadows closed around us, "I have seen Jono look at you. Have you ever looked at him?"

"Why should I, indeed, Miss Maury?"

She thought this over and then said slowly, "Do not, Anne. I remember once I asked Ivy what I asked you, and she said what you say. But you saved my life today. It would be a pity if you were to go, just when we are friends."

"I shall not go unless I am asked to go by Mr. Aengus."

I thought of Aengus Conor's trick upon me today, with the blank sheet, and was none so sure of my own statement.

Maureen, in her own way, was so positive, so sure and quiet, her reply stunned me.

"Oh yes. You can go without Father or even Maeve saying so. You can go as Ivy went."

XIII

It HAD been a difficult day entirely, what with the physical buffets and emotional shocks. Nor was my day of confusion ended by our arrival at Conor House, both of us dripping mud and dampness. Maureen sneezing as if her head would pap off, and myself in scarcely better condition. The last portion of our trip, along the beach from the village to Kelper Head, we had been fortunate enough to be met by Dr. Jonathan in the pony cart, and just as Maureen predicted, he was cross as two sticks. Though he said nothing to me of my responsibility, I felt deeply a sense of having failed him. But then, if I had obliged him and seen to his wife this afternoon, I should have failed my employer, Mr. Aengus. It was a sorry day's work and, I thought, soonest ended, soonest forgotten.

The doctor scolded his wife roundly but I read in it the tenderness he occasionally showed his difficult, if likable, charge.

"What in God's name were you doing in the bog, love? Why will you be so worrisome?"

She started to say something petulantly, and he interrupted with firmness, "Didn't you hear Maeve say that there would be company to dinner? You are the daughter of the house. Maeve should not be let to do all the honors."

"But Jono, you always say I am so—"

"I said to return with Father MacMonigle who was making a visit to your father in his sickroom."

I could have told him why his wife could not do as he told her; Father MacMonigle had gone to his church in Ballyglen Town instead, but I did not like to inject my voice into their private matters more than necessary.

She looked at me sidewise, with her tongue curled against her upper teeth like a child about to tell a lie, before she said quickly, "I did not hear you. The Mulcahy boy was

162

showing me the grandest creature just taken from the bog.
Like a toad, all puffed out and making such sounds as you
have never heard."

He sighed and jogged the patient pony.

"You tiresome girl! If you knew what you were doing
when I spoke to you, devil-a-doubt you knew I spoke!"

She said after a pause, apparently thinking this over, "I
had a thing to do and I did not do it."

I was startled, but if there was another meaning in this,
it escaped Jonathan who frowned and looked troubled as
if puzzling it out.

"You had a thing to do. You were to hurry home and be
with your stepmother when she greeted your guest. Sir
Horace Pumbleby is a mighty important guest at Conor
House."

"Oh, him. Fusty work!" She wrinkled up her nose and sank
down cosily between her husband and me. Her hips wrig-
gled into a comfortable place, which almost made me
laugh, though I knew, from Jonathan's scowl, that her conduct was not a thing for laughter. But it was so very childish!

He glanced over her tousled, wind-blown hair at me. I saw
in his grim face the gratitude and the kindness, even before he spoke.

"How will I thank you, Anne? You've been so good for
us here, there'll be no thanking you rightly."

Maureen straightened up. I felt the stiffening of her body
as she heard these words, and I knew without looking at
her, that she was eying first her husband and then me,
just as she had warned me today on the bog road.

It was not fear of this poor child-woman, but a surging,
overwhelming sense of pity that made me freeze my expression and say coldly, "It was well I came by. But I daresay Miss Maury would have managed alone. She is very efficient and could have found the path, I am persuaded, even
if I had not chanced to pass that way."

Slowly, beside me, the stiffness melted away and Maureen was her happy, smiling, mercurial self.

"Jono, Annie says I do not spoil it for Conor House."

I wished she would not call me "Annie" but I supposed
it to be her notion of an endearment, and in any case, the
name was soon forgotten in the explosion by Jonathan.

"Good God, Maureen! Let's have no tittle-tattle of your 'spoiling' it for Conor House! Have we not been meeching enough, with their lordly pride put up against their own flesh and blood?" He squeezed her mud-spattered hand, and I saw that they were friends again.

"If you say," she murmured and subsided until we had reached the door at the north wall of Conor House, and were making our way up the stone staircase, lighted by the flimsy spill carried on high by the huge O'Glaney. The cold stone was rough and chill upon my stockinged foot, but I was not the only one who suffered. There was Maureen ahead of me, sneezing a dozen times and complaining that she was late for the sugar buns.

"And the night is so peevish," she excused herself.

"Ay. It do be that peevish! But never ye mind, Miss Maury," O'Glaney's voice rumbled staunchly in the shadows ahead, "there'll be sugar buns for 'e, no matter what some-ut would be wishing. My Sara will be seeing to that."

It was coming on for that long dusk familiar in these parts, when I reached my rooms. While I was still washing myself and changing my muddy garments, Rosaleen came by and rapped upon my sitting room door.

"Miss Anne, Her Ladyship was asking after you. She'll be wishing to see you at the usual hour tonight, only in Miss Ivy's room."

Having dressed again and being decently clean, I opened the door and looked out.

"Has Mr. Conor asked after me?"

She looked vastly surprised.

"La, no, miss. He scarce ever asks about anything, but through Her La'ship. He don't like the sound of voices. They be noisy-like to his ears. He's that ill, miss. He musn't be troubled."

That ill? He was not so ill when it came to ordering about such foolish-minded creatures as myself, like the sending of housekeepers upon long walks with blank sheets of paper, and setting them to wait and be struck by the sun in deserted graveyards. Ill? Ay! But ill in the head, to be thinking up such tricks!

"Well, thank you, Rosaleen," I said, and was about to close the door when I thought of Lady Maeve's order to me. "Did you say I am to meet Her Ladyship in Nurse Kellinch's room, not the morning room?"

"Ay, it is. She'll be setting the nurse's things to rights. Then, they'll be bundled off to the Convent of the Blessed Poor, I think she said. There's none to mourn Ivy Kellinch. Seems a bit sad-like, miss." She sketched a brief curtsey to me and went her way.

As I was closing the door I thought of Maureen's words to me on the Bog Road today. How like to Ivy Kellinch was my own situation! Even the confused mind of Maureen Trumble saw it. Like Ivy, I was alone in the world and had none to mourn me, should I die as had Nurse Kellinch. Nor were there any to ask inconvenient questions, except my dear old friend and employer, Miss Nutting. And like Ivy, I was asked to concern myself with Maureen's welfare. What was it Maureen had hinted? Nay, she had said it in so many words. I might go the way Ivy had gone.

These unpleasant thoughts pricked me and remained with me during the evening, like a tooth that gives one rest, then goes to aching again just as it is all but forgotten.

Sara O'Glaney told me that Lady Maeve had been annoyed by my absence, especially as there was a guest to dinner, adding, "And the girl we had in from the village to serve tells me the outlander is smacking his lips and drunk as a lord on Her Ladyship's wine. So all's well as end's well, they do say."

I fully expected a rebuke from Lady Maeve, and I began to wonder uneasily if her husband would confess his part in taking up my time so that I could not attend to the household duties.

At that minute as we stood in the kitchen there was a rattling of chains in the wall behind. I went over, opened the little door of the sliding shelf and peered up, expecting to see the face of one of the servants in the dining parlor. I saw instead, the insolent, grinning countenance of Theo Conor.

"So she's come home from the graveyard at last! If you'd been about when I drove home you'd have gotten a ride and saved those pretty limbs."

Behind him I heard Lady Maeve's voice, horridly clear, cutting and regal. "Theo, have the goodness to do as you are asked. Tell them Sir Horace is awaiting the next course."

There were murmurs from Sir Horace, indistinct, and punctuated by titters of laughter which sounded to me a trifle drunk, and then Lady Maeve's clear voice again, which made my cheeks redden with the indignity of it.

"Not entirely, Sir Horace. And Theo is too old for such 'petticoat games' with the servants. Come back to table, Theo!"

Theo had turned his head as she spoke, and I was so angry, and perhaps so tired from the day's exertions, that I gave a hard jerk on the chain he held. For an instant I had the horrid notion that he might tumble down upon my head, putting himself in worse case than his crippled father. He laughed though, and ordered up the sweets course. I took the covered dishes from Mrs. O'Glaney's hands, set them on the shelf, and saw them rise before me. The cook stared at me.

"Do you be ill, miss? You're that pink I could warm my hands to you."

" 'Petticoat games,' indeed!" I said furiously. "For tuppence I'd take my leave of this hellhole as Ivy did!"

"Lord forgive us! As Ivy did . . . miss, you'll never be meaning it!"

"I mean as Ivy intended." To assuage my anger I set about washing dishes, very much aware that she was staring at me in a shocked way until interrupted by the presence of many dishes to dry; whereupon, she took up the cloth and set to with a will.

"Is it true then, that Ivy Kellinch was leaving Conor House?"

"Yes," I said, throwing caution to the four winds of Kelper Head. "And it's my opinion she never died of any heart seizure. Make of that what you can."

I expected an argument on this but received none. I think she must have begun, belatedly, to worry about the cause of the nurse's shockingly sudden death. Later, I heard her murmuring to herself, and when I asked what she had said, she looked at me blankly.

"Nothing, miss. Not but what there's many that hated the Kellinch woman. Why should it be but one, indeed? And her as innocent as ever a babe may be, no matter what is thought in some quarters."

By 'her' I took it she meant her favorite, Miss Maureen.

"I don't understand," I said, as I made ready to go on that errand I dreaded, for it was sure to be unpleasant. "I must go to Her Ladyship now. I trust you sleep well, Mrs. O'Glaney."

"Oh, ay. That is . . . if there's no Ivy Kellinch floating among those rocks out yonder."

"Ivy Kellinch is dead and gone," I reminded her.

"Dead," she said after me, "but not gone."

I thought grimly that Sara O'Glaney had the last word on this occasion.

I did not know why, but the presence of Sir Horace in the house seemed to take away many of its shadows, and as there were more branches of candles burning tonight and more obscure corners mercilessly revealed to the light, I was relieved that I had seen to the cleaning of the family quarters yesterday. Just as I reached the corridor opposite the morning room, Lady Maeve came out of the dining parlor with her guest, followed at a slight distance by Dr. Jonathan and Maureen, with Theo Conor on his sister's other side. Maureen sneezed suddenly, and I was amused when both her husband and her brother offered handkerchiefs, but she was holding one of her own. I suprised an odd look on Theo's face as he stared at Dr. Jonathan, almost as though he resented the doctor's attention to his own wife.

Sir Horace saw me before I could duck back around the corner of the stairs, for I had no mind to meet him in my present mood. I was too tired, and my head ached, and I was prepared for the worst from Her Ladyship.

"Jove, but I am in very best of luck tonight," Sir Horace announced, slurring the words together so that he felt it necessary to repeat them for Her Ladyship's benefit, although Lady Maeve's face did not indicate her appreciation for this service. "Very-best-luck. Must make apologies to your La'ship's pretty housekeeper. Frightfully sorry I didn't take you up today when I left Ballyglen. Truth is, could not find head nor hair of you. That's truth."

"I feel sure Miss Wicklow did not expect you to," said Lady Maeve in a voice that sent chills chasing themselves up my back. I was not used to this tone taken by my employers, nor had I earned it, until today.

"I had business in the town, sir," I said, curtseying to the group and hoping I might make my escape without more banter.

Lady Maeve motioned to me, her forefinger raised for emphasis. "I will speak with you shortly, Miss Wicklow. Meanwhile, since it is rather later than our usual hour, Sir Horace, I am persuaded you would prefer the comfort of your own quarters. Theo!"

Theo had just let go his sister's arm and was about to sneak out of the group and down the stairs, but upon his stepmother's summons, he turned back. I wanted to smile at the boyish expression of dismay upon his face, rather as though he had been caught dipping into the cook's jam jar.

"Yes, Maeve?"

"Will you escort Sir Horace to his chamber?"

"Old Jono will do so. Fact is, I am awaited in the village. A matter of—some fifty guineas."

Lady Maeve looked at him, her green eyes piercing as two Spanish daggers.

"Will you do as I ask, Theo?"

"I say," Sir Horace protested, as Jonathan started to speak to him quietly on one side and Theo, crestfallen, shuffled slowly forward. "Fifty guineas! Quite a little matter, that."

"A gambling matter," said Lady Maeve without looking at either of them. She motioned to me and I followed her up the stairs to the top floor. I looked back to see Theo and Jonathan buzzing away in a series of whispers, and was not surprised when Theo vanished from the group. I knew who would be showing Sir Horace to his quarters.

Maureen, however, stood in the hall and watched her husband take the staircase behind us, with the London guest. It was in moments like this that I felt all my old indecision about her. With her face half in shadow, her mouth hidden by the handkerchief she held to her nose, she seemed mature, thoughtful, with something of her brother's and her father's shrewdness. The devil was in these Conors, I thought, and none were exempt from my suspicions.

We were now on the floor where, at the other end of the corridor, was the door of Aengus Conor's apartment. I was surprised to find my heart beating rapidly, whether from the exertions of the day, surmounted by the two staircases I had climbed, or from some mixture of fear and fascination that the thought of Aengus Conor gave me. Anything to do with him was like playing at darts with the devil. I wondered why I felt no repulsion toward him physically, though I knew him to be crippled in body, and I felt too, with a woman's instinct, that he had—however slight—a physical desire for me. His eyes, his eloquent mouth, his hands . . . it was impossible not to feel it. As I followed Lady Maeve into Ivy's room, I wondered what Mr. Aengus was doing behind his door, in the eerie silence of his quarters.

"Are you coming?" asked Lady Maeve, not so politely as the summons sounded. I went in and we looked around at Ivy Kellinch's room.

Miss Kellinch had packed away so many things in bandboxes and portmanteaux and traveling cases that there seemed very little to do but send her things off to the charities. I set about gathering the few garments off the backs of chairs, the worn slippers off the table, while Lady Maeve watched. She looked puzzled. I realized suddenly that she had not been frowning and angry with me so much as she was concerned about this room, or perhaps the fate of its inhabitant, for she said nothing to me about my day's absence until we had discussed Ivy Kellinch.

"It would appear that you were right, Anne. She certainly intended to leave Conor House. Now, I wonder why."

"When I brought her supper, I was of the impression she had obtained money, ma'am, from somewhere. But she may have been driven away by an enemy in the house. There was the fringe in her hand when she died. As though she had caught her fingers in—"

Her Ladyship asked sharply, "You know about that?"

I explained that I had seen it in Ivy's hand before Dr. Jonathan took it away.

"Of course. That would explain why he . . ." Her voice trailed off, and she pretended to discover something interesting among the lingerie that I had not yet taken up, but I knew, when she handed me the bundle all helter-skelter, that she had merely used this as a pretext to break off her sentence. "You have some suspicions, Anne. Tell me what they are."

. . . Oh no, Your Ladyship, I thought. I am not so simple. Nor do I wish to wake up dead like Ivy Kellinch for knowing too much. . . .

"My suspicions are profitless, ma'am." I added then, considering the problem as I spoke. "It was my thought Miss Ivy drank rather too much for dinner, and then, perhaps when she walked along the cove she may have tripped and hurt herself. And then, climbing back up the headland . . ." But all the time I was remembering the black fringe. Had it been part of Ivy's own shawl? Had she lost the shawl in the surf when she fell? Or had it been part of the clothing of someone who was on the shore with her when she had her attack—if attack it was?

Lady Maeve said thoughtfully, "You may be right," and then added the thunderbolt: "Why did my stepson see you in Ballyglen Town today?"

It was clever of her; for I had become so engrossed in the mystery of Ivy Kellinch's death that I forgot the more immediate problem between us.

"I went to purchase some cloth, ma'am."

"In the graveyard?"

I made a great bundle of Ivy's discarded and outworn things before I replied, "No, ma'am. I was there to pay my respects to a long-ago ancestor of my father. Him that was called Fergan O'Carty."

She smiled ever so faintly.

"You are discreet. Well then, I must leave you and Theo to your secrets."

I looked her in the eye and said straight out: "As to that, ma'am, there was no more Mr. Theo had to do with the graveyard than a—well, than a sheet of blank paper."

This time it was she who was forced to look away and change the subject. I think my fierce conviction awed her a trifle.

"I will say no more upon your absence today, Anne. Only that Jonathan, and all of us, count upon you to take Ivy's place with Maureen. You have been told that; have you not?"

I nodded.

She looked grim. A minute later she turned abruptly, saying as she left the room, "Take everything of any use from the room and leave it with O'Glaney. He will have the turf-cutters over tomorrow. They often carry things to the Convent for me."

She left the door open, and I was at first conscious of the darkness of the corridor behind me as I made separate bundles of the different items. It occurred to me to examine everything as I took it up, but nothing seemed in the least suspicious and I decided at last that the clue to Ivy's death was not to be found among these charity objects.

There had not been a sound, even the wind was still tonight, and when I started out of the room balancing two bundles, one in each hand, it gave me a start to see Jonathan in the doorway. He took the bundles from me, but said nothing. I walked along the corridor beside him, feeling that something should be said, but fearing to broach any subject. When he stepped into a room I had never seen before, next to Mister Aengus's, I wondered, but then I saw that the same sort of contrivance which Theo Conor had built for the dining parlor was here built into the wall to connect the top floor with a linen closet below. He threw in the bundles while I watched, marveling at these mechanical wonders. Of course, the height from which the bundles dropped, and their weight made them break open in mid-air, and I took up the candlestick from a tabaret nearby, and looked down with a sigh.

"I fear we shall find it a great confusion down there. But I thank you, sir, in any case."

He smiled as we started out of the room, a smile that illuminated his rough face, showing its youthful warmth, yet not destroying its vigor and force. When he looked at me in this way, I could not but remember Maureen's face, and her words. He must have read as much in my expression, for the look vanished. I was sorry that it must be so. He looked so very disappointed of life, disillusioned and bitter.

"No, Anne. We thank you. Or—I do. We owe much to you. There'll be no confusion in that but the confusion of my own—friendship toward you. From the first you knew it, love."

I started at the term, finding it bitter-sweet upon my ears. He guessed my dilemma and said abruptly, almost rudely, "It is a term we use in the North Country. It was an accident. I did not mean to—"

"Yes sir," I said, "I understand." And I would have gone on with my work but he spoke again as we entered the corridor together.

"You think I forget Maury? My own dear lass that I care for the way a babe is watched over?" He laughed shortly. "Though it was not always so. Often and often when we were children and the high and mighty Conors passed, my little Maury, ever-watchful of Theo, scuffed sand and stones in my face and called me 'dirty urchin' because Master Theo and I were forever fighting."

"All children are cruel, I think."

"You tell me nothing. So they be! But when the Earl took me to his house, and had me shod like the Conors, like Maeve too, and dressed for their church and the like, then it was not so rude. And for a while, before the Earl shot himself over his debts, I thought I'd been made a gentleman. But he died and there was nothing . . . no word of his belief in me. And Maeve made the grand marriage and lorded it more than ever." He rubbed his face tiredly and scowled at the dim candlelight.

Hoping to change his mood, I prompted him, "And Miss Maury?"

His voice softened. "Ay. It came to be different very soon. Maureen Conor smiled at me, her that once threw rocks and put her tongue out at me. It was good. It was very good!"

"Because she was one of the lordly Conors?" I asked.

"Because—I will not lie—it may have been so. But she needed me, you see. And she trusted me. It was a grand feeling, that, to know her sweetness and her dear dependence were on me. And then, Aengus Conor set his boot upon our marriage and forbade it."

"Yet you married, in any case."

"But only after—the thing happened, and Aengus was helpless. And now all goes to wrack because they keep Maury's income from use. Only to spite me! Couldn't they use it to help all of Conor House? But no. It is part of the spite because an outlander married into the precious Conors!"

As a man, Dr. Jonathan probably did not realize how important money must be to a woman of Lady Maeve's habits, and perhaps too, she had inherited her father's profligate ways. I suspected she married Aengus Conor for the Conor money. Indeed, she had very nearly confessed as much to me. And then she had found herself bound to poverty despite herself, all that was left being her own marriage settlement and the income of Miss Maureen's inheritance from her mother. I found myself joining Mrs. O'-Glaney in her suspicion that Miss Maury's income had already been dipped into by Lady Maeve for her own use, and even for the use of her apartments, such as the morning room, which looked so different from the other rooms I had seen.

"It was good for you, sir, that Miss Maureen came to depend upon you. You must have felt her need of your approval, your opinion, everything."

He found my phrase more suitable than even I had suspected.

"Just so. She depended upon me, and maybe"—he smiled wryly—"I need that dependence, for my own peace of mind. God knows I receive little enough dependence from those in this household. So now Maureen is nearly a part of me, even a part of my skill. That is how our lives are shaped. . . . Do you understand what I am trying to say?"

"Yes, sir. I believe so."

He did not look happy about my reply but went on more rapidly, "You did a brave thing today, and I think it cost you somewhat. You look as though a good breath of air might make you faint."

"Faith, sir, I'm none so weak as that," I said sternly, not liking this surgical diagnosis of me. "It was my duty, after all."

"More than that. It was the warm goodness and strength of you, love—"

I felt myself stirred emotionally and was anxious to stop him, to put space between us, but he went on after the merest pause,

"—lovely Anne."

"She is a sacred charge upon you, sir, and upon me. Her condition makes it so." He bit his lip and put his hand up to me very slowly, as though against his own inclination. He touched my cheek, brushed his fingers over it the while I flushed and wished myself a thousand miles from this dangerous presence, this temptation where, but for

Maureen Trumble, lay the warm comfort and care of me that I had once received from my husband. I started to move and was stopped by the swiftness of his painful grip upon my waist. He would have kissed me but I turned my head away.

"No," I said hoarsely, finding it difficult to control my voice. "No. Please. Good night, sir."

I felt all the disgrace, the indignity of this struggle with him, which was compounded by an emotion in me that was greedy for my remembered love. His strength, or the use of it, however, was more than I had bargained for. Before I could summon the usual swift, easy evasion that had served me often against such designs, I found myself pinned against the damp, cold wall of the corridor, unable to retreat, and with my face held securely by one of his hands under my chin. I felt the hot, angry passion of his kiss which put me in emotional turmoil, but I presented to his embrace what I hoped was a cool indifference. He let me go so roughly I dropped the candle and scrambled to retrieve it before the wild, flaring light was snuffed. He made no effort to help me. He stalked away rapidly as I stared after him, trembling in dismay, the candle shaking in my hand. I had a strong desire to burst into tears.

I was about to go back to Ivy's room to finish my work when I heard my name called. The door of the next room was ajar and I knew without the ridiculous and insulting mistake in my name, that I was being spied upon by Aengus Conor, as was his custom.

"Anne Wexford! Come here, Anne—'lovely Anne,' I believe he called you."

I went over and pushed open the door into Mr. Aengus's room. There he was behind the door, grinning at me in the candlelit room of shadows, and by opening the door so rapidly, I had barely missed striking him with it. He seemed unconscious of his danger and looked snug as could be in his chaise longue, wrapped from toe to waist in a dusty old satin coverlet that was split with long wear. He had his nightcap on jauntily and crookedly over the tangled, graying locks, and I could see the high collar of his nightrobe covering his precious hide from night drafts. A pity he did not get the typhus and leave us all in peace, I thought angrily in that first moment. Instead, he withheld

Miss Maury's money, objected to the man who cared for her, and hid around corners hoping to see what he should not be seeing. Small wonder a kelper or someone else had tried to kill him! But I was shamed enough at my own faults this moment to give Mr. Aengus a little charity and tried to think of him as a man incapable of movement as the rest of us knew it, and therefore prone to spy upon us behind doors.

"Well, Anne, you served me most amiably today. Did you know that?"

"Excellent," I said. "Then you will not hesitate to favor me in turn, sir."

He looked surprised.

"By all means, Miss Wexford. You have but to ask it."

"Then," said I, raising my voice, "kindly call me by my name, which is Wicklow!"

"But, of course," he agreed gravely. "I daresay you wonder why I sent you so far, and on a fruitless errand."

"Not at all. I can only suppose that you conceived me in the need of exercise! The paper was blank, by the by. It fell open after I was struck unconscious, and I saw it."

"Struck unconscious!" He straightened up at this, and then, as though the trunk of his body were in pain, he winced, and settled back. It served him proper, I thought as I watched him. Anybody ought to have body-cramps, cripple or no, when he spent all his time spying on a person.

"By the sun," I explained.

"Impossible. It was not that hot today. I felt its rays in this chamber," he said, pointing to the far window, "and it never warmed my bones."

"In Ballyglen Town it was hot!" I contradicted him with relish. "And so I felt the pain in my head, and a few minutes after, when I awoke, I knew it had all been useless, some jest you played on me, sir."

"I see. Where was the pain in your head?"

I turned around and raised my hair and he touched the place, at which I let out a cry that I felt sure must awaken all the residents of Conor House.

"And how do you feel now?"

His voice seemed so genuinely concerned that I was amazed and not displeased. At once I minimized the tale.

"Very well, sir. I am tired, though. I think I will sleep well tonight."

He laughed, but more lightly, less sardonically than I remembered. It was as if he laughed with me and not at me.

"I should think so. Well, we must have no more missions such as I sent you upon. Did you see anyone in the churchyard?"

"Only Master Theo who was speaking with Father Mac-Monigle."

I waited for him to dismiss me. I could not remember when I had been so poor of spirit, but there was more to come.

He said after a little while, "Have you any fondness for my daughter?"

"Yes, sir. I have."

"Yet you let her husband kiss you."

The devil was in him after all. I was almost too tired to put up the battle I should have put up at another time. I only said with all my heart, "I did not kiss him, sir. But what happened will not happen again. I give you my word, sir."

"I believe you, Anne. Go about your business now. And I, in my turn, give you my word. No more messages to Ballyglen Town."

Exceedingly puzzled, I went back along the corridor to Ivy Kellinch's room to finish my night's work, so busy wondering what Aengus Conor and the others in this house were about, that I did not feel the ache of all my bones until I was safe in my bed an hour later.

XIV

I AWOKE next morning with a distinct tenderness at the back of my head, and a resolution to stay out of deserted graveyards, sunshine or no! It was beginning to be borne upon my consciousness that the shaft of sunlight which struck me down yesterday was a most uncommon one, to have left its "visiting card," so to speak, behind my skull.

Two cups of strong tea that tasted of smoke and peat fires did much to put me in charity with the world, and when this was followed an hour later in the kitchen by porridge and a bit of uncommonly good fish freshly caught, I felt ready for another day at Conor House.

Dr. Jonathan came into the kitchen as I was finishing breakfast, and upon hearing his voice behind me I stiffened self-consciously, careful not to turn around. He spoke, however to Mrs. O'Glaney who was sweeping the hearth.

"Would you be good enough to make a hot posset for my wife? She seems to have taken a cold and I do not want it to settle upon her lungs."

The cook began to sweep more vigorously than before. She and her husband were always over-zealous in support of the Conors against the outlander who had married into their sacred family.

"Ay, sir. Miss Anne will see to it—will you not, miss? You being so good and all with Miss Maury, and me with the mutton on."

"Of course," I said. "I shall at once."

Jonathan and I looked at each other, I without any sign that I had ever met or spoken with him before, and he, with the same indifference in all but his eyes.

"Thank you, Anne," he said, and left the room.

Sara O'Glaney sniffed, and with her bundle of broom-straws, blew up a great cloud of cinders and dust, so that she was one mass of sniffs for a few minutes.

"Well now," she said finally, watching me make up the posset. "It'll be 'Anne-this' and 'Anne-that,' is it?"

I went on with my work, ignoring her querulous tone. "Probably because, like Mr. Aengus Conor, he confuses the county of Wicklow with the county Wexford!"

She frowned and scratched her head with broomstraw.

"So Mr. Aengus mistakes your name. An odd bit of business, that. He was never one to mistake such matters, but for his own odd humors."

"Odd humor it is!"

She grunted, which I suppose must make do for a laugh.

"Ah well, but then, we must allow the "quality" their little ways. It's often so, in life."

I made up a tray with the steaming posset, and prepared as well a freshly laundered cloth for her throat, and wrapped it around a warming pan. Then I thought of the one thing which would make all else palatable.

"Are there any warm sugar buns, Mrs. O'Glaney?"

She grinned at me, in good spirits for once.

"Good for 'e, miss. That'll be the cheering up of our girl. I've a fine lot, just popped out of the fire."

She wrapped up several sugary little cakes to preserve their warmth, and my nostrils were pervaded by the pleasant smell of spices and sweet dough. I put the tray upon the little rising floor, and left it there, thinking to go upstairs to the dining parlor and haul it up for delivery to Miss Maureen, but as I started to leave the kitchen, Mrs. O'Glaney and I heard the whirring, clanking sound of chains in the walls, and upon opening the little door, saw that someone upstairs had already begun to raise the tray. I could not see who it was, as the floor upon which the tray sat was already above my head, and I did not in the least like the idea of unknown hands handling the sick girl's food.

"Quick!" cried Mrs. O'Glaney, quite as stirred as I was by this mystery. "I'd lay you ten guineas someone's meaning no good to Miss Maury."

I ran along the guardroom and flung open the door to the winding stone steps. I hurried up those twisting steps as fast as ever I had done, and was in time to see Rosaleen carrying the tray along the corridor past the Trumbles' bed-chamber.

"Where are you going?" I asked.

She was a trifle flippant, as though the protection of someone more important than I gave her permission to use liberties with me.

"That'll be for Her La'ship to say, ma'am."

"Give it to me."

She held on, but began to show signs of confusion.

"I daren't."

"Give it to me!"

Her fingers were shaking now, and I felt sorry for her, but I had no intention of repeating the suspicious actions that may, or may not, have caused the death of Ivy Kellinch. I took the tray just as we both heard Lady Maeve's footsteps approaching along the corridor.

"What is it, Rosaleen? What is the delay?"

"There has been a mistake, ma'am," I explained. "Dr. Trumble ordered this tray for Miss Maureen. She has a cold and he fears it may settle upon her lungs."

"Yes, I know." That surprised me, in the circumstances, as did her next words. "I think you may go, Anne. Rosaleen and I will manage. You may give me the tray now."

Fearful of showing my anger at her tone, and perhaps also, my mistrust, I took a breath before replying.

"Very well, ma'am. You may find the tray a trifle heavy. Let me—" I gave her the tray and stepped back along the hall to the Trumbles' door where I knocked and called out, "Miss Maureen's breakfast, sir."

I had never seen Lady Maeve in such a rage. Her hands shook as they held the tray, but unlike the terrified Rosaleen, Her Ladyship shook from fury. She gave me her most freezing setdown. "I feel sure you have many things to do, Miss Wicklow! Please do not let me detain you!"

Dr. Jonathan came to the door and opened it at that moment, and it was all I could do to keep from smiling in Her Ladyship's face. She had certainly not intended to give the Trumbles that tray. Not yet, at least.

Jonathan said in surprise, "How good of you, Maeve! Here is your stepmother, Maury, come to bring you somewhat that's going to do you good. Come in. Come in." He made way for Her Ladyship, and she had no choice but to bring the tray into the room where I heard Maureen exclaim over the sugar buns whose odor betrayed them clear across the room.

"Whoosh!" said Rosaleen, rolling her eyes at me. "It's me scalp, it is. Her La'ship do send me into a fit of the vapors when she be in a rage!"

"Come along," I said. "We'll let her bestow her vapors upon those who have time for them."

The girl and I went down to our quarters companionably enough and set to work immediately, sweeping up the latest accumulation of stagnant salt water that seeped in along the floor of the wine cellar and the guardroom. The tide had been out and it was almost peaceful for the first hour or two of our work, but gradually the distant waves approached again, and the whirlpool at one end of the escarpment wall began its first little sucking, churning sounds as the currents met.

Later, I saw Maureen and Dr. Jonathan out on the debris beyond my bedroom window, the doctor speaking very seriously, and Maureen nodding, like someone being scolded but not really listening. She had around her throat the cloth I had put on the tray, and she kept tugging at it with nervous fingers. As her husband spoke she would glance to either side of her, and then break in to point out several kelp gatherers coming up the headland, dripping seaweed and water; or she would suddenly raise her head and stare as though a gray gull overhead was the most amazing sight in the world. I could not but smile at her husband's efforts.

As I opened my window I heard him say sternly, "I forbid it, Maury! You must not. It can be dangerous. The tide may come in one day when you have forgotten. You know how you forget things."

"Yes, yes. But Jono! See the cormorant. How big he is! They nest on the terrace now and again. . . . See?"

"It is not a cormorant. It is a common seagull. Look at me, Maureen."

I moved away from the window so that I did not hear whatever Maureen replied. I was sure she would agree with him, and equally sure that in two minutes after his back was turned she would forget entirely everything he had said. She was maddening, perhaps, but oddly endearing, as well.

Presently, when I went out to fetch some clothing that had been laid upon the rocks to be aired, I saw Maureen over at the corner where the little whirlpool formed at the

joining of the escarpment to the headland. She was staring down at the churning waters as though under their
spell. I went over and stood beside her, with my hands full
of stiff, sun-warmed petticoats.

"It would be best if we step back a little," I ventured, not
raising my voice. "Think how nasty to be mesmerized
by that cold wet pool!"

I had caught her attention at last. She shifted her feet
back from the edge, asking curiously, "What is that? Mesmer—what you said?"

"That was a Doctor Mesmer. In France at the court of
the kings, long ago."

"A doctor like Jonathan?"

"No. A wicked person who made people do his bidding
by"— I wasn't quite sure how Dr. Mesmer worked, and added
lamely—"by staring at them and they did what he asked
because they could not help themselves."

"I see," she said thoughtfully. "And he was wicked?"

"I suppose he must have been, with such powers."

She shaded her eyes from the sun, and seemed to be
thinking this over.

"I—knew someone like that—once. But I do not know.
What is wicked for you, perhaps, may be good for others.
Sometimes I know my family, who love me, wish I had never
been born, for I am a great trouble to them. And it would
not be wickedness if I were to—I do not know. I am not clever
enough, I think. If I were, then I should know."

If I had not my hands full of clothing, I should have
gently shaken her. As it was, I said as earnestly as I knew
how, "No, Miss Maury. That is a wicked lie! You must never
believe it. There is not a soul in all the world who does
not love and esteem you. What you think of as being—
not clever, is simplicity and honesty, and lack of pretense.
Do you understand what I am trying to say?"

"Not—not all. Only that I think wicked things sometimes,
and I must do as I am told even if I want to do something else." She shook her head, and sighed and then
smiled. "But I am not simple, as you say. I often do things
I am told not to. That proves I am clever, too."

She put her arm through mine and took off some of my
garments from the pile I carried, and we went into the

house together. I knew I had not answered her satisfactorily, but it was so difficult to know what to say, how to make her understand, for, somehow, she believed everything backward, as though she saw life in a mirror and not as it truly was.

She sneezed several times as we were putting away the undergarments in my bedroom, and when I asked her gently to go to her room and lie upon her bed and rest, she promised me to do so. However, she used that same saucy, indifferent voice she had used with her husband earlier, and I was not surprised when I followed her out into the guardroom to see her go in the opposite direction, toward the north end of the building.

"Miss Maury," I called.

"I was going to follow Jono to the village."

"Never you mind Dr. Jonathan," I told her firmly. "He's his patients to see to, and you must not be one of them. Will you be getting upstairs now, there's a good girl."

"Wicked old thing!" she shouted, straining her voice and beginning to cough. "You old Dr. Mesmer, you!"

I laughed and made a gesture of shooing her up to her quarters.

She hesitated, turned reluctantly on one heel, and came back toward the winding stone steps. Just as she opened the stair door she squeezed her face up into what she doubtless thought was a sinister mask, and sticking her tongue out at me, hurried up the steps. I could not help laughing at her naïve tricks as I set about my work again.

Shortly after, when the first combers were feeling their way up toward the escarpment, I went out on the headland and made great bundles of the sticky, foul-smelling kelp I had cut away two nights before, and went over to the edge of the cliff and threw handful after handful into the water below. Underneath this crawling vegetation I found an old boot of very good leather, and after thinking what a pity it was that I had not the mate, to polish up and give some needy person an expensive pair, I took it over to the cliff's edge. I was just asking myself whether I should throw over the boot when I happened to glance down at the root of the escarpment where the waves were already making a great to-do against the little shelf of safety outside the escarpment door. You may conceive my astonishment and concern to behold Miss Maureen there in her day dress, with the white cloth that had protected her throat now dangling about her shoulders, and her feet bare to the icy, rising waters. She knelt as I watched, and put her outspread fingers into the foam, then arose and seemed to wash her face with this salty spray. Then she stood there as though under a spell, staring out upon the enormous Atlantic which was unusually blue today. I called to her but she did not answer. Either she did not wish to, or the rising waters absorbed my voice. I hurried inside and through the guardroom to the thick little escarpment door. Already the first foamy signs of the incoming tide had drifted into the guardroom though the partially opened door, and I squeezed through that narrow opening, to Maureen.

"Will you be coming in now, ma'am?" said I, as cross as two pins. "You will have the lung sickness for sure!" Not to mention drowning, if she remained here very many more minutes.

She turned to me and I thought for a moment that she did not recognize me, for her Irish blue eyes had a vague, misty look in them, as though they peered through me. Then she smiled, her agreeable but tricky smile, and said,

"Why, it's Anne! Don't be cross, there's a good one. Paddy said the door was sticking, and I showed him it would open. Now, we have only to close it."

I was in despair of knowing how to curb her rashness; for she spoke in a hoarse way that showed me how quickly her cold had gotten its way with her.

"Never you mind the door," I said. "Just get inside. Come now."

She came in with me, all obedience, and I saw that since it had been pushed open a trifle, Paddy was right. It would not close. Stones were caught under the outer edge of the door. I told Maureen to go up to her room, but first to stop by the kitchen and fetch me the boy Paddy, or Rosaleen or anyone who was in service at the moment. As for me, I knew we could not have half the Atlantic Ocean pouring in through this partially opened door; so I went back out on the rapidly vanishing ledge under the escarpment, and dug away under the door, to release it. I broke a fingernail in the process, and acquired a couple of bloody cuts which the sea-foam stung mightily when it washed against my hands at work.

I could feel the yielding of the door now, and called out, "Maureen, have you gone yet? Do not forget to stop in the kitchen."

There was no response, which relieved me, as I had half expected her to stay on the other side of the door, pulling and hauling at it, and catching more cold. Looking out for her, I realized, was like watching over an irresponsible baby.

I removed one more stone from under the outside of the door, and quite suddenly, with enormous force, the door swung shut. Well, I thought, feeling the first long sea-wave wash about my feet and into my shoes, at least the door would operate more easily now. I pushed against it, and found it would not yield. I had not allowed for the fact that the door must open from the leverage on the other side.

Thank heaven Maureen had gone for help! I looked back as another, much longer wave washed up against my ankles, and felt annoyed to think that I may have lost two pairs of shoes in as many days. I resolved firmly to put this to the account of the Conors and make them pay me for the loss. Something wound itself around my feet, and for an instant I thought it might be a sea-creature. But it was only the throat cloth that Maureen had dropped. I went back to pushing at the door, but got no response.

Moments were slipping away, the tide was rising, and my patience was quite exhausted. I called out, hoping someone would be on the terrace, or perhaps on the headland, but I felt like a fool at the sound of my voice, for it obviously could not compete with the roar of the breakers as they rolled up toward the escarpment, cutting me off now entirely from any dry ground. I took a deep breath and, waiting until an especially large breaker had roared, crested, and retreated, I screamed as loudly as I could in the tiny space of time between breakers. There was no response.

It was too ridiculous! I should have known I could not count upon Maureen to remember anything five minutes after she had been told. I might have to remain here until . . . It might be hours before someone came up over the headland and looked down at the base of the escarpment. Meanwhile, I should be directly under the huge battering of the waves against the escarpment.

My situation began to be serious. I tried to measure with my eye the time it would take, so that I might give myself the encouragement of an hour's grace, or half an hour, before the tide was in and churning against the wall whose prickly, pitted face I now leaned back against, to escape the ever-rising water. Just since I had been out here the tide had risen sufficiently to cover my ankles, creeping a little higher with each wave. I stepped out into the water, feeling it drag at my skirts, and looked up as high as I could. I could see the top of the headland but not, of course, the terrace. Why could not Lady Maeve be patroling the terrace at this hour, as she was during all the odd times of day or night? Stubborn, contrary woman that she was!

And Maureen! And all of them. To allow such a stupid thing to happen.

Of course, it was my fault. I knew this, but it did not cure the angry panic that arose in me just as one wave, longer, higher than the others, broke up against my thighs and made me cough and choke on its salty spray. I screamed again, with all my force, feeling the scratch and strain in my throat, and at the pit of my stomach. For a few minutes in an absolute panic heretofore unknown to me, I ran up and down in front of the escarpment wall, like a mouse in a trap, unthinking, yielding only to sheer panic. There must be some method of climbing out of here. Someone would hear me. I must find a way. . . .

I paused at last, buffeted by the waves which now came at me regularly, about every fifth to seventh breaker. My knees were trembling as they had never trembled before, and I stood staring up at the headland, wondering if I could possibly gain a footing over that sheer cliff. But soon, in precisely that spot, the whirlpool would have reached its full force. If I could get across that pool I might be able to climb up, holding onto jutting rocks, trusting to my normal levelheadedness not to grow dizzy or weak. But I was trembling so that I could hardly stand up against the crash of each wave.

And it was too far across that pool. I held onto an outcropping of stone from the escarpment, and tried to calculate how far I could leap across, but it was beyond my strength. The first, brief effort threatened to tear my arm from its socket and did, in fact, pull out the loose stone which I had been holding to. I fell back into the water which now covered me as I lay flat upon the sand below the escarpment, and I swallowed salt water, and coughed and found myself crying like an infant, in fear, and in fury. I rolled over, crawled to the escarpment, handicapped by my sodden skirts, and pulled myself up, clinging to the escarpment as to my last hold upon earth.

I began to pray, fumbling, nonsensical words, full of self-pity and pleas for help, and the wild concern for self that is natural, I suppose, in the final extremity. For a last attempt at summoning help, I braced myself to leave the wall, and staggered out into the surf between breakers. Half-drowned by the following wave that engulfed me, I dragged myself up from the kneeling position to which I had been flung, and as the breaker receded, I heard the blessed sound of a voice calling to me in sharp concern from the south corner of the terrace. I caught a glimpse of Dr. Jonathan's dark face, etched so deeply in horror that I could make out the features from my watery coffin. He leaned far out, yelled something to me, and then disappeared.

In my present state I thought he had left me to drown, and I rushed up to the escarpment door dragging what seemed half the ocean with me. I leaned against the door sobbing, shaking so that I do not quite remember what my thoughts were before I felt the door giving away before my body, just as a huge breaker broke over my head against the escarpment. I fell forward into someone's arms, and having been half blinded by the sunlight upon the water, as well as the salty lashing itself, I saw only dimly that Jonathan had caught me and carried me without effort, dripping as I was, along the guardroom to the kitchen.

There was a deal of fussing. I opened my eyes to see Mrs. O'Glaney offering me a hot mug of something that smelled like very strong spirits, and Dr. Jonathan rubbing my hands briskly so that I objected to the hurt, while choking on the hot spirits.

"Come," he urged me, smiling but still tense and grim. "Just be very quiet. You've had a trifling shock."

"Trifling, is it!" said I, trying to raise my head at this lowering description of my closeness to death. "I'll thank you to speak more respectfully of—of—"

"Now, now," he said in that voice which had often seemed vastly annoying to me in surgeons, quite as though one were a child, to be cosseted. "You'll be better in a trice."

"Poor lamb. It might have been the death of you, miss," said Mrs. O'Glaney sympathetically.

The fiery liquid which they were pouring down my throat had its effect, and for some contrary reason, I now began to resent the good cook's pity as well.

"It was my fault, entirely. I went out to bring in Miss Maury, and there was trouble with the door. I sent her to the kitchen for help, and then—I suppose— Where is she?"

Theo Conor came into the kitchen, dusting his hands.

"She is laid down on her bed, so do not concern yourself with her."

I thought of something else.

"Good heavens! We'll be flooded. The escarpment door will be open, and the tide is coming in."

"Not today," Theo said in the sardonic tone that his face used so often. "I've seen to it." He leaned back against the wall behind the hood of the fireplace, so that I could not read in his face whether he cared about the life or death of a housekeeper.

Jonathan slapped my hands aside with a laugh when he was through with them, and said, "I think the patient will live. But if it is a comfort to you, Miss Wicklow, it would have been touch and go had you been out there longer."

"Nonsense," said I. "I was seriously thinking of trying to climb the headland."

Although Mrs. O'Glaney murmured, "Tsk-tsk" in horrified sympathy with me, Jonathan and Theo laughed.

"Very likely," the latter said while Jonathan shook his head.

"I think not," he told me lightly, but his eyes were deeply concerned. It was a moment or two before Theo Conor cleared his throat in a way that could not be misunderstood.

"Maureen has been asking for you, Jono. You had better go and see to your first patient."

Jonathan stood up, brushing off his jacket and looking around for the battered old case of instruments that he had brought back from the village.

"I expect I left my case on the terrace. I came back from the village and was just crossing the terrace. . . . I wonder why I looked over? And you'll imagine my feelings to see Miss Wicklow trapped down there. Mrs. O'Glaney, you will look out for our patient here, will you now?"

"That I will, sir," said the lady phlegmatically. She glanced at Theo Conor for some reason, and as he was staring at the hearth, apparently without interest, she shrugged and said no more as Jonathan left the kitchen.

I started to rise, felt a trifle dizzy, and sat back, enjoying the warmth of the fire.

"I'm sorry, Master Theo. I know now that I should not have expected Miss Maureen to remember all that I asked."

He did not look at me but went on studying the hearth, and frowning.

"You asked her first to go to bed, I imagine."

"Yes, sir."

"And then to go to the kitchen for help."

"I believe so. I confused her. I can see that now. Probably she met someone, or something occurred to change the direction of her thoughts."

He dismissed this with a gesture.

"Highly problematical. She may have merely taken the first of your advice and gone to bed. I saw her in bed not half an hour ago. She asked me when Jonathan would be back from the village. Maeve is gone to inspect the tenant coteens and will not be back until God knows when. Rosaleen is sitting with Maury. They are playing at draughts."

"How lucky for me," I said, "that Dr. Trumble saw me. No one else seems to have done." I could not help it if this was aimed at Theo Conor. He had apparently been about the place all afternoon and never been near enough to save me.

"Ever the gallant gentleman," Theo agreed in the nastiest way. He turned abruptly and left the kitchen.

Mrs. O'Glaney and I looked at each other.

"Well!" I exclaimed. "There'll be no reasoning with that young man."

Instantly, she was on the defensive, as she and her husband always were when it came to the Conors.

"I wouldn't be saying that, Miss. It's likely that if the doctor had not been and seen you, Master Theo would. Or Aengus, to be sure. He has the habit of looking out of that window of his. There an't much that Mr. Aengus misses . . . or used to miss before his illness, I'm thinking."

"He missed me drowning," I said, still sore on the subject. "And little does my fine Mr. Aengus guess that one more accident is going to see me on my way back to London Town. And that you may put into your pipe and be smoking it!"

"It be a odd kind of accident, miss," said the cook, going on about her work and not looking at me. "Have you thought on that?"

I sat there utterly confounded. An accident of the sun in the graveyard at Ballyglen, that might be excused. An accident in the bog when I might have been killed in saving Miss Maureen. . . . And did she, by the by, know the way out of that trap, or did she not? And now this. Was it conceivable that the evil intelligence whose presence I felt in Conor House had today tried again and very nearly succeeded in destroying me?

The horror of those moments that had seemed hours, out upon the escarpment, crept over me again. And to think that some monster whom I saw each day, might have committed me to that hell deliberately, shutting the door, leaving me there, perhaps even listening to my cries and ignoring my desperate attempts to save myself!

I shall give my notice, I thought. Be damned to the salary, and to Miss Maureen and the precious care of her that I had promised! She might even be the alert and crafty mind that conceived the whole of these "accidents" to me.

A fortnight, I agreed to myself. I shall give in my notice for a fortnight hence, and then be gone from this wretched place that my mother and my father thought so kindly of.

It was only later that I laughed grimly to myself, thinking that in a fortnight all manner of calamity might befall Conor House, if so many horrors had occurred during the past four days!

XV

SUITING MY mental resolution to the deed, I did not even wait for my evening report to Lady Maeve before climbing the stairs to the top floor to give in my notice to Mr. Aengus Conor. The horror of my near escape remained with me still, as I rapped upon his door. The upper floor was always so quiet I feared my knock upon the door might not be heard by anyone else but Mr. Aengus, who was doubtless hiding behind that very door now, spying upon all who approached. He did not immediately respond, however, and I was startled by Lady Maeve's voice, sharper than usual, as she came into the hall behind me, having apparently followed me up the stairs.

"What is it, Anne? What are you doing here at this hour?"

"I came to give in my notice, ma'am," I said, not mincing matters.

She was dressed for the out-of-doors and now stripped off a beautiful glove that looked soft as cream to my eyes, while she seemed to pull her wits together. Though she gave a fair imitation of a woman completely calm, for some reason the sight of me here had unnerved her.

"Come into the north chamber whilst I remove these things," she bade me, and I followed her into the room in which Mr. Aengus had first interviewed me. Having removed her gloves she then removed her elegant bonnet, whose ribbons felt rich and fabulously expensive to my fingers. It was curious to see her like this, with a neat and fashionable coiffure; for I had always pictured her as I first saw her, with that fabulous red hair streaming around her sculptured features in the fluid artistry of a ship's figurehead.

However, she explained as I stared at her carefully combed hair with its skewering of hair-bodkins, "I was calling upon Father MacMonigle, if that is why you are wondering, Anne.

191

There was the matter of the payment for poor Ivy's grave. Naturally, we will do what we can. It is an obligation with the Conors, since she died in our service."

This was true but I was surprised that it had occurred to her and her pinch-penny husband. All this mealy mouthed talk of their poverty, and yet Lady Maeve could dress in this fashion, with such bonnets, Dublin-imported from London, no doubt, and with those gloves!

She did not sit down, and so we stood, although my recent experience out on the escarpment had knocked me about a bit, and I was hard put not to ask permission to sit in her presence.

"Now, what is this, Anne, about your giving notice? I hope it was nothing to do with—with this morning. I am forever short with people before I have had my tea."

I had almost forgotten our last meeting, her savage attempt to get hold of Maureen's tray before Maureen and her husband could receive it.

"No, ma'am. It is nothing to do with that. It is only that I fear Conor House is not lucky to me. There have been so many things. The first night I came, when a Kelper or Mrs. O'Glaney's husband, or someone, tried to get into my window. . . . And then—"

"O'Glaney tried to get into your window!" She leaned back abruptly against the table. "But that is preposterous. He is not that sort, Anne. I pledge you my word. He has eyes for no one but Sara."

I had, of course, resigned myself to the fact that my intruder that first night was not O'Glaney anxious to give me a welcome cup of the good Irish. Whether the person was a hungry kelper or someone else, I did not yet know. Her quick defense of O'Glaney, however, did not improve the situation, as I reminded Her Ladyship.

"Then it was someone else. And after that . . ." I could not tell her about the episode in the graveyard at Ballyglen, and this reduced my arguments considerably. "Well then, there was Miss Maureen caught in the bog."

"But that threat was against Miss Maureen and not you, Anne."

I was incensed at this. "But I almost died rescuing her! Is there none here who cares about me?" I asked hotly.

She smiled, a smile I was far from understanding.

"Oh yes, Anne. You may be sure there are those who care. Rather too much, in the circumstances, I should say . . . . Perhaps you are right. There may be too many complications here for one person. Obviously, that first night attempt was made by the person who sent you and me those lying missives, with the intent of speeding your departure. Someone fears your perceptive eyes, my dear Anne. Someone fears you will see too much. That must explain those first attempts. But now, I think, the real, deadly attempts have begun."

"Against me?" I asked in amazement. "But why?"

"No, not against—" She shrugged. "I thought Miss Nutting said of you that you had courage. No matter. You will give us time to replace you; will you not?"

"A fortnight," I said stiffly.

How disappointed Miss Nutting would be! And it was like running away under fire, which no Wicklow had ever done before, I'll be bound! But still and all, I felt that her hints of cowardice were but the blandishments to make me fall into a trap and stay on, perhaps to meet such an end as Ivy Kellinch had found.

She appeared relieved. "Then I think a fortnight should see us through. We are very close now to—"

"Yes, ma'am?" I prompted her. She had stopped so suddenly it was noticeable.

"—to success, my dear Anne. Conor House has been in an uproar since my husband's—accident."

"Accident or attack?" I asked quickly.

She had begun to rub the gloves repeatedly as they lay upon the table, with smoothing gestures which seemed to mark a stronger attack of nerves than I would have suspected in Lady Maeve.

"Did I say accident? I mean—attack, of course. I take it you have lost your desire to protect my stepdaughter from harm."

I was too tired to argue further with her. I started to leave, saying as I did so, "I am selfish, Your Ladyship. I desire to protect from harm only those who do not threaten me."

"Threaten you! Whatever do you mean? Come, tell me."

I had my hand upon the door into the corridor when we both heard sounds in Mr. Aengus's room. Lady Maeve looked relieved and went over and rapped upon the connecting door.

"Aengus, Miss Wicklow would like to speak with you. Will you see her?"

There were coughs and sighs and throat clearings which I took to mean that we had disturbed Mr. Aengus, but presently, we heard his voice.

"Very well. Let us see our paragon."

I went over to the connecting door and tried the door handle. It was locked. I looked at Lady Maeve whose equilibrium seemed quite unequal to this discovery; for she flushed deeply and I, embarrassed at having caught their marital secrets, pulled my hand away as though the door had burnt me. I then went out into the corridor and tried the hall door into his room, which opened promptly.

From behind the drawn and closed curtains of his bed, his voice came to me, querulous and impatient.

"Tread lightly, lightly! My head is fit to burst. The sun at this hour drives me mad. Pierces my very brain."

It was quite true that the sun, even now at sunset, was dark and dusty looking, and the portieres that kept out the great red ball of the sun were only open a few inches. It seemed to me that I stood in a shower of dust motes, as I spoke to him.

"Sir, where may you be?"

He stuck his head out from the bed, between the bed-curtains, and I very nearly committed the unpardonable sin of laughing at him; for his nightcap was on jauntily over one ear, and his right eye was completely concealed by the tassel of his cap.

"Here, girl, of course. Now, what's the complaint? Wages too small? Not enough company at the village fair? I'll flay that son of mine if he doesn't escort you proper. Have you been yet?"

"No, sir. I've been too busy avoiding accidents."

"Indeed!" He left the bed curtains parted and lay back upon a half-dozen pillows and put the back of his hand to his forehead as though his head ached in very truth. "I suppose you refer to yesterday's graveyard scene."

"Not at all. But today I nearly drowned out on the escarpment. The escarpment door closed upon me and I could not get back into the house."

He moved his head and, still massaging his brows with his lean, strong fingers, peered at me between them. I felt like a beast in a cage, to be stared at through the bars. Then he said a thing so surprising that it shook me for a moment.

"I daresay you did not see who closed the door upon you."

"*Who* closed it?" I echoed. "You believe then, sir, that it was deliberate?"

He plumped the pillows under his head, and turned his face toward the wall in irritation.

"I have not said so, have I? I merely asked you if you had seen anyone. Tell me as you would a magistrate. Was anyone about when it happened?"

"Yes," I said sharply. "You daughter, Maureen."

"Oh God! That was to be expected!" He punched the pillow so hard I saw the dust fly out and settle in the long streak of reddish sunlight down the center of the room.

We were both quiet then, I in perplexity, and he with what thoughts I could well imagine. First her attempt upon him, crippling him for life, then the mystery of Ivy Kellinch's dreadful end, and now what he must conceive to be Miss Maury's further signs of criminal insanity.

I said after a pause, "Please, sir, do not be thinking it was Miss Maureen entirely. It may have been, and very probably was, an accident. I sent her for help and she forgot. You know she does forget, sometimes. Things confuse her." I did not know why I must defend his daughter to him, but it seemed that when another accused her, I must leap to her defense. Obstinacy, perhaps. "I gave her two instructions, and she obeyed the first. That is all."

"But if you had died, Anne—" My name sounded odd upon his lips, and not unattractive. "Then once again my daughter would be an attempted murderess, as was whispered of her when I had this misfortune."

"Nonsense," I contradicted, hearing from his voice how troubled he was.

He turned back to face me, with his arm flung across his eyes as though to shield their emotion even from a servant like myself. But he could not conceal his feelings in his eloquent voice.

"I do not know how this will end, Anne, but be good

to Maureen—will you promise me that? Whatever comes of it all. Whatever happens to the rest of us."

"I have already promised her husband," I said, puzzled at this repeated effort by all to protect Maureen when they were, perhaps, her first victims.

He laughed shortly, once more on his jealous note, which I confess I did not relish.

"The Yorkshire boor. Maeve's old *bête noire*. Dear rivals that they were for her father's affections. Thinks he may cure me, I'm told. What do you think?"

"I think exercise might work wonders, sir."

He made a fantastical remark. "With you for my nurse I should not hesitate," and then went back to his old obsession. "But if you go from here as I heard you saying to Maeve, then how can you protect Maureen?"

I could not help the selfish note that crept into my thoughts and perhaps into my voice.

"I should indeed be reluctant, sir, to have Miss Maureen blamed for killing me. I shall do everything in my power to prevent your daughter's falling under suspicion, by seeing that she does not . . . cause an accident."

"Anne Wexford, you are being sardonic, and it does not become you." Nevertheless, he was smiling, one of those unreadable Conor smiles.

"A fortnight," I reminded him. "During the next fortnight I shall see to Miss Maureen's welfare if I can. That is all I promise."

He seemed to be trying to make himself look more presentable, for he straightened his night cap, and snapped his fingers at the collar of the night robe that I saw above the covers. But at that moment Lady Maeve came into the room from the hall, and said to us, "Well then, is it all settled between you? Is Anne Wicklow to stay, Aengus? You have persuaded her?"

"Wexford," her husband corrected her irritably. "Please to remember in future, my dear."

I sighed and gave up the battle. I had no doubt that I should be Anne Wexford to him to the end of time.

"We have settled upon my leaving in a fortnight, ma'am," I told her as I curtseyed and prepared to depart.

She and her husband exchanged glances. She raised her eyebrows. It was clear as day to me that she was asking him a question. He nodded and said, "Quite enough. Yes. Now, my dear—"

Both Lady Maeve and I looked at him, and he grinned in a malicious way. I felt horridly conscious of having commited a crime of judgement.

"My dears, I should say," he amended. "Let me be, and have my tea brought to me."

"I shall attend to that," said Lady Maeve, dismissing me with a little gesture.

I was the more astonished to hear, as I closed the door, Lady Maeve's voice, directed at her husband. "God of heaven, you are a fool! A fool! And under someone else's eyes, as well."

I went below wondering at this extraordinary marriage which was jeopardized by Mr. Aengus Conor's absurd attempts to wheedle me under his wife's eyes. Obviously, he desired to arouse her jealousy. But something in her voice, in her criticism, made me feel that whatever her emotion at his behavior, it was not jealousy.

In his devilish way Aengus Conor must fascinate all who knew him, for he seemed to me to stand, or sit, upon that ragged edge between evil and good, and therefore, in his presence, one was constantly aware of his curious power. But it was preposterous that anyone should imagine the man making a flirt with me, his housekeeper. I was horribly conscious of my real guilt, my as yet undefined feeling for Dr. Jonathan, which must be snuffed out at all costs, and it was this which made the little contretemps in my employer's room the more absurd. I do not say that had he been younger and in less sinister surroundings, he should not have been excessively handsome. But such a man, with his evil aura . . .

It was I who brought Miss Maureen her tray in bed that night, and found, just as I supposed, that she had forgotten about my second command, and simply gone directly to her bed as bidden that afternoon.

"Everyone is out-of-reason cross with me, Anne," she complained, blowing mightily into a handkerchief between words. "Jono says I almost got you killed and I never meant to. Truly, I did not."

Jonathan was polishing some nasty looking surgical knives

at his desk in one corner of the room, and turned to look at us. He was smiling rather grimly, I thought.

"No one is cross with you. love. But you'll favor me to listen when people speak to you. You must obey Miss Wicklow as you—"

"As I obeyed Nurse Kellinch?" she cried, throwing the bundled up handkerchief across the room. "And you may see what came to her! All because she was horrid to me."

"No," said Jonathan patiently, but it seemed to me that he was growing a trifle out of sorts. "Not like Ivy Kellinch. Obey Miss Wicklow as you'd obey me, or your father. Sure now, you can do that."

"Oh, Father!" she scoffed. "As soon as ever I put my head in his room he shoos me out. I might as well be a porker strayed onto the bog, for all his care of me. He still believes it was I and not the "kelper ghost" who stabbed him. And yet, how could he? How could he, Jono? Because he knows I was facing him when it happened, and not behind him at all." Before her husband could reply to this, she sailed quickly on another tack. "How stupid my voice sounds! Like an ancient crow. I daresay I should have laid down sooner yesterday, as Anne said."

"What is this?" asked Jonathan sharply, so sharply that I looked up with a sudden uneasiness.

She waved her hands in the air, as one who dismisses a triviality.

"But I saw a gull out on the Headland and it was dragging one wing; so I went and helped it on its way—"

"Leaving Miss Wicklow to the mercies of the high tide!"

Maureen appeared astonished at this tone from her beloved husband.

"But it is Wicklow who must care for me, not the other way about. I am not responsible for what Wicklow does when I have gone. Badad! It was only a moment . . . or two. And then I went up to my room and laid myself down."

"And never a thought for Miss Wicklow who might have drowned!"

Maureen's sunny indifference began to cloud over. Showers were imminent. She frowned, then scowled at me and then at Jonathan.

"Is it to be like Ivy?" she asked, apropos of nothing.

"I beg your pardon," I said in confusion. "What do you mean?"

"Maury, love," her husband said then, seeing that things were teetering on the ragged edge of unpleasantness, "you are chattering too much. You had no mislike of Nurse Kellinch, and well you know it."

I had the notion that he was warning her, to avert any suspicion of her animosity toward the dead woman, and it did not make me feel more easy to be the object of her veiled threats.

Her big eyes, which had stared at me in a fixed and thoughtful way that conjured up shivers through my body, now shifted their gaze. She veiled them with her long lashes and said contritely, "I meant no harm. Do not be cross with me, Jono."

"Excuse me," I said more quickly than I intended, as I made my retreat from the room. "If Miss Maureen will be good enough to let the kitchen know when she finishes with the tray—"

"I'll take it in charge," said Dr. Jonathan and I went out of the room, supposing he intended to keep his wife company as she ate.

I was disturbed when he followed me into the hall, for I was ever aware of Miss Maureen's jealousy and did not wish to arouse it.

"You've forgiven my little lass?" he asked me. "She has no notion of time, you know. She never meant harm to come to you."

"I know that, sir. I have always known it."

He closed the door behind him and leaned back against it, studying me. I did not think this, nor the closing of the door, very wise of him.

"I am beginning to consider taking Maureen away from this place, no matter how she rebels about the money they hold from her. We live upon my own earnings now. It is damnably plain Maeve and Aengus, between them, don't intend to give us what is ours, and I'm not going to risk more . . . complications that may involve Maury."

"You are wise, sir."

He smiled but his eyes did not smile, and my heart responded to them though I retained a cool manner as he pursued the matter.

"You've nothing to say to our leaving you . . . and them?"

"I have nothing to say, sir. Except that you are wise not to rely upon the inheritance which—pardon me—it is plain they do not intend to surrender."

Still he persisted, holding me more by the look in his eyes than by his words.

"But do you yourself . . . have we no hold on your good thoughts?"

I stiffened myself against the warmth of that plea and managed the equivocal reply, "You will always hold my good thoughts, sir. I am excessively fond of"—I had not intended to pause and hurried on— "Miss Maureen. She was my first friend at Conor House."

Before he could say anything more dangerous, I curtseyed, and then thought he put out his hand as if to stop me; I evaded it, going quickly down the winding steps to my own quarters.

I confess I spent the following two or three days in constant fear of new disasters, and as bad weather had succeeded out brief late-Autumn sunlight there was little to be done outside; so I found myself looking over my shoulder every few minutes, to be quite sure I was not pursued by the evil thing that haunted Conor House.

One day I was on Kelper Head with Maureen Trumble playfully helping me bring in the aired-out bed clothing before the light mizzle turned to rain. Presently, Jonathan came back from treating a lobsterman in an isolated coteen beyond the cove.

"You are only just in time to avoid a good setdown from the heavens," I told him as he made shivering motions inside the turned-up collar of his coat, and his wife giggled delightedly at his gesture.

"How funny you are, Jono!" she said between giggles.

This was certainly the better kind of love, I thought, when Miss Maureen found in the rough, busy surgeon a figure of wit and humor. Much as I admired Jonathan Trumble I could acquit him of being either witty or very humorous.

"Do stay here," his wife begged him, as she almost covered herself, including her face, with a bundle of bedclothing, despite my objections. "I'll be back quick as you may blink." She scurried off to lay the clothing inside the linen room, colliding in the doorway of the guard-room with big, fumbling O'Glaney who was drunk as a lord.

Maureen recovered herself before her husband could get to her, speaking to O'Glaney in such tones as I had never dared use.

"O'Glaney! You are a tiresome great animal! Out upon you now and sleep it off!"

"Sorry, Miss Maury. M'fault entire," he mumbled, catching up her blankets and sheets as Jonathan was attempting to gather them up and bear them away himself.

"No, no, Jono," Maureen interrupted this confusion. "Do let go. I'll be back that fast you may lay a wager to!"

She brushed past them and went on inside and Jonathan turned back to me to ask if he might help.

"No, sir," said I. "It is easier so." I have ever found men to be in the way at such times, more especially gentlemen.

O'Glaney, who had been too stupefied to avoid Maureen, was not too stupefied to recall an ancient grudge.

"Ay, me foine doctor-man. 'Tis the pretty mum here takes 'e fancy, is it? You'll be about helpin' the housekeeper, and not Miss Maury, I'm thinkin'."

Jonathan ignored him, going about picking up blankets and folding them without a look at the drunken O'Glaney who staggered out after him, still bent upon trouble.

"Them as come from over-sea thinkin' to master Conor House acause Mr. Aengus be in no case to fight 'e . . . Outlander! What's worse, Outlander that's no got two guineas to rub, nayther."

"Be quiet!" I told him, losing patience. "Go and sleep off your drunkenness."

"Och, ay, miss. It's you gives orders now, is it?" He lurched toward me.

I saw Theo Conor coming across the headland from the bog regions to the east of Conor house, and wondered if O'Glaney would obey him as he obeyed his sister. It would be a relief, for I could see Jonathan's face set in a peculiar way which I recognized from memories of my own husband. It boded no good for the scene to come as he reached out and struck O'Glaney a quick, backhanded hard slap across the chest and gestured toward the house.

"Do as you are told. Go and sleep. You are half asleep now."

"Half asleep? That, no, me foine boy. Wake enough to take you in a fine little set-to, me noble doctor-like!"

To my disgust the hulking brute raised his two fists as though to start a brawl this instant, on the slippery kelp-strewn rocks of the headland. Jonathan had his hands full of blankets and with a sigh of impatience, set them down as O'Glaney reached out for him. O'Glaney fetched him a blow that, had it not missed by a good arm's breadth, would have knocked Jonathan's head off. Jonathan, however, as I soon saw, could take care of himself. While Theo Conor approached, unseen by the two combatants, Jonathan merely put out the flat of his hand, and every time O'Glaney swung, missing wildly, Jonathan's hand slapped him back and forth across the hands, or across the face. It was amusing for a few minutes, until O'Glaney, pushed to madness by one more slap, fell against the wall of the house and in pulling himself up, drew out something from his jacket. The blade of a lobster knife flashed as the first drops of rain fell.

"Now then, me boy, we'll be seeing what's the color of an Englishman's blood, eh?"

Jonathan stared at him, his eyes narrowing in that silent, white fury which comes to few men, and then only men of such quiet stubborn temperaments as Jonathan's. He did not retreat a step, which I thought very foolish of him, as I shouted at O'Glaney, "Miss Maury will be having your job for this, O'Glaney! You'll never see the Conors more! Now, put that down."

He was beyond listening though, and so was Jonathan as I turned to him with the desperate hope of reasoning with him. Then Theo Conor reached the group of us and said, "O'Glaney, man, have you lost the power of your fists that you must take up knives? Think, man! The weapon of a little creature, not a fine fellow like yourself. Shame to you, O'Glaney!"

Both O'Glaney and Jonathan were shaken out of their impasse by this new and unexpected voice.

"I'll have his hide, and stripped for ye, Master Theo!" O'Glaney boasted. He lunged at Jonathan who seized one end of the blanket at his feet, and swung it at the giant. So sharp was the lobster knife that we all saw its blade and point cut through the blanket and emerge, shining and terrifying, spitted on the blanket. O'Glaney did not let go of the knife, and as I rushed forward to hit him over the head, waving my armful of clothing like a flail, Theo reached out between the two men, to seize O'Glaney's arm. It happened before O'Glaney or any of us was aware . . . the knife twisting as O'Glaney tried to release it from the blanket, and jerking through to slice across the palm of Theo's hand. In that instant Theo's gasp was drowned in O'Glaney's hoarse shout of remorse, "No, Master Theo! No!"

As Jonathan and I turned to Theo, The O'Glaney yelled, "It weren't my fault, Master Theo. As God is me judge, it weren't! But it's the hurt of Miss Maury I be wantin' to save. I see them two—Doctor and the female here, always a-talkin' together and a-lookin' so, and sayin' Miss Maury this and Miss Maury that. But for Miss Maury they'd be in t'other's arms now, bedad!"

Theo Conor cut into all this filth with a few words that seemed to have their effect upon him.

"Can you possibly be silent for two minutes? Well, Jono, what do you think? Did it cut more than the flesh?"

Jonathan had taken up his surgeon's case and was quickly shaking powder upon the wound. It seemed to me that there was a great deal of blood everywhere, down Theo's jerkin and breeches, and all over Jonathan's hands as he worked. And Theo himself did not look too sturdy upon his feet.

I thought a mug of water, or better yet, whisky, might help to put more color into his face, and started into the guardroom. In the doorway was Maureen, staring at us all with that blank, dreamy look in her strange blue eyes which told me that she was not herself.

"It's true; isn't it, Anne? As O'Glaney says. You and Jono?"

XVI

THEO LOOKED across at us. Jonathan was binding up his hand and merely glanced our way, proceeding carefully, methodically, but I saw that his mouth was hard and set. Theo called to his sister.

"Maury, don't be a fool. O'Glaney is drunk."

Maureen smiled, a dreadful, acquiescent smile. It cut me to the heart to see that smile and to think that, in any way, I had contributed to the unfortunate woman's misery. I was more than ever glad that I had given in my notice and should never see her and her husband again after the week. When I tried to say something, she put her hand over my mouth, and I stood there, already shivering with the events of the last few minutes, and now facing this childish mind which was twisted by the blather of a man she had known and trusted all her life. Gently, trying not to let my fingers shake, I removed her hand from my mouth.

"Miss Maury," I said, "you and Dr. Jonathan are going away to England, as soon as ever you wish. And alone. You will never hear such talk again." Ideas occurred to me as I spoke; for I felt it the most important mission of my stay at Conor House, to bring this much put-upon woman and her husband to some sort of happiness, free from the peculiar influence of her family, and perhaps, of me.

"Let us go inside and talk about the great things you will be seeing in England. Fair splendid, I swear." I took her elbow in a friendly way and she obeyed, walking inside with me. But I had a feeling that the blankness was still within her, a wall off which my words bounded in futility.

"And where will you be, Anne? They say you are leaving Conor House, for England, too."

"Not I," I said brusquely. "I shall ask Miss Nutting to arrange that I may go to France again. I have learned to love it. I shall take an oath of loyalty, or whatever, and return to the land my husband loved. It is better so." I had thought of this on the moment, and now it seemed, by all odds, the best way out for me.

"Yes," she said thoughtfully. "I would do the same. I would like to go to Yorkshire with Jonathan. How far is that from London?"

The abrupt question showed me how she still felt the danger of being near to me, and it cut me to know this.

"Very, very far, Miss Maury. York folk love their North Country so well they scorn the Londoners. But for me, it must be London, so that I may arrange for a pardon from the French King. Else I cannot return to France."

We went up the winding steps to the apartments she shared with her husband, and I was about to ask if she felt like playing at draughts, or piquet, or perhaps cared to lie down, when she went over to her husband's desk. She stepped up on the chair and sat down on his desk, swinging her feet just above the floor, like a child on a perch too big for her.

She said to me very wisely, very old, "I know how is is, Anne. You needn't explain. Jonathan would always have been happier without me. I drag him down like a—like an anchor . . . ."

"No, no, Miss Maury," I cut in. "It isn't true. He . . ."

She put out her hand to stop me. "Don't you see how it must be, in the end, if I am to make him happy?"

There was in all this talk the deep shadow of that unhappiest of mortal sins, suicide. She could not conceive the horror of such an act upon her religious beliefs, her hope of salvation, for her mind ran as a child's, thinking only of one step at a time. And she could not know, unless I explained to her very carefully, that there might be great happiness for her in the future, once she and her husband were free of the evil that hung over Conor House.

I spoke very slowly, watching her in the most minute way, to see that she understood me. "You will have Dr. Jonathan and he will have you. There will be no one that you have ever known before, none to make you unhappy. You will live in a simple, charming cottage, perhaps, in a Yorkshire cove. And—"

"I don't really like the sea," she interrupted. "It frightens me with its great roars and the way the fingers come up toward me, coaxing."

"Well then," I went on, a trifle confused. "In the moorland country somewhere, it will be even better. With flowers and heather and winding sheep paths, and fresh cream to drink and make you even prettier."

I had caught her fancy at last.

"Do you think I am pretty, Anne?"

"Vastly pretty."

She smiled and the dimples appeared to bring out the gay little way that was hers at such moments. She shook her head, but I could see that she more than half believed me, and indeed, she should have. Her mirror would have told her as much.

"If only Maeve and Theo treated me as you do. But they are forever saying hateful things, talking against our happiness, Jono's and mine. They cannot bear it that we should be happy, and now they've got even poor O'Glaney acting out-of-reason cross with everyone. . . . Do you think they want to keep my money?"

This sharp addendum to her complaint was not at all in the same tone as the other. It was shrewd.

"I cannot say, Miss Maureen. Perhaps there is no money left. I believe Mr. Aengus was at short shrift when he married your stepmother."

"That isn't true, you know." She nodded wisely. "Mama always said that when I married my husband was to have the income and Papa was to have the money itself. Then, when Papa dies, we shall have the whole of it for ourselves."

A vagrant suspicion flashed through my mind and I asked, "If you were not married, Miss Maury. . . ? If you had no husband . . . ?"

"Then Theo has the use of my money." She leaned toward me and stopped kicking her feet back and forth. Again I felt the secretive quality, a shrewdness which was unlike her, as though she had taken on the adult Conor mind that the world did not suspect her of possessing. "Maeve got money from Father when they married. She said it was to pay her father's debts. . . . Do you trust my stepmother?"

The bare truth was, I did not trust anyone in this house, and scarcely trusted myself, but I managed to say with a false sincerity that I despised in myself, "I believe she has the interests of Conor House at heart."

"Do you know what I think?" asked Maureen. "I think she has not forgotten that she despised my husband many years ago, when they were children."

"No, no, ma'am. I am sure you are wrong."

Maureen nodded wisely. "I think I am right. I shall play the game with them all, just as they wish. But I know what I think, in my brain. I know everyone wants me dead, and if it would make Jonathan happy, then I am willing. But if it is for them—no!"

I had to take a firm tone now. "Miss Maury, this is wicked, sinful talk! Tomorrow you must speak of it to Father MacMonigle. He will tell you that no one wants your death. That it will benefit no one. And it is wicked to think of taking your life."

She thought for a few minutes, while it seemed to me that the evil in the old house stopped breathing, long enough to see whether it had won its wicked way with her. She opened her eyes wide at last and said in that sweet tone I had learned to mistrust, "I think I will go to bed, Anne. I am vastly tired."

I agreed. "A very good thing all around, and I will send Rosaleen to sit by you."

She looked at me innocently. "It isn't at all necessary, Annie-girl. I shan't be lonely. I shall be . . . thinking."

"Nevertheless, Rosaleen will be of some help and you may send her out for your supper tray. It is getting on for sunset."

She shrugged. She was being too clever by half. It put me on my guard.

"Oh well, if you say so. But if she keeps me awake with her chatter, I shall send her away."

"We'll be seeing about that, ma'am. I'll send her now to prepare you for bed."

"You are horrid!" she said crossly, and kicked very hard against her husband's desk.

I did not like to leave her alone, even for the short time it took me to fetch up Rosaleen, so I went across to the dining parlor and opened the little door in the wall, where the chains and ropes dangled, and the floor of the contrivance was down in the kitchen. I hammered on the chains until Mrs. O'Glaney came and looked up.

"What in devil's name, miss? You be sending down the dust fit to smother a person."

"Would you please send up Rosaleen at once?"

"I'm after using her," she grumbled. "But I suppose it's all one in this mad house today. What with The O'Glaney a-stabbin' them as he's breeched since birth, and causing the tears to come to the eyes of one he'd as lief die for as to cause pain."

"Where is O'Glaney?" I asked.

"Sleeping it off. Where else? And Master Theo, him dripping blood like sea water, and the doctor called away to twins for the lobsterman's wife! Howsomever, if you say you'll be needing Rosaleen, the girl shall come. Get along, Rosa, like Miss was saying."

I heard a male voice down in the kitchen with her, and asked Mrs. O'Glaney, "Who is it in there? What are they doing?"

There was a scramble, the cook protesting loudly, squeaking as though she had been squeezed. "Now then, you wicked rogue, Master Theo! Out on you. You make me spill the potatoes." Then Theo Conor's head popped into the opening and looked up at me.

"Have you no sympathy for my bloody suffering, Anne?"

"None, sir," I said, but not too seriously. "It is always the way with those who interfere in other's quarrels."

"Ay. The truth. The very truth. And there's only one solace. So it's off to the village for a quick go-round with the good Irish." He waved his heavily bandaged hand at me, while, behind him, Mrs. O'Glaney clucked in loud disgust, "And staggering in like my old man, I'll be bound!"

Theo shouted at me as I was closing the door, and I looked down once more.

"If my father happens to call you tonight, tell him the wound was not so deep as a tomb but grave enough!"

"Misquoting is one of your richest talents, Master Theo," I said, and closed the door.

By the time I opened Maureen's door again, she was sitting on the edge of the bed in her voluminous night dress, dangling her bare feet on the floor. I shook my head.

"Miss Maury, you've only just got by a cold in the head

and lungs. Will you be taking your death of cold in your feet next?"

She laughed. "That would be quite unnecessary, Anne."

I did not pretend to know what that cryptic remark meant, and before I could ask, she went on, "Besides, I did not take off all my clothes. Only my gown. I shall be warmer, you see. I am obeying you precisely as though you were Maeve."

"I should hope not," I told her. "You do not obey Lady Maeve as a stepdaughter should."

"Much you know," she replied crossly.

Rosaleen came rustling along the hall, and I went out and warned her not to leave Miss Maureen alone until I came up to relieve her presently. Rosaleen was looking pink-cheeked and pleased with herself, and I had a pretty fair idea that Theo Conor had been flirting with her while giving an occasional aside to Mrs. O'Glaney.

The girl said in a saucy way, "And if 'Er La'ship orders me elsewhere, miss? She be with Mr. Aengus now and only just carried up his tray 'er very self. Said she like to prepare him for what come to his son today on the headland. Which is a bit of a jest-like, for Mr. Aengus never give that much for his son and needn't be prepared so very much, I'm thinking."

"That is not our affair," I reminded her. "If you are asked to leave Mrs. Trumble, even for a minute, you will go to the well in the dining parlor, and call down to me in the kitchen. At once."

"Oh, very well, mum. If you say so."

I listened as she went in; for I did not want Maureen unhappy, but I need not have feared. The two women went to chattering like children, and I left them there while I attended to the work.

I went downstairs to find that Jonathan had sent up word by the lobsterman's son that the birthing of the expected twins had proved to be difficult, and advising Theo Conor to go to bed and take a good rest after the blood-letting he had received today. I told the boy who recited the message by rote, that Dr. Jonathan's message was a trifle late, that Theo Conor had gone down to the village for a gay evening of carousal. Then, after giving the boy a warm supper, I sent him on his way. He was greatly excited over the prospect of having a double addition to his little band of playmates, and nearly knocked down a group of kelp gatherers who were combing the cove and the approach to the headland, for their slippery produce.

It was dusk, but the rain had let up, and there was still enough light for their work. I went out to the headland and called to the shrouded men, first in English and then in my faltering Irish tongue.

"You may take all the kelp from the headland you choose. We should be happy to be rid of it." And I pointed back to accumulations under my bedchamber window, and all over the outcroppings of rock. There were still dark trails and splotches where Theo Conor's wound had bled, and this, I think, as much as anything, inspired me to have the kelp completely removed.

"I dunno, miss," said Mrs. O'Glaney behind me. "The Conors never give the right to them kelpers up here so near the house. But there's no mistakin', it do make the washing and the drying hard, with them dirty, ugly weeds a-crawlin' over the rocks like they was feelers out of the seabed. Half the time I've a mind to tear them down myself, else they'll be fastenin' onto Conor House and draggin' of it into the sea one day."

As the kelpers set to work here and there, some in the cove, some on the sloping path up to the headland, and the rest scattering out over Kelper Head itself, it seemed to me that it was a sight out of some terrible legend of the dead. There were the humped backs of the creatures, some of them female, as I saw by their faces and their hands, but all more or less alike, shrouded in fringed cloaks fastened all about, and billed caps, with very little that appeared alive about them. They did not even talk much, so intent were they upon their loathsome work. They would follow long ropes of kelp until they reached the end of them, pulling them up, draping them over their arms and their cloaks like endless jelly serpents whose skin glistened in the earliest starlight. The more vigorous kelpers began to hack away chunks of seaweed, disturbing the overturned rocks, the bits of broken wall and even a very much spent cannon ball which had lodged for years under the debris.

I went inside and had a supper of tea and potatoes and some left-over mutton from the family's early dinner. Then

I went up and sat with Maureen while Rosaleen ate her supper.

By this time Maureen had her eyes closed but was, I felt sure, merely pretending to be asleep. I believed that she made this pretense to avoid me, which made me feel bad since I did not want her to part from me with ill-feelings. She must discover that I meant her only good, and not the harm that some whom I could not name, were whispering to her. If there was in truth any suicidal intent in all her talk, I felt confident that an outside in-fluence had planted it there, and the thought of such cowardly, murderous schemes filled me with fury.

I stood a long while looking out the window upon the headland below, watching the strange kelpers at their task, thinking again how inhuman they looked, so heavily shroud-ed against the weather, and so intent upon gathering up every shred of seaweed upon the headland. So transparent did the kelp appear under the faint, cold glimmer of the stars, that it was even observable to me on a floor above. I was relieved when the last of the kelp that had sucked up Theo Conor's blood, was gathered and draped over one kelper's arm. The end of the kelp hung down as one more bit of fringe upon the cloak and made the kelp-er himself appear oddly luminous as the sticky stuff caught the light from the storm lantern of one enterprising neigh-bor.

Behind me I heard the slight movement of cloth, the merest rustle of muslin and wool. It was startling in that room where I conceived myself to be alone except for Mau-reen in bed. I swung about quickly. Maureen was at my el-bow. Her eyes gleamed like the kelp on the gatherers be-low us.

"I used to see them do that," she murmured. "But they have not now, for a great long time. Jonathan always wanted to have it done. Before that, Father had grand notions. He was going to have the headland cleared for new quarters on Conor House. Then it happened."

"His accident?" I suggested, hoping to have her think thus of the terrible night between her and her father.

"The night the kelp gatherer beckoned to him, and he started to turn—and the kelper . . ." Her voice trailed off. I put my hand on her arm quickly, shaking her a trifle.

"No, Miss Maureen. An accident. You must not think more upon it."

"Oh, but I must. It's the beginning of everything. You see . . . it was my fault. Just as it is my fault Jonathan is unhappy now."

I could see that only stout measures would serve and I took her by the shoulders and looked into her eyes and said sternly, "They are liars who tell you that. They are—"

"Like Dr. Mesmer?" she asked me, completely confounding me.

I stared at her, losing my voice and any common sense answer that might have served. She paid little attention to me, staring down upon the kelpers below, and then saying calmly, "I think I will go back to bed now. I hear Rosaleen coming."

It was quite true. I had been so intent upon putting together all the odd fantasies that fitted into Maureen's mind, that the sound of Rosaleen's footsteps surprised me. She brought a basket of sewing and looked disgruntled.

"I'm to relieve you now, miss. Cook says I am to hem up these cloths for the kitchen whilst I'm here."

"An excellent idea," I agreed, amused at her distaste for doing what she conceived to be two tasks at once.

I asked Maureen if she wanted anything, but she had snuggled down under the bed covers by this time and shook her head.

"Dr. Jonathan will be up very soon," I promised her.

She peeped over the edge of the coverlet.

"How soon?"

"As soon as ever the twins are born to the lobsterman's wife."

She sighed. "That will be some time, I think. It is better so."

Rosaleen looked surprised. "Better, Miss Maureen?"

Maureen paused, pleated the coverlet briefly and then answered, "Ay, better for the lobsterman's wife. Jono is a very good surgeon."

I went down the stone steps to my own little parlor and sat by the fire a few minutes, like Rosaleen, with a basket of sewing, but I could hear the dim sounds on the headland outside, and finally gave up any attempt at concentrating on the household darning. I went out on the headland and asked the nearest kelper how long they would be.

He replied ingratiatingly that he had not as much kelp as his neighbor, and stood up to point out the ambitious fellow, when we both saw one of the other kelpers, standing at a distance from us, beckon to us with one forefinger. My friend and his ambitious neighbor went over to the east end of the headland, almost to the spot where the edges of Ballyglen Bog poked into the muddy turf.

The beckoner stood there watching us, and when we started in his direction, he moved toward the group of hardworking gatherers near my bedchamber window.

I followed the other two kelpers to the spot where he had been standing. There was very little sign of the sea's overwhelming sweep. Even the seaweed died quickly and odorously here, while the rocks were more or less exposed to the heavens. Some time recently a peat cutter had deposited some of his load in one place and the sharply sliced blocks were still visible in their original shape. There seemed to be an extraordinary quantity of peat, or else it was heaped higher than was usual. The stars glinted down through the shadows made by the trees at the edge of the bog, and in that dim light something pale and fleshlike was revealed under the turf. For an instant I had the horrid foreboding that it was indeed flesh I was looking upon, but one of the kelpers, grunting, knelt and touched it.

" 'Tis cloth. White cloth once, I'm thinking."

His companion pinched the cloth more deeply and then jumped away as though the cloth were alive.

"There's some-ut inside. Not all cloth."

They both backed away in different directions, step by step.

"Well then, what is it?" I asked them, and getting no reply, knelt and myself pinched the cloth. They had been right. Within the cloth was something that yielded only so far, not like flesh, but more like bone from which the flesh had mostly gone.

"A shroud then," whispered one of the kelpers. "And I'll have no part in it."

XVII

"COME BACK!" I cried so loudly and furiously that I drowned my own terrors. "You rubbishing idiots! A dead man can't hurt you. Come back!"

There must have been nearly a dozen of the kelpers upon the headland, with a scattering of fishermen intermingled among them, and drifting up from the cove; yet these fine, strong lads were all retreating in a deliberate, backward-stepping way that came fair close to making me fling their cowardice in their faces. A taunt no Irishman, surely, could endure. I seized the nearest kelper by his fringed sleeve, pulling that garment so hard I nearly had it off him.

"You there! Summon me the cook at Conor House."

The fellow must be an outlander; for he certainly was a coward.

"But . . . but mum . . . I be no . . ." He gave up this approach, upon my shaking the great hulk of him. "How is she known, mum?"

"Mrs. O'Glaney, of course! Go! Call her. Loud and louder. You understand me?"

He did. He strode off toward the house as though hoping to enlarge the space between himself and what lay beneath that rotting piece of cloth under the peat blocks. Strength seemed to flow into my veins, and courage too, upon the retreat of all those present. I knelt and tried to pick up the cloth but it tore away in my hands, and I saw beneath it, briefly before covering again, that what we feared was true. It had been a human body once. Undoubtedly the fisherman lost a week since when his corragh was swamped in a storm down the coast. And the cloth that seemed to be a covering shroud? Well, there would be reasons for that, but I did not know them at present. I could understand now, though, how Padraic, the servant boy, had found the two boots. They must have been washed off this hapless fellow. It was extraordinary how quickly the sea had reclaimed its own, for there was nothing about the portion I had seen that suggested anyone recognizable. It was much worse battered, or at least more unidentifiable, than the corpse that had washed up on the shore a few days past. Now that I realized the fleshless thing half covered by peat and rotted cloth was an unknown fisherman, I could at least conquer my first terror, for I had half-expected to see someone I knew and perhaps liked at Conor House.

It was a cold and callous thing to feel so, but someone had to keep his wits about him. I said briskly, "It is the fisherman you were searching for a week ago. Don't any of you wish to be telling his family that he is found?"

One of the kelpers, more bold than the others, muttered, "Mum, it be best they think him asleep out yon where he sunk. Maybe if you and them as lives in Conor could be about burying the poor divvil that was, it'd be best. What say ye, lads?"

There was no mistaking their enthusiasm for this arrangement. I put the wet cloth back over the exposed part of the poor creature who lay there, unclaimed as well as unrecognizable, and could not help thinking how far I had come away from the superstitious notions my parents were born with. It was saddening to feel this estrangement from the roots of my life. But so it was.

"Now, you," I said, calling to two or three of them who stood apart. "Which of you found the body and beckoned to us?"

They looked at one another. Further behind them, out on the headland near the cliff, others looked around. Getting no reply from their comrades they repeated the question to a lobsterman who came up from the cove behaving in an extraordinary manner. He was waving a giant neck-kerchief in the air so lavishly it only just missed the fire from a lantern that someone had set upon the rocks.

"I be the father of twins, and I'll be giving you all the headache tomorrow if you follow now to the village! Rory, me boy, I'll drink ye under the table and that's me wager!"

Someone said something to him, mentioning the body, no doubt, and I could hear his triumphant shout into the night air:

"Ay! 'Tis a saddening thing, to be sure! But here's gladness come in the morn like the Good Book foretells. There's one gone, but two is come into the world, and me own two, at that!"

I might have predicted the outcome. Two by two, the kelpers and the fishermen began to fall in behind the celebrating father, and in short order, if I had not caught tight hold of the two men nearest me, I should have been alone with their own dead, with the bog at my back, and the roaring Atlantic to my face.

"Now then," I said sternly. "You'll be taking this body, or what's left of it, and fetching something for a shroud, and then giving it decent Christian burial."

"Can't be doing so," said the one with the more stubborn streak. "Father Mac Monigle is gone back to Ballyglen Town."

"Well then, he shall be fetched, and in the meanwhile, this poor creature must be attended to." I was at my wits' end, but too angry to give up. "And you there, go down to the lobsterman's cottage, and if Dr. Jonathan can be spared, bring him here. He will know what to do. Now, tell me, which of you men discovered the body, and beckoned to us to come over here?"

"Not me," said the stubborn one. "And that I'll be swearin' 'til there's hell a-freeze, as the sayin' is!"

"Nonsense. One of you did." Yet, as I thought back, I remembered that these two men had been with me. They too had seen the beckoning kelp gatherer looming out of the swamp's shadows here, to point out this pitiful remnant.

The second kelper whispered something, and they both crossed themselves.

"What is it with you?" I asked before they should sneak away.

" 'E be sayin', mum, 'twas the deadly kelper beckoned. The soul of this creetur before us and nine beside. Him as is dead beckoned to us to point out the body for proper burial, out of the sea bottom."

I overcame a strong impulse to shiver.

"That's all very well, but the other day you men said you had rather a fisherman was buried in the sea than on land."

"Ay," said the fellow significantly, with a nod to his companion. "For a fisherman, ay. It be best so."

216

While I stood there, wanting to be furious with them, but succeeding only in sighing a great sigh for the world's stupidity, they left me alone with the body. The lobsterman's son, however, scrambled up the path from the cove at that moment, and it was a welcome sight indeed when I saw Dr. Jonathan behind him.

"Congratulations," I said to him when, upon sighting me, he approached more rapidly.

"Two more for this starving, desolate country," was his only reply.

"You are cynical," I reproved him because it hurt me to have the truth presented quite so boldly.

"Perhaps. I have been poor all my life. I do not consider two extra mouths to feed a matter for congratulations."

He sighed. There were lines of strain in his face, and he looked very tired, perhaps even sleepy. I did not like to burden him with fresh problems, but everyone else had failed.

"Excuse me," I said, as he pointed to the covered burden on the ground behind me. At that moment I saw the familiar figure of Lady Maeve upon the terrace of Conor House, standing there as she did so often. Her hair flew loose and unconfined in the night wind, and she was staring across the distance at us, holding a thin cloak to her bosom against the cold. I motioned to her vigorously. Jonathan looked up at her, then back to the burden there before us.

"The other fisherman, I suppose. And all his friends have taken to their heels, I see."

"Yes. But this one will need some sort of investigation."

He looked at me frowning, yet I had the impression he was agreeing with me without saying so.

"Why?"

"For many reasons. Doesn't it seem odd to you that the body should have been carried so far from the cliff and then buried under peat blocks?"

"Not only odd but impossible." He set down his bag of those oddities that surgeons carry, and examined what lay hidden from my sight beneath the rotting garments and neckcloth, or whatever the piece of white had been, that first attracted us. I was relieved when Mrs. O'Glaney came out and toward us with a lantern.

"I had the feeling," she said. "It was with me all the

day. We'll be hearing from the dead this night, said I to myself. Now the second fisherman's found, there'll be peace at Kelper Head, for the time."

It had been my experience that there was never peace at Kelper Head, at any time, but I did not argue with her. I was much relieved when she assured Jonathan and me and the lobsterman's boy who stared at us over Jonathan's shoulder.

"My Old Man will 'tend to it. After what he went and did this day, it'll serve him proper to be put to work. Dr. Jonathan, I was wantin' to tell you he never meant no harm. It was the drink talkin' and all."

"I understand," said Jonathan briefly. "Good. Let O'Glaney shroud this poor devil, and lay him away somewhere temporarily. Perhaps it is best if we lock him into the room where Ivy Kellinch lay."

"Lock?" I asked in surprise.

"Certainly. We are not quite heathen here, you know. I should very much like another surgeon to examine these remains. And perhaps someone from the Lord Lieutenant's office beside. This fisherman's body has been tampered with, if I am any judge. For some reason, it was desired that the body should be found where it was found."

I felt he was right, but the idea was astonishing all the same.

"Do you think it was foul play?"

He hesitated for a moment. Mrs. O'Glaney and I both stared at him. Then he said, "Very unlikely. Joe Herrity had no enemies. It was some—joke. Some rather nasty business, perhaps to bring trouble to Conor House. At any rate, the body has no business back here so far from where it must have been washed up on the headland. I believe it was placed here—perhaps because the kelpers and others were busy—"

I put my hand to my mouth, but the horrid notion blurted out.

"—beneath the window of my bedchamber! Could it have been there all along?"

"God in heaven!" whispered Mrs. O'Glaney, making signs heavenward with her fingers. "A joke is it?"

The lobsterman's boy took off as fast as ever he could, upon this news, and ran madly back down to the cove. I had no doubt his poor mother and the rest of the family and neighbors would soon be regaled with fresh tales of terror centering upon Kelper Head and the hapless Conors.

I was about to question Jonathan further when Mrs. O'Glaney murmured, "Hush now, miss. 'Er Ladyship is coming, and there. She's got my old man. There is a good one, man! Have you slept off the drink then! And high time."

The two of them looked very odd walking across the rocky headland, Lady Maeve with her quick, swinging grace, and her long, carelessly floating skirts, with O'Glaney towering beside her, trudging along, holding the crown of his woolly head as though he expected it to topple off at any minute.

I stepped back while the others discussed plans, just as they had discussed plans for Ivy Kellinch only a few nights ago.

I walked slowly back to the guardroom of the house, passing the spot where Ivy had fallen against me and died. Curious that the small bloody mark upon her head was under her ear rather than where she had struck the ground, upon her shoulder and arm. There were many curious things about Ivy. I stood in the doorway staring at the spot where Ivy died, wondering at her last strange hints to me that her situation was to be improved. It was as though she had suddenly come into a substantial competence; yet she was said to have no relations, no living ties. As a member of the household she must have seen and known a deal more of the Conors than I. Could it be that when she spoke to me that last evening Ivy Kellinch had just received a secret sum from a member of the Conor household? Perhaps a sum to send her away.

My thoughts returned to that bloody bruise upon her head. I looked over at Lady Maeve, remembering her easy explanation that the nurse gave notice, had been paid. And then, as she departed, leaving her bandboxes behind, were we to believe that this strong, fierce woman had dropped dead for no accountable cause? And with no money that Dr. Jonathan or I could find upon her person?

Lady Maeve gestured to me and I re-joined the group of them, averting my eyes from O'Glaney and the task he and Jonathan had set themselves. I thought I detected in Her Ladyship's voice something besides her usual calm, superior manner.

"Anne, you will have one of the rooms on the lower floor made ready."

"Is it any room in particular, ma'am? The one where Miss Kellinch lay?"

"It's of no importance. Just a room."

"A room with a lock. A workable lock," put in Jonathan as he and The O'Glaney cleared away the last of the peat blocks.

"Good God, Jono!" cried Lady Maeve, considerably to the surprise of Mrs. O'Glaney and me.

I said, "As you wish, ma'am," and went into the house to do as I was told. Rosaleen met me in the passageway between the kitchen and the little corridor where those hideous, boxlike rooms were awaiting their latest occupant.

"What is it, mum? Whatever is wrong?"

"Nothing," I said. "We have found the second fisherman who was lost some time ago."

"Och, now," she moaned, throwing her apron over her face in a silly way. "More bodies to be floating through the halls in the night."

"Nonsense. Now, go and—" I remembered then. My nerves played me false so that I nearly shouted at her. "Who is with Miss Maureen?"

Rosaleen grinned at my excitement.

"That now, mum? It's all gone and been taken care of."

I stumbled back against the wall, feeling need of support.

"How so?"

She preened and made stupid little moues with her stupid little face.

"Master Theo, out of course. He said for me to go and fetch up a tiny noggin of the good Irish, and we'd have a bit of a nip together-like, and sit with Miss Maureen 'til you come back."

"And Master Theo is with his sister now?"

She shrugged.

"Very like. He said as how he'd be there in a trice. That's what 'e said, 'A trice.'"

"But did you see him go into Miss Maureen's room and stay there?"

"Well now, how could I be doin' that? Missy called for water and it was all gone and I went out to fetch some and there was Master Theo looking that surprised you'd think I been a phantasm, like."

"I can believe it," I said flatly. "Then what?"

"Then 'e sent me down here and I come."

"But did you not see him go into his sister's room?"

She shrugged again and turned away from me toward the kitchen. It was all I could do to keep from boxing her ears.

She said curtly, "What a pother! Faith! A body would think you mislike Master Theo himself. And him that sweet to a body I'd take him for one of me own!"

I pushed her aside and opened the door onto the winding stone steps. I went up rapidly and, seeing no one, nor any light on the floor above, I opened the door of the Trumbles' room.

It was as though I had foreseen it all in a horrid dream. The bed was disheveled and empty. Nor was she hiding in any part of the room. I went about lifting cushions, overturning chairs, looking under Dr. Jonathan's desk, peering in at the big armoire, but all the time I knew I should not find her there. I examined the armoire itself with a little more care and thought, hoping to find enough clothing gone to explain Maureen's disappearance as simply a running away rather than the dreadful thing I feared.

With no more hope of clues from the bedchamber where I had left her, I went out into the corridor and started toward the stairs that led up to the quarters of Mr. Aengus, his wife, and Master Theo Conor. As I did so, who should be coming jauntily down those stairs but Master Theo himself. He scarcely looked surprised when I seized him by the arm indignantly.

"Where is Miss Maury? Have you seen her?"

I had, all unwittingly, taken him by the arm whose hand was cumbersomely wrapped in gleaming white bandages, but with his free hand he patted my arm in a soothing way that made me want to scream with rage and concern.

"Now, now, Anne, what is this? Our stout-hearted girl gone all in pieces?" For a moment I though he was mocking me, but something about his face, or voice, the merest little warmth that crept in behind the jesting tone, made for the changing of my mind, and I swallowed hard and replied after taking a breath, "Miss Maureen is gone from her room. I do not like it."

His eyebrows went up in that way which formerly seemed to me so supercilious in the Conor men, but now I supposed it to be genuine puzzlement.

"Why should she not be about the house if she chooses? It shall be the half of it hers upon Father's death. Come." He pulled me into the Trumble room whose door was wide open as I had left it, and while I stood there looking around in the vain hope of seeing something that would explain her absence, he poured me a drink from the decanter on Dr. Jonathan's desk. Obsessed as I was by the evils I suspected in this house, I sniffed at the goblet before taking a sip. He looked down at me with a peculiar little smile as though my action was at once amusing and charming to him. I felt guilty at having been caught and tried to explain. He brushed this aside.

"Let be. Let be. I'll drink of it myself. Then you can have no doubts."

He did not drink though. I saw his lips touch the second goblet, but he did not swallow, nor drink, so I followed his tactics. He did not notice. He was looking around the room. The charm, the amusement were gone from his face. It 'had, slowly and almost imperceptibly, the shrewd, ruthless look that made me think of the rest of his family at odd moments. The son had developed charms of his own, it is true, but along by them was the devil's quality that both fascinated and intimidated me in his father, and made me occasionally suspicious of his sister.

"She talked of suicide," I said flatly.

He looked at me. I had the most extraordinary feeling that he was trying to compose his face to meet this statement, that, in fact, he was trying to appear much concerned. It was like a play-actor putting on his paint and powder to help him play at some emotion he did not feel. The thought filled me with horror and repugnance toward him. How could he care so little for his only sister, that he should be forced to play-act when we talked of her danger! I brushed past him, leaving him staring at me, and went to the window. I thrust aside the portieres and opened the window and called down to Dr. Jonathan and the group who were approaching the house with their heavily wrapped burden.

"Please come, Doctor, as soon as ever you are done!"

Behind me, Theo Conor's voice was cold, sharp, and clear as glass.

"What do you think you are doing!"

I held onto the window the while I took courage and renewed hope from the fresh, chill air. After all was said, Rosaleen had not been gone too long. Maureen would surely be somewhere in the house. Without looking around at Master Theo whose sly charm had almost put me on his side, I said, "You are standing here now when you might be searching for her." Then I faced him. "Unless, sir, you had rather not find the other heir to this property!"

How ugly is his indifference, I thought; for he looked as roguish and charming as though I had not spoken, the archetype of all dashing, handsome Irishmen of storybooks, and yet he could be so unconcerned about the fate of a sister who was prone to suicidal thoughts.

"Now, Annie-girl," he began in his wheedling way. "Be the calm, good creature you are! Don't be addling your poor head with our problems." He had the sheer audacity to reach out for me, as though I might be had for the pawing. I released myself by giving his bandaged hand such a hard swipe with the palm of my own that his wrenching gasp of pain made me grit my teeth as I went from the room to Dr. Jonathan whose booted footstep I heard in the corridor.

"Good God, Anne, what is it now?" asked Jonathan in the doorway. "Is—is it Maury?"

"She's gone," I said.

He started past me. "Gone where? Speak plain out!"

"Gone," I said quickly, getting it out in a rush in the hope of easing the pain of the story. "I wanted to tell you earlier, but you were busy at the coteens. Miss Maureen talked a great deal of suicide. Of people wanting her to die."

He looked at me a little wildly, and then moved me aside with a harsh strength too desperate for apologies. The surface manners had dropped from his dark and working face and I saw the untutored, heavy-fisted Yorkshire boy as he must have looked in his youth.

"Is it you, then?" he demanded of Theo who stood

there watching the two of us, smiling the odd, knowing smile of his. I almost feared for his life, seeing him face to face with the fierce Jonathan, and looking so very pale, plainly suffering from his wounded hand which I had given such a nasty wrench.

"You were ever the honest, hearty lad of the soil; were you not dear Jono?" he taunted the desperate man who sprang at him for these last insulting words. I tried to seize Jonathan's arm but he flung me off and I fell back against the wall, dazed and trying to collect my wits, horrified at the degrading spectacle of two civilized men reduced to this state. But I need not have feared for the clever Theo Conor. He eluded Jonathan and got a chair between them, resting his arms on its high back and still grinning.

"Find her, Jono! Find your wife. Is she dead or alive? Don't waste your time on me but find her."

Jonathan seized the chair that Theo had put between them, and hurled it aside. I heard the wood crack as the chair struck the floor, but Theo leaned negligently against the wall so that I thought he must be mad to take such chances. Yet I was not so much in sympathy with him as with the man who had been driven almost beyond endurance by the laughing Theo.

"It's the devil you are, you sly trickster!" Jonathan roared. "Don't think I haven't known what ye're about!"

But almost immediately I was pleading with him: "No, no! Find her first. He is right. Let us be finding Miss Maury!"

He must have come to this realization even as I cried out at him, for he stopped, clutched Theo's injured hand in the vise of his fingers and said, "I know what ye're about, my fine cockerel, and I'll be proving it this night!" Then he rushed past me into the corridor.

I would have followed him but after a glance at Theo Conor I knew that however much I might despise him, he needed my help. He was still smiling, but white-lipped, and I felt that, whatever his crime, he had suffered enough for the moment. As he moved out into the room he did not look quite so nonchalant; yet he managed to say to me, "Go after him, by all means, Sweeting! It's what you are aching to do."

I poured him a glass of whisky from Jonathan's decanter,

and this time he drank it, his fingers shaking so that he had to bring up his injured hand to steady the glass. When I saw that he was himself again, with more color, and a return to that sardonic, lightly mocking way of his, I left him and went to search for Miss Maureen.

Jonathan had apparently taken the candelabrum off Lady Maeve's desk in the morning room to light his way, but I made do with a candle off a side table, fumbling my way along the hall with only the streak of light from the Trumbles' room to illuminate my passage. In the dining parlor I lighted my candle by the smouldering peat fire, after peering out at the icy-cold terrace and seeing nothing of Miss Maureen. My action in moving the portieres, however, aroused Miss Maury's beloved pets on the terrace, those fearsome cormorants and the seagulls who flew up in panic, skirling their protests out over the terrace and toward the Atlantic fog that lay in wait to swallow them.

As the wick of my candle caught from the fire and I raised it the better to see every corner of the heavy Jacobean room, the little tongue of light seemed to play on the eyes of the male portrait that stared at me from the far wall. In spite of my anxiety about Miss Maury, I was momentarily caught by those eyes and the light that seemed to burn in their depths. I knew the Conor look at once, gleaming, malicious, very handsome, ready to laugh at the world. It must be a portrait of the youthful Aengus Conor, looking a good deal like his son, not quite so eccentric without the night-cap that today crowned his gray locks. The face had fascinated me since my first meeting with this very odd and very lively invalid, and I was surprised to discover that the invalid of today was more interesting to me than the splendid younger man of the portrait. But this was not finding Miss Maureen, and I lowered my candle, turning away from those eyes that followed me from that portrait, amused as ever, as though hiding their own secrets.

Still a trifle uneasy under that gaze, I moved toward the open door, and stopped abruptly, aghast at the sight that filled the doorway. A kelper, stood there, fully materialized in all his blood-red, muffled strangeness, even the face—if there was a face—concealed by the shadowing hood.

XVIII

FOR AN instant neither the kelper nor I moved. I had a moment's faintness, very unlike me, and only the flicker of the shaking candle in my hand brought me to myself. The thing was so very big, so corporeal. Sure now, it could not be a phantom that Maureen had seen strike down her father! That must have been real, as this kelper was real. Before I recovered my wits a natural male voice, bog-thick with brogue, spoke from the red depths behind that hood, and I saw that this kelper, at least, was human.

"Mum, it's meself now. Tim Corcoran, so it is, come from the village, with a letter franked from Dublin to Conor House. But Dr. Jono sent me for to fetch you. He do be looking to find Miss Maury, seeing as herself has writ one of her wee threats for to throw us into the scare."

"I'll come at once. He's found her? Is she well?"

"She be elsewhere's, mum. But she did the prank all neat-like, leavin' a letter hard-fast by her shoes, on terrace. And it all has sent the lass Rosaleen into the fits, as it were."

"Oh, bother Rosaleen!" I saw that the sturdy kelper was a man of action, and followed him hastily into the corridor and then to the comfortable red parlor I had entered the night I arrived at Conor House. The fire blazed merrily and I half expected to see Miss Maury seated before it, with her limbs tucked under her skirts in the little girl way she so often chose. But I had no more time for searching the room. There was a passionate knocking upon the terrace door and I saw Rosaleen standing outside, her blond hair blowing, her face and figure like wraiths in the gathering fog. She was gesturing through the glass to the kelp gatherer who had gone ahead of me and now opened the door so that I stepped out upon the cold, wind-swept terrace where the fog puffs seemed to drift toward me from every direction. The gray and fierce Atlantic could no longer be seen, although its roar was unmistakable as was the salty spray from the great combers.

A sudden gust of wind blew out the faint light of my candle just as Rosaleen snatched at me, panting and breathless, sobbing like a naughty child who knows she is to be punished. I dreaded these signs of worse to come.

"Rosaleen! What is it? Tell me!"

"There be 'er little ring on the terrace yon. And one of 'er little shoes. And—and there be a paper. When Dr. Jono and the kelper heard me scream, Doctor come runnin', read of the paper and give it in my hands and ran below to look out on the ledge. But I won't touch the nasty thing. So I put it back where Miss Maury left it. If . . . indeed, miss, if it was her left it, and not one of them ghosts."

"Where is the doctor now?"

She sniffled and waved one hand vaguely out over the escarpment. I pushed her into the kelper's arms where she continued to cry and otherwise impede his progress as he tried to follow me. I went swiftly, but with as much care as possible, through the misty fog, remembering the edge of the terrace was unprotected. The sea and the face of the escarpment were illuminated suddenly by the opening of the escarpment door, so that I discovered I was dangerously near the edge of the terrace. I peered down and saw the great white spume of water shimmer opaquely in the light from the open door. Greatly daring, Jonathan and O'Glaney had ventured out to search, and finding nothing, were now dragging shut that door which had given me such a fright a few days ago. Vainly, the foaming waves pressed upon the closing door. Since the tide was only now coming to its height, it seemed reasonably sure that nothing ominous had been lying upon the little stone ledge of the escarpment, for it would not yet have washed away.

My shoe trod upon something that grated roughly like a pebble, and I knelt to pick up Maureen's ring which shone in the mist, a wedding ring set with precious gleaming little gems which were dainty without being expensive. I examined it with a gnawing terror within me.

Lying beside the ring, placed very carefully to weight down the paper Rosaleen had replaced, was one of Maureen's low-heeled morocco day shoes. I removed the shoe and took up the paper which crackled noisily in my hand as the wind played across its surface. There was no light except the obscure gray radiance of the fog, and I could make out only a few words in what I took to be Maureen's handwriting: . . . *for everyone, for Conor . . . for all. All I be possessed of, I leave* . . .

Was it a Will then? It sounded dreadfully like one. The wind and the moistness of the fog obscured much that followed, but I read the words: *It is best. It is best. It is best.*

This latter repetition was underscored, and followed by a final touching line which made me realize the note was addressed to her husband: *No other human being can ever come between us now.*

I was sickened by the implications in that note.

The kelp gatherer, bidding Rosaleen to "Hush now, lass, and be still!" came over to me and at the same time I heard running footsteps crunch upon the stone floor of the terrace behind us. I looked around, holding out the pitiful wedding ring in the palm of my hand. It was Jonathan, his face white and still in the foggy light. He looked unfamiliar in a borrowed dry jacket over his wet garments, his uncombed hair still damp so that a strand of it lay lank across his forehead like a dark gash.

"God be thanked! She is not there. It would not be possible in the past few hours or we should have found—" His voice broke momentarily but it was not necessary to say more on that score. He ventured after a moment, "It is all one of Maury's wretched jokes."

"Excuse me, sir," said I, "but this letter does not sound like a joke."

As Jonathan took back his wife's letter, his rough hand trembled slightly, then regained its old strength, and he folded the letter, putting it away inside his jacket. "She's written such things before. You must not fret, Anne. It is only Maury's way of getting attention; getting the love from all of us that my poor lass craves."

"That be so," said the kelper, nodding vigorously. "I disremember when first we was to make search for Miss Maury, back when she was so high. And we found her safe and singing, up the bog a way."

"Tim!" said Jonathan. "Will you take the path to the coteens? You know my wife's ways, where she may have gone. At Midsummer Eve it was the same. You remember?"

"Och, ay, Dr. Jono. We've seen the poor pretty thing afore now at such pranks. Don't ye be a worriting now, nor you, mum."

I could not quite share the feeling that we were all the victims of a rather dreadful joke, perpetrated by Miss Maureen. But they knew her better than I did. Nevertheless, I was intensely relieved when the kelper took his red visage and his overpowering red shadow away from us at a great, leaping pace.

Jonathan and I looked at each other, but I doubt that he saw me. Within the very depths of his heart he must be more filled with doubts and questions than I.

"It'll be the bog, of a certainty! My lass was ever for the bog when they fretted her. Anne, have warm things ready in the red parlor against our return."

He was gone almost before I could say, "Yes, sir," and attend to Rosaleen who—idiot girl that she was!—took this moment to have hysterics.

"She'll be gone in the bog. In the dirty bog, mind! My poor Miss Maury!"

I shook her until her teeth rattled, and half dragged her into the kelper parlor where I set her to tidying up in preparation for Maureen Trumble's return. But I had little faith in all our preparations. Deep within me was the terrible certainty that the unhappy Miss Maury had finally committed the act for which there was no rescue.

I was on my way to the stone staircase to prepare tea and sugar cakes when I thought of the master of the house, alone in his sinister darkness at the top of the house, while his daughter was in great peril—all, I felt sure, through the machinations of some greedy heir to Mr. Aengus's properties. Indeed, it was within his power to leave his holdings away from the family and thus prevent Maureen's fellow heirs from poisoning her mind with suicide talk. In any case, he should know what his family was about. I did not want to be trapped in some dark corner of the top floor, so I peered into the Trumbles' room where I had last seen Theo Conor, but he had long since gone. Nor was Lady Maeve in the Morning Room. As I passed the Trumbles' room once more, the candles in their sconces burned low, giving off smokey clues to their imminent demise. I stopped to light another and doing so glanced around from force of habit. Beneath the desk was a scattering of small papers torn very fine which had certainly not been there an hour before. Among them was a bit of paper with the seal of its sender still intact. Then I remembered the letter our kelper friend, Tim Corcoran had delivered to the house tonight. I wondered who in this household had received that letter which was so important it was franked in Dublin and delivered at this hour of the evening. The obvious recipient was one of the Trumbles. Could it have anything to do with Miss Maureen's disappearance? But no. The kelper was searching for her along with everyone else.

There was nothing for it but to inform Mr. Aengus who was master of the household, and to follow his instructions from this moment. I came out of the room and into the corridor again, feeling quite cowardly at the sight of those stairs to the top floor. Where were Lady Maeve and Theo Conor? Should I meet them in some shadowed recess now?

Before setting foot upon the stairs I felt one of those curious silences fall over the house in which even the distant tide beating at the escarpment did not seem so savage, and I could hear my heartbeat distinctly in my ears. I paused, put my head against the cold, damp wall, and waited until I should be a trifle more calm, my body more under command.

I heard then a sound so out of place in this house that for a moment I fancied I was back on Ballyglen Road, running through the bog and away from the light, silvery laughter of the dead Ivy Kellinch, if it had, indeed, been she. The sound seemed to echo from all corners of the long hall I was just quitting. I felt its inhuman, metallic quality racing down the staircase toward me, coming to me from all directions.

I chided myself silently: *Do not be making a bigger fool of yourself than you are, girl! Is it mad you are then, to be hearing sounds of the dead?*

Now, who would be laughing like that, so carelessly, so lightly that the source seemed very far away, and only the echo reaching me? Who but a madman would laugh without cause, starting so suddenly, almost as if the sound were unconsciously uttered? A madman, or a madwoman, belike.

It was then I knew I had been wrong in Ballyglen Bog. The lilting little laugh that followed me had not been the dead Ivy Kellinch. That was nonsense. It was the laugh of the one person in this house who might be liable to laugh without cause, to laugh suddenly, unconsciously, at some secret little thought running through her phantom child's mind. It was Maureen Trumble, laughing, of course.

I stood there looking around me slowly in the darkness, listening. I could not quite place the source of that laughter. It was far from me, I felt that. As I listened, it stopped as abruptly as it had begun. I went up the stairs; for it had seemed to me at the last that the sound originated above me somewhere. All was silent on the top floor, though there was a light under the closed door of Aengus Conor's room and under the door of the north parlor which Lady Maeve had evidently taken to be her quarters. Either Theo Conor was not in his own room, or the door was more firmly fitted to the ancient floor; for no light shown beneath to betray his occupancy.

I moved along the hall slowly, trying not to make a sound. I was nearing the north parlor when the tinkling light voice came again, softly through the gloomy night air, this time humming some forgotten tune out of Ireland's dim past. But I could not quite discover from which door that sound came. I went on to Mr. Aengus's door and rapped lightly. There was no response. But whatever its source, the humming stopped. I made no further sounds that would betray me. Scarcely daring to breathe, I waited a very long time. The humming did not resume.

Then I went to the north parlor, guessing that Maureen must be within this room, hiding perhaps, in some strange notion of a joke. Just as the door yielded under my fingers, the humming took up again, but behind me, in some other room. I had gone too far now to retreat, however, and still silent, entered the north parlor. At the far end of the room, on the very table where Mr. Aengus had asked me to take up the Book of Common Prayer and deliver the message from within its pages, there were two sets of candles, flickering ever so little in the slight draft of the room. Seated at the table with his back to me was a man in a long, concealing robe above whose collar I saw the ruffles of a nightgown I remembered from another visit, and there was no mistaking the gray locks that snaked down to his collar in the back, nor the tasseled night cap jauntily cocked over one side of his head. I had come upon Aengus Conor at some deviltry or other. He was bent over the table very studiously, working hard with his hands.

I was just about to cough, to speak, announce my presence, when, to my amazement, I saw him rise from the chair, still leaning over the work that occupied him at the table. In the tiny interval that I watched this, my thoughts were curiously satisfied.

"So he can walk," I thought. "Just as I half suspected. And what is he up to, I wonder."

Near at my hand was a chair which I barely noticed, so fascinated was I. But to steady myself, for I was undeniably shaking, I put my hand out and felt under my fingers the cloth of a robe or a cloak that had been thrown over the back of it. I glanced at it, and I remembered thinking it was very like one of Miss Maureen's cloaks with the hood attached. Then something so stupefying occurred at the far end of the room where Aengus Conor stood that my senses whirled and I felt I was mad.

Mr. Aengus stood up, straight and lithe and young, and having knocked something off the table, picked up the object, swearing impatiently. The object was a long strip of blood-stained cloth, and he was wrapping it about his wounded hand.

XIX

I MUST have gasped, made some strangled sound to betray my presence; for the man stopped suddenly, and in another instant, as he faced me, I saw the devilish little smile, the strange, eerie Conor face, terrifying in its attraction, like the Medusa-head my husband once described, so that I could only stare, with my mouth open, and my mind whirling as though I had lost all sense of time and space and connective ties of memory. I saw the gray hair, the amusing cap, the trappings of Aengus Conor, but the face and the trim, straight body were young, as young as his son. And the wounded hand—that was certainly Theo Conor's hand!

"You have caused us endless trouble, Anne," he told me, shaking his head so that the tassel again fell over his eye, exactly as it had when I knew him as Aengus Conor. I felt strongly the urge to laugh, one of those meaningless, mirthless sounds that Maureen Trumble made now and then.

"I—I don't think I understand, sir."

"You express the matter at its mildest, dear girl. You know you don't understand. Yet you were meant to. You were engaged from Miss Nutting for some very important uses here, but instead you dabbled in affairs that were better left untouched."

"Like murder?" I asked, so nervous I clung to the chair and the cloak under my fingers. He was right. I did not in the least understand. I did not even know to whom I spoke.

"That was our concern. Not yours."

Murder was their concern? I could believe that!

"Yes, Anne, you compounded the difficulty with your precious sense of fair play which you can only have acquired in England. We Irish are more realistic. Emotions betrayed you, and I am afraid your emotions nearly betrayed us as well."

233

I began to make furtive steps backward, preparing for sudden and desperate flight. My movements were increased when I saw that he was coming toward me, saying, "Don't you know yet whose body was uncovered tonight—so all the world would know what we thought we so carefully concealed? Aengus Conor has been dead these many months."

"No!" I almost screamed the word. No man had seemed more alive than the Aengus Conor I knew. But of course, that Aengus was the man before me!

He moved a little faster, lithe and easy as Theo Conor always moved; yet with that smiling cynicism of his father, or the man I thought him to be, that I had watched with such fascination as the shadows played over it. What an actor this man might have been! I swung around like a rat in a trap, ready to decamp instantly. But there was an obstacle behind me. Lady Maeve had come in during our incredible little scene, and stared at me now with those green eyes, her flaming wild hair loose about her head. She was directly in the path of my escape.

"Stop her," said the voice of my tormentor who was both Aengus and Theo Conor to my confused brain. "She will ruin all."

"Not so fast, my girl," Lady Maeve said coldly. "You are too mettlesome by half."

I seized Maureen's cloak and swung the heavy, full skirts across the face of Lady Maeve. As she thrust the cloak out of her way and scrambled to reach me, I ran madly out through the open door and down the corridor dragging the cloak which was entangled in my fingers. I scarcely stopped at the staircase but rushed down, using every ounce of strength to reach the bottom before the footsteps now pursuing me could know which way I had turned on the lower floor.

I fancied I heard my name called from above, in the light, cheerful voice of Maureen Trumble, but I paid it no heed. More likely, it was all part and parcel of the terrible fantasy to which my brain had been prey during the past hour. It was very cold on the main floor of the house. The window in the Trumbles' room was still open as I had left it—so long ago, as it seemed—when I looked out and called to Dr. Jonathan, and the bitter dampness was everywhere. I did not look at the cloak I dragged with me, and which had been my single weapon against Lady Maeve, but I hung it about my shivering frame, and hurried through the corridor, looking for an open door, a way out, any way out of this accursed ancient pile. The red parlor door was ajar and the door onto the terrace was open just as it had been when Rosaleen came through it. Somewhere in my confused brain I remember thinking I should give Rosaleen a scold for never closing doors.

It was quite ridiculous. I began to laugh softly to myself as I ran through the open door onto the terrace, and found myself half giggling, half sobbing as I met the slap of night air and sea-spray against my face. I put up the hood of Maureen's cloak and looked carefully around, remembering the treacherous end to the terrace, above the escarpment. There must be a way down from here. I had never explored the north end of the terrace and in all likelihood there would be a narrow servants' steps, if nothing else. All around me the fog had gathered in curious, motionless puffs, so that I was several times startled into supposing someone stood out here on the terrace somewhere, watching me, silent as the fog. I too must be silent. It was not difficult, now that I had left the creaking boards of the corridors in the house. The fog muffled the sound of my footsteps upon the stone.

I had to find some way down to the headland without their trapping me, so that I could send after Dr. Jonathan. It was imperative that I find him first; for if Maureen was actually in the labyrinth of Conor House, his search of the bog was futile, and, in any case, those of us who were sane and unconnected with the Conor crimes would need his protection. Mrs. O'Glaney would help me. I felt that, whatever her loyalty to the Conors, she would never defend murder, and what I had seen tonight must surely be a confession of murder. But how to reach the cook without having my way cut off by the two monstrous creatures who had nearly trapped me on the top floor of the house?

I had apparently thrown them off the scent for the moment. I heard nothing of their pursuit. Meanwhile, however, I saw that I had fallen into a trap despite myself, for I could find no escape from the north end of the terrace by which I might reach the lower quarters and Mrs. O'Glaney. Pulling the cloak and hood tighter against the sea spray, I moved closer to the edge where the tide was retreating now and had almost laid bare the escarpment ledge far and dimly seen below, and horrible to my memory.

In making my way toward the south end of the terrace I was careful to watch each step and so avoided stepping into what seemed to be a wild scramble of sea birds. They took off at my approach, with a great flapping sound, but one of them gave me a frightening little start I did not need, when it fluttered against me, its wings bruising my hands before it fell at my feet. The gull was crippled in some way, or perhaps stunned at having struck me in its flight, and I bent over to take it in my hands. I feared that the noise of its fluttering would bring me the attention I was afraid of. But I also thought of the tenderness of Maureen Trumble with birds, and my feeling that whether she was alive, or dead and only her phantom voice haunting me, she would be pleased that I had saved one of her living creatures. I took the flapping, squawking bird into my hands which were kept busy with its size and activity, but something in my touch made the bird stop squawking, and I felt that I had escaped detection for the time, in any case. I looked toward the house furtively, to be sure.

I saw a curious, shadowy thing in the puffs of fog, standing there like a monolith between me and the house. The fog drifted by, and while I clutched the squirming bird to my cloak with icy fingers, I made out the figure of a kelp gatherer, Tim Corcoran, from the size of him, with his fringed red cloak all grayed and pale as a shroud in the fog. The cap shielded his face, but I was determined not to be fooled twice, and called in a voice that revealed a timid and absurd fear of this good fellow, "Tim? You were looking for me?"

How tiresome of him! He stood there like stone and as I stared, the fingers of one stone hand moved slightly. What I saw now through those waves of fog was not the kelp gatherer at all but the thing I had seen earlier tonight, across the grave of the real Aengus Conor. And again, as in that twilight moment on the headland, the hand beckoned to me.

"So it was a joke again, Maury," said the voice to me across the mists, so strange, so low it was almost a whisper; yet I understood the meaning and knew what had happened. Just as I had mistaken this creature for the harmless Tim

Corcoran, so had he taken me for Maureen Trumble. I wore her cloak, and I had not yet revealed my height nor my own true voice, and in my hands was one of Miss Maury's birds. How caressing were those sounds bidding me to my death.

"But now you must do it. You said you would do it for me when I told you, and now it is time. They know Aengus is dead. I found his body myself and for our love, Maury—for our love—I led them to it. When you go, they can never touch you. And you will belong to me always. Maury? Do you understand me? Maury?"

My heart hammered within me like the flutter of the seagull against it. The kelp gatherer was closer now, appearing and disappearing in the thickness of the misty fog, close enough to touch me, to pitch me over the side of the terrace and to that death we had feared for Maureen.

Was it possible that this hideous, sweet voice calling me to my death was the voice I had heard not an hour ago, warm and compassionate as he spoke of his helpless wife? The bestial sin of him, to cosset a loved one into suicide! Thinking this I could not help whispering, "I did not know. I did not know it was . . ."

He misunderstood me. The beckoning hand came down as though to touch my shoulder, but I put the fluttering bird in the way and he withdrew his hand. He leaned nearer me and whispered with such tenderness as must break my heart if I had been Maureen, "They all believed you killed him. It cannot change now, lass. So you must not let them have you. Do you want to hang in chains at the crossroad? Or be far from me forever, in Bedlam?"

"But the kelper," I whispered. "He did it."

Jonathan chided me in that half-impatient but tender way I had so often seen him use toward his wife.

"Sweetheart, you knew who the kelper truly was, and why I did it. Aengus would not let me marry my little girl, and he had to die. You said so yourself. Now, do not tease me, love. You must do the thing you promised, so no man else may love you as I do, nor see you suffer in Bedlam. Think of eternity, Maureen. Your Jono never to stop loving his little girl. Do it!"

He reached out. I saw then by the stiffening of the muscles in his hands that he intended to push me over the

escarpment that was so close, so very close under my feet.
I felt the hands upon my shoulder but before they seized
me, I sent up the seagull fluttering at him. It struck the
kelper's cap off him.

"I expected that, love," he taunted me, as the bird
flew past, doing him no harm.

I raised my head and looked him full in the face.

We stared at each other, his eyes dilating, dreadful in
the white light of the fog, as dreadful as my own, I daresay. Inconceivably, he looked stricken as though I had wounded him.

"Not you! Not you!" he whispered, his voice so changed,
so twisted with what emotions I could only guess, that
I scarcely understood him. "Anne, Anne . . . you always
knew Maury must go—for your sake."

I asked as quietly as may be, "Was it for me that you
killed the real Aengus a year ago? And even tried to frighten
me away those first days at Conor? As I suppose you did."

He seemed indignant, as though I had misunderstood his
lofty motives.

"Aengus deserved to die. He held Maury's money and
would not see it go from him to any husband of Maury's,
especially the dirty Yorkish lad, the Outlander! But you,
Anne, I meant only to set you afright as I did the other
housekeeper, so you would not pry. I would never have
hurt you. I was very gentle—do you know how gentle?—
when I struck you in the Ballyglen graveyard. And it was
all to no purpose. Theo tricked me with his empty paper.
He very nearly caught me as well. Then you and I should
both have been lost. And Maury's fortune too."

How sincere he was, giving an indication that with any
response from me we should presently be in each other's
arms! How close in his greedy, embittered mind were death
and love!

I said, "There can be no happiness with Maureen dead.
Where is she got to? We must find her."

He brushed this aside as of no consequence, his wind-
blown garments and that sturdy body of his the more
terrible as they stood between me and any hope of escape. I thought he would shake me. He made as if to do
so, but stopped as he touched me. "Anne, you are a fool!
I daresay she is already deep buried in that accursed bog

she fancied so. Even as a child she was forever threatening. A child's trick it may be, to gain her ends. But now the bluff is called. She has done the only thing she knew to keep my love. And in a way, she is right. I will owe her much. With Aengus's body found, Theo must admit his playacting, his tricks that held Maury's money from me. Then I'll be as fine a toff as any Conor. Maury left me every farthing. You read her will here. It is all for us, love. You and me!"

He must have seen a shadow of the revulsion I felt, though I schooled myself to show him a face wiped blank of emotion, for he added more violently, "God judge me, it is so, Anne! Consider my suffering. All I did went for nothing. The whole year I never knew if Aengus was dead or not. And until his body was found, there would be no money. Until you, Anne."

"Me!"

"Ay, it was your talk of Kelper Head and the rubble there, the mystery of it. And so tonight I found Aengus's body and beckoned you to it, just where Theo must have buried it, hoping to keep Maureen's money to himself by making us all believe Aengus still lived. Had I been allowed to see our precious 'Aengus' in a clear light, I should have known at once the trick he played. But tomorrow, someone will discover our fisherman's body is really Aengus Conor, dead over a year. And my poor Maury a willing suicide, knowing peace at last, as she wished it. Then our troubles are done. Don't you see? We deserve these things from those who have kept them from us too long."

At his reasonable boast of these horrors I wanted to laugh, partly, I think, from an access of strong hysterics; for all the while I was his prisoner, his "poor Maury" might be dying. "And this would make a future for us?"

"Anne, love . . . I called you that once. Do you remember?"

"I remember."

The pain of its repetition here on the edge of eternity, cut my breath.

"Come inside where it is warm. You are trembling," he said tenderly, as though we were gossiping at teatime. "It was brutally told to you, Anne, I admit it. But when you think on the evil of Aengus and of Ivy you will not judge me harshly. You are a lass who knows how the world treats folk like you and me."

"Ivy Kellinch too?"

He had tried to force me toward the house, a fraction away from our danger, and I wanted to say nothing, to save both myself and perhaps Maureen by my acquiescence, but almost against my will I repeated the nurse's name. He stopped, shaking me gently.

"Spare your sympathies, Anne. Ivy heard me talking to Maury about suicide. She thought to marry me and share Maury's inheritance. The filth of that creature! Out of the scum of Liverpool. When I met you, I knew Ivy had to die. She would have come between us, given us no peace. I sent her off with a promise to fetch her when Maury was gone. But I knew she would talk. The thing had to be done, so I followed her to the cove. A blow just under the ear. She scarcely felt it. And my Maury, dear innocent, believed it was I protecting her, when we agreed that I had not left our room that night." He hands moved upward to my throat, caressing me in a way I found hard to bear; for it reminded me of the emotion I had once so nearly felt for him.

I willed myself to remain still, but my flesh betrayed me by withdrawing from him. He felt my shrinking under his hands and his grip tightened. I read distrust and more. I read death in his eyes for the first time since we had confronted each other tonight. The grayed red of his kelper's robe seemed more horrible, now that I looked on the true face of Conor's phantom kelper.

"Is it so, then?" he demanded in a sudden access of fury. "And all the time I thought you understood and shared my feelings. But you despise me as they do. You despise the land agent's son that had to scratch for every farthing, because he wasn't a Conor angel! Well, my lass, long, long before ever I saw you, I set my life to be in the Conor boots, and not even you will stop me."

I tried to wrench myself from him but his hands caught about my neck and in an instant the gloomy night was a blur before my eyes, and a burning agony was at my throat. My feet scuffed vainly for footing on the rough terrace floor. As if in echo there were more sounds of feet scudding across the terrace from the morning room door.

Our sounds aroused a storm of beating wings around us, as several vagrant gulls were set afright. Dark wings whirred past and out to sea cutting across my cheek and skimming the Kelper's robe. One of Jonathan's hands released its grip giving me a respite, and I gasped and choked, believing my head would burst. His hand struck wildly at one of the flying creatures so that it fluttered and dropped out into space beyond us. The moment the bird went over the side of the terrace there was a cry behind us: "No, no, Jono! You hurt it. . . ! You hurt it. . . !" and the sobbing I knew for Maureen's breathcatching, childish unhappiness.

I felt the shudder that stabbed through Jonathan at his wife's voice, her whom he thought dead of her own hand. In his moment of confusion I took my life's reprieve, wrenching hard away from him, striking out with all my nearly spent force to free myself from that iron grip of his. As Maureen screamed again, running toward us, I fell hard to my knees. I had not counted the cost to him as my struggle threw him off his precarious balance upon the edge of the terrace. I felt the merest whisper of his fingers groping to cling to me for his own safety, before the dreadful thing was done. Too late, Maureen and I reached out to save him but caught only a bit of the fringe from his cloak. His cry as he went over the edge and plunged into the foaming cauldron below was nearly drowned in the thunderous roar of the waves.

I put my cheek to the cold, wet, salty floor of the terrace and found myself weeping. Then Maureen patted me on the head as though I were a child, and her soft voice said plaintively, "Do not cry for my Jono, dear Anne. He should not have hurt the bird . . . . It was very bad of him and God punished him, so do not cry. Tomorrow you will have forgotten all about it. And Jono will belong to me forever."

XX

IN THAT MOMENT which saw the dreadful fate of Dr. Jonathan, and an end to the crimes that had plagued Conor House, I was numbed by the knowledge of his guilt, but more, by the realization that my own struggle had thrown him off balance and sent him to his death. A sorry end for that life of some talent, perhaps twisted and perverted to its fiendish purpose by the inequities of the society into which we were born.

I could scarcely believe my ears when Maureen, only minutes after her husband's death, looked up from her soothing attention to me, and cried out almost joyfully, "Here, Theo! We are safe. Poor Jono went quite mad and would have killed our Annie. So he did not do those wicked things out of love for her, at all. I should never have suspected him of such a bad thing."

Wiping my eyes upon my damp skirts that were already crusted with salty spray, I began to laugh at her logic—her incredible, wonderful logic. Her husband's penchant for the housekeeper would have been a far greater crime than his murders of her father and her nurse!

I could not stop laughing. Maureen paused, perplexed, and presently I felt different hands upon me, masculine this time, one hand thickly bandaged, but with unsuspected strength, all the same.

"Anne!" said Theo Conor's voice sternly. "Enough, now. It is over. All is safe."

"But Miss Maury said—she said—"

"Never you mind her. Come, sweet. You have been our brave girl." He spoke to me as though I were his childish sister, and I was so shocked by this that I ceased to laugh and let myself be led across the terrace to the morning room with Theo's arm around me for support, and with Maureen going ahead, calling to Lady Maeve, "It's time for coffee and

242

the sugar buns you promised. You said I should have them
if I was good and kept out of Jono's sight tonight."

Her ladyship sounded as though she had been running,
as she took my other arm and looked over my head at
Theo.

"We should have listened to Maureen. She guessed where
they would be. Is she—?"

"Right as a trivet. A little hysterical, I fancy. As who
would not be? Come and sit down. There's a good lass . . .
my brave girl."

Stiff and frozen and numb within my heart, I let myself drop into a chair at their direction, caring not in the
least where I was. But a cup of scalding hot coffee held to
my lips by that master villain of my imaginings, Theo, put
me partially to rights, and I was able to look around me,
seeing myself the center of no little attention by the three
Conors and the giant O'Glaney who lumbered into the
morning room from the corridor.

"The kelpers come for to fetch up himself, sir."

"Good," said Theo, glancing over at him and gesturing him
to go away. "Let them get about it." Theo was wearing his
own clothing, but something about him, perhaps only my
knowledge of his masquerade, made him take on a little
of the mysterious fascination of the "Aengus Conor" I had
met.

"They be saying as how he fell just inside the ledge,
Master Theo. T'won't be much of a thing to be fetching
him up. They're after findin' Miss Maury's letter on him
and another beside, that still reads, mostly."

I stopped drinking the coffee suddenly and noticed that
it had burned my tongue. I thought very hard about that
so I should not think about the man they were "fetching up"
from the ledge of the escarpment.

"Yes, yes. Give me the letter and get on," said Theo, and
O'Glaney, after passing a damp folded sheet of note paper
to him and touching his forelock respectfully, disappeared
into the dark recesses of the corridor.

"Lady Maeve," I said, thinking my first apology should
be directed to my employer. "Forgive me. I thought—"

She was looking a bit paler than usual and quite old. She
said quickly, "I understand. But we had such great difficulty
proving him guilty. He foxed us at every jump."

243

Theo, who had been perusing the damp page, looked up and smiled. It seemed to me, in these strange new circumstances, that the smile I had always assumed to be Conor deviltry, was perhaps only Irish, after all.

"You thought Maeve a lady vampire? That, I believe, was Maury's idea. You see, she saw father murdered by—the kelper, and then Maeve seemed to bring him back to life, through my little masquerade. It was confusing to poor Maury."

"He looked so like Papa," Maureen explained. "Theo is very clever. And, of course, he would not let me see him close up."

I said, "I understand how necessary it was to pretend your father still lived. If only because Miss Maureen was so universally suspected of the crime."

"Thank you for knowing that," Lady Maeve put in tiredly. "And for not believing it was to rob Maury's future husband of her inheritance."

"Oh, I'm sure that did enter her lovely head," said Theo in his light way. Yet I think the lightness was more in his words than his manner, for he looked very much more mature than I had suspected him, and nearly as tired as his stepmother. He seemed a little more the age of the Aengus Conor I had thought him in that dark room on the top floor, and less the young wastrel he had made himself out to be as Master Theo. "But the truth is, Father left the three of us well enough braced so that Old Jono's greed might have been satisfied if he had been sincere and waited out Father's consent to the marriage."

Maureen said with her customary eagerness, "But Papa had to die. Else Jono could never marry—"

"Give her a sugar bun," Theo cut in hastily and Lady Maeve plumped one into her stepdaughter's mouth. Maureen relaxed beatifically.

"As it was," Theo told me, holding up the Irish china coffee cup to me again, "not a soul but the Conors believed Maury innocent of the attack on father. Had it been known that he died, she would have faced charges, perhaps confinement in a mad—" He broke off. "Drink, Anne. That's better."

"You ran great risks." Even as I spoke I could not but remember that shocking though necessary act performed by Theo—with Maeve's aid?—in burying his father secretly, without church rites, out on the headland, so no one should suspect his death. To bury one's own father or one's husband, secretly in the night. . . . Was this why Lady Maeve, with her troubled conscience, stood for hours upon the terrace in the wind and fog and rain, perhaps paying secret tribute to her dead and unshriven husband?

I glanced over at Miss Maureen in Lady Maeve's custody. Theo followed my glance. Of the two women it was Lady Maeve who was unnerved and Maureen who behaved quite naturally, as though nothing untoward had happened.

"Do you think it hurt my poor Jono very much?" Maureen asked after some reflection, the while I shuddered at the innocent remark, and she added, "I shouldn't like to think that." She looked at me, her eyes wide with that curious and terribly purity of the child. "Maeve says he wrote those letters to you and to her so you wouldn't come to Conor and see things you shouldn't. And he was right, too. Because you came, and you did see things! But yet, it took Maeve a whole year to trap my Jono. He always said he was smarter than us Conors. And so he is!"

I could say nothing. Everything I heard was appalling to me. But Lady Maeve seemed to have recovered her capability.

"Now, Maury dear, you must banish all such thoughts and go to bed. You were ready enough to go to bed an hour since, with all your singing and humming, and worrying Miss Anne as you did."

It had been Maureen after all, whose voice drew me to the upper floor and that disclosure of Theo's masquerade.

"I sang," said Maureen, "because you told me I needn't die in the bog or go to Bedlam, or be hanged like the poor creatures at the crossroads." She smiled a little sadly as she scolded, "It was naughty of Jono to tell me that."

"Well, and it is over now," Lady Maeve went on. I could see that, like me, she was holding tight to the reins of her strength and nerves. "Go to bed and when you awaken in the morning the sun will shine and you shall have sugar buns and coffee again."

"With honey in it?" asked Maureen, ever practical.

"As much as you can hold," Theo promised her, looking at her with that merry, joking tenderness he ever showed toward his sister. "And now I think explanations can wait until this young lady has rested as well. I'll see you to your room, Miss Wicklow. . . . Or is it Wexford?" He peered at me in the ridiculous, devilish way that needed only the tasseled night cap to complete the portrait of my own personal "Aengus Conor." It was obviously an Aengus Conor that had never existed except in the brains of these two extraordinary people, Maeve and Theo, who went to such lengths to save Maureen.

Lady Maeve laughed abruptly at the "Wexford" thrust at me, and then said in a stern voice, "Don't be flippant, Theo. It was with jests like that you almost betrayed yourself. Believe me, Anne, we are not at all fiends and murderers here. But we had a delicate and dangerous path to take, suspecting but never sure, with Jonathan ever in our way, as sly as can be." Maureen was walking to the door nibbling at another bun, and Lady Maeve lowered her voice to say to me, "The moment he married Maureen and thought himself legally in control of her inheritance, we knew for sure what we had suspected the night Aengus was murdered. But there was no stopping Maureen. She was set upon marrying her Jono. And there he was all the time, pretending to protect Maury, yet pointing shreds of evidence her way so that she should think herself the murderess of her father, and all the world think so with her."

Theo offered me a drink of Lady Maeve's whisky, but I could not forget the decanter I had suspected of containing poison, and pushed it aside impatiently.

"We count upon your testimony to Sir Horace tomorrow, Anne," said Maeve. "Without that dreadful experience you went through tonight, we should perhaps never have known his motives—or his methods, when it comes to that."

"Believe me," Theo tried to reassure me as we left the room, "we did not intend it so. But when you fled from us and there was no stopping you, only Maury guessed where you might have gone to. A few moments sooner and we could have spared you considerable anguish."

I said nothing. I had a strong desire to burst into tears and only just managed to stifle this weakness. Theo and I went down the steps to the guardroom. Every bone in me ached, and my heart ached too. Theo held high the candlestick he had taken from his stepmother's desk, and its flaring little light touched on the long, white-wrapped burden carried between O'Glaney and a kelp gatherer from the headland. I heard myself give a sound that was the start of a scream at sight of the red-cloaked kelper, but Theo's hand tightened on my arm, and I choked off the cry.

We both stared at the burden between the two men, and then looked away.

I watched it pass and felt my way along the cold, salt-crusted wall to the passage outside my rooms. Theo came behind me. I had thought he would pause at my door but he came in and while I went into the bedroom and stared out at the piles of torn kelp left by the celebrating kelp gatherers, he stirred up the fire in the study and then came in behind me.

"You must get some rest, Anne."

My head had begun to ache and I touched the crown of it, then remembered the moment in the graveyard, and Jonathan's confession that he struck me so gently, not intending to "hurt" me. I said aloud, bitterly, "And I thought it was a touch of the sun."

Theo understood my allusion.

"Anne, that was hardly my plan, to have him attack you. I thought I was on guard and could forestall him when he tried to approach you. Maeve was furious when she heard. She could not see that it was Father MacMonigle at fault, entirely. Tiresome good creature he may be, but I nearly offended him getting back to you, only to find you gone and our plan with it."

"It doesn't matter. I wish that Dr. Trumble's guilt did not depend upon my testimony. That is all."

Theo laughed shortly. "You will feel differently when you read the letter that arrived for Jonathan tonight, and which doubtless made him think his luck was running high, when Maury seemed to have died so providentially."

"What letter is that?" I asked, not caring. I wished he would go away, but at the same time I dreaded being left alone with my thoughts.

He took the still damp letter from his jacket and skimmed through it. I scarcely understood what he was trying to tell me, except that, somehow, it made Jonathan more culpable.

"It is to Jono from Mother's solicitor, Sir Peveral Hammersmith in Dublin. See here, Anne . . ." But I would not look.

I did not really want to hear, nor to see. " 'My dear Doctor', " he began, then— "Read it!"

I took it from his hand and tried to put my attention to its contents. Presently, I understood the whole sinister wickedness of that man whose skill had saved so many in the community.

My dear Doctor,

Your description of your wretched and unhappy wife is lucid in the extreme. I agree with you that it is of the utmost importance that you be put in possession of Mrs. Trumble's inheritance immediately, for her further treatment, and for any other purpose which you deem proper in this regard. Irreparable harm may have come to her through her prolonged residence in a household where, frankly, I agree there is every ground for suspicion of the Conor motives in attempting to withhold Mrs. Trumble's inheritance from you, against the clear expression of intent in the will of the late Mrs. Aengus Conor. Whether your wife were alive or deceased, her inheritance became, in legal fact, a part of your own responsibility upon and after the date of your marriage.

In closing, I can only express admiration for your patience with that unfortunate creature, your wife, and your efforts to prevent her premature demise at her own hands."

How cleverly Jonathan had maneuvered his poor wife so that he appeared, to all the world, as the patient savior of an insane woman whose death might be expected at any time! Even in this Sir Peveral Hammersmith had played into his hands, all unsuspecting. Poor Maureen might have died tonight with her husband's blessing. Her inheritance would have been his!

I gave Theo the letter.

The wind had blown the fog away and stars were visible now, shining down in black and silver upon the headland. I saw the spot where Ivy Kellinch died, very nearly in my arms. I remembered Jonathan hastening down to us. How alarmed he must have been, fearing she was not dead and would betray him! And how carefully he had made it seem that his wife might be guilty, should there be any question! I could not forget the shabby trick with the black fringe from Maureen's shawl. Undoubtedly, Jonathan had put that fringe in the dying woman's hand, and then, afterward, came his meaching talk to Theo, constantly stressing his wife's "innocence" while at the same time, bringing her name into the discussion! A shabby, horrid man, when all was said.

"Please," I asked Theo, "May I be alone now? It's been a very long day."

Theo laughed shortly, the odd little laugh I remembered as part of the character he had portrayed as his father.

"Yes. I'm sure it has." He leaned over me and to my surprise, kissed me very gently on the cheek. "Thank you, dear Anne. Thank you for coming, and for being the catalyst of Conor House."

He went out of the room the while I wondered what a catalyst was.

I know not how well or ill the others in the household slept that night. I know it was a strange, dream-filled few hours for me. I slept almost as soon as I lay down, but my sleep was beset by the most extraordinary phantasms, mad perversions of the truth about the recent murders. Sometimes I saw Theo Conor as he looked in his father's guise, standing before me and lifting off his face, the flesh and all, to reveal a phantom kelper's shadowy visage.

Not once in my dreams that night did I see Dr. Jonathan's face. It was as though he had always remained just beyond the range of our vision. We could not see him because, unlike Theo Conor who could remove masks at will, the mask that we had known as Jonathan Trumble was, in truth, still a mask. Surely, none of us had ever known the real Jonathan at all. So sincere he seemed, so very deep, so honest in confessing his bitterness at the wrongs he had suffered from the Conors! Perhaps this too was the real Jonathan, just as was the fiendish murderer who killed two people and tried to drive his helpless wife to suicide, at last, after having prepared the household and the world for this very act. It must have required some dexterity to see that poor Maureen did not commit suicide before he was ready for that act.

When I was summoned to the Morning Room the next day, I expected to see Lady Maeve behind her pretty white and gold desk, and perhaps Master Theo standing negligently beside her, but it was unnerving to see Sir Horace Pumbleby in all his official dignity, ensconced at Her Ladyship's desk, with a soldier in the uniform of an English Lieutenant of the Irish-stationed corps, behind him. Lady Maeve sat somewhat rigidly in a straight white and gold chair against the further wall, and Master Theo, standing, motioned me to the remaining place at a small settee beside his sister Maureen. Of them all, only Maureen was smiling, pleasant, friendly, making a nice show of giving me room to sit. There is something, I think, in having one's childish wits only upon the minute-by-minute joys and incidents of life. How quickly are the woes of last night, the worries of tomorrow, sponged from one's memories! Almost, I envied the pretty widow, but I did not take the seat offered me, though I smiled at Maureen, trying to show her that I appreciated her attention.

"I wonder if I may stand, sir," I said, addressing the pompous but not unfriendly Sir Horace. "There is this and that I must say, and it comes easier so."

"Quite, my dear Wexford, quite." He nodded approval.

As for me, the single word "Wexford" made me scowl at Master Theo who looked across at me with the most sunnily innocent smile upon his devilish face. In despite of myself, that smile put me quite in charity with him.

"Now, let us have your story," said Sir Horace, brushing dust off his sleeve.

The most difficult part was the accusation I must make against Dr. Jonathan, but I did my best, repeating as exactly as I could, what Jonathan had said to me on the terrace the previous evening, urging me, his supposed wife, to commit myself to the raging sea beneath me.

Sir Horace interjected then, shaking his head, "I am given to understand that this is not the full extent of his perfidy, young woman. Did he not attack you as well?"

"He was . . . driven to it," I added lamely. "I believe it was the intention of Master Theo and Her Ladyship to make the doctor think his wife had already died."

"Quite so," Lady Maeve put in at a respectful glance from Sir Horace. "At sight of Maureen, whom he supposed to be dead, we thought he would betray himself, urging her to finish the—act. He did so, but not as we had planned. We did not expect him to return so soon to the terrace."

"My dear lady!" Sir Horace made soothing sounds of complete faith in an earl's daughter. "Now then, I've no doubt—no doubt in the world—that your own story of the . . . er . . . masquerade practiced by yourself and your stepson, will be accepted. All in good cause, as it were. And with your housekeeper here to testify to Dr. Trumble's confession. In any case, Her Ladyship could never put her hand, nor her—if I may say so—her extraordinary mental faculties, to any cause that was unworthy." He harrumphed into his handkerchief while Lady Maeve and Theo exchanged glances which bordered on the contemptuous, although in Theo's face I traced the verge of a grin. He took out his own handkerchief and waved it delicately before his nose, to my horror; for I felt sure Sir Horace would guess that he was being mocked, but I had overestimated the astuteness of the Royal representative.

They went on talking and I closed my ears to their voices. I wished I was already on the stagecoach for the Irish Sea, and back to that safe, quiet haven that was Miss Nutting's Academy for Select Young Females.

I should be sorry never to see the charming, devilish Theo Conor again, nor his fascinating other self, the tasseled Aengus. I should be sorry never to see Maureen, for whom I had come to feel a certain fondness. But I had very nearly betrayed the memory of my husband, in these past few weeks, in my mind, and worse, I had nearly loved a murderer. This was my punishment, and I must accept it.

Presently, the voices ceased, and Sir Horace and Lady Maeve went off to have a glass of the good Irish somewhere, and Maureen wandered out to the terrace. I started after her in panic, then saw Theo watching her. He too went after us. But we had nothing to fear. Maureen smiled and when the seagulls scattered at her approach, she waved to them and stood there as Lady Maeve had stood so often, with her hair fluttering in the crisp, sunny air.

Theo went to Maureen and I heard him say, "You must not think of Jono, Maury. It is better so. You see that now."

She swung around and faced us. There was a light in her face, a gleam, and happiness that was more than the little, childish moods we knew so well. She seemed genuinely content.

"Oh yes, Theo. You see—Jono always said that I should not mind if one of us went first, if I went to sleep in the bog some day. Because, in that way, he would always have me in his heart, and his mind, and there would be no room for anyone else. Only me. I would be closer to him than if I had been alive."

Theo looked at me. He seemed uneasy. Perhaps he guessed what was coming, as I did.

Maureen said calmly, with that beautiful glow in her fine eyes, "But now, Theo dear, it is quite so! Jono never lied to me. It is just as he said. No other woman will have Jono. He is mine forever now. I have him in my heart . . . in my mind's eye . . . just as he promised. I know it is what he would have wanted."

Theo swallowed and avoided my glance. He said suddenly, "Anne, shall we join the others in that drink?"

Before I could reply, Maureen swung around happily.

"Oh, may I, too? A very small one. And maybe a sugar bun and some coffee? It is a special day, so maybe I can have some coffee again."

"You may indeed, Miss Maury," said I, and took her waving hand. "Come now. We shall all have something nice."

Theo came and joined us on my other side. Maureen walked faster than we, hurrying like the dear child she was, to her special treat.

Theo said in a low voice, oddly unlike his casual self, "Anne, must you go? You have the look of someone about to say good-by. And I—we all have come to love you."

I was touched by his care for me. I knew of no one else in the world who might say that to me. But my determination was made. The memories here were too painful. Yet, I softened my reply, in my deep gratitude for his concern.

"I must, sir. Truly I must—for now. Sometime later, perhaps."

He was silent a few moments as we went into the house. In the Morning Room, however, he smiled again, almost his old self.

"I'll be saying this, Annie, my girl: If I had remained that old reprobate, the Aengus Conor that Maeve and I created,

I'll wager you'd not have turned me down so fast. You seemed to feel . . . something for me in that dusty room."

"What!" I demanded in a fine fury. "My respects to your father's memory, but the creature you played was the outside of enough!"

"You liked him, all the same!" Theo insisted. "I could see it—and feel it, when I touched you. And me in that silly tassel and the night cap and the gown with the frills. . . . Yes, Annie-girl, you liked that reprobate!"

I smiled to myself. It was insane, quite beyond the powers of reason, but I *had* felt something—I do not know what—for the weird fellow up in that strange room, the fellow who did not really exist.

He took my hand and as Maureen turned to urge us to hurry before the buns were gone, he insisted, "I shall always believe it, Anne. And some day, do not be surprised if the fellow with all his whimsies, including the tasseled night cap, goes calling upon you at your precious Miss Nutting's. You may even come home to us—with that gentleman."

I gave him my warmest smile, for I knew myself fond of him, or of that other self, and said, "Perhaps."